RECAPTURED PASSION

Gray Eagle took Alisha's face in his hands and kissed her gently. "Allow Shalee to send Alisha away," he coaxed. "You speak and think as white, my love, but you are now Indian. I have been patient as you asked; I have not forced you to become my wife again. But I love and desire you. And touching is the sharing of love."

"What about my feelings?" Alisha defended herself.

"You have no desire for me?" he demanded a little too harshly, fearing her answer.

"I am trying to—"

He severed her sentence. "Trying! Love is not a chore to be done, Shalee. Love comes to a heart and body, or it does not," he stated in a tone that made her even more nervous. "Do you feel such things for me?" he demanded.

Trapped, she murmured, "I don't know."

"Then we shall find the answer," he threatened huskily. Then he pulled her into his arms—and took her mouth with his own. . . .

BESTSELLING ROMANCES BY JANELLE TAYLOR

SAVAGE ECSTASY   (824, $3.50)
It was like lightning striking, the first time the Indian brave
Gray Eagle looked into the eyes of the beautiful young settler
Alisha. And from the moment he saw her, he knew that he
must possess her—and make her his slave!

DEFIANT ECSTASY   (931, $3.50)
When Gray Eagle returned to Fort Pierre's gates with his
hundred warriors behind him, Alisha's heart skipped a beat;
would Gray Eagle destroy her—or make his destiny her own?

FORBIDDEN ECSTASY   (1014, $3.50)
Gray Eagle had promised Alisha his heart forever—nothing
could keep him from her. But when Alisha woke to find her
red-skinned lover gone, she felt abandoned and alone. Lost
between two worlds, desperate and fearful of betrayal, Alisha
hungered for the return of her FORBIDDEN ECSTASY.

BRAZEN ECSTASY   (1133, $3.50)
When Alisha is swept down a raging river and out of her savage
brave's life, Gray Eagle must rescue his love again. But Alisha
has no memory of him at all. And as she fights to recall a past
love, another white slave woman in their camp is fighting for
Gray Eagle!

*Available wherever paperbacks are sold, or order direct from the
Publisher. Send cover price plus 50¢ per copy for mailing and
handling to Zebra Books, 475 Park Avenue South, New York,
N.Y. 10016. DO NOT SEND CASH.*

BRAZEN ECSTASY

BY JANELLE TAYLOR

ZEBRA BOOKS
KENSINGTON PUBLISHING CORP.

ZEBRA BOOKS

are published by

KENSINGTON PUBLISHING CORP.
475 Park Avenue South
New York, N.Y. 10016

Printed in the United States of America

FOR:

PESHA FINKELSTEIN,

my talented editor and good friend
who emends my verbal silver
into brazen gold. . . .

&

ADELE LEONE,

my indispensable agent and great friend,
whose exceptional skills prevented
"growing pains". . . .

ACKNOWLEDGMENT TO:

Hiram C. Owen of Sisseton, South Dakota for all his help and understanding with the Sioux language and facts about the great and inspiring Sioux Nation. My endless gratitude and friendship.

BRAZEN ECSTASY

Love tho' forbidden, still rapture's delight.
Hatred burning brightly in prejudiced night.
Boldness alights, permitting all to see;
The fierce battle raging for BRAZEN ECSTASY. . . .

Chapter One

Black Hills, South Dakota, March, 1782—A gust of icy wind impatiently yanked at the neat braids and doeskin dress of the Indian princess who had pulled aside the buffalo-hide flap to catch a breath of fresh but biting air. Her pert nose and creamy cheeks were instantly chilled by the glacial dampness that heavily laced the fierce breezes swooping down from the nearby mountains like some ravenous bird of prey carrying out his daring attack upon a helpless victim. Even after years in this Plains climate, each winter her tawny flesh stubbornly returned to its natural ivory cast as if subtly reminding the Oglala and other tribes that she was half white.

Yet she was accepted and respected as the half-breed daughter of the powerful Blackfoot chief Mahpiya Sapa and as the wife of the legendary Sioux warrior and future Oglala chief, Gray Eagle. She had long since stopped wishing for her satiny skin to remain a golden caramel shade, for her forest-green eyes loudly proclaimed her white blood to anyone who gazed into them. Thankfully, after five years in her husband's camp, she was considered an Indian by many tribes. If only their rival and enemy tribes would also ignore her white blood. Hadn't she proven herself Indian in heart and essence? Perhaps one day all tribes would view her a worthy mate for the formidable and invincible man whose life and heart she shared.

All in all, these past five years had been peaceful. She had long ago stopped thinking of herself as Alisha Williams, the English girl who had entered the domain of the valiant warrior Gray Eagle and challenged all he knew and felt to win his heart. Days of denial and pain had ceased many winters ago; only love and acceptance dwelled within their hearts and tepee. A passionate and powerful love had conquered all differences between them. For the remainder of her days, she would live and love as Princess Shalee.

Shalee's green eyes studied the leaden sky that hovered ominously above the winter camp at the base of the Paha Sapa, the sacred Black Hills, which offered protection from the harsh winters in the Dakota Territory and sufficient grasses to feed the animals during the lengthy period of waiting until the open plains were once more covered with lush bunch and buffalo grasses. When Mother Nature renewed her face with the coming spring, her people would return to their summer camp near the prairie where the buffalo herds would graze, generously supplying them with the main source of their livelihood.

Yet another snowstorm was threatening to whiten the face of Makakin at least one more time before it finally yielded to the verdant beauty of spring. Shalee's gaze shifted toward the lofty black mounds to the west, still sleeping beneath a heavy sheet of white. But for the persistent evergreens, the trees were naked, shuddering with cold as if silently pleading with Makakin to place a warm garment of green over them. Without a doubt, the River Spirits had won her ear; although slightly cluttered with hunks of ice and an edging of it, its middle ran freely and swiftly, aided by the melting snows from the majestic

Black Hills. But soon it would be warm and inviting outside. Inevitably life would forcefully renew itself.

Shalee lowered the flap and secured it against the frigid fingers that wanted to sneak inside to warm themselves at the price of chilling the tent's inhabitants. She quietly walked over and knelt beside the child sleeping upon the thick buffalo hides, hides captured by the skill and daring of her husband, hides tanned by her own deft hands. Pride and pleasure flooded her singing heart. She had learned so much since coming west in 1775. She possessed a husband whose virility was envied by all women, whose cunning and coups were envied by all men. Her softened gaze roamed the face of their child. How fortunate could one woman be? How could a heart contain so much happiness and pride without bursting from fullness? She knew. She had defiantly and brazenly challenged all odds to win this once forbidden ecstasy. She would allow no person or force to endanger it.

Without awakening Bright Arrow, Shalee lovingly stroked his shiny hair, which was as sleek and black as the raven's wing. Even amidst the winter demands, his firm body was a rich coppery shade that she almost envied. His closed lids prevented Shalee from gazing into eyes as dark as precious jet, eyes that frequently sparkled with boyish mischief or glowed with pride at his lineage: a proud heritage of dauntless chiefs, a heritage which he did not fully understand at his tender age of four winters.

The Fates had certainly been kind to Shalee, to Alisha Williams. They had artistically interwoven the threads of her life to present her as a worthy mate, although white, to the indomitable warrior who had stolen her heart at their first meeting, even though they had been avowed enemies. Some day soon, her beloved would follow Chief

11

Running Wolf as leader of the awesome Oglala; some distant moon in their wonderful future, their son would also become a Sioux chief. Such realities thrilled and awed Shalee. So few women were granted these great honors and joys: wife to a chief and mother to a future chief. It made her feel like royalty, like an English queen who had borne the future king of her land and people. Often, such thoughts were even frightening. Each moon, she would pray that no one would ever declare her son unfit to become chief because of the white blood given to him by his mother; such a disgrace and rejection would surely break his heart and hers. His father, her cherished lover, would die in battle over such a loss of face. So far, no one had challenged Bright Arrow's right to future chiefdom. But would things change when that eventual day arrived? Surely not, for Bright Arrow would match the legend of his father.

Yes, she happily concluded, the Fates were on her side; no trace of the white man's heritage flawed her son's visage. Judging by his present appearance, he would become his father's image. His father's image. . . .

Shalee's mind mentally traveled the short distance to the Ceremonial Lodge where the O-zu-ye Wicasta, the famed warrior society, was in deep conference over their imminent plans to return to the open plains as soon as the last snows melted. She was eager to feel the warm sunlight caressing her face and body as she diligently worked beside their tepee. She could close her eyes and envision the seemingly endless grasslands waving in the breeze. She longed to smell the freshness of the reborn lands and forests, to sniff the fragrance of the wildflowers, which grew in abundance, to gather heady herbs to use in her cooking, to stroll leisurely along the riverbank, and to make passionate love among the

12

wondrous offerings of nature. Despite the hardships of living in the wilderness, they led such a peaceful and exciting existence. A frown creased her lovely brow as unbidden worries flickered across her mind.

She couldn't forget the troubling words of the visiting party of Cheyenne braves three moons past. After nearly two years of peace following the fierce battle and necessary destruction of Fort Pierre, more and more white settlers and soldiers continuously flooded the Indian lands in every direction. As before, with her own group of settlers, new animosities were raging. Only the harsh winter had briefly halted this new uprising of danger and death. Why was peace so impossible? Why must people, Indian and white, be so greedy and evil? A human life was so precious, too short to spend in bloody warfare. How she wished she could experience life as it had been here before the whites invaded this unspoiled land of the mighty Sioux and his brothers.

She had witnessed and learned enough to know that the white man would never cease his advance; nor would the Indian yield what had been his for countless years. Fear and torment knifed her heart as she defensively pushed such agonizing thoughts from her mind. The Cheyenne had always been friendly to the Sioux, as was the Blackfoot tribe. The braves had warned of the close proximity and already budding hostilities of Fort Henry, to the north of the Black Hills, as well as of the persistent building of Fort Meade near the mighty Missouri River, near the summer camp of the Oglala. God, how she prayed history would not repeat itself. . . .

Shalee did not fear for her life and safety, nor for that of her son. How could she be afraid when her husband was alleged the greatest warrior ever to ride the Plains or to battle their aggressive white foes? The Sioux were powerful and brave; she didn't fear her own fate. But a warrior's life was open to death's greedy invitation every day, each time he left camp to intentionally or unsuspectingly confront this deadly foe who demanded both his lands and life. For a long time, she had relaxed in her tranquil surroundings; now, the threat of the white man was rapidly growing like some fatal disease that determined to consume all in its path.

Being white, she could not always agree with the ominous, lethal actions taken by the Indians toward the white pioneers, for many were good people. Many whites had come here in good faith, looking for new beginnings and to revive their hopes and dreams. Many had been led to believe the Indians would indifferently accept their presence and the confiscation of parts of their lands. Many had no other place to go. Many had been driven from other lands or from the now independent America. Poverty, religion, political disagreements, and such had sent many whites hurrying to this so-called promised land. Time hadn't changed the reasons behind the heavy influx; the victory over England for independence had. Once the English Crown had been conquered, the Americans almost instantly turned their wide gazes to their West, its conquest challenging them now.

Somehow the victory over her fellow Englishmen didn't trouble Shalee; the threat of victory over her present and chosen people did. "Please, God, don't let them recall I am white," she fervently prayed against that disastrous possibility. "Just permit me a few more years and even my color won't matter to them." But would that day truly come? she fearfully wondered.

Shalee went to her own sleeping mat to lie down, as was the custom of the Indian during this time of day whether it was winter or summer. She closed her eyes and forced her taut body to relax. His skills honed to perfection, Gray Eagle entered so quietly that Shalee did not note his presence for a few moments as he remained motionless to study her. As he silently knelt beside the mat to prevent disturbing her, his manly scent assailed her senses. Her eyes opened and fused with his obsidian ones. He smiled down at her, his smoldering gaze engulfing her exquisite features and holding her eyes captive as he had once done with her very life.

A radiant smile filled her eyes and teased at her soft lips, inviting him to join her upon the mats before their son awakened. The power and passion of his love had never ceased to enflame her body and to stir her heart. No matter how many times they made love, it was always unique and overpowering. They never grew weary of touching or possessing each other; it was as if they couldn't have enough of each other. Such had been the pattern of their great love since the beginning many moons ago.

He stretched out his lithe frame beside her sleek one. Propping himself upon his left elbow, Gray Eagle continued his slow scrutiny of his woman. At twenty-five winters, Shalee was more beautiful than any living creature he had set eyes upon during his thirty winters upon the face of Makakin. Her presence and possession enlivened him more than the breath of the Great Spirit that filled his lungs or the food supplied by Wakantanka. She was like the air, the water, the forces of life; she was vital to his happiness and completeness. How had he survived without her? How could he survive if he ever lost her?

He chuckled softly, bringing an inquisitive look to her alluring eyes of leaf green. No power or man existed who could defeat him or steal his love from his side. If necessary, he would challenge the Bird of Death himself before yielding her over to his hands! He had seen her and taken her; she was his for all time. Forever their bloods were joined to exist within their children and their children's children after them. The line of Gray Eagle would continue as long as Wakantanka existed: forever. But there was only one son to carry on this line; he needed others, for a warrior's life dangled before the Bird of Death each new sun. He needed more than one powerful son to ride at his side to defeat the white man who threatened all he loved and owned. If Shalee hadn't borne another son after losing their first child during a tragic accident, he might believe she could not accept his seed. But Bright Arrow had grown within her body. He was healthy and untouched by evil spirits. Surely that meant they could have another child someday.

He grinned at his wife; there was but one way for his seeds to enter her body and to lodge there. He lovingly caressed her cheek, skin as soft as the hide of a newly born fawn. Her eyes burned with the same flames that filled his taut body. He sat up, then gently pulled her to a sitting position. His eyes glowed with merriment as he unlaced the ties upon her *heyake* and lifted it over her head. He deftly unknotted the strands that held her *cehnake* in place. He tossed it upon the discarded dress, then quickly divested himself of his own garments and breechcloth.

Shalee eased back to rest upon the plush skins as her husband pulled another buffalo hide over them to guard their privacy and to prevent a chill. No matter how long Shalee lived with him, she would probably always retain her natural air of modesty. Gray Eagle glanced over at their sleeping son and whispered into her ear, "Our son sleeps, Little One. No spark from the fire will touch his mat or from his keen mind to halt our joining," he teased, nibbling upon her ear between words and chuckles.

Shalee smothered a giggle at his playful remark. "Had I not been so naive, my love, you would have been denied the joys of teaching me so many things," she seductively jested in return, her teeth painlessly seizing his chin as her laughing eyes met his beguiling ones.

"What things did I teach you, Grass Eyes?" he questioned in feigned innocence.

"To love you more than life itself," she began, her tone husky with deep emotion. Her hand traced the proud lines of his handsome coppery face as she murmured, "To know every part of you better than I know my own body . . . to live only for you and our son . . . to boldly touch you wherever I wish. . . ." At that provocative statement, she allowed her hand to trail over his powerful shoulders, down his strong arms, and across his chest. Such vitality and strength were evinced beneath her exploratory hand. He looked as if some talented artist had melted rich cinnamon, blended it with a clear liquid, then poured it into a sensual mold to produce a frame of hard and sleek perfection.

Her brazen hand drifted down his lean side, over his narrow waist to briefly hesitate on his firm buttocks whose masterful skills could drive his manhood into her and grant such blissful ecstasy. One finger traced the length of the shaft that intoxicated her senses and that instinctively responded to her light and stimulating touch. Her hand gently closed around his erect manhood, and, with agonizing sweetness, leisurely and rhythmically moved up and down its full length, causing his virile body to tense and shudder, drawing a low moan of passion from his wide and sensual lips. Confident in her love and talents upon his mats, she smiled wantonly and

17

vowed, "For training me how to please you . . . for teaching my body to greedily accept yours whenever you're near me . . . for being the one man who stirs my heart and soul to desire no other . . . for giving me pleasures I never dreamed possible . . . I love you with all my heart, Wanmdi Hota. For as long as I live and breathe, I will belong to only you."

Gray Eagle's mouth closed over hers in a hungry and tantalizing kiss. He tasted the sweetness that was freely offered to him, demanding more and more of its precious nectar. Soon there was no inch upon her face that did not tingle from a fiery kiss. As if blazing a new trail into paradise, his lips began their seeking trek down her throat to wander from one passion-taut breast to the other, discovering the delightful treasures of her pliant body and heated response.

His moist tongue circled and circled each nipple as a voracious vulture over a recent kill, patiently awaiting the right moment to devour his object of interest. Suddenly deciding to land upon the right one, he sucked hungrily as if drawing life-sustaining fluid from it, only to move to the left one and repeat this intoxicating action, which caused her head to roll from side to side as a wildfire raged within her body.

She didn't know how long he feasted upon her body before his lips sought sweetness from her mouth. His hand slipped over her flat stomach and drifted down into her auburn forest. His actions became a journey for a new quest of exquisite pleasure, seeking out each path and mound and cave there. Mindless with overwhelming need for him, her body arched and moved to assist his deliberate search for sublime ecstasy. Enticingly and purposely, his advance party of skilled fingers probed and prepared the way for his triumphant journey's end.

Shalee's hand stimulated the leader of this exploratory expedition, urging him to join the busy members of his search party. The feel of his throbbing, fiery manhood within her hand thrilled and intrigued her, knowing the ultimate job it would perform within her writhing body, wondering when he would loosen its powerful force to do it. When her starving body could no longer withstand its callings for appeasement, she coaxed him to complete his intoxicating quest.

He entered her gently, but the height of their shared passion demanded a fierce and immediate union. The previously slow and tender strokes became strong and swift as their bodies pounded together, almost savagely demanding their brazen ecstasy to come forth instantly. As if ascending the hazardous peaks of the Black Hills, they bravely and vigorously climbed higher and higher to reach their goal.

As if all the snows upon those mountains had melted at once, wave after wave of pleasure washed over them, carrying them along with its potent force. To prevent her outcry of sated passion from awakening their son at this vital moment, his mouth captured hers and ravished it with a heady kiss which seemingly had no beginning or ending. Determined to obtain every treasure of this journey, he worked until every spasm ceased and total fulfillment was their reward.

Drained and breathless, he rolled to his side to avoid placing his entire weight upon Shalee, pulling her along with him. No matter how rushed he was, he never released her before a long time had passed. After sharing such a moment, a too hasty retreat could spoil it. The touching before and after were important; the shared closeness and warmth added to the precious union as their bodies gradually cooled.

Such love and tenderness had never gone unnoticed by Shalee. Her heart surged with love as she snuggled into his protective embrace, savoring the disappearance of a fierce hunger that was now quieted and sated. This lingering at her side during the peaceful aftermath inspired a greater love and need for him. She felt as safe and excited as a new butterfly resting in a warm cocoon after a stormy metamorphosis. During the heat of their desperate struggle to quell their starving senses, only passion ruled their bodies. Before their union, over-powering desire controlled their reasoning. But after-wards, that was the time for love and tenderness to be shared and enjoyed. Sated bodies and love-swollen hearts reached out to touch and to claim the rewards of their preceding trek.

"Do you know how much I love you?" she asked softly, turning her auburn head to meet his tender gaze.

He caressed her cheek and murmured with vivid self-assurance, "Yes, Grass Eyes, I know. No two bodies or hearts are as wisely matched as ours. The Great Spirit surely knows and sees all, for He sent to me the only woman who could ever give me such joy and pleasure. Sometimes I think He rewarded my coups and obedience far more than I deserved."

"Never. I am the lucky one, the honored one, that He allowed me to win your love. Even as your white captive, I would be happy beyond my wildest dreams. I refuse to even think what my life would be like if I had never met you."

"The Great Spirit guided you to me, Little One. He called your feet from across the great waters and over the lands to rest at my side and to enter my sacred life-circle. If this were not so, the forces of evil would have torn us apart many winters ago."

When she pulled her haunting gaze from his to stare unseeingly at his broad chest, he astutely knew to where her thoughts had flown. "We endured many pains and separations in past moons, Grass Eyes, but never again. Have we not shared five peaceful winters of love and happiness?" he said, gently scolding her for retreating to times long past when they had tragically resisted this powerful and fated bond between them.

Meeting his gaze, she spoke softly with a strained voice, "It was not the past that cast a shadow over my heart and eyes, Wanmdi Hota. Sometimes I fear we are too happy and too much in love. I fear something or someone will cruelly tear us apart, out of jealousy or for cruel spite. My very soul trembles each time I hear of new whites and their hatred toward us. Their evil victory would be half won with the death of Wanmdi Hota himself; they know this, my love. I fear their hatred of you and their vindictive resolve to defeat the legendary Gray Eagle. Each time you leave camp, I nearly hold my breath until you return. Each time I make love to you, I fear it will be the last. I could not live without you," she cried out as her mounting anguish and apprehensions poured forth.

He held her tightly and rocked her like a small child who desperately needed comfort. "The words of the Cheyenne caused such feelings," he concluded aloud. "I should not have told you their childish fears. The white-eyes have never defeated me; they never will, Grass Eyes. The Great Spirit guards my life and honor; He will not permit my enemies to slay me. He has placed the safety of our people, our Indian brothers, and our lands within my hands. His shadow falls over me in battle; I cannot be slain by white dogs who steal our lands and bring their evil here. Do you doubt my courage and honor?" he questioned, knowing she did not, knowing it was a woman's way to fear for the man she loved above her own life.

"If there was only one man in the world who could not be conquered, it would be you, my love. Yet, each man must join the Great Spirit when He calls to him. Does any warrior know when that voice will speak to him?"

He laughed and replied confidently, "It will be many, many winters before the Great Spirit calls the name of Wanmdi Hota. Until our son is old enough and skilled enough to take my place, I will remain here to lead and protect our people. No man will ever take you from my side and no enemy's weapon will take me from yours."

"But what of other powerful forces, those beyond yours or the Great Spirit's control? Look how the whites flood our lands. Do you not see there is evil as well as good?" she argued his logic.

"Each time, have I not conquered the evil? Each time, have I not been stronger and more cunning? Even the mighty white fort could not withstand my strength or keep you from my side. Each time I have faced danger and defeated it. Until Bright Arrow takes my place, it will also be this way."

There was no hint of idle boasting or arrogance in his mind or voice. True, there was no warrior who could challenge him and win. True, he had always been victorious over all forces. But the time came when even great men fell beneath the joint forces of many enemies who were determined to defeat him. Gray Eagle's power could not be ignored or accepted by his white foes; they would press and press to defeat him, knowing the result of his death upon the Indians. He stood before them like an immovable oak tree; they wouldn't rest until they discovered some way to destroy the legend that inspired

22

more daring and spirit than those of all other warriors combined. Perhaps if he were only a regular warrior . . . no, if he were, he would not be the man who had claimed her heart and life.

She smiled. "You are right as always, my husband. What have I to fear when I live under the wing of Gray Eagle himself? Perhaps one day I will become as brave as you, my love. Until then, you will have to be brave enough for both of us," she teased, eyes dancing with love and mischief.

"You are as brave as I am, Shalee. Many times you have proven your great courage and cunning. Gray Eagle chose his woman wisely. You are as gentle as the newborn fawn, as cunning as the fox, as brave as the great bear, as playful as the otter, as mischievous as the raccoon, as . . ."

As he hesitated to think of another playful comparison, she quickly injected, "And frequently as annoying as the buck who is smart enough to outwit the great hunter Wanmdi Hota?"

"When has any buck denied my arrow's finding its mark?" he jested.

"Just last moon, you said they were hiding from your keen sight," she playfully reminded him.

"Only because spring calls them back to the forests. Soon, we must follow them and hunt the buffalo. Before you number twenty-six, we will be camped in our summer village near the great river where Wi awakens."

Excitement and eagerness filled her. "I can hardly wait."

"There will be much work to be done, wife. You will be too weary to roll in the newborn grass with me," he hinted slyly.

"Never will I be that tired. Do you prepare me for

excuses of your own?" she laughingly retorted, running her finger over his lips.

"Excuses? I know no such word," he parried her jest.

"Yes, you do. I taught you all the English words you did not already know. Do you recall what 'seduction' means?"

He eyed her curiously, grinning devilishly. "That is one I shall never forget. Why?" he probed, his eyes glowing with intrigue.

"If you become so weary that you call upon some 'excuse' to discourage me, I shall teach you what it means, not just tell you," she saucily warned.

"With a threat like that, I shall certainly feign weariness and think of some 'excuse' to use," he informed her. "So, you would 'seduce' your own husband if he fails to feed you properly?"

"Not before warning you first," she came back between giggles.

"Is this my warning?" he asked, joining her game.

"Your first and last, Noble Eagle of the Sioux. Still, it might be fun to . . ." Her words were cut off by the voice of their son as he rushed forward to topple between them.

"Our son demands his share of our love and attention, Grass Eyes."

Amidst laughter and tickles, the three tussled and played upon the sleeping mat for another hour. The sport was ended when Bright Arrow looked at his mother and announced, "I'm hungry."

Gray Eagle and Shalee quickly exchanged amused glances, recalling only too well how their hungers had been sated. "Patience, Bright Arrow," he gently reprimanded his growing son. Shalee smiled at him, then at her son before rising to fix their evening meal.

Chapter Two

It had been two uneventful weeks since the Cheyennes' visit to the winter camp of the Oglala when they came again to discuss the new happenings near Fort Henry, spring lending the opportunity for dire events to begin. Shalee tensed the moment she saw them weaving their way between the conical abodes, heading straight for Chief Running Wolf's tepee, the largest and most colorfully decorated one in the entire camp. She hesitated in midstep to observe them closely, her heart thudding heavily with dread. Why had they returned so soon? What heralds of gloom did they bring upon their tongues?

Running Wolf stepped outside to greet them, confronting the stoic warriors on one of the warmest days since winter had begun. Several daring birds were singing their hearts out as if entreating Mother Nature to make her changes this very day. Audacious shoots of green could be noted in their fierce struggle to pierce the slowly thawing ground. Why did such dark forces shove their unwanted presence into this time of rebirths, spoiling its beauty and tranquility? Peace, must it carry such a heavy price?

Running Wolf invited the warriors to enter his tepee, then turned to motion for the rigid Shalee to come forward. Propelled by the sheer power in his voice and gaze, Shalee hurried over to his side. He asked her to find

Leah Winston and to send her to his tepee to prepare food and drink for his guests. She smiled and nodded to her father-in-law, a man who held her affection and respect. He ducked and entered his tepee, leaving Shalee poised there alone for a few moments in deep thought.

Leah Winston . . . each time she spoke or worked with this particular girl who was the white slave of Running Wolf, strange qualms gnawed at her. Leah had been a gift to the aging Running Wolf from White Arrow, Gray Eagle's lifelong companion and best friend. Leah was quiet and mysterious. She responded to commands with respect and quickness. She was alert, agile, and smart. Between her obedient attitude and intelligence, she had fared well since her capture last summer. Taken by White Arrow and given to Running Wolf, she had not been subjected to physical abuse or sexual degradation. Perceiving her good fortune, Leah had made certain she retained her lofty and safe position as slave to a wise and tolerant chief.

But at the first moment of Leah's arrival, Shalee witnessed the dismayed look of disappointment that briefly flickered in Leah's eyes when she realized the virile and notable son of the chief already possessed his own tepee and a woman. In Leah's disheveled and dirty state, the resemblance between the two women went unnoticed by all except Leah. There was just a slight shade of difference in their green eyes; their auburn hair matched tints perfectly. Yet Leah's mussed and grimy locks concealed this similarity, as did Shalee's natural vitality and freshly scrubbed waves. Both women were the same height and weight, though childbirth granted Shalee the more favorable bosom. If not for her days upon the open plains, Shalee's skin would also match the creamy coloring of Leah's. At a distance, and if they were dressed alike, Leah might be mistaken for Princess Shalee! But not on closer inspection. Shalee possessed more beauty, vivacity, and warmth than Leah did; that inner glow and gentleness were blatantly lacking in the reserved and calculating Leah.

As Shalee's mind reflected upon the ambiguous Leah, the truth suddenly dawned upon her. Why hadn't she solved this puzzle sooner? The Oglala—especially Running Wolf, her small son, and Gray Eagle—were responding to the similarities between Leah and herself! Of course, that was why they casually accepted her presence! And that conniving and cunning Leah had recognized this point and was using it to her advantage. That explained her ready acceptance of her captivity, her friendly overtures to Bright Arrow, her sickly-sweet treatment of the aging chief, and her nonchalant truce with Gray Eagle himself! She was gradually and unsuspectingly edging her way into their confidence and friendship. To prepare for a future escape? To become an accepted member of their tribe? It was almost as if Leah was striving to become Princess Shalee!

Alarm washed over Shalee and she curiously trembled, not from the chill in the spring air. It was more like some imperceptible warning tingled up and down her spine. How could a mere white captive hope to replace her? What evil mischief danced within Leah's keen mind?

Shalee walked to the stream where Leah was kneeling, washing clothes in the icy stream, her hands red and chapped from her frosty chore. She watched the white girl for a few moments. That same inexplicable and eerie feeling assailed her again. Only one other time had such a feeling ensnared her: the day when she had discovered Matu's deception, the ruse that gave life to the lie that she was a half-breed Indian princess. If one could be grateful for the misfortunes in another's life, Shalee was relieved that only Gray Eagle and White Arrow knew the truth about her—that she was not the daughter of Black Cloud and his white captive Jenny. Odd and frightening, she hadn't thought of herself as white in over four years. Why did Leah stir up such perilous memories? What harm could this woman who resembled her cause?

Without turning, Leah broke into her thoughts as she acknowledged Shalee's presence. In a tone as crisp as the morning air, Shalee related Running Wolf's orders and then turned to leave. Leah stood up and presumptuously called out, "Shalee."

Shalee halted and turned to face the woman. *"Sha?"*

Knowing Shalee could speak English, Leah impetuously questioned her in that language. "Why do you so despise me, Shalee? You also carry white blood. Does it mean nothing to you?" Leah reeked of temerity and envy.

Startled by her impertinent words and boldness, Shalee simply stared at her for a time. "My white blood makes me no less an Indian in heart or by choice than if I were born Indian, Leah," she stated in a clear voice. "My love and loyalty lie with my people, the Oglala. I do not despise you. You are obedient and respectful; you work hard and well for Chief Running Wolf. He is waiting for you to serve his friends," she remarked, dismissing the alarming subject and brassy girl.

"Your words say you do not hate me, but your eyes and actions speak a different story," Leah challenged her in a manner Shalee found disturbing.

"You are a captive and I am an Indian, wife to the next chief. How should I treat you? I have not been unkind or abusive to you. Why do you dare to question me in this insolent way?" Shalee's green eyes were fathomless and her manner rigidly controlled, carefully masking the turmoil and anger that filled her. Why would this bold-spirited captive risk all she had to verbally assault an Indian princess?

"Perhaps my people are your enemies, but I am not. Neither am I some unfeeling and mindless animal. I wish to be your friend." She calmly delivered her unexpected offer. Leah's smile and voice were entreating, but her eyes revealed emotions that Shalee didn't wish to read.

"Friendship is something earned, Leah, something special and mutual. A friend is someone to trust. I do not comprehend you or your ways. It is unnatural to so willingly accept enslavement as you do. Yet, I do not hate you. To me, skin color does not determine my feelings."

"What is there to understand? I simply choose safety over brutality, peaceful submission over dangerous rebellion. I can never return to my people, so I wish to become a part of this tribe. I don't want to remain a lowly slave forever!" Leah made no attempt to cover the vehemence in her tone or eyes.

"It is impossible for a white slave to become an Indian, Leah. Do not fill your heart with foolish dreams. Running Wolf will become impatient if you tarry much longer. Where will your safety and peace be then?"

"You would like to see me punished and sent away, wouldn't you? Why? Because I look like you and you don't want me around to tempt your husband to take me into his tepee when his father dies?" she blatantly added, recklessly enlightening Shalee as to the wanton emotions she harbored toward her love.

Astounded by this baneful girl's charges, Shalee inhaled sharply and glared at her. "Running Wolf will live many more years, Leah. I have never desired the punishment of any helpless white captive, not even a surly and hateful one like you. You present no threat to me where my husband is concerned, whether you favor me or not. No force or woman could halt our love. Even if I died this very day, Gray Eagle would never look upon you with love or lust. You are white; he would die before touching a white woman. In all the years I have known him, not once has he touched or looked upon a white woman with even lust in his eyes or heart. If you try to catch his eye, you will pay dearly for that wicked and unforgivable deed."

"If you dared to tell him of our talk, he would only think you filled with hatred and jealousy. Would you slay me with your own hand?" she taunted.

"My husband is a warrior, a leader with many matters of great importance upon his mind. I would not trouble him with the foolish rantings of a white slave. But if you dared to openly flirt with him, I wouldn't have to slay you; he would, after severely punishing you. If Running Wolf even suspected you had cast your lustful eyes upon his son, you would be sold this very day. Have you not noticed Gray Eagle has only one wife? I am the only woman he has ever loved or desired. Ask anyone if you doubt my claims. Even if I ceased to breathe this very moon, he would never replace me. Mark my words well, Leah; to fall in love with Gray Eagle would be a deadly mistake."

"Did he tell you how he removed a porcupine quill from my hand the other day?" Leah sought to unsettle the confident woman before her.

"Yes, Leah, and how he placed healing salve upon it," she added to prove there were no secrets between her and her lover.

"Did he also tell you how slowly he did it and how long he held my hand afterwards?" she quickly retorted.

30

"There is a tiny shaft pointing backwards upon a quill, Leah. If it isn't removed carefully, a serious injury could occur. From the wound, infection can set in and even fever and death can follow it. Some quills are dipped in poison. Close study after a piercing would reveal if that shaft was harmful since the area quickly turns blue." Shalee coldly and methodically dispelled each of Leah's insinuations.

"Then I'm to assume the shudder that shook his body at my touch was from relief?" Leah continued this harassing debate.

"If there was a shudder in that tepee, it was yours, Leah, not his. Your lust and dreams have blinded you to reality. Wake up, Leah, before you push too far and find yourself releasing that lust beneath countless braves," Shalee ominously warned her. "If you speak of such things again, I will inform Running Wolf of your dangerous game. Do as you're told, now."

Although Shalee had spoken her last word calmly, Leah recognized the stern tone that indicated she was saying too much too soon. If she couldn't get to Shalee through feigned friendship, she must find some other way to discredit her. She was gradually winning over the old man and the child, but Gray Eagle would require more time and cunning. First, Shalee must be dealt with in some disparaging manner. She had to break down Shalee's confidence and destroy her perfection in the eyes of her people, especially her husband. She must discover Shalee's weaknesses and use them against her. Somehow, she had to make it appear their roles were reversed! She must make herself more desirable in every way: appearance, manner, intelligence, company, gentleness, and courage. Somehow, she had to worm her way into the tepee of Gray Eagle. Once there, she would find the means to replace Shalee in all ways . . . even if she had to lethally rid the tepee of Shalee! Shalee had everything she wanted, and she would eventually take it all! There were ways to vanquish any obstacles, even live ones. Perhaps she could force changes in her personality and behavior, then arrange some unsuspecting accident. . . .

As Leah strolled back to camp, her mind was racing with a variety of schemes. One thing for certain, she must remain in Running Wolf's care until she could enchant Gray Eagle. That husky warrior would never take her once she was touched and soiled by countless braves. Thankfully the old man was beyond desiring her upon his mats! But if Shalee was right and Gray Eagle was unreachable, there was still White Arrow. . . .

When Shalee arrived in her tepee, she anxiously paced for a long time. She was relieved that Gray Eagle was out hunting and Bright Arrow was with Shining Light and her son. How dare that little witch actually relate plans to pursue her husband! How dare she speak to her in such a brazen and wanton manner! Yet Shalee decided it was best if she handled this problem herself. Not because she feared Gray Eagle's disbelief or mockery, but because she didn't wish to place Leah's life in danger by revealing such a reckless scheme. If her husband would simply punish Leah and send her away, Shalee would have told him immediately. But his anger and pride would demand more from an offensive white woman who had dared too much. On the other hand, if she kept silent, Leah would continue her wicked games with the people she loved. What to do? Nothing for the present. With luck, Leah would realize the danger of her ploy and cease it.

The thudding of several horses' hooves instantly alerted Shalee to the hasty departure of the Cheyenne warriors. In spite of her recent encounter with Leah, Shalee hastened to Running Wolf's tepee to learn the news. As was the custom, the Indian princess called out before entering a tepee with a closed flap. When the chief's voice bade her enter, she ducked and responded. Going straight to the fire and sitting down upon a thick mat, Shalee pressed him in Oglala for answers she feared to hear.

Irritated that she had not learned enough of their language to translate their words, Leah busied herself clearing away the remains of the meal she had served. Still, she furtively observed the genial interaction between Shalee and Running Wolf, hoping to discover some clue as to how to disrupt it when the right moment presented itself. Shalee's poise and her ignoring of Leah's presence vexed her. From Shalee's manner, Leah's words had not distressed her in the least! But wait, my lovely princess, they soon will. . . .

Shalee anxiously and attentively listened to the troubling words from Running Wolf's lips. The reports were not good. Many white settlements had been established along the great river that flowed through the Dakota Territory and past the large settlement called St. Louis. Far worse, the two forts in the area had been completed and well armed. The Bluecoats were determined to have a stronghold in this opulent land. To further add to these distressing facts, the villages of the Cheyenne and the Oglala rested between the two powerful forts. The only good news she heard concerned the white man's weapons; so far, no faster-loading or better rifle had replaced the sluggish flintlock. But the cavalry had been observed in almost desperate practice with those deadly sabers that swung from their waists, as well as in hours of target shooting to increase accuracy

33

and loading speed. Advanced in the preservation of food, the cavalry could store enough supplies to withstand a lengthy time period.

Running Wolf appeared annoyed that the harsh winter had not prevented the white men from continually increasing their stores of weapons, ammunition, and food. While the Indians had been camped for the winter awaiting the time to return to the Great Plains to replenish their stores, the white men had been replenishing all winter! Soon it would be time for the spring buffalo hunt. Would the Bluecoats take advantage of their scant rations and their preoccupation with this vital hunt? Would they press their upper hand at that critical moment? The camps would be open to successful attacks while the braves and warriors were away for many weeks. Plans must be made to protect their families and villages during this time.

Their talk was not interrupted by Leah, but by Bright Arrow as he raced inside and fell into his beloved grandfather's lap. The old man's eyes glowed with love and amusement as he laughed and teased this happy and energetic boy. He besieged the chief with countless questions about nature, his people, and the coming hunt. Bright Arrow was very intelligent and forward for a child of four years. Without a doubt, this mental advancement was the result of the endless hours spent with him by his father, his mother, and Running Wolf. When Running Wolf finished answering his questions, Bright Arrow instantly pleaded for him to repeat the stirring tales of his numerous coups. What did it matter that the boy knew each one? He never tired of hearing the exciting and daring tales again and again. The illustrious man chuckled and began his stories.

During the telling of the third one, Leah came forward

to hand Bright Arrow two pieces of *aguyapi* filled with dried nuts and specks of fruit. She smiled as she offered the treats to the small child, knowing he would delight in them, and knowing Shalee would not, since it was nearing the evening meal. Yet Shalee astutely did not call attention to their quarrel by halting Leah's intentionally divisive action.

Bright Arrow laughed and thanked her, manners having been drilled into him as into all the Oglala children from birth, as were respect and patience. At this moment, Bright Arrow's impatience and audacity were showing. The proper time for a gentle reprimand would come later, in private. Bright Arrow was indeed smart, but what small child could know of such devious schemes to impress and to blind him? Not wanting to appear petty before the chief or stern before her son, Shalee remained silent and calm. Leah instantly realized this small ploy had failed, for Shalee had refused her dangling bait.

When Bright Arrow stuffed the first pone into his mouth, Shalee laughed softly and chided him, "There is no raccoon here to steal your *aguyapi*, my greedy son. Eat slowly or your throat will reject such swiftly eaten treats. Perhaps your grandfather should use the second one to teach you how to eat properly," she merrily threatened.

Bright Arrow's boyish laughter filled the quiet tepee. "*Sha*," he joyously accepted her rebuke, placing his left hand in hers and smiling into her eyes. Ever so slowly, he politely nibbled upon the second pone as he listened to the voice of his grandfather, not once rudely interrupting him. But each time the chief hesitated for a breath of air during his narration, the excited child asked many questions to which he already knew the replies.

Two days later, Leah made another bold attempt to

35

unnerve Shalee. Soundlessly coming up behind Shalee and placing her burdens of wood sling and dirty clothes to either side of the unsuspecting Indian princess to endanger either path of retreat, Leah moved to stand beside Running Wolf as if merely waiting to speak with him.

Shalee finished her remarks and turned to leave, helplessly falling over the carefully and deviously placed wood sling. Shalee instinctively cried out as she toppled to the stony ground, soiling her dress and scraping her hands. Gray Eagle, standing and talking not far away, rushed forward to assist his wife and to check for injuries. Leah quickly seized the frantic moment to drop to her knees and profusely offer deceitful apologies for her carelessness.

"I'm so sorry, Shalee. Are you hurt?" she hurriedly questioned, her face and voice laced with feigned concern and remorse.

Shalee was helped up by her husband. She glanced at her torn and dirtied dress, then at her bleeding hands. Eyes chilled like pools of frozen green ice glared at Leah. "Perhaps Running Wolf should turn you over to the women for training, Leah. Such carelessness is dangerous and avoidable. An old person could have been injured badly by such a fall," she subtly warned the white girl, both aware of the abuse Leah would find under the women's watchful eyes and stern hands.

"But it was an accident, Shalee! I would never harm you or anyone here. I was in a hurry and didn't think clearly," Leah lied, forcing false tears to slip forth as if she were being wrongly and maliciously tormented.

"Accidents are for fools and enemies, Leah, not white captives. There is no valid excuse for such recklessness. Make certain it does not happen again."

More crocodile tears spilled down the white girl's cheeks. "Have I not been obedient and respectful? Have I not worked hard and done all asked of me? Have I ever caused anyone harm here? It is unkind of you to berate me so cruelly. I had not thought you like this," she murmured, unaware the valiant warrior also spoke perfect English. She merely assumed Shalee had taught him enough English to grasp a cunning word here and there, but not enough to comprehend each word; for his expression never revealed this fact to her.

The keen mind of Gray Eagle perceived the strong undercurrents that flowed between the two women. There was an enmity here that he had not observed before. The accident was a careless mistake, but why was his gentle and tenderhearted wife reacting so strangely to it and to this obviously frightened and contrite captive? This wasn't like Shalee. Something about this white girl was troubling her spirit. The glimmers of anger and repulsion in Shalee's eyes could not be concealed. Shalee had never been a vengeful or impatient person, even with just cause. But both emotions glittered in her stormy gaze as she stared at the offensive girl, who was weeping and apologizing. He was dismayed and perplexed by this new mood in his woman. If anything, Shalee had always been overly kind to and tolerant of white female captives! Why was this situation different?

He gently pulled upon her arm and suggested they tend to her hands. Her eyes softened the moment they touched upon his face. She smiled and nodded. Gray Eagle glanced at Leah, failing to pierce her false mask. She smiled ruefully at him and wisely lowered her head. The action went unnoticed by the retreating Shalee.

Leah cautioned herself not to smile victoriously or to sing with joy over her apparent success. She forced a

37

subdued and melancholy air to further her air of having been wrongly abused. She slowly walked away to perform her tasks, sensing she had instilled confusion in the stalwart warrior.

As Gray Eagle tenderly washed the blood and dirt from Shalee's hands, he remained silent and alert. Retrieving a parfleche from the edge of the tepee, he opened it and withdrew the pouch of healing ointment. He carefully applied it to the scrapes to halt the bleeding and to relieve the discomfort. After replacing the parfleche, he came forward to sit beside her.

"Shalee?" he inquisitively began. His brow was furrowed in deep speculation and his mood was serious. "Is there some trouble between you and the white girl?" He came right to the point of his concern.

Shalee's gaze shifted from her hands to his handsome face. "Trouble?" she echoed, allowing herself time to ponder a logical explanation.

Shalee had never been able to conceal anything from Gray Eagle's eyes or sharp senses. He immediately knew there was without her replying. "Tell me what private war you carry on with a lowly slave," he softly demanded, watching her closely.

Shalee deliberated this tense situation. Would she sound foolish and spiteful if she related her concerns? She had underestimated Leah; the white girl had cunningly made her game appear innocent and harmless. Could she voice aloud her unproven suspicions and fears? "There is something about Leah that disturbs me, Gray Eagle. I cannot discern what haunts me, but I do not trust her. I fear she is crafty like the fox, but I cannot guess her sport," she replied honestly, but withheld her doubts and Leah's words. Why, she wasn't certain.

"Has she disobeyed you?" When Shalee shook her

head, he asked another question, "Has there been another accident?" Again Shalee shook her head. "Does she defy my father or show him disrespect?" Once more, Shalee was forced to shake her head. "Then I do not understand, Grass Eyes," he concluded in rising bewilderment.

"I can't explain it, Gray Eagle; it is just a feeling I have. She cannot be trusted. You are a warrior and a hunter; do you not have inexplicable and strange feelings that come to you and seem to warn you of some future problem? Do you always comprehend such gnawings upon your mind?" she continued artfully, without revealing too much.

"It is so, Grass Eyes," he readily agreed. "But my father needs Leah to care for his needs. How can I punish her for feelings that haunt you? How can I send her away when she has done no wrong?" he reasoned.

Shalee held up her hands and asked, "This is not a wrong, my husband?"

"Do you wish me to punish her for an accident?" he asked, baffled. "She learned a great lesson; surely she will be more careful now."

Shalee decided not to argue his valid but mistaken conclusion. "You are right, my husband. Perhaps I am being silly. Maybe my spirits are plagued with a desire to return to busy life, like Makakin. The winter has been slow and long. Perhaps I am simply tense and bored," she laughed to excuse her behavior and attempt to change the subject.

"Perhaps I should take away your restless spirit and great energy," he jested, igneous eyes burning like two smoldering black coals.

"When we have eaten and Wi goes to sleep, I will remind you of your generosity, my love," she playfully announced, passing her hands over his shoulders and down his arms to grasp his hands. "Do you really know how much I love you and need you?" she murmured passionately, feeling an odd need to remind him.

"If your words did not tell me, your eyes would, Little One. Perhaps I should go and fetch our son so we can eat early. My body grows hungrier for you than for *wasna*." He grasped her face between his hands and kissed her soundly.

As his lips eased over to nibble at her ear, her hand moved to touch his groin. "You are right, my love; he strains with eagerness and hunger," she whispered, drawing a moan of desire from him.

"Do you ever grow weary of me, Gray Eagle? Do you ever desire to have another woman to sate your great needs?" she abruptly asked, stunning him.

He leaned back and gazed into her limpid eyes. The imploring look there increased his astonishment. "You speak with an honesty and concern that confuse and alarm me, Shalee. I have no need for another woman. You are the air I breathe and the food of my body. How could I ever grow weary of possessing only you? You are my love, my life, my heart," he vowed huskily.

She smiled, tears glistening in her eyes. "A woman needs to hear such things, my love. Sometimes the showing of such feelings is not enough. Women are foolish and weak creatures," she declared, laughing and kissing him.

He chuckled heartily and shook her playfully. "Hear me well, woman; I need no other female to care for me in any way. How can a man grow weary of a female who is fresh and exciting each time he possesses her? Where would my body gain strength to sate another female once you have lain with me? You leave no space for thoughts

40

or desires for another. Is that not true for you?" he teased, tugging upon her braid.

"It will always be that way for me. No man shall ever touch my heart and life as you have. Still, it is the Indian way to take more than one wife or woman," she reminded him.

"Only if one woman cannot fill his needs. Such is not true with us. You are the only woman I need or want. When Wi sleeps, I will prove this to my doubting wife," he taunted, a beguiling and promising grin claiming his arresting face and entrancing eyes.

She flung herself into his possessive embrace and hugged him tightly. She was indeed foolish; Leah was no threat to their great love, no woman was. It would always be this way between them, for their hearts were bound as tightly and securely as the arrowhead to a slender shaft. She sighed contentedly, snuggling up to his warm and inviting body. His heady aura invaded her senses. Flames of desire licked greedily at her smoldering womanhood. Her breasts grew taut with need. Her lips ached to have his ravish them.

Ever so lightly and provocatively she stroked his firm chest with her parted lips, her warm and ragged respiration calling out to him. Tremors passed over her as she sought his lips to fill the yearnings upon hers. Following several devastating kisses, he struggled to gently break her hold around his waist. "I will return shortly," he huskily declared, then quickly left their tepee.

As promised, he was at her side within minutes. He lifted her shapely body and carried her to his mats. With undeniable eagerness, he began to undress her. "What about our son and the cooking?" she halfheartedly debated with the powerful needs within them.

41

He grinned. "Bright Arrow will remain and eat with my father," he mirthfully announced, completing his chore. As he jerked his own garments off, she laughed.

"Did you tell him why you wished our son to remain there?" she asked, her face flushing with desire and lingering modesty.

"He is wise; he knew without words. He is also kind, for he yielded to our great needs," he cheerfully replied, coming to lie beside her.

Within moments, they were ensnared by the silky strands of love. As his lips enflamed her from head to toe, his masterful strokes drove her into frenzied response. Over and over he plunged into her receptive body, her lips encouraging him to claim them time and time again. He halted briefly and withdrew to enable his mouth to ecstatically torment her breasts. Then, he tenderly drove his manhood home once more, steadily increasing his depth and intent.

The peak attained, her body was assailed by the relenting shudders that conquered it. Just after he exploded within her and was intoxicatingly draining every drop of his release, Leah called from outside the sealed flap. Startled by her voice and untimely interruption, he stiffened and halted his movements. "*Sha?*" he nearly shouted in annoyance.

"Running Wolf went to the meeting lodge. Bright Arrow is sick. I did not know what to do," she related her words in English.

The beautiful moment spoiled by her no doubt devious intrusion, Shalee also tensed in moody irritation. Gray Eagle gazed down at her and shrugged his shoulders in appeal. "Bring our son here while I dress," Shalee suggested to cover her vexation. "If he is ill, I must tend him," she added, her vivid disbelief clear to him.

He nodded and arose to pull on his garments. He unlaced the flap and faced the white girl with her demurely lowered lashes and bowed head. "I'm sorry to disturb you, Gray Eagle, but your son cries with a stomachache. I have no medicine to give him. It is not permitted to enter or approach the meeting lodge." Thus she promptly issued her nettlingly valid logic.

Without speaking to her, Gray Eagle brushed past her and headed for his father's tepee. When he found his son lying upon the mat clutching his painful stomach, he knew why Bright Arrow had not come to the tepee himself. He comforted his son as he lifted his taut body to carry him to Shalee. Once more he ignored Leah as he swept past her bearing his light and precious burden.

Leah returned to Running Wolf's tepee and danced around in glee. Running Wolf couldn't have assisted her scheme better if he had fed the child countless fruit pones himself! How timely his trip to the meeting lodge had been! Leah had listened to the sounds of passion sifting through the hides of Gray Eagle's tepee for a while before selecting the best time to dispel their fiery union. But she hadn't counted on their passionate joining's being so entrancing they couldn't hear her call out as they found such blissful relief! She had planned to interfere at the most critical moment, but had been denied that malicious pleasure. Still, the peaceful aftermath had been ruined.

Leah halted her merriment to drop upon b⸍ mat, opposite from Running Wolf's. In ᵗʰᵉʳ Eagle tortured her mind and body an⸍ happiness. Overwhelming lust cou⸍ for that perfect specimen o⸍ thoughts filled her mind, h⸍ long denied during her e⸍

breasts ached and her lips craved a mouth to torment and pleasure them.

Dusk filtered into the tepee as she squirmed in frustration upon the sleeping mat, pleading for slumber to halt the fierce cravings of her wanton body. As she unconsciously wiped glistening beads of anxiety from her upper lip, her hand brushed against a swollen breast. The accidental contact drew a sharp intake of air and a soft moan from her parted lips. How she longed for Gray Eagle to caress her body and to ravish her, laying waste to her aching desires. Entrapped in her world of heady desire, she failed to hear the silent return of Running Wolf.

Low moans and tell-tale breathing came from the white girl smoldering from the flames of unrequited passion. Leah had miscalculated Running Wolf's potency or ability to mate with a woman. He was still virile and desirable. Suddenly his member throbbed with a fierce craving to sate himself with the captive girl who could not refuse him any wish or command. Seized by overwhelming desire, off came his garments. Astonished by this sudden surge of new life, he eyed the protruding member, then smiled as he lovingly stroked it. After two years of vexing impotency, he was dizzy with the heady reality which throbbed within his hand. Bedazzled, he could do no less than prove his sexual prowess had mysteriously returned.

He went to Leah and lay down. Frightened by his sudden appearance and by his naked body upon her mat, e tried to roll aside. *"Hiya!"* he ordered her to prompt ⁻nce. The tone of his commanding voice and the on in his eyes warned her to submit to nted. She whined and pleaded, knowing oiled if this old man ravished her.

Running Wolf grinned as he yanked off her dress and breechcloth.

His eyes glazed with rising lust as they fell upon the ripe, full breasts. He lay upon her, sucking greedily and none too gently upon them. His wrinkled hands roamed her body, testing its appeal and need. He parted her thighs and pushed a finger into her moist recess to check its preparation. He chuckled as he withdrew the finger covered with wetness. Still, Leah pleaded for release. Not wanting to be distracted or swayed, Running Wolf's hand covered her mouth briefly as he demanded, *"Iyasni,"* for silence.

Terrified by the strength in his body and her precarious position of enslavement, she willed herself to silence and submission. Her safety and truce were too vital to endanger by resisting him. She suppressed a scream as he drove into her body, which felt shock, because of her lengthy abstinence. He halted momentarily as he smiled his pleasure at her supposed previous purity. Then, he diligently worked upon his pleasure. His manhood was large and firm for his age and size. As easily and skillfully as he had plundered enemy camps, he plundered her body.

Her lustful moisture made his fierce drivings easier. Back and forth his hips drove until he spewed hot liquid into her body, each spasm felt by the enraptured Leah. Her tight womanhood sent him into a frenzy as he ravished it. As his body reeled with the force of his successful task, he chewed painfully upon her erect nipples.

Yet Leah did not cry out. Strange, but after the initial sharp entry, her womanhood greedily accepted his savage invasion. As he moaned with satisfaction and excitement, curious delight filled her at her power to so move

45

this important man. He was like a small child; and she, a savory treat. Over and over he helplessly sampled her delights, creating strange feelings within her. She realized the powerful chief was crazed with pleasure from her body. Like some starving animal, he was voraciously devouring her and sating his hunger. The pain had given over to a pleasant and thrilling sensation. Each time he drove into her, it was like stroking sensitive nerves that tingled and begged for more caressing. The oddest part of all was when he began savagely to pound his manhood into her and to gnaw upon her aching breasts—the rougher he became, the greater her pleasure! The agony soon became intoxicating; the delightful pain became an addicting drug that she craved more and more.

As one unfamiliar with savage joinings but who had been denied any recent union with a female, Running Wolf did not recognize a bewitching fascination in the actions of the white girl beneath him as she arched upwards and coaxed his throbbing manhood to forcefully stab into her inviting recess with even greater power. He nearly went wild with desire when she grasped his graying head and moved his mouth from breast to breast as if denying one sweet mound more satisfaction than the other. He was dazed and enflamed when she writhed beneath him, her longings increasing with more and more pain. As his torrid member exploded within her eager and demanding body, he sucked and chewed upon each nipple until it was raw. Yet Leah never resisted this treatment; her actions pleaded for more, enslaving him.

When they lay spent upon the mat, Leah savored this mysterious and exhilarating experience. If Running Wolf could incite her to such mindless delights, imagine what his virile and strong son could do to her body! Whatever it took, she would bring Gray Eagle under her control and spell. The chief was sleeping peacefully. Leah propped herself upon her elbow to study him more closely. Evidently he wasn't as old as she had imagined. In fact, Running Wolf hadn't lost all his ruggedly handsome looks and physical appeal. She hadn't noticed before, but he was very appealing: his face and his body.

Her eyes traced every line of his still robust frame. As they touched upon his manhood, she realized it was large even in its limp state. Her gaze glued to it as if willing it to new life. Deliriously heady about these wonderful new sensations, Leah's fiery body resisted sleep for a long time.

The following day, Leah and Shalee carefully avoided each other, each fearing the other would read emotions that both wanted to remain hidden until brought under control. That night, Leah and Running Wolf repeated their animalistic joining. Another day passed as Shalee and Leah successfully prevented any meeting between themselves.

That night, Leah realized something new and enthralling; the chief was watching her and trailing around her like a male dog after a bitch in heat! It was obvious the greedy old hound couldn't wait until bedtime! So, the lowly white slave had powerful magic between her legs! That realization sent shivers of malicious pleasure over her. With a little effort and time, she would have him eating out of her hand. She would weave a tight spell around him and soon he would be *her* slave! Then, she could do as she pleased, as long as she pleased him upon his mats. She would possess a great hold over him. Once drugged by her, he would obey her every whim or risk finding a limp body beneath him! She would become an intoxicating habit he would not resist or deny. When he was bodily enslaved to her, she would entice him to buy a white slave to do the chores, allowing her more time and energy to see to his other needs. She smiled.

The flap already laced tightly, Running Wolf sat down beside her as she completed her last chore. Never had any female, white or Indian, so matched his sexual prowess or lusty appetite. He could hardly wait to take her again. His palms itched; nervous perspiration gleamed upon his body. He licked his lips in anticipation. His manhood throbbed to be released from the now tight breechcloth. He was too mesmerized by her behavior to recognize the danger or the shame in his carnal lust.

Leah seductively and tauntingly unlaced her doeskin dress to expose her breasts to his gleaming eyes. When she felt he had tormented them sufficiently, she unknotted his breechcloth and let it fall from his body. She grasped the member and delighted in its warmth and hardness. Soon, the vicious union was taking place for the third night in a row. Having been Running Wolf's captive since last summer, Leah wondered why he had waited so long to demand his rights upon her mat. But already her lust for Gray Eagle filled her with dissatisfaction. During their second joining of bodies, she had closed her eyes, as she did now, pretending he was his son. This action served to increase her responses and desires, leading Running Wolf to think he held great power over her body.

As she watched him sleep, she smiled wantonly as her mind returned to plotting a perfect scheme to entrap his son. If need be, she would rid herself of this problem at the same time she destroyed Shalee. Now that she knew of her sexual prowess and was honing her skills each night, her confidence grew by leaps and bounds. It was time to put her plans into action.

Chapter Three

It was four days later before Running Wolf became aware of what was taking place within his mind and body. But this knowledge didn't come from within his distorted brain, it came rather from the distressed perception of White Arrow. At first, White Arrow resisted the signs his instincts detected. When he could no longer deny something evil was in the wind, he made it his purpose to investigate his suspicions without drawing any attention to them.

He furtively observed Leah and her growing air of self-assurance, which bordered upon arrogance. He watched Running Wolf as his gaze lustfully followed nearly every move the white captive made. Although a grown man, who was skilled upon the mats himself, embarrassment and dismay filled him as he twice observed the bulging crotch upon the aging chief. White Arrow keenly read the enticing looks sent to the chief from the daring white girl. He was unsettled as Running Wolf helplessly responded to her sensual callings. When Running Wolf made any attempt to remain in his tepee to be near Leah, White Arrow knew he had guessed correctly. But to make absolutely certain there was no mistake, White Arrow dauntlessly and covertly wandered near Running Wolf's tepee at night. The sounds and words that greeted his alert ears sickened him. He hadn't been wrong after all. . . .

So he had been in grave error last summer when he presented this evil girl to the chief to be his slave, nothing more! Now she was using some powerful magic from her body to make a fool of their great chief! Gray Eagle was still visiting in the camp of the Cheyenne. For an instant, White Arrow wished he was with his friend. What would Gray Eagle think and do when he discovered this repulsive situation? As his best friend, could he relate such offensive news? Should he?

The saddest part of all was that the chief didn't realize what was taking place. The moment that thought came forth, White Arrow knew what he must do. Now, as they stood by the riverbank during the afternoon sun when others were resting, White Arrow didn't know where or how to begin. This revolting matter was private and touchy; it must be handled gingerly.

His dilemma was solved when he turned to witness Running Wolf's anxious pacing. Each time the chief halted and glanced toward camp, White Arrow knew what he wanted: to be upon the mats in his tepee with that conniving Leah! Was he so ensnared by her fiery blood that he couldn't see what was happening to him? White Arrow's hesitation and embarrassment gave way to annoyance and boldness.

Before he knew what words were forming within his mind and mouth, they had angrily spilled forth. "Is your lust for Leah so great that you can no longer stand still for a cloud to pass over Wi's face? Does your manhood throb with such need that you must lower yourself to sniff after her like some animal with the mating fever upon you? Since when does the noble Sioux chief desire to ride between a white whore's legs rather than upon his war pony or on a hunt? Is her magic so great that even the great Running Wolf cowers before her and pleads for entrance into her evil cave? Do you believe the other warriors will not soon question why their chief hides in his tepee when he is needed in the meeting lodge or upon the hunt? My face is stained with dishonor for bringing such evil to your tepee."

Astounded by White Arrow's audacity and stinging words, it was some time before his statements and concern settled in the chief's mind. When they did, he was stunned to comprehend his actions and weakness. "Why do you speak this way to your chief, White Arrow?" he began, unable to pull forth the best words.

"Because you are my chief and the father of my best friend. Because I love and respect you. Others have not noticed this magic spell she has cast over you, but soon all will see it. Do not dishonor yourself or your son by falling prey to such weakness. The Great Spirit opened my eyes to this brewing trouble so I might warn you of its results. You are chief; she is a lowly white slave, Running Wolf. Yet she calls and you obey. It should not be this way. I have spoken as the Great Spirit commanded me. Never will these words leave my lips again."

"I am ashamed, White Arrow," the chief admitted, lowering his head. "I am not worthy to be chief of the Oglala, for I allowed myself to become the slave of a slave."

White Arrow studied the slump-shouldered man before his gaze. Suddenly Running Wolf looked old and tired. He sought to remove some of the sting barbs his words had inflicted. "Is it not said that an aging man can fall prey to the mating fever when he needs to prove his manhood and prowess? Has the fever not passed now that your prowess has been proven and the truth fills your

51

mind? Can you not resist her magic now? Once more, Running Wolf is chief and Leah is the slave. Is this not so?"

Comprehending the meaning beneath the words of White Arrow, Running Wolf smiled and nodded. "The Great Spirit opened your eyes, White Arrow, and now you have opened mine. The fever has passed," he agreed.

The two men talked for a while longer. Both were certain no one else knew of his brief madness, but Shalee did. Neither would ever speak of this tormenting matter again. The decision was made; in a few weeks, Leah should be sent away. The two powerful warriors grasped forearms and smiled into each other's eyes.

"You are a true friend, White Arrow. I will not forget this coup, which must remain a secret. You have saved the life and honor of your chief."

"I accept your gratitude, Running Wolf, for I know you would do the same for me. We will find ways to make her appear a useless and troublesome slave. No one will question her sale."

When Running Wolf returned to his tepee, Leah wondered at his coldness and rejection of her advances. He called her names she did not understand, but the tone of his insulting voice was infuriatingly clear. When she seductively stroked his groin to entice him, he slapped her hand away. His eyes filled with venom and fury, he sent her falling backwards with a stunning blow to her face.

Leah got his message; he was finished with her. Something, or perhaps someone, had broken her spell! He was showing her he was in full command of himself and this situation. The hatred and repulsion upon his face, now distorted with rage, warned of her precarious departure. She had revealed weakness and defeat to him; he would never tolerate it again, nor her continued presence. She dreaded to ponder the length of her stay here. The person who had foiled her plans would pay dearly. . . .

Shalee lay upon her sleeping mat alone, but her warring emotions would neither grant her peace of mind nor sleep. Although she had kept her distance from Leah for many days, she had witnessed the changes in the vile female: the conceit and the baffling confidence. Two nights ago, she had learned why. After Bright Arrow was fast asleep, she had gone to visit Running Wolf, as was her custom every two days. Before she could call out for admittance, Leah's voice and words singed her ears. Shalee couldn't believe the things she was hearing. She was instantly grateful very few understood English. Her temptation to force her way into the tepee and expose the wanton girl's intention was halted by the humiliation Running Wolf would endure. For two days she had fretted over how to handle this degrading situation. Gray Eagle would be furious; he would kill her with his bare hands!

What could she tell him when he returned in two more moons? She had never been able to conceal anything from him. Shalee couldn't bring herself to approach Running Wolf with her proven suspicions. Learning she could never attain Gray Eagle, Leah had apparently settled for the chief. She didn't have to wonder how. She knew.

Later that evening, Running Wolf came to visit Bright Arrow and Shalee. He practically invited himself to eat the late meal with them, then stayed until it was very late. As Shalee observed the Oglala warrior with his grandson,

53

enlightenment filled her; happiness quickly joined it. Running Wolf had seen the light and was denying Leah's charms. She could detect the renewal of fierce pride and strength within him. Shalee quickly decided Leah had lost her battle and would soon be gone. Running Wolf would never tempt himself to another self-betrayal or to unforgivable weakness. His brazen ecstasy had ended. . . .

That night both Shalee and Running Wolf slept peacefully. But Leah did not. She was busy planning her revenge on White Arrow, for his look of fierce hatred informed her of her new enemy. . . .

When Gray Eagle returned home, he was greeted by a cheerful father and an ecstatic wife. Running Wolf was asked to join them for late meal, to visit and to discuss Gray Eagle's trip to the camp of the Cheyenne.

The evening was long, but enjoyable. When Running Wolf finally bid them goodnight and left, Shalee fell into her husband's arms and covered his face with kisses. "I missed you greatly, my love. Our mat is cold and empty without you."

"As it should be, Grass Eyes, then you will love and desire my presence even more," he teased, closing his arms around her. Later he would tell her he must ride to the camp of their Sioux brothers, the Sisseton Tribe, at first light on the next sun. For now, he craved to hold her and savor her love.

Their need overpowering, they joined quickly and fiercely to quench this thirst within them, to drink of their shared love and passion. As Shalee nestled into his embrace, she whispered softly, "There is more you did not tell me, my love," alert to the solemn mood that now claimed him.

"Have I no secrets from you, Grass Eyes? Should I rename you Eagle Eye?" They both laughed.

"One name and two endearing terms are sufficient, my love. What news did you forget to tell me?" She returned to her greater concern.

He sighed heavily and propped himself upon his elbow to gaze down into her liquid green eyes. "When Wi shows his new face, I must ride to the camp of the Sisseton to tell them many things," he reluctantly told her.

Disappointment filled her eyes and clouded them. "But you just came home," she promptly argued against his hasty departure and another separation.

"I am band leader, Shalee. It is my duty to relate the words spoken in the camp of the Cheyenne. I will be out of your sight for only three moons. When I return, we will break camp and return to the Plains. You will one day become the wife of the chief. You must learn to share me with my people and my duties," he playfully scolded her.

Disregarding his words of jest, she replied seriously, "I know, Gray Eagle. But often this sharing is difficult and frightening. I wish you could remain at my side day and night forever. Even that would not be long enough," she added, drawing his head down to fuse his lips with hers.

Running his tongue over her lips, he enflamed her senses once more. "You must learn patience, Little One; you are Indian now. Soon the buffalo hunt will take me from your side for many weeks. Should we not enjoy our times together, no matter how long or brief?"

"I'm going with you this time," she casually announced. "When you halt at night to rest, I will lie at your side."

55

"The buffalo hunt is dangerous, Shalee; the work is hard and bloody. What of our son and my father?" he tenderly reminded her of her other duties.

"Shining Light can take care of our son, and Leah can see to Running Wolf's needs. I wish to be with you," she petulantly vowed.

"What if you are with child then?" he unexpectedly and unwittingly asked. Unable to take the hurtful words back, he kissed her to remove their sting.

When the heady kiss ended, she met his rueful gaze and softly entreated, "If you desire another son, Great Eagle of the Sioux, you must work for it. Place your seeds within me and I will pray to the Great Spirit to plant them there," she encouraged, revealing no anger at his words.

How they both longed for another child, a child who was yet to be conceived, no matter how many times they had joined since Bright Arrow's birth. "The Great Spirit knows and sees all, my love. When the time is right, He will grant us more children. You will see," she comforted him, knowing each prayed for this gift each day.

"If you are not with child, you can come on the buffalo hunt with me," he acquiesced, to lessen her sadness and pain.

She laughed and remarked, "Perhaps then new life will grow within me as it does upon our lands. We will find an albino skin to wrap around our new son when he is born."

"Your face beams like Wi's. When he is born, we will name him Sun Cloud until he seeks his vision and new name."

"Sun Cloud . . ." She rolled the name upon her lips. "Yes, he shall be called Sun Cloud. He will shine brightly before our people and rain upon our enemies," she commented with rising joy.

"Sun clouds reveal the power of the Thunderbirds. Our new son will draw his strength and cunning from them. First, we must make a new child," he suggested roguishly, leaning forward to kiss her.

His kiss was leisurely and deliberate, driving all thoughts from her mind except those of fusing her body to his. He trailed his fingertips from her throat to her groin, then slowly returned to her breast. His movements caused her stomach to tighten and her pulse to race. To be so strong, his touch could be as light as a feather and as warm as the sunlight. Each spot he touched tingled and glowed. How she dearly loved this man who had once been her fierce enemy, who had stolen her purity and heart, who had given her joys and pleasures beyond belief. Was it wrong to be so happy?

Wrong, no; but perhaps dangerous. It seemed as if some evil force could not tolerate perfection and ecstasy. It always sought some malicious way to destroy or to damage it. Annoyed by such dire thoughts at a moment like this, she cast them aside to concentrate upon her lover. She eagerly returned his fiery kisses and gave him the same pleasures he was giving her. Her hands roved his body as some dextrous expedition exploring and mapping it. How wonderful he felt, so firm and smooth, so warm and responsive.

She giggled as his tongue circled her breast, anticipating his attack upon her defenseless peak. She moaned as he teased it with his teeth, his hands roaming freely over her body. The blissful tension and sweet ecstasy were always present. If possible, she could remain entwined with him for days or months or years. Was there another love as powerful as theirs, a passion as fiery and fulfilling? She doubted it.

He was in a playful, tempting mood tonight. Each time he eased into her, he would slowly withdraw until she begged for another stroke. He laughed in total abandonment. His woman. She would always belong only to him. But their game soon became serious as their fiery passion flamed hotter, threatening to fuse their souls together. His strokes became rapid and his kiss evinced his rising fervor. Each inch of her cried out to feel the rapture only Gray Eagle could grant.

His body shook with intensity as he followed her release. His control cast aside, he pursued her over the summit into the tranquil valley. Reluctant to withdraw from her body so soon and not wanting to place his full weight upon her, he propped his elbows on either side of her head and gazed down at her. Such love and tenderness were reflected there. Her heart swelled with those same emotions. "Forever," she murmured.

"Forever," he happily agreed, kissing her lightly. They talked for a while before relenting to slumber and wonderful dreams.

Shalee waved as her husband and his band of warriors rode off early the next morning, heading for another talk of battles and hunts. When they were out of sight, she turned and entered their tepee to sleep a while longer. As she lay down, she could smell the heady odor of her lover still clinging to the mats. She pressed her face to that spot, inhaling his lingering essence as she drifted off to sleep.

When Shalee and Bright Arrow finally awakened, the day passed slowly and uneventfully, too quietly, since Bright Arrow was entertained nearly all day by his grandfather. It seemed more like days than hours before night descended once more.

The next day was warm and sunny; April would soon reveal her lovely face. This fateful day began much like yesterday's uneventful one, but it did not end that way. Shalee decided to take advantage of the nice weather to wash garments in the river, which was around seven hundred feet from the last tepee in their winter camp, the one which fed the narrow stream that flowed peacefully beside their campground. Eager for exercise and diversion, Bright Arrow tagged along with his mother.

Today, Shalee allowed her auburn hair to flow wild and free down her back, secured from her ivory face with a beaded headband. She and Bright Arrow held hands as they leisurely strolled along, her garments loosely thrown over her other arm. They halted by the bank and watched the swirling power of the swollen river, which was nearly over its bank because of the melting snows from the nearby mountains. Shalee warned her son to stand clear of the slippery bank, for the forceful water could easily carry a person away. Even a skilled swimmer could not defeat its present power.

Shalee dropped the garments and knelt to test the water's temperature. She quivered at its still icy tinge. Perhaps it would be best to carry water to her tepee and warm it first. Surely her hands would be numb within minutes if she plunged them into the frigid water. The way the currents were tearing at anything weak or loose, they would no doubt yank her garments from her hands and steal them.

When a red fox with white-tipped ears and tail came to the other side to drink, Shalee pointed him out to her son. They laughed and watched him as he shook his head as icy water rushed up his nose. The fox held their full attention too long, much too long.

Not far away, two pairs of eyes were watching the woman and child at the riverbank. "You really think that's the Eagle's son, Starnes?" one man apprehensively and excitedly questioned the other.

"Look at his *wanapin*. It's Bright Arrow all right," the second man concluded, smugness filling him.

As Bright Arrow half turned to speak to the woman, the silver arrow dangling from his neck captured the sunlight and sent shimmers that caught the first man's attention. "You're right, by damn! You still think we can grab him before any alarm could be given?" he worriedly pressed.

"Half the warriors are gone and the rest of 'em are sleeping this time of day. We could have 'em and be gone afore anyone knows what happened," the other confidently stated.

"What about the woman? Our horses can't bear that much extra weight."

"From the looks of 'er, she's just a white captive. 'Sides, she ain't no more good after them Injuns have had 'er. We'll have to kill 'er."

"I ain't never kilt no woman afore. I'll take the boy and you deal with 'er."

"Don't make no never mind to me. If she was any good, she wouldn't still be alive and feeling so cheerful. Sh-h-h, they're heading this way. Get ready. When I give the word, you grab the boy. Mind he don't make nary a sound."

When Shalee and Bright Arrow stopped within feet of where the two soldiers were concealing themselves, the deadly plan went into motion. Well-trained and determined, they acted too quickly for Shalee to react or to cry

60

out for help. Starnes spoke the only Sioux word he knew to catch their attention, *"Hiya."*

Both Shalee and Bright Arrow turned simultaneously to see who shouted "no" at them. A band of steel closed around Bright Arrow's squirming body and a large hand over his mouth as the first man seized and imprisoned him in an iron grip. Shalee only briefly saw her danger coming, too late to avoid it. The rifle butt crashed into her temple. Instant blackness claimed her as the forceful blow sent her backwards into the awesome river. Within moments, she disappeared from sight.

Bright Arrow struggled with all his might to pull free and to save his mother; he could not. He stared at the spot where she had gone down, not to surface within his sight again. He was quickly bound and gagged, then hauled away to their horses. He was placed before the largest and strongest man in the dark blue garments with sunny yellow trim. Tears eased down his cheeks into the nasty gag, not from fear, only from heartrending agony. The men walked their horses a safe distance before galloping headlong for Fort Henry to the north. It was only too clear what the infamous Gray Eagle would trade for his son's life. . . .

Another pair of eyes watched this fierce and tragic battle, but their owner did nothing. The green eyes shifted from the spot where the two riders had disappeared into the trees to the riverbank where one obstacle to her success had been removed for her. Leah smiled as she tossed Shalee's garments into the bushes to conceal them, then casually returned to camp. Suddenly she was deliriously exhausted and wished to rest a while. . . .

Running Wolf was the first to discover Shalee and

Bright Arrow were missing. Several times later that day he walked the short distance between their tepees to visit with them, each time to find they had not returned. Dusk was rapidly approaching and the chilly winds were picking up; the threat of one last snow flurry hung heavily in the unpredictable weather, which was common for this time of year and this area. Some intangible feeling of danger refused to leave his mind.

He made his rounds of the tepees where he hoped his dearly loved family were visiting, to find neither person. As if winter was resolved not to yield easily or graciously to spring, the winds increased their force and the spidery clouds drifted closer toward the camp. Eventually only heavy gray sky sprinkled with fleecy cirrus clouds could be seen in every direction above the land. Worry rose higher and higher as time passed.

Running Wolf summoned the aid of several braves to search for his family; they, too, discovered no sign or news of them. The search spread out into the surrounding area: the nearby forest and the riverbank that barely contained the turgid flow of violently agitated water.

Moon Gazer gave a loud yell from downstream. The others hurried to where he was squatting. His dark gaze was bright with distress and fury. Running Wolf, his heart heavy with panic and anguish, dropped to his knees to study the signs that Moon Gazer was pointing out. He-Who-Stands-Tall-Like-The-Tree added another torturous clue to their rapidly formulating conclusion: from the nearby bushes, he held up the buckskin garments that had been tossed there to conceal them. He told of the boot tracks left there, and the significance of that additional clue needed no further deliberation.

Moon Gazer traced the boot tracks to where two horses

had been hidden and noted the direction their enemies had taken. Talking Rock traced a more ominous trail to the edge of the turbulent river. Knowing how futile his visual search was, he frantically strained to scan each side of the riverbank for a lengthy distance. Accidentally ensnaring several blades of stained and withered grass as he retrieved a tormenting clue, he hurried to where Running Wolf was anxiously talking with the other braves.

"The Bluecoats have dared to steal the wife and son of our great warrior and my son! Their fort that stands upon the face of Mother Earth will be destroyed for this unforgivable deed! We must prepare to ride!"

His hate-clouded eyes scanned the leaden sky overhead. "We must not wait for Wi to guide us. When the snow comes, their trail will be lost to us. Moon Gazer, summon two braves and ride swiftly to warn my son of this new treachery. Talking Rock, call the warriors together. We ride for revenge and to rescue my family."

Talking Rock sighed heavily, wishing he was not the one to deliver the bad news to his chief and friend. In a distinct voice whose strain could not be controlled, he stated, "The Bluecoats did not take Princess Shalee."

All eyes focused upon the stalwart brave and exposed their confusion. Several colorful beads dropped to the hard earth as Talking Rock displayed the object he had been holding behind his back: the severed, bloodstained headband of Princess Shalee. Talking Rock could barely master his quavering voice as he informed the stunned group, "Her trail leads to the mighty river; it does not return. The blow that placed her blood upon her headband and broke it was a fierce one. The signs say she fell into the water and was quickly swept away. She was taken by surprise, for there was no struggle."

Running Wolf instantly protested. "Perhaps she was injured and the Bluecoats carried her off!"

Lines of anguish furrowed Talking Rock's forehead. "It is not so, Running Wolf. The weight of her limp body would have changed the depth of the Bluecoats' tracks upon Makakin's face; it did not. My keen eyes searched the hands of the mighty river that hold her fury back; there is no sign of her. The currents are swift and demanding; the water is cold and icy. Injured and weakened, Shalee could not have saved herself. Surely she walks with the Great Spirit now. We must avenge her and return Bright Arrow to his people." He sought to turn their minds from the obviously lost Shalee to the endangered son of Gray Eagle.

Not that they doubted the skills or words of Talking Rock, but the warriors rushed forward to discern the clues for themselves. A cry of agony rent the air as Running Wolf could not disagree with Talking Rock's statements. Still, hope did not give in to despair so easily. "Man-Of-Two-Feathers, take braves and search both sides of the river. If she lives, she must be found quickly. Come, we ride," the furious chief ordered, turning to lead the way.

In less than twenty minutes, Moon Gazer was heading toward the Sisseton Camp with his gloomy news; Man-Of-Two-Feathers and his small band of braves set out upon their futile search of the river banks; then, Running Wolf and Talking Rock left with a band of valiant men painted for war. Leah watched them ride away in different directions. Perhaps Bright Arrow could be rescued; if not, she would gladly bear the noble Eagle another son. A cruel sneer twisted her lips as she delighted in the knowledge that Shalee was lost to that puissant and compelling warrior. Soon, he would require a female to soothe his anguish and to sate his needs. Who better than a female who strikingly resembled his lost love? . . .

It was two suns since Gray Eagle's departure, and three more days had passed before two groups of Indians thundered into the winter camp of the awesome Sioux, joining another one, which had returned empty-handed the day before. As if mystically ordered to utter silence, the warriors wordlessly and solemnly headed to the Tribal Council as the call severed the silence: *"Ku-wa, Oglala, Oyate Omniciye!"*

His heart thudding and his senses tasting a fear he had never known before, Gray Eagle sat down upon his mat and crossed his sinewy legs. So many emotions racked his towering frame that he dared not speak. His mind in a vicious turmoil, he could not think clearly. His warring thoughts kept returning to an agonizing day over five winters ago when other Bluecoats had attacked his village and stolen Shalee, then Alisha Williams, from his side. That time, he had humiliated the soldiers, destroyed their wooden fort, and retaken his love. But this time was different: His only son was a prisoner of the white dogs and his cherished wife's fate was unknown. The Bluecoats did not need to slay him to destroy him; the loss of his only son and wife would accomplish that seemingly impossible feat for them!

Gray Eagle's imploring gaze went to the bowed head of Man-Of-Two-Feathers, his aura speaking louder and clearer than his words could. If he was to control his wits, Man-Of-Two-Feathers' report must come last. Gray Eagle swallowed several times to force the lump from his throat before he could speak. The others remained silent, knowing how difficult this situation was for their great warrior, sharing his anguish and fury.

"*Michenkshe?*" Running Wolf tenderly spoke to his somber son.

"Speak, Father; tell us how to return Bright Arrow to his people." Gray Eagle encouraged the dull-eyed man to handle this trying episode, suspecting his turmoil would perilously glaze his wits.

Their gazes met and locked, each feeling the pain in the other. As Running Wolf spoke, Gray Eagle noted the weariness and dejection in his father. "The fort is strong, my son; there are many Bluecoats there. This act will call for much strength, cunning, and bravery. Perhaps I am too old and weak to lead my people this time," he slowly announced.

"You have enjoyed the breath of the Great Spirit for only sixty winters, Father. Your body speaks of strength; your heart of courage; and your mind of cunning. It is not so with me. My keen senses are dulled with sadness and worry. Even my courage wavers before such deadly odds," Gray Eagle stated, but his warriors did not believe such words. There was no man braver or more cunning and daring than Gray Eagle. No man could boast of coups to match his in number or in greatness. Once the shock of this deed wore off, he would also realize these truths.

"We watched the white man's fort as Wi awakened and until he slept once more. I saw no way to enter there and hold our lives safe. The trees are lashed together so tightly, no eyes or arrow could sneak through them. They are so tall, no warrior could sneak over them. Even at night, it would be impossible, for the cunning Bluecoats

66

have sharp lances pointing downward from the top of the wooden guard around them. Many white-eyes guard the fort in all directions. They have many weapons and supplies. No plan comes to my old mind," Running Wolf stated regretfully.

Next came a question Gray Eagle had to ask, "Do you think Bright Arrow lives?"

As if reflecting a war dance, glittering images moved within his eyes. "Though we stayed hidden, the Bluecoats knew we were there. They knew we would track them to their hiding place. Three times as Wi gave his light, Bright Arrow was shown to us from the small wooden tepee at the top of the pointed trees where the Bluecoats stand guard. Your son is brave; he does you great honor. Not once did he cry or call for help. He stood straight and tall beside his enemies."

Gray Eagle sighed in relief: alive and well. But a difference more deadly than their skin colors separated the Indians from the whites there. "The white-eyes spoke no words to you?" he pressed.

"Each time they revealed Bright Arrow, they spoke only your name: Gray Eagle. They call for you to come and talk. Their meaning is clear; they want the son of Running Wolf, not the son of Gray Eagle."

"Man-Of-Two-Feathers," Gray Eagle addressed the other frightful subject. "Speak of your search." He could not bring himself to say her name, dreading the effect of it before his warriors.

Man-Of-Two-Feathers cleared his throat loudly. "We searched the riverbanks on either side for countless lengths of our strides. We found nothing."

"Nothing?" Gray Eagle echoed incredulously. How was that possible?

"Princess Shalee could not be found. There were no tracks leading from the riverbanks," he added, knowing what the others would deduce from those words. To give lingering hope, he said, "Perhaps the snows covered any trail she made when she left the water."

Gray Eagle withdrew the broken headband from his waist. He looked at it for a long time. The dried blood had flaked and fallen off the hard, smooth beads; but not before he had viewed it. His mind's eye could still envision that ghastly sight when it had been reluctantly placed within his grasp in the Sisseton Camp. Could she still live with such an injury and exposure to the freezing water? His keen and troubled mind said no, but his pain-riddled heart screamed yes. What had she said to him so recently? Something about evil often being more powerful than good? Something about the fear of being too happy? No, he would never accept her death until he viewed her lifeless body!

His body assaulted by conflicting emotions, his fathomless gaze shifted from one man to the next until it halted upon the face of his father beside him. "Perhaps I have become too proud and confident in my coups. Perhaps the Great Spirit seeks to teach me humility and trust in Him. Perhaps He tests my courage, patience, and faith. If He has called Shalee to live at His side, I will avenge her death. But I will never mourn for her until she rests upon the death scaffold before my eyes. If it is as you say, Father, there is but one way to save the life of my son."

Running Wolf started to interrupt his son, but controlled his outburst, as it was not their way to halt the flow of words from another during council. Gray Eagle continued. "The Bluecoats view my name as their most

68

feared enemy, not the man Gray Eagle himself. They will not rest until it is sung with the Death Chant. Without Shalee and my son, my heart will slowly die. I must prove my courage and faith in the Great Spirit; I must trade my life for that of my son. Perhaps Wakantanka has chosen Bright Arrow to be the next leader of the Oglala, not Gray Eagle. If He so wills, both our lives will be spared. Bright Arrow's safety and life must be considered before mine. Moon Gazer, begin a new search for Shalee. If she lives, Wakantanka will lead you to her. I will ride to the fort. This bitter deed must be done quickly."

Sleep did not come to Gray Eagle that night; his barren tepee was oppressive and lonely. He lay upon his back on his mat, his forearm resting over his closed eyes. There was no decision to be made; the events settled the matter for him. If he refused the demand of the Bluecoats, the body of Bright Arrow would be tossed outside the wooden fort. Many times the Bluecoats had brutally slain innocent women and children; yet they called his people savages! Was there no mercy or kindness within the white hearts that invaded his lands? Was there no price too great to pay for their greed? For certain, his sacrifice could be endured far more easily than that of his wife and son. He could not live with such cowardice and shame.

For the first time in Gray Eagle's life, tears eased from his jet eyes and slipped into the midnight braids on either side of his face. How could his heart bear such grief or his mind such torture? Time and time again, vivid images of Shalee's face flashed before his mind's eye. Her smile enticed him; her green eyes glowed with love and vitality. His warring senses could almost hear her happy laughter, which bubbled like a gentle waterfall. The fresh scent of her hair and body called to him from the mat and her possessions. How his arms ached to hold her, his lips to kiss hers. How could he breathe when she was his air? How could he live when she was his heart? Pressing the headband to his quivering lips, he murmured soulfully, "Shalee, my one true love, you must be returned to me; or I must come to you." What did his pride matter now? If she was dead, he might as well be dead, too.

Some monstrous evil had thrown him into a dark and bottomless pit to bury him alive, if this now wretched existence could be called living. Shovel after shovel of grief and bitterness were tossed upon his helpless body until he felt he couldn't breathe. For years, the green-eyed, auburn-haired, fair-skinned English girl had lived as Princess Shalee, his cherished and honored wife. Their ageless love had grown stronger than the surging white waters of death from the snow-swollen river and blazed hotter than the fiery sun that warmed the domain of the Eagle himself. But some treacherous and mighty force had stolen her from his side.

During their tormenting journey toward perfect love and harmony, he had rescued her many times before from the awesome hands of death and danger. Somehow, some way, he must find her again. But could he this time? Was the Bird of Death more powerful than the mighty Eagle? Had he taken her beyond his reach this time? How could he ever endure the permanent loss of his brazen ecstasy? He could not. Devastated, he allowed the tears to flow freely as his powerful body shook with anguish.

Chapter Four

The very instant there was sufficient light the next morning, Gray Eagle left his tepee to join his father. Leah had been awaiting this very moment and had mentally practiced her ploy well. Disregarding custom, Gray Eagle threw the flap aside and entered his father's tepee to find only Leah present. Without a word to the white captive, he turned to leave.

Leah called out to him, "Gray Eagle." When he halted and turned to gape at her, she hurried forward and spoke rapidly, "I'm so sorry about Bright Arrow and Shalee. I wish there was some way I could help. You must eat before you ride away; you will need strength to conquer your enemies," she stated, offering him *wasna* and wine from the buffalo berries. "This will warm you and give you energy." Phony tears and a quavering voice were used to further her ruse.

Gray Eagle's steady gaze went from the items in her trembling hands to her teary eyes. For a brief moment, he couldn't look away. Cunningly, Leah had enhanced her resemblance to Shalee. Before he could master himself, anguish was mirrored in his black eyes. His mind so deeply troubled, he did not realize Leah was wearing one of Shalee's dresses and her favorite beaded thongs to secure her auburn braids.

Having studied Shalee closely, Leah presented his frozen gaze with an expression and smile that matched

71

her rival's. She wisely did not speak, knowing her deeper voice would break her deceptive spell. She merely stood still and silent as those compelling eyes in his arresting face stayed glued to her upturned features. Abruptly his eyes chilled and he shook his head to clear it of some strange image that clouded and disappeared before he could comprehend it. *"Hiya!"* he stated harshly, refusing the food and dismissing her.

As he whirled to leave once more, Leah's softened words repeated, "I'm truly sorry for your pain, Gray Eagle. I pray you will find them quickly and safely."

Without responding, Gray Eagle was gone. Leah smiled in satisfaction. The first seed was planted. When his physical and mental torments became too great to bear, the seed would sprout and take hold. If he couldn't have his precious Shalee, he would soon desire the next best thing! She quickly changed clothes, aware of the danger if someone recognized Shalee's garment. When no one was around, she would return it to where she had stolen it some days past.

By midmorning of the second moon since leaving his camp for possibly the last time, Gray Eagle sat majestically upon his mottled Appaloosa just out of range from Fort Henry. He sat alone and proud without a trace of warpaint upon his handsome visage. He wore no *wanapin* and carried no weapon for the Bluecoats to demand, to be later exhibited as a boastful war trophy. What a magnificent and intimidating sight he was, sitting like a bronze statue upon a spectacular beast of white and gray.

Gray Eagle waited for the imminent battle of wits and words with his self-acclaimed enemies. A bitter taste teased at his mouth. There was no excitement or anticipation to this coming challenge; there was no eagerness to prove his great prowess. There were no coups to be earned this vile day. For his illustrious career to end in this humiliating manner tore viciously at his pride. It was unimaginable for a warrior to be forced calmly to hand his life over to his enemies without a fierce battle for that honor! He had never considered or envisioned a death not in honorable battle or with a weapon in his hands. To enter that hostile fort was like rashly walking into the outstretched arms of the awesome grizzly; yet, he must do just that. Perhaps his self-sacrifice required more honor and courage than a terrible battle.

The heavy gate to the fort slowly opened enough for a sutler to slip through, then instantly closed and locked once more. Confident in his safety, the man walked toward the lone rider who awaited him. It was not an Indian or a half-breed who was approaching him; it was a white man dressed in fringed buckskins, a fort peddler with hair like a raging fire. His feet were encased in knee-high moccasins and his wiry hair by a skin hat. He was tall and solid. If fear or respect lived within him, his movements and expression hid it.

Within two feet of the legendary warrior, he halted and looked directly into the obsidian eyes that seemed to pierce his very soul. He didn't ask if Gray Eagle spoke English; he addressed him in fluent Sioux. This situation a foregone conclusion, few words needed to be spoken aloud. The gravel voice stated brusquely, "Our leader Major Hodges offers a trade: your life for your son's. Do you accept his terms?" asked the huckster, whose trade depended on Hodges' whims.

Without even batting an eyelash, Gray Eagle nodded.

73

"The exchange will be made at the gate; you walk in and the boy walks out."

"No. You will bring my son to the edge of the range of your firesticks. When the signal is given, we will trade places." Gray Eagle issued his own terms, his expression stoic and his tone firm.

"No way," the man disagreed. "You and the boy could flee for cover while your warriors harass us with countless arrows."

"In the range of your firesticks, you could slay both Bright Arrow and Gray Eagle. Only one of us will die at the hands of the white-eyes. I do not surrender to you until my son's safety is clear," he calmly asserted.

"If you refuse these terms, his body will be sent out to you."

The possible bluff failed to alter Gray Eagle's decision. "Tie a long rope around his waist. When he walks past gun range, I will walk toward the fort gate. You hold a firestick to my back and the Bluecoats to my heart. When I am between you and the fort, release the rope and let him return to my people who wait nearby. Then if your tongue speaks two ways, only my life will be in danger. You will give me your word, not the word of the Bluecoats, to free him when I am between you and them. If you lie, I will slay you before they fill my body with their black balls," he confidently warned, his ebony eyes piercing his challenger's stolid frame.

The man indifferently pondered this wily suggestion. "The skills and daring of Wanmdi Hota are well known. Once the boy is free, your honor will demand you attempt escape, maybe over my dead body. It will be as you say only if I bind your hands behind your back first," he said, all too clearly acknowledging his sullen respect of

74

this warrior's prowess and total lack of fear.

Their gazes met and locked. "Do you fear the power of Gray Eagle so much you must even the odds with your thongs?" he taunted the white man.

Mocked like some coward, the white trader snarled indignantly, "I fear no man, not even a living legend. But only a fool would turn his back upon a desperate wolf. You would probably die in your hasty flight, but you might also escape. The legend ends here and now, Wanmdi Hota. I am a fighter; I would rather best you in battle. But the stakes are too high to chance losing you. I know it must stick in your craw to be defeated in this humiliating way. What fighter wants to die empty-handed or without a chance to defend himself? You have my word of honor the boy will be free if your hands are bound."

Gray Eagle's gaze drilled into that of the white trader. One who depended upon his instincts and perceptions for survival and victory, Gray Eagle felt the proud white man would keep his word, unaware that his keen senses were perilously dulled by this weighty affair. Regardless, would the others allow it? "I accept your word. But if the others do not, how will my son go free?" He cunningly sought to prevent all traps.

"I'll stop the first man who tries to prevent it; you have my word on that, too. I don't give over to killing babies for any reason."

"What of the second or third man?" Gray Eagle pressed.

"Them too if necessary." Once more their gazes fused and locked, each man assessing the strengths and weaknesses of the other should the occasion call for such knowledge.

75

"It will be done; Wanmdi Hota has spoken," the deep, rich voice agreed.

"I'll return shortly. If you have any last words to your people, speak 'em now," the man advised, for some curious reason.

"It has been done. Bring Bright Arrow out to me."

The gate opened and closed once more. Time passed, then this action was repeated. Gray Eagle's heart sang with relief and joy as his eyes touched upon his son. A rope was secured around his waist and was held tightly by another burly soldier. The trapper came forward. Gray Eagle dismounted and remained where he was. Jed Hawkins pulled a length of rawhide from his belt and bound Gray Eagle's hands, much tighter than necessary. Hawkins unhurriedly walked back to where the soldier was waiting with Bright Arrow. He took the rope and wound it around his strong hand several times before signaling to Gray Eagle.

"Walk toward me," he insolently ordered, all eyes trained on them.

Before he complied, Gray Eagle called to his son, "Bright Arrow, your grandfather waits behind me. When the white man releases the rope, run to him as swiftly as the *wapiti*. Do not come near me or halt your race. Do you understand? Can you run swiftly and not look back?"

The white man stiffened in suspicious outrage. "I gave my word the boy would be safe!"

"I accept your word, but not the evil ones of the Bluecoats. My son will obey me. It will halt any trick. You heard all I told him. When I am in place, toss him the rope so he will not trip over it," the intrepid warrior commanded as if he were the one in charge of his

76

own capture!

"Fine! Let's get this over with!" the other man shouted in annoyance, the playing of a deadly and traitorous game with the life of a child not being to his liking. Far worse, the lies he was being forced to tell soured in his mouth. He spit as if to eject the foul taste.

"*A'ta!*" Bright Arrow exclaimed in alarm and distress, seeing his father's hands bound.

"Obey me, Bright Arrow! I must remain to speak with the white men. When the rope slackens, race swiftly to Running Wolf!" he commanded forcefully, praying his son wouldn't hesitate in the face of danger or halt if the white trapper called out in his tongue.

"*Sha, A'ta,*" the small boy acquiesced.

With Bright Arrow walking ahead of him, Hawkins came toward Gray Eagle. In like manner, Gray Eagle purposefully strode toward him. They passed within three feet of each other, but were too close to the fort for any daring action. Gradually taking one step at a time, the noble warrior sidled toward the ominous fort, his keen eyes watching both the fort and the retreating Hawkins for any hint of deception. When their previously indicated positions were reached, both men halted. The rope around Bright Arrow's waist strained as he attempted to continue his movements.

"Release the rope and draw your weapon," Gray Eagle called out across the short distance between them.

Hawkins drew his flintlock pistol, but didn't release the rope. The fort gates shouted "betrayal and danger!" as they were flung open wide and six rifles were trained on the stalwart body of Gray Eagle. The rope around his left hand, Hawkins was half-turned to aim the pistol in his right hand at Gray Eagle. One daring movement and his body would be assaulted with many rocks of fire.

But a turbulent storm was already assailing the towering frame of Gray Eagle. Even in war, a man did not give his word of honor and then break it. Hawkins must die! Before anyone could react in the flurry of events that happened next, the deed was done.

"Chula!" the resonant voice cried out to his horse, then ordered the animal to attack the white man near Bright Arrow. The massive animal charged the creature who was endangering the life of his beloved master. With six firesticks pointing at Gray Eagle, he knew it would be foolish to move. His own escape must come another time, if the Great Spirit willed it. For now, he must force the white-eyes to keep their word, without recklessly yielding his own life.

Chula reared and flailed his hooves, great snorts coming forth in warning. Hawkins fell backwards in an attempt to avoid those deadly weapons. "Run, Bright Arrow!" the concerned father called out once more as the agile beast continued his brave attack.

The alert child yanked upon the restraining rope, pulling it free from Hawkins' hand. He ran like a squirrel scampering to safety. Oglala warriors had instantly stepped from the trees at the first sign of treachery. Bright Arrow ran into his grandfather's arms. Gray Eagle watched as the offensive rope was yanked from his slender, sturdy body. His eyes locked with Running Wolf's; he nodded in relief and resignation, then shifted his fathomless gaze to the dead man beneath Chula's hooves.

"*Chula, ya!*" He commanded the cherished animal to return home to safety. The beast instantly obeyed, his hooves thundering upon the hard ground as he sped away into the forest. As ordered, the Oglala had also withdrawn into the forest to deny the whites their grief over the coming loss of their famed warrior. Gray Eagle looked at the six rifles trained upon his body. As he glacially stared into the eyes of each man in turn, he could read their tension and fear.

For the briefest of moments, he was tempted to start running, to force the soldiers to fire upon him and end this lethal game quickly. He could not show such cowardice, nor could he permit his retreating son to hear the call of death take his life. He remained where he was, as the soldiers did. Gray Eagle was amused by their timidity in approaching him. Was he not bound? Did they not hold firesticks in their hands? Were there not many of them and only one of him? These white-eyes were cowards!

Finally, an entire detail of armed soldiers came hurrying out to surround him. Since Hawkins was the only man who could speak Sioux, they were at a loss to communicate with this powerful warrior, ignorant of his ability to speak fluent English! Hawkins' trampled and mangled body was futilely checked for life. None found, a prompt burial was ordered. Several nudgings of firesticks to his broad back instructed Gray Eagle to move forward.

Once inside the fort, he was taken to Hodges' office. All but three men left and the door was closed. Gray Eagle stood in the middle of the small room, his muscular frame intimidating all three men even though they presumed he was helpless. The guard remained in front of the door, his rifle directed at Gray Eagle's gut. A strange-looking man sat in a chair to his left, while the barrel-chested leader of the Bluecoats strolled around Gray Eagle several times.

Hodges' eyes scanned him up and down, back and

front. "So, this is the infamous Gray Eagle," he contemptuously sneered. "He don't look so awesome now, does he?" When his hands punched a firm muscle here and there to test the might of this so-called invincible warrior, Gray Eagle neither moved nor spoke. His gaze remained stoic, set upon the back wall. He suppressed an amused smile when Hodges fumed at the absence of trophies upon his body. He knew the white man well; they relished such bloody souvenirs.

Hodges stepped before the warrior's line of vision; yet it seemed to drill right through him to continue its gaze upon the back wall. Hodges' nerves tingled with pricklings of vexing fear. He suddenly delivered a forceful blow into the unprotected stomach of the infuriating Indian who revealed no speck of fear or weakness. The only response from the brawny, intrepid warrior was a rush of air from his flaring nostrils!

"Damn you! I wish Hawkins were here to tell you what I plan to do with you, you red bastard! Your people'll get their great warrior back again, piece by piece," he threatened bravely, though he quivered inside.

Gray Eagle's expression never changed. Laughing wildly, the smug major stated, "Come over here, Don Diego. Get yourself a glimpse of a real live savage. Is this why your gov'ment wants to rid itself of this wild frontier? Did they send you here to check it out? You can see it ain't worth much. Full of bloodthirsty redskins, wild animals, places where nothing won't grow, and work that'll kill the best men!"

"If it is so bad, *amigo,* why did *you* come here?" Don Diego de Gardoqui, official representative of the Spanish Government, asked in a polite and direct tone. "Though this territory belongs to Spain, there are more Americans

80

and French here than my people."

"That why you want to sell 'er? She's closer to us than Spain. You can't rule a growing land like this from across an ocean."

"I did not say my government wished to sell this vast wilderness to your people," Don Diego corrected him, toying with his thin mustache of sooty black before thoughtfully stroking his goatish beard. His complexion was fair and as smooth as a baby's, his perturbed expression revealing his displeasure at Hodges' crude manner.

The white men spoke in circles; this land belonged to the Indian, not the whites or the Spanish, as he called himself. Dressed in black and adorned with expensive silver, this man did not look like the others here. Diego's speech and garments were different, the astute warrior noticed. Some unknown power and smugness flowed from him. It was clear the Bluecoat leader respected and feared his rank. Alerted to this curious fact, Gray Eagle listened to their words closely.

"Why do you boast so highly of only one man's capture? When one leader is slain, another can easily and quickly take his place. I do not understand your immense fear of this solitary warrior."

Rankled, Hodges scoffed, "Only one man? Caesar was only one man! Genghis Khan was only one man! Alexander The Great was only one man! William of Orange was only one man! Your beloved Columbus was only one meager man! It only takes one such man to fill hearts with dreams of greatness and mindless unity! Gray Eagle is such a man! Every warrior in this territory would follow him to Hell and back if he commanded it!" Hodges snapped, then flushed red at his rude outburst. "Forgive

81

me, sir; I forgot my place," he hastily apologized, witnessing the disapproving scowl of the willful Spaniard.

"I see you are an avid student of history, particularly of war heroes and overblown legends. If this Indian is the great leader you seem to think he is, why did he walk into your trap?" Don Diego reasoned skeptically, his voice insultingly humorous. "Leaders such as you mentioned were not above sacrificing even their families for achieving their greatness. For a man to trade his life for that of only one small son cannot make him so cold and fearsome as you allege him to be. I see no war god standing before me, only a mortal man who has unselfishly and perhaps bravely given his life for his son's."

Hodges could hardly restrain his boiling temper at this dressing down. Yet Don Diego's safety and pleasure were in his hands. The failure to grant him every whim could be a costly mistake. His orders were to make certain he had anything he desired, anything.

Don Diego walked around the rigid warrior. He inhaled sharply at the sight of the blood that dripped from the fingertips of the Indian's hands, hands turning blue from a severe lack of circulation. "Untie him!" he abruptly demanded.

"Untie him?" Hodges repeated incredulously.

"The bonds are too tight. Soon his hands will die," Diego caustically remarked, perturbed by the childish fears of the commander of this fort.

"What does that matter? His whole body will die soon. He's dangerous, Don Diego," the major clamored, chafed by this imperious Spaniard.

"To justly execute one's enemy is expected, sir; childish games of brutality are not. Your guard holds a weapon; you wear a pistol at your side. Surely two armed men can overpower only one man," he panted. How dare this strutting peacock in blue and yellow question his authority!

Hodges thought he would smite the Spaniard if he said "only one man" one more time! "I said untie him!" Don Diego repeated himself.

Rage-stiffened and crimson-faced, Hodges stammered, "As you wish . . . Don Diego. I don't . . . like this. He's dangerous and sly."

Hodges took a knife from his desk drawer and sliced through the blood-soaked bonds. He yanked off his yellow bandanna and wiped his moist fingers upon it, then his knife. He seated himself behind his desk, at a safe distance from the insidious warrior, rashly tossing the stained knife upon his desk. He observed Gray Eagle as he flexed his fingers, then lazily crossed his arms over his brawny chest, ignoring the blood that discolored the sienna-colored buckskins and his coppery flesh. Hodges began nervously to fidget as those obsidian eyes bored into his, never having experienced a more forceful and intimidating stare.

"Keep your gun on 'im, Clint. He's fast and cunning."

"Come, come," the Spanish official chided him. He stepped to Gray Eagle's left side and asked, "Do you speak English?" When the brave remained silent, Don Diego added, "Do you understand it?" Often men could understand tongues or words that they couldn't speak. Nothing.

"Don't get too close now that he's free, sir," Hodges warned, irritating Diego with his bristling caution.

Don Diego slammed his fist upon the desk. "So far, Major Hodges, I have seen nothing to fear! He is only one man! What can a helpless prisoner d . . ."

With lightning speed and accuracy, the carelessly discarded knife was in Gray Eagle's grasp, Don Diego was imprisoned in his hold, and the blade was at his throat. Gray Eagle yanked the Spaniard aside, placing the justly terrified man between himself and his white foes.

"What the . . ." Hodges cursed in panic and surprise. "Damnit, Diego! I told you he was quick and dangerous! I shouldna cut him free. Only one man, you said. Well, your life's in his hands!" Hodges exploded before thinking.

"Talk to him, fool! Don't just stand there babbling like an idiot! You can't allow him to harm me! I'm here under your protection! If anything happens to me . . ." Diego left his vivid threat hanging in the ominous air, ignorant of the character of this honorable warrior.

Hodges stared at him. Where were all that arrogance and courage now? Only one man, he mentally scoffed. Gray Eagle wasn't just a man; he was a war god, a terrifying legend come to life. Hodges was sorely tempted to let the warrior slit Diego's miserable throat, then shoot him. That way, he would simultaneously be rid of two nasty problems. Diego had flaunted his rank and pranced around like he owned this place. He had demanded the warrior's release. Let him squirm a while!

"Aren't you forgetting he killed the only man who could speak his savage tongue?" Hodges reminded the tense man struggling to breathe without nicking his throat with the deadly blade touching it.

"Surely there's some way to communicate with him!" he shouted.

"No need to. It's clear he's trying to escape!" Hodges declared. Was the man also stupid? Could he allow this annoying snake to cost him his greatest victory, the capture of Gray Eagle without a single casualty? Hawkins didn't count; he was just some trapper down on his luck.

"Then open the door and let him go, *embecil!* Are you crazy? He could kill me!" As a gleam of pleasure flickered in Hodges' eyes, Diego warned again, "I would think twice about such a foolish act, sir."

"You mean just let him walk out? Zounds, Diego! That's Gray Eagle himself, and I captured him! Now, you want me to free him!"

"My life is not worth his capture. Release him immediately!" the shaky voice thundered.

Gray Eagle pointed to the rifle in the guard's shaking hands. His meaning was clear. "Lay down your gun!" Diego shrieked at him.

The guard's eyes shifted to his commanding officer's scarlet face. He waited for him to speak. Hodges cursed as he panted, "Put down the gun, Clint."

The guard moved to the desk and laid his weapon there. Gray Eagle motioned to the rope hanging upon a peg on the side wall, then nodded at the soldier. Hodges fumed as he bound and gagged the youthful guard. He turned to Gray Eagle and sneered. "What now, Your Highness?"

Gray Eagle sent forth the sound of a horse. "You want a horse, do you?" Hodges jested sarcastically.

"Give him one quickly, Hodges! Don't make him angry! That knife's sharp and he might get nervous."

Hodges glared at the offensive man and stated daringly, "If you hadn't demanded I free him, your hide wouldn't be in danger. I'll expect a big reward for saving it."

85

"Your punishment will be greater if you lose it," Diego sneered.

As Hodges moved toward the door, Gray Eagle shifted the knife to point directly into his jugular vein. One false move from Diego or any attempt to lunge at him would send the tip into his throat with no hope for survival. All three men recognized the warrior's strategy. Hodges opened the door. Gray Eagle called out, "*Wasichu.*"

Hodges turned and glared at him. "What now?" Gray Eagle's gaze slipped from one man to another who was nearby, then nodded to have them moved back. Seething, Hodges called out, "You men there, get over to the cookhouse on the double."

They stared at him strangely, but quickly obeyed. Gray Eagle's keen gaze walked over the front section of the fort, halting upon the guards in the towers on either front corner. His next tacit message was clear. Gritting his teeth, Hodges also ordered them to the cookhouse. A flicker entered the major's eyes, hinting at a deliberation of wily betrayal. The warrior caught his eye, smiled knowingly, and shook his head in warning.

"You filthy red devil! I'll take you again someday!" he boasted.

Hodges called for a horse to be brought to the gate and left there. When all appeared in readiness, Gray Eagle shoved Diego through the door and practically dragged the little man toward the horse. At his nod, Hodges himself was compelled to open the front gates. Catching the reins over two fingers, Gray Eagle backed out, leading the horse and hauling Diego. A safe distance off, Gray Eagle's triumphant gaze taunted the raging Hodges. The dauntless warrior released Diego and handed him the knife as a souvenir.

Gray Eagle nodded his head and smiled triumphantly. He mounted up and rode off. Diego stared at the weapon in his trembling hands, then at the back of the retreating warrior. Hodges rushed up. "Why didn't you stab him?" he shouted in disbelief. "You could have killed the Eagle himself!"

"For the same reason he did not slay Don Diego de Gardoqui himself! Savage he might be, but a man of honor and great pride. I greatly underestimated your intrepid legend," Diego confessed.

"Savages have no honor! You had the knife; why didn't you use it?"

"For a man so aware of his cunning and skills, you also underestimate him. If I had tried, my blood would be upon the ground, not his. You do not seem to realize something he obviously did; I'm no fool, Hodges!"

Diego went back toward the fort. Hodges glanced toward the forest. There was no need to pursue Gray Eagle; once away from the fort he could disappear into the forest like just another tree! He whirled and stomped back toward the gates. Another day, my feathered foe. . . .

There was great rejoicing and astonishment when Gray Eagle rode into his camp the next afternoon. The Oglala gathered around him and sang his praises. With awe and joy, they listened to how he had beaten his enemies at their own game. Bright Arrow was held in the powerful arms of his father. Several times the boy hugged his neck. Gray Eagle complimented his courage and wits. The boy laughed and puffed up with pride.

"Am I a warrior now, Father? Have I earned a feather?" he excitedly cried out.

"You have earned a feather, Little One, but it takes

87

many feathers and winters to become a warrior. You must be patient. There is much to learn and many skills to practice."

"Can we look for Mother now?" the child abruptly asked, bringing fresh pain to Gray Eagle's eyes and heart. "We must find her and tell her of my first coup. The Bluecoats hurt her."

"You must tell me what happened by the river the day the Bluecoats captured you," Gray Eagle gently encouraged, trying to sound calm.

The boy related the same events the braves had reasoned out from the signs. "Where is Mother?" he asked when he finished.

"I do not know, Bright Arrow," Gray Eagle replied honestly. "Others have searched for her many moons. They could not find her."

Distressed, Bright Arrow shrieked, "She is hurt. We can find her," he declared with childish confidence and blind hope.

Gray Eagle looked at his father. "Has Moon Gazer returned yet, Father?"

"Yes, my son. Nothing," he sadly announced.

When Bright Arrow insisted upon their own search, Gray Eagle smiled and stated, "The Great Spirit will watch over her until we can find her. Do not fear, Little One; she will return safely to us."

Four days later, Gray Eagle was repeating those same words to Bright Arrow. But Bright Arrow's mind did not understand why his father could not find his mother and bring her home. There was nothing his father couldn't do! Twice he cried for Shalee; another time, he beat his small fists upon Gray Eagle's chest, demanding he find his mother. His violent outburst spent, his wide gaze met his father's as he unexpectedly asked, "Is Mother dead? Did the Bluecoats kill her? Did she drown in the river?"

The dreaded words hit Gray Eagle with staggering force. "I want my mother," the child wailed, sensing something terrible in his father's actions and mood.

What could he say to this small boy who was hurting so deeply? It was wrong to stir false hopes in him. Surely she would have been found and returned to him by now if . . . his eyes became dewy at that thought. "I cannot bring your mother home, Bright Arrow. If the Bluecoats slew her, the Great Spirit is taking care of her now. He would not leave her alone. If she is not returned soon, we will know she has joined the Great Spirit."

"The Bluecoats are bad, Father. She fell into the water and I could not see her. Did the Great Spirit save her?"

"I do not know, my son. But he spared my life so I could return to you."

Bright Arrow cried himself to sleep in his father's arms. It was nearly dawn before slumber overtook the grieving warrior.

When Bright Arrow realized his grandfather was absent for the second day, he beamed with suspense. "Has Grandfather gone to find Mother?" he asked, brown eyes glowing, ravaging his father's heart.

Gray Eagle looked down at him and smiled. "Perhaps he will find Shalee," he replied, unable to tell his son Running Wolf and White Arrow were visiting the camp of the Sisseton, along with other representatives from each tribe. He should have gone with them, but he could not leave his son to bear his troubles alone. Too, his heart was not upon the continuing warfare with the whites. He and Bright Arrow needed this time together, for soon there would be no denying the reality of Shalee's permanent loss. Gray Eagle felt he must send word to Chief Black Cloud about his alleged daughter's tormenting disappearance. But surely he was also at the meeting in the Sisseton Camp. When the critical talks ended in two more days and his own father returned, he would visit the Blackfoot camp with his dire news.

As usual since his escape from the fort, Leah came to bring their food and to do their chores. Under the guise of sympathy and respectful obedience, Leah performed her daily tasks with warmth and concern. She seized every opportunity to take advantage of Bright Arrow's needs: feeding him, caring for him, entertaining him, and even comforting him. So enwrapped was he in his own sufferings, Gray Eagle failed to absorb her ploy. But the conniving Leah knew exactly what she wanted and was doing.

While Running Wolf and White Arrow were away, she knew she must use every wile and chance she possessed to enchant both Bright Arrow and his valiant father. Under normal circumstances, such a deed might be impossible or at least very time consuming. But with the agony and loneliness of Shalee's death to plague them, both males were susceptible to her devious schemes. The child was responding quickly and openly to her resemblance to his mother. But Gray Eagle was resisting any pull upon his aching heart.

Leah craftily avoided as much contact with the other Indians as possible, doing her chores during their rest period each day. If anyone had noticed how she was gradually likening herself to Princess Shalee, there was no outward show of suspicion. How she wished she did not have to return to Running Wolf's tepee each night. But the stalwart warrior made it clear she wasn't to sleep in his, no matter if she behaved like his slave. A matter of

90

time was all it would require. But did she have that precious item? No, for Running Wolf and White Arrow would vanquish her and her dreams the moment they returned! Somehow, she must cautiously rush her victory. All she needed was one union with the virile warrior to ensnare him!

Leah's body quivered and her pulse raced when Gray Eagle's somber gaze lingered upon her face for a few moments, the first time since that one morning in Running Wolf's tepee. She smiled timidly, intentionally brushing her breast against his arm as she moved past him. Her fingers would lightly touch his as she handed him his food. She moved and swayed provocatively as she carried out her chores, chores performed with talent and perfection. Surely he was noticing her abilities and beauty? Surely his sexual needs for a woman to sate his fiery blood were attacking his senses? Men were so emotionally different from most females; they did not require romantic feelings in order to appease physical needs. With tempting efforts and appealing qualities, surely his seeds would be pleading to spill into her willing body within a few days?

That very afternoon, Leah threw her cautions to the winds. It was time, since it was too quickly fading, to let him know just how receptive she was, how much she desired him. Her expressions increased in warmth and frequency. Her smoldering gazes became inviting and imploring, her smiles and moves enticing. Having observed him closely, Leah knew his routine by now. She knew exactly when and where he bathed in the still chilly water. With daring and planning, he could find her in a most compelling situation. She shuddered at the thought of the frigid water; then smiled wantonly, dreaming of how her body could warm itself afterwards. It was perfect; how could this emotionally weakened man resist the likeness of his wife, rising naked and inviting from the stream?

Determined to carry out her shameless scheme the next day, Leah's mood was cheerful and serene. Gray Eagle's was not. Haunting memories plagued his mind and heart. His body yearned for that of his beloved Shalee. He wondered if this aching pain within his heart and loins would ever cease. He raged at the forces that had stolen his love. Too, guilt was harassing him: guilt over his inability to protect the woman he loved, guilt over the physical stirrings that the white captive encouraged in his loins. If only she did not reflect his love . . . if only his manhood did not cry out for the appeasements it had enjoyed nearly every moon . . . if his spirit was dead, why did his desires not die? Yet, he would master this repulsive lust. He could never take a white woman to his mats, no one except the white bird of his ravaged heart. When the time came and he could no longer resist the urgings of his traitorous flesh, he would sate himself upon some receptive Indian maiden. Perhaps one who had also lost her mate would be agreeable to his physical yearnings and his needs for a woman to care for him and his young son. Never had he endured such loneliness and agony. What could fill this devastating void in his life and heart? Why had she left him alone? Was death not a selfish betrayal? How could he bear to see another take the place of Shalee in his tepee and upon his mats? Could he? No, his aching heart cried out.

Instantly his tortured mind argued, but what of the many needs of your son, what of the chores to be dealt with, and what about the throbbing needs of your manhood? It had been almost twelve moons since his last view of the bewitching woman of his heart. It seemed an endless span of torturous time. It was illogical to believe he would glance up one moment and find her standing before him, smiling with outstretched arms. But how he longed for such a blissful moment. No, there was no female alive who could take her place, not even one who reflected her face like a murky pool!

At the first meal this curious day, Leah had placed her hand upon his cinnamon-colored chest and smiled sadly into his eyes as she whispered, in English, "My heart weighs heavy to see you suffer so greatly, Gray Eagle. Is there nothing I can do to ease the pain in your heart and life? How I long to remove those dulling lights from your eyes and the haunting shadow from over your head. Whatever your needs, I am here to serve you." Leah had played heavily upon her expressions and tender voice. Gray Eagle wondered what she would think if she had known he could understand each word she uttered.

But Gray Eagle was the one in error now. To her astonishment two days past, Leah had witnessed an incredible scene. Having concealed herself in the bushes near the stream to relieve herself, she overheard Gray Eagle and Talking Rock as they passed within hearing range of her alert ears. To her shock and resulting pleasure, Gray Eagle was teaching Talking Rock English! His fluent and easy command of her language astounded her. It played right into her wily game. . . .

As if still unaware of this talent, Leah called upon her wits to verbally entrap the man she desired. She would offer solace to Bright Arrow; she would speak highly and affectionately of Gray Eagle and the Oglala. She would supposedly speak to herself, words she wished him to hear and respond to with favor.

It worked, but not in the way Leah hoped and plotted.

It made Gray Eagle more and more aware of her growing desire for him, of his son's rising dependency upon her, and of the stirrings her words and moods brought to his body. With the guilt and sexual yearnings came gradual resentment: resentment of her allure, resentment of the fact that she was here and not his Shalee, resentment that she dared to resemble his unique woman, and resentment that she was revealing her willingness to lie upon his mats! To remove her temptation, he and Bright Arrow joined Talking Rock and Little Flower for the late meal that night. By nightfall, he had artfully and defensively avoided her for the remainder of this trying day, the worst he had endured since Shalee's loss. A deadly reality was forcing its way into his heart: Surely it was past time for hope.

Very late, Gray Eagle went to the Ceremonial Lodge. He needed solace and communication with the Great Spirit. He sat cross-legged before a small campfire surrounded by large rocks. He removed a peyote button from a pouch and placed it in his mouth. Slowly he chewed the dried cactus button that produced hallucinations and euphoria, and what was believed to be contact with the Great Spirit. But that particular button had aged beyond its great power. The needed visions did not sate his desire for answers; instead, they produced images of Shalee, reflections of days past when they were together and happy. The impaired cactus button did not produce its normal aftereffects of tranquility and well-being; a terrible emptiness and anguish still burned within him. Fleeing the embittering dreams of Shalee in the Pezuta Tipi, Gray Eagle stumbled and swayed as he made his unsteady and slightly drugged return to his own tepee.

Little Flower had pleaded for Bright Arrow to spend the night with their son, to enliven the sad-eyed child.

Gray Eagle collapsed upon his mat, throwing his arm over his closed eyes. His mind floated upwards, seeking communication with Shalee at the Great Spirit's side. . . . He spoke her name several times in a slurred tone.

Leah had observed him in what she presumed to be an intoxicated state as the noble warrior staggered from the large tepee to his own. She knew Bright Arrow was not there. The unlaced flap swayed invitingly in the night breeze. Did she dare to seduce him in this irresistible state? Apprehension and suspense filled her. Time was so short. If she could lie with him just once. . . .

Summoning her courage, Leah checked to make certain no dark eyes were around to note her brazen trip to the tepee before her. She hurriedly crossed the shadowy distance and quickly entered the tepee, lacing the flap against any invasion of their privacy and her wanton intent. She forced her quivering body to move forward to halt beside the sleeping mat. Gray Eagle was mumbling incoherently, except for one antagonizing name. Her green eyes narrowed in envy of the woman who could so enchant this pinnacle of manhood and prowess. She bitterly vowed that he would soon forget she existed!

Leah's lustful gaze noted the pile of carelessly discarded clothing. She knelt and allowed her hungry eyes to feast upon the masculine beauty stretched out before them. Dangerous fires licked at her body; her womanly recess tightened and moistened. Her nipples surged erect with desire. She licked her suddenly dry lips, lips craving to taste of the sweet flesh before her.

The time was ripe for plucking this virile creature. Leah removed the doeskin garments from her freshly scrubbed body. To forestall his awakening, she lightly trailed hands softened with healing balm over his chest and across his stomach, causing him to wiggle beneath the feathery touch. She eyed the smooth firmness of his bronze flesh. He was such a splendid male animal. Resolved to sway him, her hand reached for the sensitive shaft, which she considered a man's weakest part. She traced the length of the shaft which intoxicated her senses. It spontaneously responded to her touch. Her hand slipped around it as it instinctively grew large and taut, sliding leisurely up and down the flawless surface to stimulate it, working carefully not to wake him.

As the protruding member surged with life, its warmth increased. A moan escaped the parted lips of the still dazed Gray Eagle as Leah intentionally enflamed his hazy senses. His mind was precariously clouded by the deluding peyote. He automatically responded to this exquisite dream of his beautiful and gentle Shalee. His body was ensnared by the intoxicating sensations in his throbbing manhood. Gray Eagle's hips arched upwards to freely offer himself to the vision of the woman he loved and desperately needed.

Passionate moans rumbled in his throat and chest as his right hand sought to caress the body within his hazy reach. His left hand seized a firm breast and teased the taut nipple between his deft fingers, the right one wandering into her auburn hair. How he had missed his love, but now she was home again. . . .

Leah thought she would go mad with the fierce cravings consuming her body, yearnings he was torturing and increasing. Her body a sheet of fire and her nerves tingling, she voraciously savored the feel of him. His body shuddered with overpowering needs. Thrilled by her heady effect upon him and blissfully accepting the pleasures he was giving her, she worked enticingly and generously as she stroked, delighted, and teased the masterful object held lovingly in her hands.

His deft and seeking hands worked just as feverishly to please his beautiful Shalee. In a wild frenzy, Leah's hand rapidly and gently ascended and descended upon the flaming shaft connected to the squirming hips that plunged it upwards time and time again in search of the stimulating pleasures she freely offered it. She willed herself not to lunge upon it as she was sorely tempted to do. Impatient to feed her great hunger for him, she avidly entreated his full and promising member to demand its right to empty its contents into her. Surely he could not withstand her imploring actions much longer.

Impassioned to the fullest degree, Gray Eagle reached for his love and drew her up to him, covering her mouth with his, ravishing it before doing the same to the creamy mounds that burned his chest. His mouth and fingers sought to drive her wild with the same fires that burned fiercely and brightly within his barely restrained body. She groaned and writhed upon the mats, yielding completely to his onslaught.

As his mouth seared her lips and her face, Leah made an irrevocable mistake. Her throaty voice pleaded for him to take her, to allow her to push painful memories of Shalee from his mind, to sate his great needs within her fiery body, to permit her to take the place of his lost love. His mind battled to sober and clear quickly. He stiffened and pulled away as he realized it was not Shalee driving him mindless with love and passion. Shalee was dead; Leah was brazenly seducing him!

"Hiya!" he harshly rejected her as his body struggled to master its flames and desires. He shuddered at the ache that painfully knotted his defiant manhood. He struggled to find strength to resist this brazen temptation until his

97

senses could return in full force.

Leah rubbed her naked and shapely body against his, pulling upon his neck to return his lips to hers. She urgently pleaded, "Please, Gray Eagle. My body and heart burn for you. You need me. Let me ease the hunger in your manhood and your heart. You can take me anytime you desire me. Treat me as you wish: hurt me, take me, use me. I don't care. I must feel you inside me. Please. Shalee is gone forever. Yet your body burns for what Leah can give. It will be our secret. Take me," she desperately coaxed. Before he could react to her stunning words, she resolved to tempt him beyond control or rebuff. Her hand closed around his still erect member and she stroked it feverishly.

Unbidden but pleasing agony swept over him. He shuddered. Carnal cravings pleaded for hasty release, for he was precariously stimulated. He seized her soft shoulders and tried to push her away from the torrid shaft that practically demanded to be left where it was. His mind raged a fierce battle with his body. "*Hiya, Leah,*" he repeated, his strained and difficult reluctance encouraging her. Leah did not obey his shaky command.

Weakened and aroused, Gray Eagle was briefly tempted to permit his body this humiliating but desperately needed release. For the first time since Shalee's irretrievable loss, he was experiencing an emotion other than anguish and void. Was his ravaged heart enjoying this degrading punishment, for surely submitting to this castigator with Shalee's likeness was a purgative penalty? Were his heart and body separate warriors? Could one defeat the other? Could a physical victory of the body assuage an emotional defeat of the heart?

Back and forth his distorted and deluded mind fiercely

wrangled for what seemed ages while Leah worked greedily upon the traitorous flesh, but only moments actually passed. He could not betray Shalee in this repulsive manner. He firmly shoved upon Leah's body to end this demented agony.

"Please, Gray Eagle. Don't you see how much you need this? He is filled with fire and war. Let me cool his fever and give him peace," she seductively wheedled, knowing he was swiftly gaining the strength to halt this madness. She struggled to regain her enticing position, but he would not allow it. "How can you deny him this way? Greater pains will attack him if I do not please him. Let me feed him." Her hand reached for the shaft.

Gray Eagle painfully seized her wrists and snarled, *"Hiya! Ya, Leah!"*

"How can I go when I need you and you need me? Plunge him into me until our bodies cry out in pleasure," she urgently coaxed.

"Ya, Leah," he stated again, his voice now distinct and cold.

"You are cruel, Gray Eagle! Why do you create such fires within me if you will not put them out? Don't you realize I love you? No man matches your beauty or prowess. Each time I see you, my body burns to have yours. You need a woman to take care of you and Bright Arrow. He needs a woman to comfort him," she declared of the stiff extension that seemed to point accusingly at her. "If you cannot bring yourself to enter my body, then let me drink of its sweetness. Let me drain the fires that burn within him."

Her brazen words shocked and disarmed him. How could a female speak so wantonly and plead for her enemy to ravish her? What strange lust crazed her mind? Was his prowess so large she could not resist it? Why was

99

she willing to deny her own vivid needs and simply sate his? Did she believe there was great magic in his seeds, or perhaps in her skills? Her glazed eyes were glued to his manhood as if mesmerized by it. In spite of his resolve and control, the traitorous warrior flamed anew and stood proud and tall before her visibly appreciative gaze.

She lunged for the object of her lust. He threw her backwards to the hard ground and pinned her there. How dare this lowly white slave tempt him to such a betrayal of his lingering love for Shalee! Leah continued to plead for their union. Furious with himself and her, he rashly debated if he should brutally stab his manhood into her many times and punish her evil lust and rash actions! For once, Gray Eagle was irrationally and vindictively compelled to savagely rape a woman, this infuriating and reckless female! If he hurt her badly, then she would leave him alone! She would then avoid him! Then she could not entice him to respond to the likeness of Shalee within her!

The weight of his shoulders upon her wrists caused her to wince in sadistic pleasure. As if a message from the Great Spirit, slivers of light from the full moon entered the ventilation opening and blazed across Leah's face and body. A bold invitation gleamed in her eyes. A smug and taunting smile curled her lips. Suddenly she did not even slightly remind him of his lost love. Just before losing his temper and vengefully ripping into her womanhood, control and reality assaulted his warring emotions and conquered them.

"*Ya, Leah,*" he ominously warned, resentment and fury flashing menacingly in his igneous eyes. The lines upon his face were harsh and unrelenting. Danger permeated the oppressive atmosphere. It was staggeringly clear the battle was lost to her, for now.

There was but one thing to do, graciously and proudly yield defeat. As he moved to sit upon his mat to await her departure, she slowly sat up and reached for her garments. After pulling them on, she looked down at him. "Perhaps it is too soon for you to take another woman. When the time is ripe, come to me and I will please you beyond your wildest dreams or needs," she confidently vowed. "Shalee is gone forever, but the needs of your body are not. I will never refuse you any pleasure you seek upon me. I have loved you and desired you since the first moment I saw you. Send for me, Gray Eagle, when your hungers become too great to bear."

With those provocative statements, Leah calmly left his tepee. As she stretched out upon her sleeping mat, fury was the first emotion to lie with her. Gradually it deserted her company for vanity to take its place. She smiled as she realized her daring act had accomplished several vital facts: Gray Eagle had found it nearly impossible to reject her advances; in time, he would weaken even more as his body's needs increased with a lengthy denial and he helplessly recalled her many skills; he had temporarily mistaken her for Shalee; with effort, she could force that delusion to happen more frequently and be timely; he had not appeared to reject her as a white woman, only as a woman who desired to take Shalee's place. The situation wasn't hopeless after all, she promptly decided.

Little did the rosy-eyed Leah know how deeply Gray Eagle loved and missed Shalee. Little did she realize how great his pride and strength were. But Gray Eagle was all too aware of his emotions. . . .

Chapter Five

The lovely creature feverishly thrashing upon the buffalo mat was totally unaware of the multiple dramas taking place around her. Her body burned with the fiery illness that raged within it, pressing upon her chest like some heavy mound of dirt. The bleeding from the jagged wound upon her right temple had finally ceased its steady flow into her auburn hair, which was fanned out around her head. From all appearances, the ointment and bandage were doing their best to deny infection, to ease the pain, to seal the laceration, and to reduce the swelling and purplish cast upon the ivory skin. She babbled incoherently during her delirium, always in English. She called for people her rescuers did not know; yet, she never cried out the names that should have been upon her lips.

Shalee had been enslaved in the fiery world of blackness for the past four days, since the pair of black eyes filled with panic and love had touched upon her limp body entangled in a log jam at the river's edge. Relief and fear washed over him as he glanced down to sight the beautiful face of Shalee barely held above the greedy water's surface by long strands of flowing auburn hair entangled in the branches.

He thanked Napi for leading his feet to where this lovely creature was fiercely, but unknowingly, resisting the calls of the Bird of Death. How had she come to be swept away by the forceful and deadly currents of the river? The Oglala camp was situated two days' ride to the west of their camp! The river that moved past that camp joined with this one many, many steps from here. Even if she had accidentally fallen into the rushing flow, how had she been carried so far away from the Oglala Camp and still survived? Surely the Great Spirit watched over her and had spared her life.

But she was injured badly. Either some treacherous enemy had attacked her and the Oglala village or some heavy branch had smashed into her skull after she fell into the water. If not for her loose hair, which had ensnared itself upon the upper branches of the floating log, Shalee would be dead now. He had carefully stepped forward into the icy water and untangled her hair. He lifted her seemingly lifeless body in his strong arms. She was so cold and numb; her lips and flesh were tinged like the blue heavens. Placing his ear to her chest, he could hardly breathe until he detected the faint thudding that seemed to shout of hope.

In spite of the heat from her body, she shuddered with a perilous chill as he lay her upon the ground. He must act quickly or she would die anyway. Taking his knife, he cut her saturated clothes from her body, then removed her moccasins. He seized the blanket from his horse's back and dried her, roughly teasing the flesh to regain some warmth and blood flow. He called her name many times, but she was too deep in her illness to hear him or to waken. She coughed as the frigid water inflamed her lungs and denied her enough air to breathe easily.

The troubled warrior stripped off his buckskin shirt and put it over her naked frame. He then removed his leather leggings and placed them upon her lower body.

Because of his towering height, the legs were long enough to cover her chilled feet. Dressed only in a breechcloth, the biting winds nipped at his bronze flesh. As he feared, the snow began to fall, lightly at first, but steadily increasing in force and amount. He must get her to his village swiftly, for she was sinking fast. He wrapped her garments in his damp blanket and carried her to his horse. He laid her across the animal's broad back before him, hoping the position would send blood to her upper and lower body. Tearing a strip from the bottom of her own dress, he secured it tightly around her head to halt the flow of blood from the gash there. He kneed his horse into a gallop to make camp as soon as possible, the fleecy snowflakes filling each track he made, later to wet the earth and cause it to ooze into the impressions and obliterate them.

For three torturous days, the frantic warrior and his sullen wife had aided the medicine man in his attempt to save the life of the daughter of their own chief. Two messengers had been sent on their urgent missions to Chief Black Cloud in the Sisseton Camp and to Gray Eagle in the Oglala Camp. Both should be at her side very soon. But as two more days passed, neither man approached the winter camp of the Blackfoot Tribe. The warrior left in charge of the camp wondered at this curious event; he had no way of knowing the two braves had been slain before delivering their messages. His mind plagued by the sufferings of the woman who would have become his wife if not for Gray Eagle, Brave Bear had little encouragement to consider the feelings of his past rival where Shalee was concerned. Memories of his love for her returned to stir dangerous tenderness within his heart.

As fiercely as he tried to conceal and master his deep affection for the girl upon the mat, he failed to do so. Each time Chela caught him gazing longingly at Shalee with such worry and love in his dark eyes, resentment and jealousy flared in her mind. It was bad enough this half-breed girl had stolen her rightful mate many winters ago, but to linger in the heart of her present mate was too much to generously accept. She had been pledged to Gray Eagle, but Shalee had invaded his heart and life and taken him from her. To appease Brave Bear's loss of her hand, Gray Eagle had given Chela to Brave Bear for a mate. Indeed, Brave Bear was a worthy and excellent replacement for Gray Eagle, but both men had lost their hearts to the half-white girl lying upon the mat in her own tepee, perhaps dying.

Chela wondered if she should fervently pray for Shalee's death to end her magic spell upon both men. If she had not been proven the daughter of Black Cloud, she would still be Gray Eagle's offensive white slave; and she, Chela, would be Gray Eagle's proud mate. These past five winters with Brave Bear had been good ones, even happy ones. Why did Shalee have to intrude upon this enforced compromise and remind Brave Bear of his love for her! What was keeping Gray Eagle away? Surely he could come to his injured wife's side within five or more moons! Was the meeting in the Sisseton Camp so vital that both Shalee's father and husband would allow her to die without coming to check on her?

If Black Cloud would hurry home, Shalee could be taken to his tepee, away from her husband's desirous gaze. Even if Gray Eagle and Shalee had argued and she had run off, why would he refuse to come to her side knowing she was gravely ill? Chela was bewildered and vexed.

It was true she and Chela had established a mutual acceptance of each other. They could not be called friends, for too much had happened between them in the past. Neither had forgotten that Chela had attempted to stab Shalee to rid Gray Eagle of her magical spell. Nor had they forgotten how Shalee had boldly argued against the lashing Chela received for her reckless act. When Shalee visited her father in the Blackfoot camp or Chela visited her family in the Oglala camp, both women were polite and genial. Chela had even come to ignore the fact that her husband had loved and desired Shalee as his wife before losing her to Gray Eagle during a fierce challenge. Chela could not deny that Shalee and Gray Eagle were deeply in love, for she had viewed their attraction and passion many times. Chela scolded herself for blaming Shalee for Brave Bear's weakness for her; yet, the venomous teeth of the green monster continued to nip at her heart and mind.

Shortly before midday, Shalee quietened most noticeably. Brave Bear jumped up from his seat by the campfire and raced to her mat, fearing her breathing had halted for all time. He sighed heavily in relief. "The fever has broken, Chela. Napi will spare her life. Still, I fear for her safety, for she is very weak and pale."

Chela joined him at Shalee's side. "She is strong, Brave Bear. If Napi wills it, soon she will awaken and return to her husband's side," she stated factually, but tenderly. "Gray Eagle and Black Cloud will be happy we have taken such good care of her, if they ever return," she added snippily. "What words could be more important than news of Shalee's survival? If I had been injured and lay dying, would you not rush to my side?" she asked.

"My mind does not understand the slowness of her family," he replied, not wishing to scold them by name. "Even now, she could still die."

"It often seems love and passion must yield to war and a man's honor. Does the face of a chief honor his rank before his love, even when she lies near death? I had thought Shalee was more important to Wanmdi Hota than even his own life. Why does he linger?" she reasoned aloud.

"I do not know, Chela." To soothe the lines of resentment from her brow, he smiled and stated, "If my wife were gravely ill, I would go to her side the moment such news touched my ears." He caressed her cheek. Chela had been a good mate. It was not right for dreams of Shalee to bring sadness to her brown eyes or trouble between them. "He will come for her soon. We will help her to get well quickly to return to her family. Do not overtire yourself, wife; you carry the son of Brave Bear," he proudly reminded her.

She smiled. "This time, it will not be a girl. You will have a son to follow you after you follow Black Cloud. My dream told of a strong son riding at your side, my husband. It will be, for Napi has revealed it to me."

A firm believer in dreams, Brave Bear beamed with joy, joy to be short-lived when Chela was delivered of another female child in six more months. Still, the dream helped him master his longings for Shalee. "Look!" Chela excitedly shrieked.

Following the line of her gaze, Brave Bear watched the lids of Shalee's eyes struggle to open. Moments later, green eyes blinked several times in confusion before closing again to send her back into the land of much needed rest. Chela and Brave Bear exchanged smiles, knowing the illness was relenting to Shalee's battle for life.

Off and on all day, Shalee came and went many times. Her body felt so weak and heavy; she ached everywhere. She was thirsty and groggy. She drank from the strange cup placed to her lips, a white object that sometimes contained water and other times contained a soupy liquid whose flavor escaped her. She snuggled beneath some unknown furry coverlet. She wondered where her uncle and the others were. Who were these odd-looking strangers who were caring for her? What had happened to her? Where was she? This dwelling was unfamiliar, large and round with a pointed ceiling. Such mysterious words and images filled her mind. Yet she was too dazed and confused to reason them out.

She would fight to rise above the weightiness of her eyes and body to see who was touching her head and causing such agony there, but she could not order her eyes to open or her body to respond. She strained to catch the curious words she could not understand, but to no avail. Each time she would almost grasp reality, fatigue would send her spiraling downward into some black void.

Inevitably, longer periods of awareness and logic came to Shalee. Twice she had attempted to call to the woman near a fire encircled by large rocks, but could not bring the words from her parched throat before that dark night closed in upon her. The fact that she was and had been very ill became a frequent first thought upon awakening each time. The pain in her head was slowly receding. She was feeling better and a little stronger. But where was Uncle Thad? Why wasn't he caring for her? Was he also ill? Did that explain why these two strangers were tending her?

That night, for the first time in eight days, Shalee slept peacefully. When she opened her eyes the following morning, a man with reddish-brown flesh was kneeling beside her, smiling at her. Her baffled gaze scanned his unusual dress: fringed leather garments, knee-high leather shoes, and a necklace of some animal's claws. Around his flowing mane of raven-black hair he wore a leather band that bore colorful etchings. Her gaze returned to his nice and relaxed features. She met his smiling eyes, her confusion vividly written in the green depths of hers.

"Who are you? Where am I? What happened?" she asked one question after another, halting breathlessly from lingering weakness.

Brave Bear stared at her. Why was Princess Shalee looking at him so strangely? Why did she speak to him in the white man's tongue? "Shalee?" he hinted in befuddlement, worry edging into his gaze and voice. Her gaze slipped to his mouth as he asked how she felt in his language.

"I do not understand your words," she replied, feeling apprehensive, but not frightened. This unfamiliar man made no attempt to harm her and he had been tending her while she was ill, so why should she feel intimidated by him?

He spoke again, the rapid words spilling from his lips like water rushing over a cascade. Her puzzlement increased, for he acted as if she should comprehend his language. She shook her head and stated once more, "I cannot understand your words. Where is my uncle?"

The man's brow furrowed and his eyes studied her intently. Chela came to join them. Shalee's eyes shifted to the lovely young woman who sat down beside the strange bed upon the dirt floor. The woman smiled and spoke in the same unknown tongue. Both people seemed friendly and polite, so Shalee remained as calm as possible under these perplexing conditions. She tried to sit up, but was too weak. The man touched her shoulder, indicating she should remain down. He smiled again, then pulled the furry blanket up to her neck.

She smiled in return and thanked him. She needed some means of communication. She touched her chest and said, "Alisha."

Brave Bear and Chela exchanged curious looks. When Brave Bear tested his suspicion by asking her if she could understand his words, she did not reply in Sioux or Blackfoot, but in English. He touched her arm and stated, "Shalee."

She waited a moment, then repeated her name. Brave Bear, knowing her English name, shook his head and stated firmly, "Shalee." This process was repeated several times until Shalee stared at him. Was he offering her a name in his tongue? Did Alisha mean Shalee in his tongue? Or did he have her confused with another person?

The man touched himself and stated, "Mato Waditaka," then touched the woman's arm and stated, "Chela," then touched her arm again, stressing, "Shalee."

To prove she understood this much of his tongue, she repeated their names correctly, but with difficulty. When she touched herself, she emphasized, "Alisha. Alisha Williams."

Brave Bear shook his head either in disagreement or in resignation. To argue would serve no purpose except to drain her scant energy. It was clear she did not know she

110

was Shalee, nor did she know their language! The injury upon her head and her lengthy stay in the world of blackness had driven such knowledge from her mind. Perhaps when she fully recovered, the memories would return. . . .

Chela and Brave Bear discussed this dreadful state. What would Gray Eagle do when he found her like this? Suddenly Brave Bear said, "Wanmdi Hota?" Only more confusion clouded her green gaze. As they debated their next move, Shalee drifted off to sleep.

Chela stared at the ashen-faced Shalee. "What will we do, Brave Bear?" she inquired anxiously.

"We must send another message to Gray Eagle if he does not come soon. It has been eight or nine moons since she left his camp. Why does he not come for her? Perhaps when she sees him, the cloud upon her mind will vanish. We must be careful not to frighten her," he advised. "Once more she is white. Yet, she does not seem to fear or hate us. We must walk lightly until the Great Spirit heals her mind as well as her body."

Another day passed, then another. Still, Gray Eagle did not arrive. Word did arrive from Black Cloud, but only to say he would stop off in several other camps before returning. No mention was made of Shalee! Brave Bear did not think it his place to question his Chief's strange behavior, but he deeply resented it.

Shalee had regained some of her strength and could sit up for a short time. When she could learn nothing from these genial strangers, she was forced to accept their assistance and care. Perhaps there had been some terrible accident and she was a lone survivor who had been found injured by these friendly people. But why could she not recall such a terrible event? Perhaps the wound upon her

111

head had driven those painful memories from her mind until she was strong enough to accept such a tragedy.

But something alarming was taking place today. The lovely woman named Chela with dark braids and coppery skin was watching her intensely. What were the emotions that warred within her chocolate eyes? It quickly became apparent it had something to do with the excessive friendliness and assistance of the ruggedly handsome man. Were they sister and brother or husband and wife? If they were married, why did he look at her in that way that suggested attraction and affection? While she was weak and shaky, he had held the curious cup for her to drink from and the bowl while he actually fed her that reviving and unknown broth. His smiles were tender, revealing a fondness she found dismaying and puzzling. Noting Chela's disapproval and annoyance, Shalee tried to accept his aid with politeness and to prevent too much friendliness. Yet she couldn't help but smile radiantly at him for his kindness. Too, he was attempting to teach her some of his words.

While he was out that afternoon, Shalee steadily grasped the bewildering resentment and feminine spite in Chela. Her soup was served cold and her water warm! Pains shot through Shalee's head when Chela suddenly yanked the bandage off, for it was stuck to the dried blood and clear liquid that had dried to form a protective scab. The perplexing and intimidating woman indifferently tossed her a clean bandage to replace herself, whirling and leaving Shalee alone.

Dread began to edge into her mind. Who were these people? Why was this young woman suddenly becoming so cold and cruel to her? Likewise, why was the man becoming more friendly? Were their changes related?

What could she do? Where was she? How should she respond to these mercurial and strange people? How could she comprehend this mysterious and alarming situation when there were so many questions without answers? If only she could remember the accident or attack that had brought her here!

Two radiant suns had crossed the sky since the drama between Gray Eagle and Leah had taken place. Enough time to make another attempt to sway the fierce resolve of Gray Eagle, Leah smugly concluded. Her second plan had failed miserably; it was time to use her first one! The day was sunny and exceptionally warm for early April. Leah timed her strategy perfectly. As Gray Eagle rounded the last large tree that stood near the spot where he normally bathed at this time of day, Leah climbed from the water to halt abruptly before his line of vision. As planned, she shrieked in surprise at being caught naked and glistening with water from her recent bath, but she made no movement to cover her body. As if hypnotized, she guilefully stood motionless and silent, her eyes locked upon Gray Eagle's narrowed gaze.

Taken off guard and confronting the naked beauty within a few feet of him, his gaze swiftly roamed over Leah from dripping braids to slender ankles. On his return journey, his eyes hesitated briefly at the dark triangle of hair that guarded her womanhood, then also lingered upon the breasts with their protruding nipples. When his gaze reached her face, Leah was careful to hold the innocent and tender mask in place. Yet her eyes sent out a bold invitation, or rather a desperate plea.

"God, how I want you, Gray Eagle," she murmured, keeping her voice soft and silky as tears sparkled in her

113

eyes. "Why must you torture me and tempt me every day?" she deceptively accused, feigning misery.

Torture and tempt her? his spinning mind scoffed. His respiration ragged, he turned and walked past her into the forest, needing to dispel the imitation of Shalee that reached out to him from Leah's visage.

Leah's time was gone. Success called for desperate measures. She seized her garments in her hands and raced after him. When she called his name, he abruptly halted and turned to glare at her in stern warning. But she fell against him, her breasts crushing into his chest, her upturned face entrancing him with its resemblance to Shalee's.

The clothes dropped to the ground. Attacking his male ego, she panted wretchedly, "Aren't you a man anymore? Did you also lose your manhood when you lost Shalee? Aren't you still the greatest warrior alive? Who has the power to stop you from taking what you need? No one! Will you force your manhood to wither and die because she died? Doesn't he rebel against your harsh denials? Why don't you feed him? You are the leader; no one can stop you!"

Five winters ago before Shalee had entered his life and drastically changed him, Gray Eagle would have reacted violently to such words and conduct! She dared to question his manhood and rank! She dared to speak to him in this disrespectful tone! His mind was plagued by a new guilt born within his mind this very day; now, she was also mocking his lagging prowess! Why hadn't he questioned the Bluecoats about Shalee's attackers and demanded their lives in exchange for those of the two leaders at the fort? It was surprising he had escaped at all considering the dullness of his wits that infuriating day!

114

Now, this white female taunted him! She actually gave voice to the guilt that tormented him, accused him, denied just revenge! She dared to flaunt her body before his starving senses! His manhood was intact; his forbidden arousal proved it! He should slay her where she stood!

Yet, he did not. He simply stared at the brazen woman before him who was boldly offering him the ecstasy he was missing. Leah cried, "I love you and want you! Please let me ease the pain within you. Does your manhood weaken before every woman except Shalee? She is dead! She cannot give him pleasure or take away his aching. I can, Gray Eagle. Please let me prove it," she huskily entreated, her hand freeing the engorged member from his breechcloth.

She audaciously moved her hands up the powerful arms and stroked his muscular chest. He angrily knocked one hand aside, but the other one shamelessly trailed down to touch his manhood. As Leah hurriedly seized Gray Eagle's hand to place it over her taut breast, she daringly grasped his manhood to lovingly stroke it. Infuriated by her assault upon his warring senses and weakened emotional state, he slapped her errant hand aside as he jerked his hand from her bosom.

Had her senses flown away like a bird? What was this mad obsession for him? Was she utterly bewitched by him? Stunned, he could not believe what he was witnessing. How dare this bold she-wolf believe she could behave in this offensive manner!

His body ached for sweet release; his heart yearned to halt the pain and emptiness which ravaged it. But it was not just any female he needed. He could not submit to this foolish deed just to sate his animal lust.

115

An unnatural rage to chastise himself consumed him. He needed to lash out in anger, to feel something besides pain and loneliness, besides guilt and lifelessness, to hurt someone as he was hurt, to make someone or something pay for his loss. Gray Eagle knew he wanted to feel something other than the endless agony and mindless grief which were steadily sapping his vitality. But release with Leah could not vanquish his emotional battle. When she tried to entice him once more, he shoved her aside in mounting rage.

From a distance, someone shouted his name over and over. His temper about to explode, it was several moments before his mind cleared. The stark reality of how this encounter would appear staggered him. The voice called out again. Anxiety washed over him. His shame would be mountainous if viewed like this, being wantonly enticed by a white slave. He glanced at Leah's naked frame and passion-flushed face. He was innocent of wrong, but it would not appear that way!

Dizzy with unbridled passion, Leah resisted his second rebuff. She fondled his chest and brushed her breasts against him, knowing her last battle would be lost if he refused her. The male voice called out again, this time nearer. He had to halt her madness and prevent a humiliating scene.

He forcefully pushed her backwards. She pleaded and reached out to him, inspiring him to knock her to the hard ground.

"Hiya!" he declared firmly, but cautiously quiet. He quickly refastened his breechcloth and disappeared into the forest, furious with himself for even permitting a scene which could possibly stain his reputation.

Was he so blind and sad that he could allow his keen

senses to dull for even a brief moment? It was not Leah's place to punish him, nor his own. He was relieved the Great Spirit had intervened once more. What was happening to him, to his pride? Was his mind slipping away from him? His loss of Shalee was taking a terrible toll upon him. "Shalee, my love, I need you," he murmured.

Leah shuddered with frustration and fury. How could he deny such fiery desires? Suddenly the voice called his name again. Rage filled her as she discovered what had broken her spell. She snatched up her own clothes and dashed into the concealing bushes. From far away, she heard the vibrant voice of Gray Eagle as he answered the call for him. The other man turned and headed in that direction. Her body flamed and ached. She swore to herself, there will be another time, my handsome warrior; I will have you yet . . .

Gray Eagle's jaw dropped and his eyes widened as he listened to the incredible words from the Blackfoot brave. He shouted in joy and gratefully slapped the brave upon his back. He hurried to ask Shining Light to care for Bright Arrow for a few moons. When she heard why he must leave, tears of relief and happiness filled her eyes.

Before Leah could return to camp, Gray Eagle was riding hard and fast for the camp of Black Cloud to retrieve the bird of his heart. He thanked the Great Spirit he had not been tempted to possess Leah, for he belonged only to his one love.

Shalee had watched Chela closely for the past few days; the strange woman failed to respond to her smiles and friendly overtures. She panicked at this stark change. Was she a prisoner here? Were these the fierce

117

and deadly savages her uncle Thad and the other settlers had spoken of so many times? All she knew was that they were most unpredictable. She tried to stand up the first moment she was alone, but her weakness was too great to support her light body. She dejectedly sank to the furry skin, tears of confusion and fatigue blurring her vision. What now? she wondered. If she could only recall what frightful episode had placed her in their hands. . . .

Chela and Brave Bear met the frantic rider as he galloped into the edge of camp. Brave Bear spoke first as he dismounted. "Why have you not come sooner, Gray Eagle? Shalee tempted the Bird of Death many times during these past moons."

Gray Eagle read the anger in the warrior's voice and eyes. "I did not know she was still alive until Deer Stalker came to me the last moon. We searched for her many suns, but could find no trace of her. We have mourned her death. Where is she?" he impatiently demanded, annoyed at this delay.

When Brave Bear told him of the first two messengers, Gray Eagle was dumbfounded. "No brave entered my camp before Deer Stalker. Why did you wait so long to send a second message? My heart has been heavy at her loss!"

After a few heated words were exchanged, the problem was solved. Brave Bear hurriedly related how he had found her and cared for her. He spoke of his confusion at the ignoring of his previous message, words that had obviously, he saw now, never arrived. He then spoke of her recovery. Lastly, he hesitantly began, "I do not know how to speak such words, Gray Eagle. Shalee is not Shalee now."

Baffled, Gray Eagle questioned his meaning. "She calls

herself Alisha Williams. She speaks only the white man's tongue. She does not understand our tongue. She does not know Brave Bear or Chela. When I spoke the name of Gray Eagle, she did not respond to it. The wound upon her head has stolen thoughts of us," he concluded aloud.

"Perhaps she has been confused since awakening, but when she sees me, she will remember," Gray Eagle confidently declared, then asked to be taken to her.

When the two men and woman entered the tepee, Shalee glanced up. Confusion clouded her green eyes as the stranger rushed forward and embraced her, then devastatingly kissed her upon the lips! She instinctively jerked away from him. How dare this man treat her in such a manner! She stared at the handsome creature with bronze skin and sparkling jet eyes. No recognition of him could be noted in her face. He smiled and caressed her cheek. She slapped his hand away and withdrew from his disturbing nearness.

Bewildered, he murmured, *"Shalee? Waste cedake."*

She stared at him. He had called her that same name, but his tone was tender and mellow! Who was this man? Why did he treat her this way? She instantly demanded, "Who are you? Why did you kiss me? Where is Uncle Thad? Where am I?" she frantically added, panic exposed in her naked gaze and quavering tone.

Gray Eagle stared at her. She was looking at him as if he were some stranger! He touched the bandage upon her head and asked if the wound hurt. He spoke in Sioux, and naturally she did not understand.

"Why do you call me Shalee? They also called me by that name," she remarked curiously, nodding to Brave Bear and Chela. "Who is this girl you mistake me for? I am Alisha Williams. Where is my uncle?" Tears of

119

frustration welled in her eyes. As one slipped down her pale cheek, he brushed it away. She retreated from his touch.

"I am Gray Eagle; you are Shalee," the warrior stated in English.

Her gaze widened. She sighed in relief; this man could speak English. Now, perhaps she could get some answers to her many questions. "Gray Eagle, where am I? What happened to me, to my wagon train? The others couldn't speak English; they could tell me nothing."

Again, the warrior stared at her. "You do not know me?" he asked incredulously.

Eyeing him closely, she shook her head. "Surely I would recall if we had met before," she reasoned aloud, sensing some mysterious distress in him. "Where are my uncle and the others? Was there some accident I do not recall?" she asked in dread, compelled to hear his explanation.

"You fell into the river; it carried you here," he replied.

She pondered that news, then asked, "Where am I? Why isn't Uncle Thad here? Why do you behave as if I should know you?" she pressed, intrigued. Something imperceptible told her he was serious and honest.

"I am your husband," he calmly replied, watching the effect of that declaration upon his wife.

"My . . . husband?" she echoed. "That's absurd! I'm not married. I've never laid eyes on you before today," she argued, alarmed by his grave look.

Alerted to the extent of her injury, he softly stated, "You are Shalee, my wife of five winters, five of the white man's years," he clarified.

"Five years? Your wife?" she repeated. She searched

his face; nothing. "How can I be your wife when we've never met before?"

"We met at your uncle's fortress five winters past. We loved and joined. We have a son, Bright Arrow, four winters old." He added a new fact, hoping it would spark a memory in her rebellious mind.

"A son? I have no children! We're strangers! Why do you say such things? I wish to return to Uncle Thad. Take me to him right now!"

"The white man you called Uncle Thad has been dead for many winters. Why have you forgotten such things? Did the injury by the Bluecoats do this?"

"Bluecoats? I do not understand. I saw Uncle Thad only a few days ago. Why did you say he has been dead for years?" she demanded, fear racing through her heart and panic through her mind. What were these Indians doing to her? Why did they tell her such vicious lies?

"The Bluecoats stole our son and wounded you. You fell into the river and were brought here. I searched for you many days, but could not find you. I feared you dead until Brave Bear sent word to me you lived. He said you spoke and acted strangely. Now, I see the meaning of his words."

Her gaze shifted to the other Indian who must be Brave Bear, then back to the one who had identified himself as Gray Eagle. "You must mistake me for someone else. I am not your Shalee; I am Alisha Williams."

"Shalee is the Indian name we gave you when you came to live with us. You married me five winters ago; we have a son. Do not resist the return of such beautiful memories, Grass Eyes. I love you and need you. My heart lost all hope and joy when I feared you dead."

His strange words disturbed and dismayed her. Why

121

did he persist in his error? Yet, his eyes pleaded for her to agree; she could not. How could she be married to this man and not recall him? A son? Impossible! Yet he was serious! Was she dreaming or still delirious?

"How can I be your wife, this Shalee, when I do not know you?" she reasoned.

"The blow to your head has taken such thoughts from your mind. I speak the truth, Shalee," he vowed earnestly.

"How can such things be? I do not know you," she stressed, becoming highly agitated as he persisted with his unbelievable tales.

"When the wound heals and you return to your people, you will remember," he confidently stated. "Do not unsettle yourself. You are still weak and ill."

"Return to my people? You said Uncle Thad was dead." She seized what she believed was a slip of his tongue.

"Your people are my people, the Oglala. We will return to my camp. When you see our son, your mind will clear."

"I'm not leaving here with you! I want to go home," she panted.

"My camp is your home, Shalee," he stated, near exasperation.

"No! You're lying! Why are you doing this to me?" she wailed.

"You are my wife, the mother of our son. Soon, you will recall such things."

"This Brave Bear sent for you?" she questioned. He nodded. "If all you say is true and I am your wife, why did the woman Chela treat me so cruelly?" she unwittingly demanded, assuming this revelation would halt their malicious game.

Gray Eagle turned and glared at Chela. He demanded an explanation of Shalee's claims. Chela paled, then flushed in guilt. Shalee watched this interaction with rising curiosity. Both men verbally assailed the trembling female. Shalee wished she could understand what was going on.

The handsome Indian turned to face her. "Chela reacted from jealousy. Before we joined and Chela joined him, you were promised to Brave Bear; she feared he was desiring you once more."

Startled by this explanation, Shalee stared at each person in turn. "How can such things be true? I am a stranger here! Are you an Indian?" she abruptly questioned, astonishing him.

"I am Oglala, but the white man calls us Sioux. You came to my lands many winters ago. We loved the first moment our eyes touched. You are my wife. Can you deny your own son?" he reached for one ray of hope.

"I have no son! How can I have a son when I'm not married!"

Gray Eagle reached for her hand, but she jerked it away. "Shalee . . . how can I reach you when you reject my words and love? We must go home. Our son needs his mother. Many nights he has cried himself to sleep fearing you are dead. Does his pain mean nothing to you?"

"But I'm not his mother. Can't you understand, Gray Eagle? You have me confused with another woman. Perhaps you are blinded by grief over her loss. I'm sorry, I'm not your Shalee!" she frantically shouted at him.

"For five winters you have lived as Shalee. You bore our son. Even if the thoughts are gone from your mind, the reality has not fled. When you look into his face, the

123

truth will shine clear."

"What is your son's name?" she unexpectedly asked.

"Our son's name is Bright Arrow," he replied.

She mulled the name over in her mind as she observed the warrior before her. "How can a woman bear a son and not remember him? How could I live as your wife for five years and not know you? It cannot be."

Was the Great Spirit punishing him for his betrayal of her love, of himself? She was like a stranger to him, the irresistible stranger he had first met many winters ago! "Tell me, Shalee, what is your last thought?" His scowl was replaced by a grin.

"I don't understand." She expressed her confusion.

"What is the last thing you recall?" He clarified his meaning.

"We were on the trail, heading west. We were camped for the night, just past a settlement called St. Louis. Why?" she inquisitively probed. Who was this earthly god whose looks rivaled those of the mythical Adonis? How could a total stranger stir such unknown feelings within her? A quiver of uncertainty raced over her.

"You do not remember coming here and building a great wooden fortress with your people? You do not remember our happy life together? How? Why?" he sadly inquired, frowning slightly.

"We haven't arrived at our destination yet. We still have many weeks to travel. Now that spring's arrived, we should end our journey soon," she panted, alarm and suspicion mounting gradually. Why was she even bothering to banter with this vital and distressing creature?

"It is winter, Shalee. Your people came many springs ago. By the white man's counting, this will be the spring

124

of 1782. We mated many winters ago. I swear upon my life and honor you are my wife and I love you," he vowed, torn between joy and pain.

She swayed and paled. "That's impossible! This is 1776!"

"By your time, we were joined in 1777; our son was born in 1778. I beg you to call your memory home. We have mourned you for dead. My heart has never endured such pain and emptiness. I need you, Shalee." She shot him a skeptical look.

"Surely you don't expect me to believe I have forgotten five or six years!" she exclaimed in rising alarm, petrified by his confident and gentle aura. What vicious and intoxicating game was the bronze creature playing? Why? If all was lost to her, could she go along with it?

"It is true, Little One," he replied as calmly as he could, his arresting expression tender and sincere. "I love you and rejoice at your return to me." He flashed her an engaging grin.

"I don't believe you; I can't," she whispered, quivering noticeably.

"I can prove my words if you allow it," he entreatingly offered.

Weakened in body and dazed in mind, Shalee fainted.

Chapter Six

After Shalee revived, the distressing and mind-staggering debate continued for hours, with Shalee resisting the claims of the handsome warrior who towered over her, who vowed such strange and terrifying facts and feelings. The many days of torment and loneliness had taken an awesome toll upon Gray Eagle, and then to recover his precious love only to discover that she defied his words and emotions—all this played havoc with his patience and understanding. Even if she could not recall such things at present, soon she would! He spoke the truth with clarity and logic. Why did she insist he did not? What was behind the fear that glittered in her lucid eyes?

He talked, reasoned, and chided until his frustration and anguish could take no more. "I do not understand you, Shalee! Never have you behaved this cruel way before!" he suddenly exploded, his nerves taut and at his wit's end.

"Cruel way!" she shouted back at him. "I lie here ill to the point of death from an accident I cannot recall, then you smugly swagger in and casually declare I'm your lost wife when we're total strangers! You actually claim this impossible marriage has lasted for five years and we have a son! You say I've lived in an Indian village for nearly six years! You say my uncle and people are dead! You boast of fierce war against other whites! You shout of love for me! All lies! A little bump upon my head couldn't drive so many things from my mind! Perhaps a few days or weeks, but five to six years? It cannot be true!"

"I do not understand such things either, but I speak the truth! Why would I speak of such matters and feelings if we were truly strangers? Do you not question why Brave Bear and Chela knew your face and name? Do you not question the passage of many moons upon your body? Would you accept my words if I can tell you every mark upon it?" He abruptly seized a point of proof.

She paled, then flushed a deep scarlet. She demurely stammered, "That . . . would be simple . . . since . . . I've been unconscious and . . . at your mercy for . . . I don't recall how long!" she finished in a huff.

Taken back at her stinging insinuation, he angrily stormed, "I arrived this very sun! Your charges and insults are painful to me!" He promptly tempered his fury with tenderness, noting the undesirable effect of his outburst. "Do you care nothing for the suffering I have also endured?"

"They could have told you such things! I have only your word you have not taken advantage of my illness," she debated his logic.

"Before the evil firestick of the Bluecoats crashed into your head and drove our love from it, you would not have questioned my word or my honor. Such a painful loss does not change the truth. How can I help you when you turn your heart and mind against me? Look at me, Shalee. Our love was strong and beautiful; how can you forget such feelings? Why do you hurt me this way? Have I not suffered enough thinking you dead for many moons?"

Her gaze met his, then obediently traveled his striking

face and virile frame several times. If there was some inexplicable barrier before her mind, she honestly struggled to vanquish it. Who was this magnificent creature who spoke such imploring and disquieting words, whose entrancing eyes pleaded for her agreement? What if he was telling the truth? What if he was her husband and they had a small son? What if five years of her life were missing? What if she did have a husband and a son . . . that would mean they had . . . he had . . .

She blushed, then paled and shuddered as if suddenly very cold. A trembling hand lifted quivering fingers to stroke her lower lip as she continued her futile scrutiny of the beguiling man before her troubled line of vision. Her hand balled into a tight fist, the nails driving painfully and unnoticeably into her palm. Her chin quivered; her eyes darted about in rising dismay. Her respiration quickened as her shrewd mind deliberated this situation. What if he is telling the truth? the portentous words screamed across her warring mind. "I . . . don't . . . remember you," she finally confessed, unable to call him a liar as he gazed so tenderly into her frightened features. "I don't remember you," she whispered raggedly, tears flowing down her cheeks. "How can I instantly accept a man and a life I cannot recall simply because you vow they are facts? For all I know, this could be some monstrous charade and you my worst enemy."

The awesome reality of their dilemma struck him as lightning hurling into a sturdy oak tree. It was agonizingly clear she honestly didn't know him or recall the past winters and the love they had shared! He pulled her into his powerful embrace and promised, "Do not worry, Grass Eyes. When you are well, the darkness will leave your mind."

For an instant in her great distress, she submitted to his comforting arms and words. As he placed numerous kisses over her face, terror filled her. She jerked away from him and shrieked, "Don't touch me! I don't believe you! I've never seen you before in my life!"

Stunned by the vehemence in her tone and the coolness in her wide eyes, he gaped openly at his wife. "I don't know what evil trick you're trying to pull, but it won't work. I'm not crazy! Let me go home, please," she begged earnestly. "My uncle will reward you if you take me back to him," she optimistically coaxed.

"He is dead! All at your fortress were slain during a battle! I rescued you and married you. From your people, only you and the scout Kenny live," he stressed, bringing a new fact to life.

"Joe Kenny? Where is he? Take me to him," she quickly demanded, sidetracking him with a suspenseful command.

Stunned, he shook his head and sighed loudly. "Kenny left many winters ago. He lives in a wooden tepee many, many moons from here. He took Mary O'Hara to wife. Do you recall nothing of such times?" he quizzed, dreading her next words.

"How would you know Mary's name? How could Joe marry a child?" she challenged, recalling the girl of fifteen she had briefly met in St. Louis not long ago. True, Mary and Joe were friends, but married? Impossible!

"The white girl was young many winters ago, Shalee. *Koda* Kenny told us of their joining when he came to our camp long ago."

"*Koda?*" She repeated the strange word.

"It means friend. Kenny and Gray Eagle were *kodas* long before your moving tepees came to my lands. You have also forgotten you speak my tongue as I speak yours." He dropped another mysterious clue.

"How can I when I didn't understand anything they said to me?" she disagreed.

"I taught you my words during these winters you have forgotten," he calmly replied, smiling with newly gained patience. Surely the loss of so many thoughts was distressing and frightening. He must be firm but gentle with his woman until they returned to her. "I will teach you my words again," he stated, a beguiling smile tugging at his lips and softening his eyes.

"If what you say is true," she slightly relented, "what happens if I never remember these past five years?"

His brow furrowed and his eyes narrowed in deep thought. Hearty laughter then spilled forth as he nonchalantly declared, "Then we will make new memories. I will teach you such things again."

"But if we're . . . married, how can I . . . live with a stranger?"

"Many times you told me Gray Eagle was the only man who stirred your heart to love and your body to passion. It will be the same this time," he confidently promised, his smoldering gaze bringing a modest flush to her face and overly warming it.

She tore her gaze from his. What would this stranger demand of her and from her if she left with him? Her hands twisted over and over in her lap as frightful emotions and suspicions darted in and out of her mind. Marriage meant sleeping together. . . . "I can't," she mumbled, more to herself than to him.

130

"You can't what, Shalee?" he curiously probed, witnessing her alarm.

Without looking up at him, she responded, "I can't be . . . your wife. I don't know you. I don't love you." The words that came forth cut into his heart like a sharp blade. "You wouldn't . . ." The words caught in her throat, refusing to be spoken aloud. After all, he could forcefully take her home with him. If so, a friend would be easier to deal with than a carelessly made enemy. From her observations, he actually believed she was this Shalee!

"Gray Eagle wouldn't what?" he probed once more, needing to understand her many fears and doubts.

Compelled to know his intentions and to test his vow of love, she asked, "Would you . . . force me to . . . to sleep with you?"

"A wife always sleeps upon the mat of her mate," he replied softly.

"But I'm not your wife!" she panted apprehensively, such news petrifying her.

"But you are," he corrected her, lovingly stroking her tangled hair.

If she possessed the strength, she would have jumped up and fled this portentous scene; she did not. "What will you do with me?"

His look was inquisitive. Enlightenment dispelled it. "I will love you and protect you as before," he huskily vowed.

"The same way you did when the Bluecoats injured me, if what you said is true," she blurted out, needing to ease her tension.

The statement was like a savage blow to his heart and pride. "I was not in camp when they sneaked to our

131

village and brought this evil with them. I would freely offer my own life to protect yours," he vowed, his voice strained and his gaze somber. His forehead knit and his jaw clenched as his gaze fell to his lap. "Forgive me for the anguish and fear you now endure, Little One."

Such a strange and magnetic sadness permeated him that she could not resist responding to it. She touched the large hand which rested upon his knee and spoke softly, "I'm truly sorry, Gray Eagle. I do not mean to hurt you. Can't you understand my feelings? This whole situation is so confusing and frightening. You say one thing, but my mind says another. I cannot instantly accept such wild claims, even though I suspect you might be telling the truth. You speak of bonds and love which are unknown to me. Yet, you act as if I should fall into your arms and put my faith in you. How can I when I don't know you?"

When his gaze lifted to fuse with hers, she read such intense anguish there. She didn't understand why, but it irresistibly drew her to him. "Perhaps in time when I'm fully recovered from this accident, I'll remember these things. Until then, you must understand and be patient with me. If you love me as you vow, would that be so impossible?"

He gently captured her upturned face between his hands and gazed lovingly into her entreating eyes. "Do you not understand how greatly this pains and troubles me, Shalee? Gray Eagle is also confused and frightened," he hoarsely admitted, surprising her with his candid confession.

"Why should you be afraid?" she asked, bewildered.

"I fear your loss. I fear you will not come to love me again as before. I fear you will reject me and our son. I fear the lack of love and desire in your grass eyes. I fear the doubts and resistance I sense within you. I fear you will never recall our happy moons together. More so, I fear you will prevent new ones.''

Had she loved this intriguing man so deeply that her loss could torment him this much? Did he love her so much that he would actually die for her as he had vowed? How could one forget such powerful emotions? Pains thundered through her head. She uncontrollably screamed as she clutched at her forehead, reeling and paling from the agonizing twinges.

He caught her and held her tightly. ''Shalee! What is wrong?''

''My . . . head. It hurts so much. I must lie down,'' she breathlessly panted, the stress of this predicament attacking her injured body.

He lowered her trembling body to the mat and covered her. ''Rest, my love. I will watch over you and care for you,'' he said, caressing her cheek. His eyes were clouded with worry and his voice was laced with it.

''May I have some water? My throat is so dry.''

Before fetching the cool liquid, he tested her brow for a new fever. Finding none, he sighed in relief. As she sipped the water, she observed him. How could she deny his concern and tenderness? Yet there was so much she did not understand. How had she come to be married to this man?

When he stood up and left the tepee, she implausibly felt afraid and utterly alone. How could she understand this contradiction? She felt safe under his eye; yet she was frightened of it. No, not afraid of him; afraid of his words and his effect upon her. He was the most handsome and vital man she had ever seen. A curious

133

warmth filled her as she called his face to mind. His noble and majestic visage could rival that of a king. The effect of his smile and igneous gaze inspired unknown emotions within her. His body was bronze, smooth, and hard. Agile muscles rippled when he moved. He was indeed an earthbound god. How could he possess such tenderness when he reeked of power and strength?

Each time he had touched her, the spot had burned or tingled. Why? If she truly feared and doubted him, why did he have this intoxicating effect upon her? Could the modest and naive Alisha Williams fall in love with a man so different from herself? Had she actually created a child with this arresting Indian? She struggled to bring a child's face to her mind's eye. She could not. If she had carried such a child within her body for months and then given him birth, why couldn't she recall such a wonderful moment in her life?

The Indian returned. He knelt beside her and offered her a cup of some dark liquid. "Drink this; it will help you sleep. When you awaken, I will pray your mind also awakens. I love you, Shalee."

Tingles raced over her suddenly warm body. She almost choked on the sweet liquid in the cup. She handed it to him, their hands making contact. She stared at the spot, then up at him. He captured her gaze and would not release it, drawing her deeper into the inviting pools of black magic. His head came forward and his mouth seared hers. Her senses reeled wildly at the delightful and unknown sensations that washed over her. When the pervasive and heady kiss ended, she looked at him oddly. Her fingers moved over the lips that had so gently ravished hers. She stared at them, then met his piercing gaze. "Why did you do that?"

Amused, he laughed. "Because my lips have hungered to feed there. Such loneliness has tormented me. I need to hold you, to kiss you, to make love to you. But your fear of me is too great. You would hate me for taking what my heart yearns to have. It is easier for you to resist me, for you do not recall the love and passion we shared. It grows green with life in my mind. I want you, and I dare not take you."

Her heart and pulse raced madly as she listened to such stirring words and looked into such compelling eyes. To halt such wanton feelings, she lay down and asked, "What is your son's name?"

Knowing she was trying to change their line of thought and feelings, he smiled and replied, "Our son's name is Bright Arrow."

"Yes, you told me before. What will he say and feel when I do not recognize him?" she unexpectedly asked.

His gaze grew somber. "He is but four winters old. He will not understand such things. He will feel great sadness and pain, as I do."

"Can't you explain this situation to him?" she reasoned, not wanting to hurt any child, especially not one who could possibly be hers.

"You are twenty-five winters old and have much wisdom; yet, you cannot accept such words when I speak them to you. How then will a small child understand and accept such words?"

"Twenty-five . . ." She struggled against the power of the sleeping potion, for she needed to question his claim. She could not.

"Sleep, my love. We will talk after you rest. You are still very weak. You will have much to think upon and to accept. I will remain nearby."

Her vision was blurring; his voice was sounding far away. Soon, she was fast asleep. Gray Eagle's hands freely roamed the body that had haunted his dreams for many torturous days. How long would she force him to deny his cravings? It would be a terrible mistake to take her before she came to love and desire him again. But how long could he control the fires that raged within him each time he looked at her or touched her? Disgust and anger filled him as he reflected upon the moments of madness with Leah. Never again would he allow his traitorous body to betray either himself or his one love.

Slowly Shalee pulled herself up from the black depths of slumber. She sighed and stretched, feeling rested and cheerful. The moment her eyes opened, they touched upon unfamiliar surroundings. Her confusion cleared quickly as the supposed dream was accepted as bold reality. The handsome Indian left his place by the fire to come to her side, smiling. He hadn't been a dream after all! No, he was very real, too real.

"Has the pain stopped?" he asked, lightly touching the bandage around her head. She nodded, watching him closely, recalling every word he had spoken yesterday.

His expression grave, he added, "Still, you do not know me?"

Almost reluctantly this time, she shook her head. A look of rueful resignation claimed his face. "Another sun and you will know me," he lightly hinted, his smile returning and broadening.

"Perhaps." She spoke for the first time, agreeing with his words.

"We must eat, then return to my camp," he stated in a mellow and resonant voice. At her look of panic, he added genially, "Many others have mourned your loss. We must share the happy news of your return with them. Our son's heart will sing with joy, as mine does. The Great Spirit has spared your life and returned you to us."

As she nibbled at the roasted meat handed to her, she was relieved to realize it was rabbit. Dreading to confront a past she did not recall, she lingered over the meal. When she could stall the inevitable no longer, she returned the dish to him. He smiled warmly and held out his hand to her. She hesitated before placing her small and cold hand within his larger and warmer one.

He pulled her to her feet, then held her arms until she steadied. "How far away is your camp?" she asked, feeling she must say something to break this strange aura that engulfed them.

"Two day's ride. We must travel slowly; you are still weak. You will need much rest and care. Come, Shalee, we must leave."

After a few steps, her legs trembled and threatened to give way. He caught her and lifted her into his strong and strangely disturbing embrace. As if bearing the weight of a fleecy cloud, he headed for a mottled horse. "I can walk," she argued weakly, her body burning each place it touched his.

She flushed as he gazed down at her. "Even if your legs were stronger, I would prefer to carry you," he teased roguishly. He halted by the magnificent beast and placed her feet upon the ground. As he agilely leaped upon its back, she instinctively seized its mane to prevent slipping to the ground. As he reached for her and lifted her up to sit before him, he playfully jested, "Did I not say you were still weak? Your pride and innocence have returned. I had forgotten how your face could glow like the fire and your pride could stand as tall as mine."

She fused a deeper red, bringing more laughter from him. "Why do you make fun of me?" she scolded him.

"I do not, Grass Eyes. My heart sings to have you within my life-circle once more. I should have realized the Great Spirit would allow no evil to steal you from my side. You are mine once more, as it should be."

"You make it sound as if you own me!" she panted, fighting the emotions that raced through her mind and body.

"Once I owned your heart; I pray it will be so again. Until it is so, my love is great enough for both of us."

As she retreated to defensive silence, he spoke to the two people who had saved her life and cared for her. She listened to the mellow voice whose words she could not understand. Her head jerked upwards and she asked, "Will you thank them for saving my life and doctoring me?"

He smiled. "*Sha, Pi-Zi Ista,*" he replied in Sioux.

"What?" she asked in ignorance.

He laughed in good humor and clarified, "Yes, Grass Eyes. It is good to see you have not changed in many ways. I will speak the words of kindness for you. Later, I will teach them to you again."

She smiled and thanked him. Before realizing what she was saying, she stated honestly, "You don't know how glad I am you can speak my language. I would be terrified if we couldn't communicate."

His chest rumbled with laughter. "Such a skill was how I first learned of your love for me," he informed her between chuckles.

"I don't understand," she murmured, intrigued.

"For a long time, you did not know I spoke the white man's tongue. You told me many secrets about Shalee

138

and her love for Gray Eagle," he jested, his onyx eyes dancing with merry mischief.

His words increased the mystery. "Why didn't I know you could speak English?" she probed, baffled by his reaction.

Her innocent question had a curious effect upon him. She felt him tense as he stated in a tightly controlled tone, "We will speak of such times later. We must ride."

As if some mask had been placed over his features, she could not pierce the suddenly stoic expression and forcefully blanked eyes. It was obvious he didn't want to answer that particular question. Why? What was he hiding? Why had he abruptly placed a guard upon his lips and face? Twinges of suspicion flickered over her mind; yet, they refused to land long enough to be viewed.

As they rode off, she asked, "Why won't you answer my question?"

He glanced down at her. "Many things happened long ago, things you would find hard to understand until I can tell you all. First, you must have time to gain strength and to witness my love since you cannot recall it. When the time is right, I will tell you all you wish to know."

Having no choice but to rest against his powerful frame, she fell into the arms of deep thought. What would she find hard to understand? What memories did he fear to revive or repeat? Why did he need to evince his love before revealing their past? Calling to mind the tales of this wilderness and the Indians who lived in it, the reality of her being white and his being Indian struck home.

She bolted upright and panted, "We didn't meet as friends, did we?"

Shocked at her accurate guess, he couldn't master his

139

emotions or expressions quickly enough to prevent her from viewing them briefly. "We met as . . . enemies?" she couldn't help but ask at his guilty look.

If he lied now, she would know it. He couldn't risk casting doubts upon his honor and verity. "Yes, Shalee, we met as enemies. But our love overcame our differences; it was stronger than the white man's hatred for me, for such feelings never lived within your heart. Even now when you do not recall me, such hatred does not live there," he stated with confidence, touching her chest near her madly racing heart.

Shalee's next thoughts were too swiftly pursuing the truth of his first words to allow his last ones to sink in. He captured her chin and forced her eyes to meet his. "Is that not still true?" he tenderly demanded, his stoic mask falling away as he struggled against the dread that filled him.

"Of course I don't hate you," she replied, drawing a rush of air from him. Had he been holding his breath in anticipation of an affirmative reply? "When we first met, did you hate me?" she boldly ventured.

"No. But I fiercely resisted the feelings you instilled within my heart and body. I had not known the love of a woman before you. I did not understand the strange way you made me feel or the thoughts that entered my mind. I resented the weakness I felt for you, my foe, for I did not understand it. But the time came when the Great Spirit opened my eyes and revealed such things to me. From that day to this one, I have loved no other woman. The Great Spirit showed me that my love for you did not bring defeat or weakness to me. It brought great joy and pleasure. I have loved you more than words can explain, Shalee. When I feared you dead, it was like taking the air

140

I breathe, the food that gives me strength, and the heart that gives me life. Do not ask me to speak of those first days when I resisted this love and desire for you."

"You think I would hate you if I learned the truth, don't you?"

His troubled gaze looked upwards and he inhaled deeply with great difficulty. "Yes, Shalee. Without the protection of your love, you could not understand such times," he confessed unwillingly.

"Then do not repeat such tormenting events. If we met as enemies, then fell in love, we both must have changed greatly. I should discover you as the man you are now; show him to me. If it is to be, he is the one who will earn my love this second time," she offered, feeling she could do no less.

His eyes squeezed shut as he exhaled loudly. She did not refuse his possessive embrace, for he seemed to need this small show of comfort and understanding. Understanding? The word boomed across her mind as ominous thunder before a storm. Was she being understanding? Or was she only thinking of her own feelings? If what he said was true—and she could not disprove it— surely he was suffering too. She was not the only one affected by her loss of memory! How would she feel under these same circumstances? What if the husband she loved had suddenly returned from the grave, but could not remember her? Their love and life together? Their child? What if he acted as she was now behaving? Yet could she behave any differently? No matter the truth, to her they were all total strangers! Still, she must be fair to him. Surely she owed him that much, a chance to prove his claims?

Gray Eagle was thinking along these same lines, but

from the opposite point of view. Shalee had endured much and her mind was confused. He must be loving and patient. He must earn her love once more, as she had challenged. A new challenge, a heady and stimulating one, a desperate and priceless one, a provocative and enlivening dare: to win her love a second time. . . .

They rode in relaxed silence for a long time, each caught up in similar thoughts. Off and on, Shalee dozed in his arms. But when she had reasoned upon the matter at great length, she decided she must have loved this appealing man greatly to forgive the sufferings he had subtly hinted at, and to marry him and bear his son. He was magnetic and compelling, but could she fall in love with him? A second time?

Gray Eagle's mind was racing with enticing ideas of how to enchant this woman again. His prowess and manhood would be tested, challenged. He thrilled to the sport she was presenting. Suspense and exhilaration flooded his body and heart. Cunning ploys came to mind. He grinned. He would attack her senses with skills and cunning to shine brighter than his prowess upon the battlefield. His keen mind and smoldering body anticipated this stirring game.

He halted at dusk to make camp for the coming night. She needed rest, but she also needed time before facing new challenges and problems. He dismounted and handed her down. He spread his blanket upon the ground and suggested she sit and rest while he built a fire. She readily obeyed his words, unaware this was the duty of a woman. Feeling drained by her first day of activity, she lay down.

He dropped to one knee beside her prone body after the fire was going. He smiled, offering her some food and water. She sat up and accepted it, ravenously hungry for the first time since regaining consciousness. She returned his smile and thanked him. He sat down beside her while they ate in silence. Later, he sat gazing into the colorful flames while she lay upon the buffalo skin, watching him.

Aware of her eyes upon him, he remained motionless, hoping she was feasting upon the masculine vision he presented. Recalling days past, he knew her opinions of his looks and prowess. The flames danced upon his bronze frame and face, inspiring the desired effect in her. She wondered if the glow in his black eyes came from the fire's reflection or some other place. When she realized she was boldly staring at him, she turned to lie upon her stomach.

"What animal does this skin come from?" she abruptly asked, fingering the furry mat, shattering the magical silence.

He laughed as he flung himself down beside her, propping his chin upon his hands. With great enthusiasm, he told her about the awesome beast known as the buffalo. He told her of suspenseful and daring hunts, of how they used every part of the animal for some purpose, of the importance of this animal to their way of life. She was amazed by his explanation, for nothing of the animal was wasted or tossed aside. At her request, he told of his camp, his customs, his family, and his people.

She turned her face toward him as she made her next request. "Tell me about Gray Eagle. Who are you? Why did I select you to love and marry?"

"The Great Spirit blinded your eyes to all other men and made me irresistible to you," he promptly jested. "He sent you to me as a reward."

The glow in his eyes danced merrily as he laughed. "To reward me or you?" she teased in return.

"Both. For he also blinded my eyes to all other women; I could see only you. That is how love should be. Do you not agree, Little One?"

She ignored his question to ask another one, "How old are you?"

"Thirty of the white man's years."

"You said you don't have any brothers or sisters?"

"None by blood, but a friend who is like a brother to me."

"Who is the chief of your tribe—that is what you call them?" She continued her questions along what she considered safe ground.

"There are seven tribes in the Sioux Nation; Oglala is the most powerful. We are Oglala. My father is called Running Wolf; he is chief of the Oglala," he said, pride and respect shining upon his face.

She leaned over to stare fully into his face. "Your father is chief and your tribe the most powerful; yet, you say such things without vain pride. Does that mean you'll be chief after him?" she queried, amazed.

"Yes. You will be wife to the next Oglala chief," he added, grinning.

"Me?" she asked, then realized the magnitude not only of his importance but also of her own. She shook her head as if dazed. "Alisha Williams, wife to a chief? That sounds too incredible to believe," she absently murmured.

"To my people, you are Princess Shalee, wife of Wanmdi Hota, my name in Sioux," he playfully elucidated.

"Wanmdi Hota . . ." She tested the name upon her

144

tongue. It stirred no memories, but, "It has a nice sound to it. Wanmdi Hota," she tried it once more, then smiled. "Do I call you Wanmdi Hota or Gray Eagle?"

"Most moons you call me something else," he hinted mischievously.

"I probably shouldn't ask, but what do I usually call you?" She took his tempting bait. If he really was a stranger, why did this closeness and rapport seem to come so readily and easily? Perhaps he was irresistible!

"Perhaps I should not say; it might embarrass you. Your face could flame like the fire. It might be you will choose it again," he teased her.

Joining his merry sport, she studied him closely. "Let's see . . . what would I call you?" She gave it some thought, then laughingly hinted, "Black Eyes, since you call me Grass Eyes?" He shook his head. "If I'm Little One, you might be Tall One? No?" she hinted as he shook his head again. Enjoying herself, she pondered his name and personality. She beamed as she stated, "Gray Eagle, warrior of the sky?"

He laughed. "You have called me such before, but your keen mind must think harder," he huskily suggested, enjoying himself and this sport.

What would a woman call her husband, her love? She smiled smugly as she offered provocatively, "My love?"

His expression told her she had guessed correctly. "I see you have not lost your wits and cunning, Grass Eyes," he complimented her intelligence.

The dangerous words had left her lips before she could halt them. "Are you my love?" She quickly pulled her gaze from his and stared at the fire beyond him. Whatever had possessed her to say that?

"I was, and I hope to be again, Shalee," he insisted

145

upon answering. "Open your heart to me," he huskily entreated.

She trembled as she informed him, "It's too soon, Wanmdi Hota."

Why had she used his Indian name? Had her view of him as a man suddenly altered, so that now she saw him primarily as an Indian? She was tense and afraid. He could not press her, not after sharing such warmth. "Do not worry, my love; I will not force such feelings upon you. They must come freely, as before."

She looked at him. "You are kind, Gray Eagle. Thank you."

"Rest, Shalee. This sun has been hard for you. There are many suns and moons to talk again. If you have forgotten all else, remember I love you. In time, I pray you can return this love."

"I will try, Gray Eagle; that is all I can promise you right now," she replied honestly. "There is so much I do not understand or remember. The loss of five years of one's existence is terrifying."

"I can ask for no more. Sleep. I will guard you."

Surprisingly, slumber came quickly to her. As the night chilled and the cover slipped from her shoulders, she instinctively gravitated to the warmth of his body and snuggled there. He smiled to himself as his arms encircled her and held her tenderly, sharing his warmth and love, though she didn't know it. Soon, peaceful slumber claimed his cheerful mind and singing heart. His ecstasy had been returned to him and he would brazenly conquer it. . . .

Chapter Seven

Shalee awakened to the carefree chirping of birds in the nearby spruce trees. There was a slight nip in the air this promising morning. She nestled closer to the object beside her, which radiated magnetic heat. Her eyes hastily opened as she realized her hand was moving over firm, smooth flesh upon a rich bronze chest. Her head jerked backwards and she gazed into the smiling face of Gray Eagle. She relaxed and smiled. "You startled me. For an instant I didn't know where I was," she confessed demurely.

As if suddenly realizing she was in the disturbing stranger's arms, she reluctantly moved away. "You were cold. I shared my body heat with you," he informed her to calm the uncertainty that gleamed within her green eyes.

"Thank you. Will we reach your camp today?" she asked, needing to dispel the heady aura around them.

"I think it best to camp here today. There are many things we must speak of before you return home. You need another moon to accept a life you do not recall. I do not wish to hurt our son," he said, reminding her of another trial to be confronted.

"What can I do? I could pretend to know him and to love him, but I can't talk to him. I will be as much a stranger to him as he will be to me. You said I was intelligent, but I cannot possibly learn your language in one short day. What will you tell him?" she worriedly asked, imagining the anguish of a small child when confronted with a mother who suddenly could not pick him from a group of unfamiliar children.

"I will tell you about him. I will point him out and teach you his name in Oglala. I will say you are still weak and need much rest alone. He can stay in the tepee of Talking Rock and Little Flower. After the shock has passed, he will enjoy the game of teaching his mother to speak again. I will say the injury claimed your words."

At the mention of two new strangers, she panicked again. "Everyone will be strangers to me! I don't know any of your customs, or how to cook your foods, or to choose them. I'll be like a baby there!"

"Do not distress yourself, Shalee. Others will care for you until you are well. They will teach you all you must know," he encouraged.

"Did your people like me?" she abruptly inquired.

"*Sha.* Yes," he translated the word.

"*Sha* means yes. At least I know one word," she stated in exasperation. "You must teach me as much as possible," she entreated seriously.

"*Waste cedake,*" he murmured tenderly.

"What does that mean?" she quickly responded, thinking her lessons had started.

"I love you," he repeated in his stirring voice.

She flushed. "What is Bright Arrow's name?" she hurriedly asked.

"Wiyakpa Wanhinpe," he replied.

"*Waste cedake, Wiyakpa Wanhinpe,*" she repeated. "Did I say it correctly?"

"*Waste cedake, Wanmdi Hota,*" he teased lightly.

"What month is this?" She changed the subject again.

"At the fort, the Bluecoats called it April." He wisely dropped his line of pressure.

"April, 1782 . . . it sounds impossible. Five whole years gone."

"When the Great Spirit wills it, they will return."

She met his somber gaze and probed, "Will they, Wanmdi Hota?"

"Sha. The *wilhanmna* told me."

"*Wilhanmna?*" she echoed inquisitively.

"Dream. Not once did my visions say you were dead. Each time I dreamed of you, you were smiling at me and holding out your arms to me. My faith was small; you were calling for me to seek you out, but I was too sad to understand the vision," he explained.

"But dreams don't always come true, Wanmdi Hota," she argued, practicing his name at each occasion.

"They do when the Great Spirit sends them as messages."

"How do you know the difference between a vision and a dream?"

"Often I do not, as with the message you were still alive. When our searches failed to find you or a clue of you, I lost hope. Brave Bear sent word to me and your father, but the braves were killed by white trappers. When the second brave came to my camp, my heart sang with joy at his news."

"My father? My father is dead. I do not understand."

"You are Princess Shalee, daughter of Chief Black Cloud of the Blackfoot Tribe. The village we left on the last sun was the camp of Black Cloud. The warrior who found you was his son." He slowly began his incredible tale.

"They think I'm an Indian? The man who saved my

149

life believes I am his sister? Why?"

"It is a long tale, Shalee. You are not Brave Bear's sister. Black Cloud has no sons; Brave Bear has no mother or father. Black Cloud chose him as son and next chief when he was two winters old and his parents died."

"But you just said I was Black Cloud's daughter," she refuted his confusing words.

He told her of how Black Cloud had once captured and loved a white girl named Jenny, a female with green eyes and fiery hair. A daughter was born to them, then kidnapped at two winters by the whites. "When you came to our lands, you carried the mark of Black Cloud. He says you are his half-breed daughter. That is how Gray Eagle could marry Alisha Williams. They did not see a white enemy; they saw Shalee, daughter of a chief, member of the Sioux Nation. He did not come to your side when you lay ill, for he did not get the word of your injury, just as I did not get it."

"I was right! They did mistake me for someone else. You couldn't have married me if not for their mistake, right?" she probed curiously.

"No. But I would have captured you as my slave and loved you in secret. As Shalee, we could join," he stated matter-of-factly, leaving out many details she didn't need to know yet.

"What mark are you talking about?" She seized upon a previous clue.

He touched her left hip and stated, "There, there is a symbol upon your body that proclaims you Shalee. The Blackfoot Tribe marks their children to show their name and tribe in case they are captured or endangered."

"What mark? I have no mark there," she said, denying his claim.

150

He pulled himself to the edge of the mat and drew the sign in the dirt: a crescent moon with two stars. "This mark is upon the hand of Black Cloud and the body of Shalee."

"Impossible! I have no such drawing upon my hip."

"It is there. Look with your own eyes," he suggested.

She felt the place mentioned. Something was there, perhaps a scar. "How do you know?" she foolishly asked.

He chuckled. "You are my wife; I know every mark upon you."

She flushed again. She gradually became aware of a tangible clue in his tone. "You do not believe their mistake, do you?"

He sighed and shook his head. "I said nothing. I wanted you and loved you. I wanted Shalee to wife, not Alisha to lowly slave. My love and desire shut my lips to rejecting their mistake. Only White Arrow knows you are not Shalee."

"White Arrow? The man you call brother and friend?"

"Yes. He is your *koda*. The truth will not pass his lips. You must tell no one, Shalee. The honor and happiness of Shalee, Bright Arrow, and Gray Eagle will die at such words."

"You married me knowing I'm not this Shalee?" she persisted.

"*Sha.* Love does not see the color of skin or the hatred behind it. A man cannot live without his heart; you were and are my heart."

Who was this man who loved her so deeply, who would risk and sacrifice so much to have her? "You said we met as enemies. Tell me about the first time."

She knew he didn't want to, but he hesitantly complied. "The whites who came to our lands with you

151

built a wooden fortress. They hated me and my people. They killed Indians for joy and hatred. When I traveled near your fortress, three white eyes captured me and placed a rope around my neck. They took me to your fortress to be whipped and slain. Your heart was pure and gentle. You took a firestick as they whipped me and mocked me; you would not let them do such evil and cruelty. When they held me captive, you secretly brought food and water to me; you placed medicine on the wounds of their whip. I loved you and wanted you that very day. But my heart was filled with anger, so I refused such feelings."

"My people did that to you? Uncle Thad? Joe? The others?"

"*Koda* Kenny had gone from the fortress many moons before that sun. The man you called Uncle was hunting in the forest. He could not stop them; they were many and he only one man. He did not resist their vote for my death."

"You're lying! Uncle Thad would never kill an innocent man! Why are you saying such cruel things?" she shouted in dismay.

"Hear me, Shalee! He did not torture me, but he did not free me," he added to soften the sting of his prior words. "He spoke against such cruelty, but did not have the power to halt it. He was a good man."

His words had the desired effect and she relaxed and listened. "They voted to kill me; they had killed others."

As his words settled in, she asked, "Did I free you?"

He smiled. "You would have before letting them kill me, but White Arrow helped me escape. Later, I took you captive."

"I was your prisoner!" she shrieked.

"For many moons, until Black Cloud claimed you as

152

daughter. Then, we were joined. You lived in his camp many moons. Brave Bear loved you and wished to join with you. I fought a challenge with him to win you. That is why Chela was cruel to you; Brave Bear's love still lives within his heart. Chela is Oglala; we were to join. But I met you and loved you. It is not the white man's way to have more than one wife. I gave her as mate to Brave Bear when he lost you. Both men Chela had desired loved you."

That certainly explained both Brave Bear's and Chela's actions! "You actually fought over me?"

"I would not give you up without it. For five winters we have been happy. But many more whites and Bluecoats came to our lands. They fear the name and power of Gray Eagle. They tried to kill you and steal our son to destroy me. I was forced to trade my life for our son's. But the Bluecoats' victory caused dangerous pride in their hearts. I tricked them and escaped the fort. But you were gone and feared dead. For many moons I mourned you. But you are alive and here now."

"You didn't want to tell me how we met because you were afraid of how I would feel about you?"

"*Sha*. Love came easily and swiftly, but not acceptance and understanding."

She reasoned for a time. From nowhere a heartrending thought struck her forcefully: Her people were all dead; they had brutally tortured him; she was the lone survivor, captured by him. Did that mean . . .

God, how she hated to ask her next question, but it was necessary. "What happened to Uncle Thad and the others?"

"They were slain during a raid," he replied under duress.

"By the Oglala?" she asked, praying he would say no.

153

"Sha," the dreaded answer came forth.

Agony seared through her. This was the dark secret he had feared. She had married the man who had massacred her people? How? Why? She sat up, fighting to breathe and to think clearly.

"We were enemies at war, Shalee," he offered to no avail.

"How could I marry the man who killed my people?" she reasoned.

"You have forgotten the cruelties of your people. You do not recall our fight to love and live in peace," he quickly explained, then went on to relate many terrible events.

"No more!" she screamed, covering her ears to such wicked news.

"For five winters we have been happy. Does one year weigh more than five?" he demanded, after pulling her hands away.

"Please, no more," she pleaded sadly, tears of anguish flowing from her pain-filled eyes.

"You must know of the good moons that covered the bad ones," he insisted. He hurriedly spoke of many such times, but she resisted his words. When he came to the birth of their son, she halted her weeping. Their son? She forced herself to hear him out.

He continued until breathless to the day of her disappearance. "Five winters of love and peace, Shalee. Do not close your heart to them."

"You should not have told me such terrible things. They were best forgotten. Perhaps I could understand and forgive them over a span of time, but to hear them all at one time . . . that one year far outweighs the other five," she vowed in anguish and disbelief.

"You asked. I could not lie to you. If I had, your keen mind would never trust me again. With all I feel and know, you loved me," he stressed.

She stared at him, seeing him in a much different light. "Did I?"

Her words and look became lances hurled into his heart, wounding him deeply and painfully. "If I say yes, you would not believe me. You are right; I should have spoken falsely." At that conclusion, he arose and left her side. It was a long time before he returned from the forest.

He sat down at the fire he had made. His broad back was to her as he stated, "The Oglala raided your fortress, Shalee. I killed no one there; I came back for you."

She stared at his powerful shoulders and midnight mane. The problem was that she had recalled many things her people had said and done along the trail. Blending them with his words of justice, she didn't know what to think or to feel. Revenge? Justice? Self-defense? Survival? There were so many warring factors involved. Had she forgotten white atrocities that made his dim in significance and brutality? Had there been so much love between them that nothing else mattered? More love than hate? More happiness than tragedy? Pains ripped through her head. Her senses reeled beneath them. She rested her forehead upon her knees and moaned.

"Are you in pain, Shalee?" the rich voice inquired.

"Yes. My head is aching. It's like someone is beating it with a rock."

"I have medicine. Do you want it?"

"Please. I can't stand this throbbing," she faintly admitted.

He placed yellow powder in a cup made from a buffalo

horn and mixed water from a leather skin with it. He offered it to her. She took it with trembling hands, sloshing some of its contents upon her borrowed dress. She swallowed it rapidly, then handed the cup back to him.

"You must rest, love. The wound is fresh and still painful."

She stretched out upon the furry skin and was soon asleep. Watching the tears roll into her hair, he knew he was facing his first defeat in this new battle to regain her love. His keen mind had made a terrible error in judgment. How could a gentle heart understand such black words, which carried no evil to prove them?

"Great Spirit, help me or I will lose her again," he fervently prayed.

When Shalee's dreamy mind began to feel sweet and inviting sensations, she unknowingly responded to the lips that tingled against hers and pressed closer to the compelling body that drew her forward as an insect to a succulent flower. Her arms eased around the narrow waist above her prone body as her hands explored the rippled surface there. Warm air whispered past her ear and something moist and soul-trembling played there. Whatever touched her lips and burned them was incredibly pleasing and stirring. Soon, her breasts throbbed as some unknown spirit blissfully drank from them. What magical torch was enflaming her womanhood? What madness seized her hazy mind and inspired both pleasure and sweet torment?

She struggled to find the clear surface to this enslaving black ocean that carried her body upon its turbulent waves and tranquil dips. Why did her mind resist the halting of this wanton dream? Why did it fight to savor it a while longer? It was wrong to dream of such unbridled passions, wrong to desire them in reality. Why was she thinking such thoughts about the savage warrior who claimed to be her husband? How colorful and daring her imagination had become since meeting him! She must awaken and stop this wanton fantasy. First, she would steal one last kiss before vanquishing her intoxicating and tempting illusion.

When the pervasive kiss ended and she slowly opened her eyes with a contented smile upon her lips, Gray Eagle's face was within inches of hers. She froze as he continued to kiss her ears and lips. It wasn't a dream? She had actually felt and enjoyed a reality? This Indian had truly enticed her body to feel such things and her mind to think such wanton thoughts? What great prowess and magic did he possess? When his lips brushed over her breasts before taking one into his fiery mouth, she gaped at his audacity. The dress Chela had loaned to her was one used after bearing a child, for it laced from neck to waist to permit the feeding of a baby, allowing his hands and lips easy entrance to her quivering body.

She didn't know which emotion was stronger: fear, anger, distress, or wanton pleasure! She shoved his head away as she screamed, "Stop it! How dare you do such a wicked thing! Let go of me!"

His eyes were glazed with some heated emotion, his body was taut and excessively warm, his respiration was heavy and erratic. What fever was upon this robust man? She feared to comprehend it and to witness it. A plea clouded his ebony eyes as he raggedly entreated, "Do not deny us what we want and need, Shalee. It has been many painful moons without you. My body burns to love you. Do not reject me. Do you not feel how it was between us? Can you not feel what we shared? Do not be afraid. I will

157

not hurt you. We have shared many such moons upon my mat. Let me prove the love was greater than the hate, the pleasures more than the pains."

What was he saying? What were these intense feelings that raced through her body and mind? She did not understand, for she did not remember. Returned to a day long before meeting him and discovering such wild and wonderful sensations and such powerful love, she was confused and alarmed by this moment. Yet her instincts and burning body understood and pleaded for what her mind denied.

Terrified, she used the only argument she could think of, "Would you rape your own wife?"

"Rape!" he echoed in disbelief. "I desire to make love to my wife, to bring forth the memories of how it was between us. Love does not hurt the other, only denying such love. My heart and body ache for yours. Do yours feel nothing for mine?" His challenging gaze captured hers.

How could she honestly say no? She couldn't. Yet she instinctively knew the peril of saying yes. "I am confused and frightened, Gray Eagle. I do not understand you or this situation. I cannot yield my body to you simply because you claim I'm your wife. To me, you are a stranger! Husband or not, I do not know you! Please do not force yourself upon me. If you do, I shall hate you and fear you forever!" she warned ominously.

He stared at her, his heart stormed with doubts, his body flaming with great need. He desperately wanted and needed her, yet he dared not seduce or force her. "It does not matter what I feel or need? You think and feel only for Alisha. Where is my Shalee and the great love we knew and shared? Would that I could slay the Bluecoat who drove her from my life!" he vengefully thundered in anguish. The throbbing need in his manhood was so fierce that he disappeared into the forest to spill his torment upon the ground there.

When he finally returned, there was something different in his aura. He was moody and sullen. He neither spoke nor glanced her way for what seemed eons. His pride was immense, but suffering. Just as his tortured mind had reached the agonizing point of accepting Shalee's death and loss, Alisha was returned to him. But Shalee was missing. In her place was a resentful and unfeeling white girl! Would his precious Shalee ever climb from the black hole that imprisoned her within this white girl? How long could he endure Alisha's mind and soul within the body of his Shalee?

Yet Shalee had once been Alisha. Would this new Alisha finally become his old Shalee? How long and painful would such a struggle take? Would they be called upon to relive the same evils and torments they had once endured along their first journey to love and acceptance? After this torturous separation, how could he be patient and loving toward Alisha when his heart and body demanded Shalee? Why was Alisha fighting him and the return to life of Shalee? He was her husband, a husband who needed her desperately. Why was she hurting and punishing him? How could he prove their love and passion when she refused his words and touch?

The two emotional upheavals that Gray Eagle had so recently and closely endured sapped his understanding and denied his keen wits. First, his heart had been ripped from his body with her death. The salt of loneliness and grief was applied to the open wound. Another dash had been added by the unforgivable fear over Bright Arrow's life. When the wound had festered and pained him day and night, it had suddenly been teased with a healing balm: Shalee was alive. Before the injury could begin to heal, it had become infected: Shalee was not alive; Alisha was, and she did not know or love him! A perilous fever was gradually building around the injury that she would not tend.

He turned and looked at her. She was like a frightened and timid fawn sitting upon the buffalo mat. His heart lurched in tenderness and sadness as tears slipped down her pale cheeks and she whispered almost inaudibly, "I'm sorry, Gray Eagle. I honestly do not mean to hurt you so deeply. But I cannot help how I feel. Please be patient with me. I'm trying to understand what has happened to me. I'm trying to deal with it, but it takes time. Is that so hard to comprehend and accept?" she implored dejectedly.

In his absence, many troubling thoughts had plagued her warring mind. He remembered her and their love; she was his wife. It was only natural he desired her, that he needed reassurance from this woman who had unexpectedly returned from the grave. If matters were to be resolved between them, it would require effort and understanding from both sides. When she told him her thoughts, he nodded in resignation, then smiled. But the smile was tempered with a sadness that tugged unmercifully at her.

She arose and went to stand before him, the top of her auburn head halting near his heart. She smiled and remarked absently, "Now I know why you call me Little One. I'll try very hard to remember, Wanmdi Hota," she promised, her alluring eyes coaxing the same compromise from him.

He caressed her cheek; this time she did not withdraw from his touch. He smiled and said, "This time is hard for

160

each of us, Shalee. If only I did not so clearly recall what has passed between us. If only such love was not lost to your mind. It will be as you say. It will be hard not to touch you, for I yearn to do so. I do not wish to frighten you. But my heart cries out to remove the coldness in your eyes and heart."

Her arms went around his waist and she rested her cheek near his drumming heart. "Perhaps it will not take me long to love you again, Wanmdi Hota. Even now when you seem a stranger to me, I feel safe and warm in your arms. Your touch and kiss cause me to feel such strange emotions. But they're confusing and frightening. Love must come before passion. Do you understand this?"

He inhaled with difficulty as his arms encircled her and held her possessively. "*Sha*, Little One; I see and hear your words and fears." He leaned back and captured her face between his hands and lifted it to fuse their gazes. "If the love we shared is gone forever, we must seek a new love. For now, it is enough you are alive and here with me."

When she smiled through misty eyes, he kissed her lightly. Before he could release her, she hugged him fiercely and thanked him. He smiled, tugging playfully upon her braid. For now, truce was more important than his torment and disappointments. "Are you strong enough to ride?" he asked.

"Yes. *Sha, Wanmdi Hota,*" she corrected herself.

He laughed in rising spirits, for it was ecstatically clear she was trying. After a quick meal, they mounted up to ride as far as her strength and injury would permit. For a time, serenity rode with them. . . .

Chapter Eight

It was late afternoon when he reined in his horse near a wide stream. He slipped nimbly to the damp earth, then grasped her slim waist to help her down. Well-trained and loyal, the huge animal began to nibble leisurely at the new shoots of green beneath his unshod hooves. The small hands of the white girl upon the broad shoulders of the Sioux warrior slid down the well-muscled chest as her feet touched the surface of the ground.

He smiled as he instructed, "Drink and rest, Shalee. If you are too weary to ride further, we will camp here for the night." The tremors of fatigue within her as she held tightly to his forearms told him of her need to rest the night here. Still, it would be best to allow her this choice.

"I'm sorry to be such a bother, Gray Eagle, but I am exhausted. This is the most exercise I've had in days. I know you must be eager to get home; perhaps I will be better after a short rest."

"Both your mind and your body must be prepared to face the unknown when we reach our camp. A long rest will be best for you," he hinted.

The unknown? What better way to name what she would soon face? "You're right. Shall I help you gather some firewood?" she offered.

"No, you sit and rest. I will return soon. Chula will guard you," he stated cheerfully, rubbing the nose of his beloved animal. He spoke softly to the Appaloosa, as if the splotched creature could actually understand his commands.

He spread the buffalo skin upon the ground and left her alone. She knelt to drink water from her cupped hands, then moistened her face hopefully to refresh her lagging energy. Admiring the mottled beast, she rubbed his neck and "talked" to him. Surprisingly, he permitted this stranger's touch and neighed as if responding to her words. She laughed as he nuzzled his mouth into her opened hand.

"I'm sorry, Chula, but I have no treats for you tonight." She pulled a handful of newborn grass and held it out to him in genial invitation.

He pulled it from her light grasp and chewed upon it, careful not to bite her hand. "You and your master are well matched, Chula," she absently remarked, noting their similarities in uniqueness and magnificence. Both were strong and proud; both were well-trained and alert. A noble air emanated from each, as did tenderness and great strength. They were like color to a flower, a perfect blending of unity and beauty.

"Well, well . . . what do we have here, Charlie?" a raspy voice came from behind her.

Shalee whirled, her shock matched only by theirs. As two pairs of eyes walked over her lovely face and shapely body, she gaped at the two men dressed in deep blue uniforms edged in bright yellow. "Who are you?" she asked, alarmed at the way the two soldiers were leering at her.

"I'll be damned, Starnes! It's her! That gal we knocked in the river!" the other man exploded in astonishment. "You must be a mighty good swimmer, gurl," he complimented her incredulous survival.

Starnes was too busy gaping at the beautiful girl to hear Charlie's remarks. Eyes as green as priceless emeralds upon a face of flawless white satin were focused upon him, fear and confusion written in them. "She's white all right," the man called Starnes finally spoke. "How'd you get here? What's your name?" he demanded angrily, sounding as if she shouldn't be alive!

Both men glanced around. "You here alone?" Charlie asked.

Shalee didn't reply. "You speak English, gurl! I asked you a question!"

The tone of his voice crushed the barrier upon her speech. "Of course I speak English," she replied without even realizing she had spoken.

"How'd you get outta that river? I didn't know anyone could swim that good. You're a long way from the Sioux camp. What'cha doing out here alone?"

"What river?" she echoed, stealing time to reason upon their words and intent. Were these the men who had attacked her?

"Come off it, gurl! You know I smashed your skull and tossed you into the river! I ain't no fool!" he snapped in annoyance.

"I don't remember you or the accident. The blow must have caused me to forget. Some Indians found me in the river and cared for me. They're sending me back to the Oglala camp. Is that the same as the Sioux?" she inquired, her words convincing and her look innocent.

Both men glanced around again. "What Indians? We didn't see nobody."

"They went hunting. They left me here. I'm still weak," she demurely explained, for some inexplicable reason feeling that she should behave in this dumb-witted way. Why would soldiers attempt to kill a white woman? Where was Gray Eagle? Would they try to kill her again? Why?

"Why did you say you injured me and threw me into the river? I'm white like you. I don't understand. Why didn't you rescue me?" she probed.

Starnes laughed! Charlie gaped lecherously! "From what I see now, we musta been in too much of a hurry that day," Starnes commented, his eyes glowing with an emotion Shalee resented and feared.

"They said you stole a small boy. Why?" she asked, wondering why she needed to hear such facts from these two evil men.

Starnes' chest rumbled with laughter, a soul-chilling kind that taunted her ignorance. "We captured the son of Gray Eagle himself. But that fool Hodges let him escape right under his stupid, fat nose! We'll get him again; this time, the Eagle won't get away. We'll slit his miserable throat first!" he boasted, his eyes cold and scornful.

"Who is this Gray Eagle? Why would you kidnap his son?" she pressed.

"Who is Gray Eagle? You must have lost your senses, gurl! He's a legend in these parts! They ain't a white man or Indian around who don't fear him. He's the Devil himself, if you ask me! You was living in his camp!" he snarled scornfully.

"I told you; I don't remember anything before my wagon train was heading here. I don't know how long I've been their prisoner. The last time I remember, it was the summer of '76," she ventured persuasively, feeling she shouldn't tell them more than that.

That caught Starnes' attention. "Where were your

people heading?"

"I think the scout called it Pierre," she replied.

"When?" he instantly asked another question, intrigued and enflamed.

"June of '76," she replied, as if that were yesterday.

"You don't recall nothing since then?" he demanded.

"No. Why?" she asked, staring curiously at him.

"Th ; here's April of '82, gurl," he answered, smiling again

"Seventeen-eighty-two?" she repeated. "But that's . . . six years! You're saying I've forgotten six years!" she panted as if dismayed.

"Don't worry none, gurlie. We'll take you to Fort Henry with us. If you was captured that long ago, your people's all dead," he casually stated, as if such news meant nothing to him.

"Dead? All of them? My uncle and everyone?"

"If Gray Eagle's warriors attacked you, he don't leave nobody alive. He hates us as much as we hate his guts! One day, he'll get his due. He rides like he owns this entire area, like he's some god. Trouble is, they all think he is! They won't be so cocky and brave when we fill 'em with lead!"

"This Gray Eagle, he's a powerful man?" she hinted inquisitively.

"Powerful? There ain't no word to describe him and his power. There ain't a man alive who ain't heard his name, who don't shudder in they's boots or moccasins when it's spoken. You best be glad you don't recall him and his coups! He hates whites; he kills everyone he sees."

"Why didn't he kill me? If what you said is true, I've lived in his camp for five years," she debated softly.

"You's probably taken captive by one of his warriors. They like white women, if you know what I mean," he suggested, a leer dancing in his features. "You been a white slave all these years. No wonder your mind don't want to remember such things. You kin rest easy now; Charlie and me'll take real good care of you," he promised, his meaning all too clear.

"Why do you fear and hate the Indians so much?" she unexpectedly asked, praying the fierce warrior would hurry back.

"She's surely touched in the head, Starnes! Injuns are red devils, gurl! They torture and massacre whites!" Charlie snapped irritably.

"But you said you attacked me. We're both white. Why?"

"Like I told you, gurl, we wuz in a hurry. If we'd knowed you be this purrty, we'd found some way to take you along that day."

"If you say the Indians are cruel and savage, how do you explain kidnapping a child and injuring me?" she argued boldly.

"We took him to trade for his father. We didn't have time to fool with you that day," Charlie snapped indifferently.

"Rescuing me wasn't important, but abducting this baby was?" she demanded for clarification. "Did you exchange him for his father? Did you execute this awesome warrior you described?"

"Nope! I told you; he got away again," he sneered, irate at that fact.

When she asked him to tell her how Gray Eagle escaped from the fort, he snarled, "We ain't got time to stand around jawing all day! But we shore got time to

167

rescue you. Don't matter you been living with them redskins all these years; you're still a fine looker. 'Course we'll expect to be paid for our time and trouble," he hinted, eyeing her from head to foot.

"How can I pay you when I have no possessions?" she reasoned as if naive.

He chuckled and stepped forward. "They's other ways to pay us, gurlie," he informed the panicky Shalee.

She slapped away the dirty hand that stroked her cheek. "Take your filthy hands off of me!" she ordered.

"Listen to 'er, Charlie. She's as brave as she is tough. A woman who could fight a raging river like that must have lots of energy. What'cha say we find out right now?" he threatened.

"You wouldn't dare touch me! You forget yourself, sir!" she shrieked, her breeding and temper showing.

"I'm not the one forgetting nothing, gurlie; you are. You been a whore to them savages for years. Now it's our turn to enjoy you. Let's take 'er, Charlie."

Drooling in anticipation, Charlie stepped forward and grabbed her arms and pinned them behind her back. Starnes seized both sides of her dress and ripped it open to the waist. "Look at that, Charlie, like two piles of white snow. Them Injuns shore had a fine time with you, gurlie," he crudely stated, fastening his mouth to one breast.

Shalee twisted and tried to pull free. Horrified, she watched him as he began to unfasten his belt. "You can't do this!" she screamed at him.

"First, me, then Charlie's gonna enjoy you, my wild fluff. If you don't wanna get hurt, you best relax and . . ."

There was a singing whish and loud thud that silenced

168

his threat and actions. His body lurched forward, knocking all three people to the ground. Shalee and Charlie scrambled from beneath Starnes, both seeing a yellow-tipped arrow imbedded between his shoulder blades. Upon her knees and clutching the torn sections of dress tightly together, Shalee stared at the ominous shaft. Charlie made a dash for the woods to the place where two restive horses pawed nervously at the dirt. A scream sent Shalee's gaze in his direction, just in time to see him fall forward with a similar arrow in his back. A shadow to her right seized her attention. She whirled to confront her impending fate. Stunned, her gaze widened and she stared.

Gray Eagle slung his bow over his shoulder and stepped from the trees as calmly as if taking an afternoon stroll! He went to Charlie to test for life. Finding none, he moved to Starnes' body. Assured of his vengeful triumph, he came to her, dropping to one knee. He scanned her face with concerned eyes. "Did they harm you?" he asked quietly.

Unable to pull her gaze from his, she did not reply. His eyes slipped to her torn dress and he frowned. "Did they harm you?" he asked again.

Unable to speak, she shook her head. "They were the men who tried to slay you and kidnapped our son," he unnecessarily informed her.

"You killed them," she murmured in a ragged whisper, still staring at him.

"They would have raped you if I had not stopped them," he declared, confused by her accusation and look of fear.

"Why didn't you frighten them away?" she asked incredulously.

169

"If I had spoken a threat, his knife would have been at your throat before his eyes moved. They would not have run without a fight. I possessed the advantage of surprise. I used it. They were evil men, Shalee."

"They were terrified of you. If they had seen you, they would have run like cowards. You murdered them," she charged irrationally, alarmed by this brutality.

"I avenged the harm brought to you, to our son, and to me. If not for the Great Spirit protecting your life in the river, they would have slain you many moons past! If they had seen you with me today, they would know you are the woman of Gray Eagle. Another moon, your life would be in danger again. They seek to destroy Gray Eagle by slaying those he loves. You saw and felt their evil; why do you deny the cruelty of your kind?"

That was exactly what she was doing! She couldn't bring herself to accept the bleak reality that had threatened her—not from him, but from her own people! "I don't understand, Gray Eagle. I'm white like them. Why would they do such things to me? Why do they fear and despise you so much?" she cried out in confusion and fear.

"Such hatred from them and love from me was why you chose me over your own people, Shalee. I am not your enemy; they are. They call us savages, but who was the savage here today? They say Gray Eagle is evil and cruel, but who has shown you real evil and cruelty? You are Indian now. You are my woman because you wished it so."

Her eyes darted about wildly as his words settled in. He was right. "I believe you, Gray Eagle. Can we leave this place?" she pleaded. "Can you help me remember?" she added. a tinge of desperation in her voice.

"If I had the power, I would return your mind this very day. I cannot, Shalee, only the Great Spirit has such great power."

"But I want to remember. Why can't I?" she wailed sorrowfully.

"Perhaps there is some meaning to this problem. We must wait for the Great Spirit to end it. Do not fear, Little One, for I will protect you."

"You did. I was so afraid. They said such terrible things. It wasn't true, was it?" she pleaded.

"What truth do you speak of?" he asked in bewilderment.

"He said I was . . . a whore to your people. What happened when you first captured me? You said we met as enemies."

He smiled and vowed, "Upon my life and honor, no man has touched you or taken you but Gray Eagle. I was the first, and no man has taken you since that moon. This I swear."

She flung herself into his arms. She wept as he covered her face with comforting kisses. She drew upon his strength and love for solace. There was so much she did not understand about this brutal war between the whites and the Indians. Even if she had lost her memory, she felt she could trust this man whose arms were around her and whose lips offered such tenderness and warmth.

Pulling a length of rawhide from the band around his waist, he laced it through the holes upon her bodice and secured her dress once more. She watched him as he deftly performed this kindness. She returned his smile when he finished. "Let's ride, Grass Eyes. We must camp in another place."

Without looking at either body, she allowed him to

171

place her before him and ride away from the ghastly scene. They rode for two more hours before halting again. Weakened by her exertions and the weighty episode, she was carried to a grassy spot and sat down. He quickly fetched the buffalo mat and placed her upon it. She was fast asleep before he could build a warm fire or they could eat.

Gray Eagle allowed Shalee to sleep until she awoke of her own volition the next morning. Unaccustomed to the reality of such intimacy between them, she returned from excusing herself with a pinkened face and averted eyes. She sat down near him and smiled timidly.

His grin was mellow and warm as he apologized, "I have nothing hot to feed you, Shalee. We must return to our camp and make you well." He handed her pones of what he called *aguyapi* and two small tightly pressed hunks of *wasna*, dried meat mixed with berries and some type of oil to hold it together. Although the bread pones and *pemmican* were cold, they tasted good and filled her rumbling stomach.

When she questioned him about the foods she was consuming, he related how they were made, telling her she had done this task many times, promising her that she would learn the process once more. When he touched the buckskin shirt he was wearing and told her she had made it for him, she was amazed.

She studied the leather garment with its fringed sleeves and tail, with its intricate beading across the upper portion. She reached out and fingered the design near his collarbone. "I did this?"

He grinned and nodded, pride and affection shining in the depths of his jet eyes. "You have many skills you have forgotten. If you cannot recall them, you will learn them as easily a second time as you did the first. Your mind is keen and quick; your fingers are skilled and cunning. No warrior has such garments as Gray Eagle," he complimented her.

Worry lines creased her brow and squinted her eyes as she realized how much she had forgotten and how out of place she would be in his camp. How long would it take to relearn the skills and knowledge of five lost years? How would she fare in his camp without them? She shifted uneasily upon the mat. How would she be greeted upon her return from the dead, a startling return as a white woman? How would they feel when they learned of her predicament? She couldn't speak their tongue or adhere to their ways and customs when she didn't recall them. As a white woman, would she be resented and rejected? Anxiety gnawed upon her nerves.

"What troubles you, Shalee?" he asked, observing the range of emotions that crossed her face during her deep reverie. When she revealed her thoughts and worries, he smiled and entreated, "You have earned their love and respect; they will not take them away. They will help you find yourself."

"How, when I can't even communicate with them?" she sighed in despair at the awesome challenge she was accepting. What else could she do?

"I will teach you my words. I will teach you all you have forgotten," he vowed with self-assurance.

"You are a very complex and puzzling man, Gray Eagle. I'm not certain I understand you. I've never met anyone like you before," she stated, pulling an amused smile from his sensual lips.

At the sight of his teasing grin, she laughed and remarked, "Under the circumstances, I suppose that

173

isn't true. Still, it *is* like meeting you for the first time," she modestly confessed.

"If such is true, Shalee, I pray your heart responds this moon as it did the first moon our eyes and life-circles touched. You spoke words to me long ago; you said you loved me even at that first look. You said I made strange and happy feelings in your heart and body. Before you knew the union of our hearts and bodies, you did not understand them; they confused and frightened you. Many moons later, you smiled and said they no longer confused or frightened you; you loved and desired me, only me."

Emotions that confused and alarmed her? She had found him irresistible at their first meeting? Didn't that explain the very way she was feeling right now? Was this how it all began so long ago? Did she dare to ask him about their private life together? No, not yet. . . .

She reached for a safer topic, "You said this was called a winter camp. What did you mean?"

Guessing her motivation, he calmly explained the life-style she questioned. He told of their life upon the Great Plains near the original French settlement and fort of Pierre. He told of the mighty river that had no beginning or ending in his lands: the Missouri. He talked about their summer camp and the way of life there. He related how they camped at the base of the sacred Black Hills for protection from the harsh winters in this wilderness, for safety from winds and snows, and for lingering grasses to feed their animals. When the grasslands were reborn and the buffalo returned to them and the other game to the nearby forests, they returned to the place of their summer camp until the snows threatened to conceal the Eagle's domain once more. He chuckled as he commented that

174

that was how she had described his lands.

"You live this way every year, moving between the two camps?"

"*Sha*. It has always been that way. Before the white man and Bluecoats came, peace ruled our lands. We hunted and worshipped the Great Spirit. We were free and happy. Life was content with this pattern. But the whites came and destroyed this sacred circle of life. They kill and maim. They steal our lands and claim them as theirs. They burn our villages and murder our wives and children while we hunt or defend ourselves against other bands of hostile Bluecoats. They burn the face of Mother Earth and bare it to the sun and winds. They butcher many creatures of Wakantanka just for their skins, not for food or garments as He planned. They enter villages when the warriors are gone; they steal and rape. They have made themselves our enemies; they did not come in peace. They will not rest until they have driven us from these lands and have taken them. They have firesticks to send evil balls into the hearts of our best warriors, firesticks whose thunder frightens the buffalo and sends them charging far from our hunting grounds. Each summer we must pursue them further away from the danger of the white man's long-rifles. Now, our lives are ruled by war and our minds by cunning and hatred. It should not be so."

She listened to the tortured words and fierce emotions coming from this man who claimed to be her love. She was touched by the logic and the troubles he presented to her. How could she deny that her people were pouring into lands the Indians had held for hundreds of years, destroying and taking them by force, denying any offers of peace or friendship? They were enemies at war, and

175

she was caught in the middle of it. As before? What great love or ghastly horrors had caused her to side with him and his people over her own? She couldn't bring herself to ask him to tell her.

"My people hate and fear *you* most of all. Why, Gray Eagle?"

"I am a proud and daring warrior, Shalee. I have many coups to declare my prowess and rank. The Great Spirit smiles upon me and shows me honor. He guides me and protects me. For this, my name and skills are known to both the Indian and the white man. They call me a legend, a Devil, a powerful evil to be conquered. They think if they destroy Wanmdi Hota, they will destroy the strength and unity of the Indian. They are wrong. If they send my feet to walk the Ghost Trail, another warrior will take my place. I hold no magic in my body to halt my death. Only my cunning and courage protect me, as Wakantanka desires. I lead the Indians because they trust me and favor me. But another great warrior could take my place," he told her without false bravado or immense arrogance.

Perhaps it was true that a great leader never viewed himself as a demigod or immortal, only as a vessel chosen to lead his people. Surely her husband was such a man. Her husband . . . pride and respect flowed within her at that thought. Recalling the envious and terrified tone and expressions of the two white men, she realized this man must possess immense courage, stamina, strength, and daring. It would require such qualities to earn that look of reluctant respect and intimidating awe she had witnessed. Alisha Williams had loved and conquered this intoxicating legend? Without a doubt, men feared him and women desired him. She suppressed a pleased gloat as she comprehended that she was surely a much envied woman. She was the woman who shared the life-circle of this vital and powerful man! How she wished she could recall their wondrous life together . . . how she wished she could remember what it was like to . . . she suddenly flushed at her wanton thoughts.

He chuckled and lifted her chin to join their eyes, alluring green meeting rich ebony. "You wonder what it was like between us?" he asked as if reading her mind. When she rosed an even deeper color, he laughed mischievously and hinted, "But you are afraid to ask me about such times?"

"Naturally I'm curious about our life together. But I think it would be best to . . . to . . ." she faltered as she sought the words to explain her feelings. "I know you'll tell me the truth about us, Wanmdi Hota. But I think I would find such words alarming. I think it would be best to move slowly."

"You wish to watch me for a time, to learn Gray Eagle's ways with your own ears and eyes?" he asked to make sure he was understanding her.

"*Sha*. If I'm to feel at ease with you and learn to . . . love you again, it should come from me and not from your words. I would feel pressured and obligated to behave the way you described. I couldn't relax if I felt you expected certain things from me. Do you understand what I'm trying to say?" she anxiously questioned, dismayed at not knowing how to get her real points across.

"You are not ready or willing to be my wife so soon," he concluded.

"I'm sorry, Gray Eagle, but I can't. Not yet. I have to get to know you again. I know this situation must be as

177

difficult for you as it is for me, but I cannot simply become the wife of a man I don't know. Please forgive me. Please understand," she beseeched him.

"It is hard, Shalee. My heart knows great pain at your loss. I hunger to reveal my love to you. I have given this much thought. It is hard to think of what fills your mind and heart. It is hard to accept your withdrawal when fires flame within me, fires only you can put out. Yet, you do not reject me. You try to reach out to me. For this, I will learn patience until love also burns within you. The moon will come when you love and desire me again," he vowed in self-assurance, smiling into her eyes.

"Yes, I'm sure it will," she agreed. "Tell me what I should say and do when we reach your camp."

For a lengthy time, they discussed and planned their story and actions. When the matter was settled, they mounted up and rode off. He halted shortly after two o'clock and gazed down at her. "The camp is near."

She tensed in dread and anticipation. She forced a smile. "Please help me not to offend anyone. Most of all, please don't let me hurt Bright Arrow."

He smiled tenderly. "Such is not in your heart, Shalee. This new challenge will grow easier with each new moon." He kissed her lightly at first; then, the kiss deepened as she helplessly responded to him and to the solace he offered. Afterwards, he held her tightly for a moment. "All will be as before when the Great Spirit wills it." With that promise, they entered the camp during the period of afternoon slumber.

"Where is everyone?" she asked, glancing around at the numerous conical dwellings in a camp which appeared deserted.

"My people rest at this time of day. They work in their

178

tepees. We will see our son first."

Again, she uncontrollably stiffened. Her son . . . which feeling was greater: suspense or dismay? How could she forget so many vital facets of her life? God, help me, she prayed, for this unknown terrifies me.

They halted before a tepee and his feet slid to the ground. He called out in words she did not comprehend. A masculine face appeared, followed by a lovely feminine one. Surprise and pleasure filled both pairs of eyes as unknown, but genial, words spilled forth from their lips. They smiled at her and chatted; the young woman embraced her fondly. It was obvious they were relieved to see her alive. Affection and respect greeted the startled Shalee.

As Gray Eagle's voice grew solemn, she wondered what he was saying, what words were inspiring the looks of shock and distress on those two strangers' faces. They both stared at her, then listened intently to the words of Gray Eagle. Several times they asked him questions, shaking their heads sadly as he replied. When they spoke to her, Gray Eagle translated their words. She smiled and thanked them for their offers of help and sympathy. Their tones waxed grave and quiet. The woman disappeared into the tepee, to return with a small boy with raven braids and coppery skin. His dark eyes widened as he stared at her.

Then tears and laughter burst forth as he lunged forward to encircle her legs with eager arms. He babbled in excitement and happiness. He raised his arms in a vivid plea to be lifted up to her face. In panic, her gaze flew to Gray Eagle's somber face. He softly informed her, "Your son wishes to hug and kiss his mother."

She glanced down at the entreating boy. This was not

179

the son of these two Indians; this was her son! She did not recognize her own child? Tears filled her eyes as she wavered in distress. "Pick him up, Shalee. Hold him tightly. He needs such contact with you," Gray Eagle advised to shatter her fearful indecision.

She instantly obeyed him, gathering the child into her arms. Bright Arrow looked at her and smiled. He flung his little arms around her neck and hugged her fiercely, clinging almost desperately to her. Gray Eagle softly translated his rapid flow of words as the boy wiped away her tears. "He says you should not be sad or afraid. He says you are home and safe. He says he will care for you. He swears . . . revenge upon the Bluecoats who harmed you."

Shalee's gaze met Gray Eagle's, each knowing revenge had already been taken. "My son? Our son?" she whispered incredulously.

"*Sha*. Our son, Shalee," he murmured, his heart touched deeply as she embraced Bright Arrow.

She lay her tear-streaked face against the dark head and hugged him tightly, swaying from side to side in a comforting rocking motion. But the words of solace and assurance came forth in English. Bright Arrow's head jerked upwards and he stared at his mother. His small hand touched her lips and he asked why she spoke in the white man's tongue. His brow furrowed in confusion at the look upon her face and her refusal to answer. "*A'ta?*" he called to his father, sensing some frightful problem.

Gray Eagle placed one hand upon the boy's back and one around Shalee's shoulder as he spoke to him. The child's eyes widened in puzzlement as Gray Eagle explained, "Your mother is injured, Bright Arrow. She is very weak. She must have rest and food to make her well

180

again. When the Bluecoats struck her head and knocked her into the cold water, the firestick hurt her head where the words of the Oglala lived. The blow drove them from her keen mind. She must learn to speak and to hear Oglala again. You are smart and cunning. You must help me teach your mother our tongue."

This was a trying problem for such a small child to comprehend. "My mother does not hear my words? She cannot speak our tongue? How so, Father?"

"Have you forgotten the story I told you many times about Shalee? When she was two winters old, the whites stole her from the camp of her father Black Cloud and took her far away. When the Great Spirit called her feet back to the land of her people, she had forgotten the words she learned as a child. She spoke the white man's tongue. Often when you dream, the dream is forgotten when you awake. It is this way with your mother; her life with us is like a dream. The blow hurt her head. When she awoke many moons after falling into the cold river, her life was like a dream and she cannot recall it or the words I taught her. We must help her learn our words and ways again. Can you be brave and cunning? Can you teach her such things? One day, the Great Spirit will remove the cloud upon her mind and she will remember all."

Most of what Gray Eagle said was absorbed by the child. But one fact fortunately did not enter his mind: that his mother did not know any of them! Such an incredible fact was not within the range of his comprehension.

"It will be a game, Bright Arrow. It is a challenge. We must see who can teach Shalee the most words," he tempted.

The child laughed, enticed by such a delightful sport.

"I will win, Father. Bright Arrow will teach her all Oglala words," he boasted.

When Gray Eagle interpreted the child's words, Shalee smiled and hugged him once more. *"Waste cedake, Michenkshe,"* she murmured.

"You cheat, Father," he teased merrily when his mother said she loved him and called him her son.

Upon translation of this, they all laughed. Perhaps this situation wouldn't be so distressing after all . . . Shalee's softened gaze fused with Gray Eagle's smoldering one. He read the gratitude and serenity revealed there. He smiled and nodded knowingly. "Never forget, Little One, you are loved and needed here," he whispered, for her ears alone.

She smiled, slipping her arm around Gray Eagle's waist as he took the boy from her arms. Bright Arrow initially resisted his next words, which asked if he could remain with Little Flower and Talking Rock for a few days while Shalee regained her strength. An obedient child, Bright Arrow gave in to his father's explanation and logic, for even his youthful gaze and mind could note his mother's weakness and confusion. When the matter was settled and Gray Eagle was leading Shalee toward their tepee, they confronted a white girl.

Shalee and Leah stared at each other. "I don't believe it! I thought you were dead! How did he find you?" the young woman shrieked, her disbelief masking her hatred and bitterness.

Bewildered and stunned, Shalee asked, "Who are you?"

Leah's gaze widened in astonishment, for the look upon Shalee's face declared her ignorance. Leah's eyes shifted to Gray Eagle's belligerent face. "What's wrong with her?" she demanded, sounding as if she had the right to an explanation.

Gray Eagle shoved the offensive slave aside and pulled Shalee toward their tepee. Shalee hung back as she glanced over her shoulder at the ashen-faced, infuriated white girl. "Who is she, Gray Eagle? Why were you so rude to her?"

"She is a white slave. It is not her place to question me," he snarled from unleashed anger at the memories of Leah's brazen attempts to seduce him, to dishonor him, to humiliate him with a self-betrayal during his madness and grief. How dare she approach his love and shout at her! How dare she behave so brazenly to him!

"A white slave? You mean she's a prisoner here?" she pressed.

"She belongs to my father. She serves his needs. He is old and has no wife," he half-explained.

"She's your father's . . . woman?" she blurted out in disbelief.

"*Hiya!*" he forcefully and repulsively stormed before thinking or mastering his outrage at her innocent assumption. "Running Wolf would never defile himself with the touch of a white slave! No Oglala warrior would dishonor himself in such a manner!"

Astounded by his fury and stinging words, she declared, "But I am white, too! Did you defile and dishonor yourself with me?" her own temper flared to match his. "Is that how you view me? How you truly feel about me? Why did you marry me if such hatred lives within your heart?"

Catching his error, he quickly responded, "You are half-Indian! You are the daughter of Black Cloud."

She halted her denial, pondering the contradictions in his words—past and present. "Why was she so shocked to see me alive? Is she a friend of mine? Were we

183

captured at the same time?"

"Leah, your friend? What madness is this? Leah was captured last summer by White Arrow and given to my father as slave to do his chores. She has never been your *koda!* She is but a slave."

"Why are you acting this way? How can you be so cruel to a helpless prisoner? Why do you hate her so deeply? I do not understand you. She looked upset; she sounded concerned about me. Why didn't you answer her question or allow me to speak with her?"

"She is not concerned about you. She is only upset you have returned to my side!" he sneered, dropping a clue he wished he could take back.

"Why would my survival offend her? We are both white."

"Leah is strange. Trust me, Shalee; she is not your *koda.*"

Something in the way he looked and spoke sent suspicions racing through her mind. Why would this Leah be unhappy at her return? Why was her husband being so defensive and angry? "Is there something between you and Leah?" she helplessly asked. "Is that why she resents my return?"

His head jerked around and he gaped at her. "Leah and Gray Eagle? I would die before taking her to my mat in your place! Speak of her no more."

But Alisha Williams could recall all too well the stories about men and their carnal needs, how widowers flocked to easy women soon after the deaths of their wives, as did men whose wives were heavy with child. Was he embarrassed to admit Leah had played this role for him when he assumed she was dead? Was he afraid Leah would tell her such things? She studied the fierce look upon his face. "You're saying Leah has never touched

184

you?" she softly demanded.

A brief look of uneasiness flickered within his gaze before he stated clearly, "My manhood has never entered her womanhood. Why do you ask such a thing?"

He spoke with such honesty and vehemence that she could not resist believing him. Perhaps he had only been tempted to take her; thus, his defensive guilt. "You do not believe the words of Gray Eagle?" he probed.

"Yes, Gray Eagle; I do believe you. Still, something passed between you out there," she insinuated boldly.

"I have slept with no woman but you, Shalee, not since the first time my eyes touched upon your face. Leah has cared for our son since you were lost to me; she has gathered my wood and cooked my food. She has been a slave to me and Bright Arrow, but she has not been a woman to me."

"You don't find her pretty or appealing?" she annoyingly went on.

"She favors you; that is all," he unwittingly confessed.

Her eyes widened in enlightenment. "You desired her, but you didn't touch her?"

"I want and need no woman except you," he vowed truthfully.

"But Leah desires you, doesn't she? She thought she could win your affections if I was out of the way? Isn't that true?"

Trapped, he confessed, "Yes, Shalee; Leah desires Gray Eagle. She offered herself to me many times while I grieved for you. I am a man; my body burns for such things. But I did not make love to her." He used the white man's term for clarification.

"Is she in love with you?" Shalee demanded, jealousy and anger rising strangely within her.

"She spoke such words, but they meant nothing to me. She tempted me many times, but I did not take her. I took no woman; my heart ached for you. She wished to replace you, but I refused."

"If she had been Indian, would you have refused her?"

Taken by surprise, he inhaled sharply. "My heart and mind say no, but my body cannot answer truthfully. In time, perhaps. My thoughts were not clear while I suffered your loss. It is enough that I love and desire only you."

She wisely did not sneer: when I'm around and available! So, one rival had been Indian and another possessed white skin . . . how many more rivals would she learn about soon? How many more women would grieve over her unexpected return to life? Fury filled her. Gone less than two weeks and other females tempted him to forget all there had ever been between them! The grieving widower, my foot! Shalee didn't realize she could not place Gray Eagle in the same category with the men she had known in England while growing up or the men she had met here in America. . . .

"Again I feel I should have spoken falsely to you, Shalee. The truth causes more troubles than a kind double-tongue would. If you could remember me and our love, you would understand; you would trust me. I am deeply troubled and pained by the things I see in your eyes and sense within you."

"How do you expect me to feel, Wanmdi Hota? I return to find another woman hotly pursuing you?" she angrily shouted.

"Hear your own words, Shalee; Leah desires me, I do not desire her."

"It's the same thing!" she argued irrationally.

186

"No, Shalee; it is not. I want and need only you, Little One. I love you, Shalee," he vowed huskily.

"If only I could remember," she wailed in renewed despair.

"In time, my love, the Great Spirit will open your mind," he offered.

"When? I don't know what to think or who to trust! Do you know how that makes me feel?"

"I am trying to understand. It is difficult. You must help me."

"Help you? How can I help you when I can't even help myself?"

"You are weary. You must rest. This time is hard for you, Grass Eyes. But it is also hard for me."

Why was she being so selfish and unfair? He was right. Who was this quicksilver man? Why did he fluctuate between tenderness and brutality? Why did he both attract and repel her? What was happening to her? "I am tired. May I rest now?"

"*Sha. Istinma.*"

At her confused look, he stated, "Yes. Sleep."

She went to lie down. He touched her cheek and smiled. "It will end soon, Little One."

"Will it, Gray Eagle?" she asked, not really offering a question.

"*Sha.*"

She smiled faintly and closed her eyes. He was ducking to leave when she opened them to add, "I'm sorry, Gray Eagle. I truly am."

"*Waste cedake, Shalee. Istinma, Pi-Zi Ista.*"

She smiled, knowing those few words by now, and slept.

Chapter Nine

Persistent drumming forced its rhythmic beat into Shalee's slumberous mind, pulling her to awareness. She sat up and glanced around. The intruding noise was not the threat of some ominous storm; it was some sort of music. Unsure of her position, she didn't know if she should remain where she was or if she should look outside. Who were these strange people? What was expected of her? Who was the mercurial man who had urged himself into her life a few days ago, who fiercely desired to do the same with her heart and body? She rubbed her sleepy eyes and sought to clear her wits.

Gray Eagle ducked and entered the tepee, walking directly to her. He sat down cross-legged before her. "The *can cega* has disturbed your rest?"

When he realized her puzzlement, he grinned and said, "Kettle drums. Our people celebrate your return to us."

A celebration without the guest of honor? As if reading her skeptical thoughts, he added, "I told them you were weak from our journey and still injured. I knew such a large gathering might frighten you. They will sing and dance and offer prayers of thanks to the Great Spirit. Do you wish to go out and speak with them?"

A look of sheer terror flooded her sea-green eyes. "No!" she shrieked almost instantly, imagining hundreds of strangers and what they might expect of her. "I . . . think it would . . . be better if I met them a few at

188

a time, Gray Eagle. Is that all right? Will they be offended if I don't attend tonight?"

"*Hiya, Shalee.* They know you are hurt and weak. I did not tell them of your lost memory; I pray returning home will also return your thoughts," he speculated.

She reluctantly told him, "I'm sorry, Gray Eagle, but I remember none of this, not even you and your son." What if her memory never returned? How long would it take before this place seemed like home and the Oglala her people, before this man and child seemed her own family?

"Why do you call him my son each time? He is our son," he stressed. "You must stop resisting such facts. You must think of him as your son, our son. I am your husband and this is our home. You must practice such thoughts," he encouraged.

"Is Bright Arrow all right? How is he taking this strange news?"

"He is a child. He does not see or feel the greatness of this problem. But he will if you treat him as a stranger. His mind is keen and quick; he will know something is wrong. He will hurt deeply, as I do. You are brave, Shalee; you must conquer your fear and doubts."

"That's very simple for you to say, Wanmdi Hota, but it is difficult for me to do. So much has happened since I regained consciousness. You've told me so many incredible and tormenting facts. I need time to adjust to them. The only life I remember died years ago; now I'm confronted with a life and family I can't even recognize. Put yourself in my place."

"How is it possible to become Shalee?" he asked, losing her meaning.

"I meant, try to imagine how I feel and what I am

thinking. What if you woke up one morning and I told you the same things you've told me? What if I were a complete stranger to you; yet, I vowed to be your wife? What if I placed a child before your eyes and said, Gray Eagle, this is our son? What if I told you all your people were dead? What if you were surrounded by whites and couldn't understand a word they were saying? What if the last thing you recall as yesterday happened over five years ago?"

"I would know you spoke the truth. I would know the Great Spirit was holding my thoughts in His grasp, deciding when it was best to return them. I would fight to bring them back into my heart and head. I would accept those who love me and need me. But I am a warrior, not a woman. I do not feel or think as a *winyan* does. You are afraid and confused. You must try even harder than I would to recall your past."

In some ways, he did understand; in others, not at all. Men were ruled by a physical nature and logic; women, by emotion in both areas. But perhaps she wasn't trying hard enough. Her life and happiness were not the only ones in the balance here; she must think of others. "All right, Wanmdi Hota; I'll try to be brave and helpful. I'll fight as you said. But you must teach me how; help me," she entreated seriously.

"I will, Taopi Cinstinna," he vowed cheerfully.

"Is that my name?" She began her studies.

"It means Little One. Shalee is your name. Do you feel strong enough to meet Running Wolf? His heart was heavy at your loss; to him, you are also his daughter."

"How do I say his name?" she asked, her question revealing her agreement.

"Suntakca Ki-in-yangki-yapi," he replied in a vital tone.

190

"It takes all that to say Running Wolf?" she asked in dismay, wondering how she would ever learn such a complicated and guttural language.

He chuckled. "It means, He-Who-Runs-Like-The-Wolf. Soon, you will say it with swiftness and ease," he confidently flattered her.

She repeated it several times, each time the saying becoming easier. She smiled at him. "Does he know I can't speak Oglala anymore?"

"I have told him. He is confused. He feels shame at not protecting you while I was at the Sisseton Camp. He wishes to see you are here and well."

"Why does he feel responsible? He isn't to blame for the evil of other men, white or Indian," she reasoned, brows lifting inquisitively.

"The success of the cunning and daring of the Bluecoats burns at his pride. He is chief; you were under his care and protection. He allowed the Bluecoats to injure you and to steal our son," he calmly expounded.

"But we're safe; you rescued both of us. He should be relieved and very proud of you," she softly debated.

"He knows pride in me for tricking the white soldiers and relief in finding you. But he searched for you many moons; he believed you dead. His skills and his faith in Wakantanka suffer at his mistakes."

"I think I understand," she murmured thoughtfully. Men were such proud and stubborn creatures. Why did they believe everything hinged upon their courage and intelligence? An attack was an act of violence, not a dishonor. Or so Shalee mistakenly assumed, unaware of the importance of such actions and beliefs.

"I will bring Running Wolf to see you," he stated, rising agilely.

"Wait!" she hurriedly shrieked. "I need to freshen

191

up first."

"Freshen up?" he queried her befuddling English term.

"Wash my face, brush my hair, and change my clothes. I look awful," she concluded aloud, scanning her dirty and torn dress. "Surely I have other clothes here?" she suddenly asked.

He grinned. *"Sha.* There," he said, pointing to where her garments hung upon a side pole. *"Ku-wa,"* he called for her to follow him. *"Mni,"* he offered, handing her a water skin and a softened piece of deerskin. He searched until he found her porcupine quill brush and two leather ties for her braids. He selected his favorite dress and moccasins, offering them to her.

She smiled and thanked him. As she hesitated, he glanced at her askance. "Is there another need?" he asked.

She pinkened, then lowered her gaze. "I need . . . privacy to bathe and dress," she hinted modestly.

Hearty chuckles escaped his smiling lips. "You do not need my help?" he jested mirthfully.

Her glow brightened as she shook her head. "I will wait until you are ready, then bring my father." He smiled and caressed her flushed cheek, then casually strolled outside, sealing the flap behind him.

She could detect his shadow upon the skins. Yet she felt she could trust him to remain there until she finished. She hurriedly stripped, bathed, and dressed. Noting the beauty and softness of the garment, she beamed in pride, recalling his allusion to her sewing talents. She pulled the moccasins on her bare feet and laced them snugly. She brushed her lengthy auburn tresses and neatly braided them, securing the ends with

192

the beaded thongs. She studied the lovely headband before securing it around her forehead. She twisted this way and that to scan her manner of dress. If this exquisite attire seemed natural, she did not realize it.

She walked to the flap and called softly through the leather barrier that separated them, "I'm ready, Wanmdi Hota."

He returned to observe her appearance before fetching his father. His eyes gleamed and flamed at the sight before them. He smiled and inhaled loudly. "You are beautiful, Shalee. My heart sings with pride and love."

He came forward with the grace and speed of a jungle cat, drawing her into his arms. His mouth came down upon hers, savoring the sweetness there. Caught by surprise, she swayed against his tall and hard physique; her senses reeled madly at the taste of him and the warring sensations that assailed her body. The kiss seemed eons long; yet it was brief and staggering. He leaned back and visually traveled her face. As she trembled, she stared up at him.

He sobered quickly, not wanting to alarm her. He slowly and reluctantly released her. "Your beauty drives all other thoughts from my mind," he promptly excused his siege upon her senses. "I pray Wakantanka returns your thoughts quickly; I fear my understanding and patience wear thin. Such great love and need are hard to deny and to master," he confessed with a beguiling grin.

Bewildered by the powerful waves that threatened to carry her away upon some unknown and turbulent sea, she swallowed loudly and remained silent. What a potent and perilous attraction this man possessed! He was right; it would become harder each day to deny the feelings he stirred!

"Your eyes and silence tell me you resist the feelings that fill your heart and body when we touch. Am I so . . ." he faltered as he searched for the correct English word to explain his disappointment. "Am I so repulsive to you, Shalee? Do you wish you were not my wife?"

She was stunned by the questions that she dreaded to answer.

"No, Wanmdi Hota, I do not find you offensive. You are the most handsome and stimulating man I've ever seen or met. But the feelings that plague me when you look at me this way or touch me are confusing and alarming because I don't understand them. I know we have a son, but I remember so very little about . . . love. Is that what I feel when you kiss and hold me?" she candidly asked.

"My innocent and beautiful Shalee, how I long for you to recall what lived between us. There was a bond, which drew us together long ago; that same bond cries out for you to yield to it, to imprison yourself within the circle of our love. Do not fear or reject the feelings I stir within you."

"This new bond must have time to grow, Wanmdi Hota. Surely the first one didn't ensnare us overnight? When I yield to it, it must come from my heart and not your words. Do you understand?"

"*Sha.* I ask only for you to let it have freedom; do not so fiercely resist it. My memory is alive and green. Never has any battle asked more from me. My heart pleads for a swift victory, but not at such a great price."

His meaning was clear to her, clear and compelling. She smiled. She boldly caressed his taut jawline. "You are a very unique man, Wanmdi Hota. More and more I see how easy it must have been to love you. With the combined forces of you and my emotions against me, your victory shouldn't require too long," she confessed.

He laughed mirthfully. "It will be so, my love; it will be so."

He brushed a light kiss upon her lips and left. She sighed, wondering at her unnatural and wanton streak. Wanton, she echoed in absurdity. How could it be wanton to entice your own husband? Were these feelings that assaulted her called love and desire? Did her heart or body recall things that her mind could not? Were they struggling to defeat her warring brain? Why? .

The meeting with Running Wolf was initially stressful. Guilt and amazement laced his speech and manner, while confusion and reserve tinged hers. Gray Eagle translated his apology and good wishes for her recovery; he did the same for her genial understanding and encouragement. After a short conversation, Running Wolf stood up to depart. His last words pleased and warmed Shalee. She smiled as her husband repeated them in English.

"My father says he watched you change from a white woman to his daughter once before. He will do so again. He freely offers his life in exchange for the protection of yours."

Tears clouded her eyes. "Thank him for me. I can't explain how much his words and acceptance mean to me. Perhaps my return won't be so difficult after all."

The aging man with his noble features and proud stance smiled and nodded as her words entered his ears in Oglala from his son. He left, standing taller, as if some weighty burden had been removed from his once powerful shoulders and dauntless heart.

"How old is your father, Wanmdi Hota?" she asked

when they were alone.

"Sixty of the white man's years. Each winter his body grows weaker and his sight and mind duller. My heart is heavy to view such changes in him. Soon, I will become chief. War demands keen eyes and senses, just as the whites demand that war. I wish it were not so, Shalee. My heart yearns for the peace and happiness that their coming has taken from us."

"Changes of any kind are frequently painful, Wanmdi Hota. Still, life demands them. From what I have observed and learned, you will make a great chief. But I wish this war wasn't with my people. It pains me to think of such hostilities and hatred."

"*Kokipa ikopa, Shalee,*" he encouraged her, then promptly clarified, "Do not be afraid, Shalee. No harm will come to you again."

"When I'm with you, I'm not afraid, Wanmdi Hota. I wish my journey back to you wasn't so difficult for both of us."

"The light in your eyes and the smile upon your lips removes much sadness from my heart. I feel the courage and daring that grow within you. You will battle this darkness and win. As with me, Wakantanka's shadow falls over you, as many times in the past."

"I hope and pray you're right, Wanmdi Hota."

"You will see, Little One; you will see."

Shalee's first test of courage and intelligence came that following day around midmorning. "Shalee?" Leah's voice called from just inside the tepee opening. "May I come in and talk with you?" she asked politely.

Shalee turned and glanced at her, paying close attention to their resemblance. She had no way of

196

knowing Leah's brazen entrance was an unforgivable breach of Indian etiquette. She nodded and waited for the tense white girl to approach and sit down beside her.

"I must hurry. They'll be furious if they find me in here with you," Leah stated mysteriously, heavily lacing her words with fear and furtive accusations.

"Why would they be so angry, Leah? I don't understand. Leah is your name?"

"Yes, Leah Winston. You're a princess here; they guard you like a treasure. You've always been so kind and friendly toward me. I had to make sure you're all right. Do you need anything? Is there something I can do for you? They forget you're half-white, too. They refuse to believe you don't hate or scorn me as they do. Whatever will become of me now? My only friend and protector can't even remember me," she wailed, sobbing and wringing her hands.

What did she mean by "protector"? From whom?

"Don't worry, Leah. I won't let them harm you. I'm at a disadvantage here; I honestly don't remember you or them. Tell me everything you can. What was it like here before my injury? I don't even remember who or what Indians are. I saw a few from a distance on our journey here. But I heard such terrible tales about them. I'm confused. Gray Eagle certainly doesn't match those horrible stories," she unwittingly stated.

"Only because you don't remember the awful things he . . ." Leah played her game well, instantly scoring a critical point in her favor. She halted at the precise moment to prevent actually lying, but she boldly insinuated a ghastly time that Shalee was fortunate not to recall. "I'm sorry; I shouldn't have said that! He's your husband," she hastily pretended to rectify her curtness

197

and cheeky outburst. "Is there something you need?" she added, artfully changing the topic.

"I need the answers to many questions, Leah, five years of questions." Shalee softly demanded for the dismaying subject to remain open. Did she need to reevaluate her mysterious situation?

Five years? "I can't talk about such things, Shalee; they'll either torture me or kill me," Leah vowed fearfully, secretly gratified. "When did you first meet Gray Eagle?" she suddenly asked.

"I don't know. The last thing I vividly recall happened on the way here from St. Louis. He told me we met right after I came here."

From St. Louis? The baffled Leah asked, "Did he tell you how you met?" A white settler? But she was an Indian princess, wasn't she?

"Yes," Shalee bravely replied. "But something must have happened afterwards. After all, I loved him and married him," she reasoned.

"Did you?" Leah asked, viciously sucking upon the oblique wound like a greedy leech. There was a riddle here to be solved!

"What do you mean? He said I was his wife," Shalee inquisitively replied, pondering this girl's baneful insinuation and motives.

"You are his wife. I meant, did you really love him?" Leah boldly ventured. "How did Princess Shalee get hooked up with whites?"

"I must have!" she exclaimed. "Why else would I marry him?"

"Maybe he didn't give you any choice. You're a princess. He lusted for you. Perhaps he forced you to marry him," Leah craftily hinted.

198

For some unknown reason, Shalee didn't argue her alleged identity. But the words "lusted for you" had a disturbing effect upon her. Was it carnal lust that had compelled his challenge and their marriage, not love? Would she know the difference? "He said you're a slave here. How do they treat you? What's Gray Eagle really like?" she queried, trying to piece together her own puzzle.

"Physically, you can judge him yourself. He's handsome and virile. But he terrifies me. It's no exaggeration, Shalee; there's not a more feared man alive than him. He is power. He's a living legend. Every eye and ear train upon him when he speaks or moves. Our people fear him. His tribe thinks he hung the moon itself. Other Indians won't even challenge him. He's not a chief yet, but he rules this entire land at the mention of his name alone. He's the last man I would anger or resist. Now, do you see why I'm stupid for even being here?" Her tone was resentful, but . . . but what?

"Why are you?" Shalee unexpectedly asked, guarded.

"The warriors are out hunting. Most of the women are too busy to care what I'm doing. As long as the chores are done by nightfall, I could be a ghost for all they care! It's so hard to play the coward and fool, Shalee. But I would do anything to avoid torture. I force myself to be obedient and helpful. Everything will be all right until . . ." Again, she dramatically halted, lowering her gaze as if embarrassed and greatly distressed, as if modesty or terror froze any remaining words.

"Until what, Leah?" Shalee probed, too sensitive and naive to avoid Leah's cunning trap. Was there some point to be made?

"I must go! Send for me if you need anything done,"

199

Leah stated, making a move to leave, hoping her ploy to cause resentment had worked.

Shalee caught her arm and held it tightly. "I want to know why you're so afraid of him."

Leah pulled out all the stops, believing Shalee wouldn't confront Gray Eagle with her lies. "He would kill me if I told you what . . . I can't, Shalee. I must leave before they find me here."

"Whose safety concerns you more, Leah: mine or yours?"

"Your life is in no danger! You're Black Cloud's daughter and Gray Eagle's wife. I'm only a despised slave. I can be punished or sold if it suits them. Running Wolf is a savage, but he doesn't abuse me if I work hard for him. I can't risk being sold to a man who would . . . you know what I mean!" she breathlessly finished.

"You sound as if you resent me. I thought you said we were friends." Shalee wavered between sympathy and suspicion.

"We are! The problem is you don't remember that fact. All you know and feel are the colored words of your husband," Leah sneered, mentioning the man with contempt and fear to inspire mistrust.

"You're saying he's lying to me, deceiving me?" Shalee pressed.

"How can I answer that? I have no idea what he's told you."

"Some things agree with your words; some do not. Tell me your side of this matter so I can understand," Shalee beseeched the baneful Leah. What did Leah have to do with her? With Gray Eagle?

"I can't. You might tell him what I said, and he would . . . he would kill me," Leah exclaimed in false

200

panic, deliberating how far to press this first time. "How did you become a chief's daughter?"

"If I promise I won't repeat anything you say, then will you tell me everything you know?" Shalee offered a compromise. How could they be good friends if Leah knew so little about her? Very odd . . .

Leah gazed at her intently. "You aren't the Shalee I know. I can't decide if I can trust you," she guilefully fenced.

"You have my word, Leah. Whatever you say will remain between us, whether I believe it or not," Shalee added, subtly telling the girl her words would not be instantly and rashly accepted.

Leah hurriedly related the details of the precarious life of a white slave in an Indian camp. She told of her capture last year and her life in the Oglala camp. But she artfully wove a false tale of friendship and acceptance between them. "Many times we did our chores together. We washed clothes in the river; we filled water skins and gathered wood. We prepared food and skins for winter. I watched over Bright Arrow when you were busy. We shared many days together. We talked about our people, about lots of things women discuss. You were so kind to me, Shalee. I don't know what I'll do now. Now that he has you back, he'll get rid of me." She slyly dropped a false clue.

"Why would my return encourage him to send you away?"

"Are you blind, Shalee? Look at us. See how much we favor each other? If your husband died and another man who looked like him was within your reach, what would you do? How would you feel about him?" she suggested. That insinuation struck a raw nerve.

"What are you trying to tell me, Leah?" Shalee felt compelled to ask, warily observing this complex girl.

"You are such a naive woman, Shalee. Women are ruled by their hearts; men are ruled by their loins. Even sadness doesn't halt the needs of their bodies."

"I'm still not sure I follow you," Shalee murmured, her heart racing, her stomach knotting.

"Gray Eagle assumed you were dead. He is a virile man, Shalee. He needed a woman to take care of Bright Arrow, to do his many chores, to . . . ease the hunger in his . . . body for a woman. He saw you in me. I am but a slave here; I cannot refuse any command."

"What was his command, Leah?" Shalee persisted, anger and jealousy mounting within her, unwillingly recalling the currents that had passed between Leah and Gray Eagle on her return.

"There is only one way to ease such hungers, Shalee."

"Did you and Gray Eagle . . ." Shalee flushed, unable to complete her question. Had he lied to her, disarmed her?

Careful, Leah cautioned herself. Don't go too far. "When the word came of your survival, the timing couldn't have been better, Shalee. In just a few more minutes, he would have . . . I need not finish."

"Then you didn't sleep with him?" Shalee pressed in curious relief.

Leah fumed at her rival's vivid reaction to that fact. To wipe the pleasure from Shalee's face, she declared, "He put on his clothes and shoved me aside as some suddenly repulsive whore! I hate him. I am not some mindless, unfeeling animal to be treated that way. You should be glad you don't remember him and your life with him."

"I think you should leave now, Leah. It could cause trouble if they find you here. Perhaps we can talk

202

another time. I'm still weak and I need some rest."

Leah smiled sadly. "I'm sorry, Shalee. I didn't want to tell you such things. Please forgive me. I hope we can become friends again."

"We shall see, Leah. First, I must deal with more pressing matters. I have a son to consider."

"Don't worry about Bright Arrow. He's a wonderful child. You'll adore him whether you remember him or not," Leah happily exclaimed, needing to leave on a lighter note. "Call me if you need anything at all." With that deceptive offer, she left.

Shalee was tense and drained. What she needed was the peace of mind and optimism Leah had stolen. Innocently or intentionally? Shalee hadn't missed the gleam that filled Leah's green eyes at each mention of Gray Eagle's name. Did it hint boldly of fierce hatred or carnal desire? Was Leah happy or sad at her return? If such a moment of weakness had taken place, who would have been the tempter and who the victim? Leah, Leah Winston . . . are you friend or foe? Another piece to a trying puzzle that was coming together slowly and perilously. . . .

Much later, Shining Light came to bring Shalee some nourishing soup. She smiled and stated, *"Kokipi sni, Shalee. Koda,"* she claimed, pointing to herself.

Why should she be afraid of this amiable woman who offered her friendship? There was no reason. She smiled warmly and agreed, *"Koda."*

Shining Light wished she could speak with Shalee and ease her worries and doubts. Their language barrier made her solace and encouragement impossible. Only her actions could speak for her.

When Shining Light left, Shalee was calmer. Surely Leah had exaggerated or was merely consumed with fear at her own precarious situation. Shalee couldn't deny the warmth and affection in the eyes and manner of Shining Light, or the love in Bright Arrow's twinkling eyes. Where was he? Why hadn't he come to visit his own mother?

As if she had actually called out to him, Bright Arrow excitedly burst into the quiet tepee. He ran to her and flung his arms around her neck. He chatted rapidly, holding out a necklace. She watched him in rising intrigue and pleasure. Her son . . . she caught his face between her hands and scanned it. He allowed her eyes to walk over his face, her touch warm and gentle.

He was a small image of his father. She could detect none of her features in him. Perhaps that was a stroke of good luck, considering he would someday become an Indian chief. Her son, a kingly chief? How strange that sounded as it echoed through her mind. He appeared a happy child. His ebony eyes sparkled with life and mischief. His body was sturdy and healthy, tanned to a vibrant copper shade. His hair shone like the sun reflecting off a raven's wing. He was a handsome and vivacious lad.

She smiled and hugged him. "I am proud to have you for a son, Bright Arrow," she murmured, her heart instinctively and helplessly reaching out to him.

At her English words, he looked up at her. Puzzlement clouded his features. *"Ia Oglala?"*

Tears misted her eyes. "I'm sorry, my son, but I don't understand." As she observed the distress upon his face, she wept. "God, how I hate hurting you and troubling you this way." Her embrace tightened.

The perceptive child smiled and hugged her fiercely in return. *"Kokipa ikopa,"* he offered in love.

Shalee knew those words well by now; still, how could

she not be afraid? He nestled his head to her breast and held tightly to her as she rocked back and forth, weeping softly. Gray Eagle entered and halted abruptly, wondering at the agonizing sight before his eyes. He came forward and squatted before them.

"Shalee? What troubles you?" the emotion-tinged voice asked.

Bright Arrow's head jerked around and he exclaimed, "Why is Mother crying, Father? Is she in pain?"

He lovingly tousled the dark hair as he said, "She hurts because she cannot speak to her son or hear his words. We must be patient, my son, she is still very weak."

"But she is my mother!" he argued unnaturally, the situation tormenting his childish mind. He held up the necklace and declared, "I brought her a medicine *wanapin* to make her well."

"The Great Spirit will know when to make her well again," Gray Eagle vowed.

"But I want her well now," the child stressed impatiently.

Shalee asked what her son was saying. Gray Eagle met her teary gaze and explained about the necklace and his confusion. "He hears my words, Shalee, but he is too young to understand such matters."

Shalee lifted his chin and vowed earnestly, "*Waste cedake, michenkshe.*"

Bright Arrow hugged her and shouted with glee, "See, Father! The *wanapin* has made her well!"

"No, Bright Arrow. I taught her those words. You must help me teach her more." He reminded the boy that he asked for help with this problem.

Bright Arrow gazed at his mother and asked if she understood him. When her gaze shifted to his father's face for translation, his heart lurched. "Why did the Great Spirit make her head white?" he demanded angrily.

"Come, Bright Arrow, we will talk while Shalee rests," Gray Eagle coaxed.

Abnormally defiant, the child lifted his chin in rebellion. "No. I will remain here and make her well again."

"It will take time for the injury to heal, Bright Arrow. Your mother is weak. We must leave and talk quietly," Gray Eagle stated sternly, his disapproving glare noticed by both people.

"What's wrong, Gray Eagle?" Shalee inquired in mounting concern.

"He wishes to make you well this very moment. He refuses to believe his own mother cannot remember him or speak with him."

"Please tell him how sorry I am. What is happening to me?" she cried out in torturous frustration, forgetting Leah's taxing visit.

"Do not unsettle yourself, Shalee. I will make him understand. Come, Bright Arrow; we must not upset her," he firmly ordered.

Bright Arrow whirled to face Shalee. He flung his arms around her waist and clung tightly to her. Between sobs, he shouted over and over, "No! No! No! I will stay with my mother! She needs me!"

Gray Eagle attempted forcefully to extract the child from her arms. His distress increased. "Leave him a few more minutes, Gray Eagle; I'll try to calm him down. This must be frightening for him."

But the stalwart warrior realized her distress was quickly matching his son's. He must end this agonizing confrontation. "Come, Bright Arrow!" he stated more firmly, a hint of impatience and harshness lining his voice.

It required physical strength to break the child's desperate hold around Shalee's exhausted body. Gray Eagle imprisoned his son's wrist in one powerful grip and lifted the squirming child. Gray Eagle spoke to him once more. Whatever he said, the child ceased his struggles. Large tears eased down his cheeks from sad eyes. The anguish upon his face ripped into Shalee's body like thousands of sharp needles.

She stood up, swaying with renewed weakness from her emotional upheavals. Distraught, she stroked the child's hair and offered him her love and excuses. "Do not do this to him, Shalee! Do not entreat him to reach for what you cannot give! He is suffering enough; do not make the suffering greater. I must reason with him. Rest; I will return later."

"But Gray Eagle . . ." she began.

"Silence! I know what is best here! Your white words fill him with defiance and pain! Must all suffer so greatly at your loss? Think of our son! He does not understand why your mind wishes to be white and not Oglala!" Gray Eagle irrationally vented his own frustration and anguish upon her head. It didn't help matters any that one of his warriors, a close friend, had been brutally murdered and his body mangled by saber wounds that very morning. Shalee had no way of knowing the pain that knifed through her husband at that moment.

His words rained upon her like harsh blows. She shuddered and paled. Wide-eyed and terrified, she backed away from his unleashed fury: fury and cruelty that matched Leah's insinuations! His glare spoke far louder and more clearly than his previous words of love and tenderness. She gaped at this stunning facet of her alleged husband. Contact with a side-pole halted her instinctive retreat from such vehemence and coldness.

In the middle of his exasperated outpouring of grief and tension, he witnessed a look and an action that instantly silenced him. Those were the responses he dreaded. "I did not mean to speak so harshly, Shalee," he swiftly apologized. "My mind wars with my heart this day. When I have spoken with our son, I will come to speak with you."

"Don't bother! We have nothing further to say. I would not force my disgusting English upon your Oglala ears. Do not concern yourself with the feelings of a selfish white girl. I don't need your understanding or your help. Get out! I want to be alone." Tears welled in her eyes, tears that she struggled to contain there. Her fatigued body trembled with anguish and weakness.

"My tongue was swift and cruel, Shalee. I did not mean to say such things."

"I think you said exactly how you feel inside! You don't care how I feel or what I think! All you care about is how it interferes with your life! It doesn't matter that mine has been torn asunder. Just go away and leave me alone!"

As Bright Arrow witnessed the tense scene that he could not comprehend, he whitened and shook. Gray Eagle glanced down at him. "I will return soon. Our words bring alarm and fear to our son." He turned to leave. He must speak quickly with Bright Arrow and leave him in the care of Shining Light. He was panicked by the destructiveness of his words and behavior, unaware of the helping hand of Leah behind it.

The moment the flap ceased to waver after his hasty departure, Shalee's vision blackened and she slipped to the hard ground, yielding to its protective shroud.

Chapter Ten

Shalee was gradually aroused by the feel of a cool, wet cloth upon her face. She opened her eyes and looked up at Gray Eagle. "What happened?" she inquired, her look of concern suddenly deserting her eyes for a frostiness to fill them. She pushed his hand away and remarked, "I'm fine. You needn't bother."

"I have hurt you deeply. My wits are slower than my tongue this moon. Much trouble has tormented me this day. It was cruel to cool my temper upon you. I ask your forgiveness."

She stared at him. "I do not understand you, Gray Eagle. You're like two different men: one my friend and one my enemy. I never know who I will be facing each time we meet. If you hate the whites so fiercely, why did you marry me? You say one thing, then the opposite; you behave tenderly one moment, then brutally the next. I don't know whether to fear you or to . . ." she didn't complete her sentence.

"To love me," he supplied the correct ending. "Once you did both, then only love ruled your heart. There is no need to fear me, Shalee; I have enough fear for both of us. And I despise this fear and weakness."

She forced the challenge to his words back into her throat. "How is Bright Arrow?"

"He is calm now. It is hard for him. But a child's mind can be distracted from cares he does not grasp. Your injury is unreal to him except when he views it. That is why I have kept him away. There is no need to let him suffer as we are suffering."

"You blame me for this problem, don't you?" she accused.

"I blame the whites," he parried.

"But I'm white." She instantly countered his attempt to answer without answering. "Who are you, Gray Eagle? Did I ever truly know you?"

The words she spoke needed no explanation. "The same is true of you, Little One. Who are you? You are two women in one body. I see and speak with Alisha, but Shalee is there for a moment. Why do you imprison her within your mind?" he entreated earnestly.

"Is that what you think, I'm doing this intentionally? I'm not! I don't know what's happened to me or why. Maybe there were things my mind needed to forget," she declared unthinkingly.

"What things would you wish to forget?" He pounced upon her words, piqued by that unexpected discovery.

"How should I know? Are there?" She threw out another challenge.

"Your words are strange, Shalee. We were happy. We shared much love. I do not understand these doubts and resistance."

He went on to relate why he had been so upset earlier. He pleaded for her understanding and forgiveness. He discussed the demands of this matter upon each of them. His gaze narrowed and hardened when she surprisingly asked if Leah was taking care of their son. "Our son stays in the *tipi* of Moon Gazer and Shining Light. Leah is Running Wolf's slave, not mine."

Recalling her promise to Leah, she mastered her uncertainty in another way. "Who cared for you and him while I was thought dead?"

"My father was gone; Shining Light and Little Flower had much work to do. Soon we return to the Plains. The white slave cared for our son and cooked for us. Why?" he asked, perceiving some odd tone and mood. Why all the interest and questions about Leah Winston?

"How is Leah treated here?" She asked another question, ignoring his. She shifted uneasily beneath his discerning, piercing gaze.

"She is a captive. She works. She is not punished for she does what is commanded of her," he replied indifferently. "Why?"

"What is commanded of her, Gray Eagle?" she persisted.

"You wish to know her tasks?" he asked incredulously, suspiciously. Something foul was in the wind!

"Yes," she declared succinctly, eyes wide and searching.

When he finished his description of the life and duties of a white slave, she asked in that same odd tone, "Is that all she does for you?"

"She is not my slave," he repeated firmly, lips taut.

"She was while I was gone," she refuted. "She's a pretty female. She even favors me. Have you never thought of her as a woman?" She noticed the tic that appeared and quivered in his jawline. Anger?

Enlightenment washed over him. Did she suspect his guilt and weakness? "Once before you asked such questions. I have not taken her to my mat. That is your meaning?" he icily implied.

211

"Did you ever want to take her to your mat?" she challenged, using his own words to voice her unspoken charge.

"*Hiya!* What madness fills the darkness in your mind?" he sneered, eyes blazing with tightly leashed fury.

Either one or the other was mistaken or lying! When he eyed the doubt in her angry eyes, he stated, "Upon my life and honor, I have not taken her or any woman. Why do you question me this way?"

"I wished to test your claims of love for me. Leah is lovely, and she was available. I am naive, Gray Eagle, but not enough to be unaware of the needs men have. I only wanted to know if you replaced me while I was gone." It was time to halt her vexing probe.

He broke into amused laughter. "You are jealous? Of a white slave? How can this be so? No female can match your beauty or gentleness. How could a man cast his eyes upon another when his heart burns for only you?" His expression and tone were cryptic.

"Does your heart burn for only me?" she asked seriously.

"*Sha*, Grass Eyes, for only you. My heart, my mind, and my body see only you. I would prove this if you would allow me," he hinted huskily, his gaze and tone convincing.

Panic danced wildly in her gaze. Reading it, he shook his head and sighed heavily. "Why, Shalee? Why do you deny such love?"

"I'm honestly trying to work this thing out," she stated sadly, wishing she had denied Leah's visit.

"No, Shalee, you are resisting it. You hold to fear and doubt. You will not reach out to me."

She tensed as he leaned forward and kissed her. "See? Coldness fills you like winter when I touch you, but fires like the summer sun burn upon me. Let my heat melt your snow," he urged tenderly.

When he leaned forward this time, she did not turn her face away. She allowed his lips to explore hers. Surely he held the answers to her doubts. She inhaled raggedly as warm and stirring air filled her ear as he nibbled upon the lobe. His mouth returned to hers, plundering it with skillful devastation. His kisses deepened and intensified. A strange glow spread through her body. Her arms slowly eased around his neck and held his lips more tightly to hers.

It did not matter that the doeskin garment was between her breasts and his hand, the blissful sensations could not be denied. Shalee didn't know when her hem was lifted and his daring hand began an exquisite expedition in that private region, but a stirring ecstasy sang within her mind and body. The small peak beneath his thumb grew taut with desire. The passage where his manhood yearned to travel moistened with rising passion. Determined to end her resistance, he worked gently and deliberately. Soon, she moaned with hungers she did not recognize. She clung to him to sate the needs that plagued her fiery body.

He lifted his head and gazed down at her, ebony eyes smoldering with bright fires. "It is time to end this agony that torments us. We must join our bodies and love as we have many times."

His words panicked her. "We can't. It's too soon. Please don't."

"I burn with need for you, Shalee," he coaxed futilely. Her speculative jab hit home before she could halt its careless toss, cooling his passion and enflaming his temper, "Like you burned with anger and hatred moments ago! If you truly love me, give me time to know you again. Which is greater, Wanmdi Hota: your lust for me or your love for me?"

"If the love was not greater, I would take you without your agreement! My body hungers for yours, but I wish to feed your needs, not your hatred."

He was up and gone before she could think clearly. What was this tension and aching within her? Why did she suddenly feel empty and sad? Why did she want to run after him and beg him to return, to begin a new assault upon her senses? What was this fierce craving in her breasts, upon her lips, deep within her womanhood? Was this the fiery agony he had mentioned? Was this the calling of passion to be sated? Did his body feel this same torment of denial that hers did? No wonder he was upset and angry! It wasn't fair to build a fire, then toss cold water upon it! But pride and confusion held her glued to the mat. Too many discrepancies flourished here!

It was dusk when she realized she wasn't alone. To her astonishment, it was not Shining Light who brought food and drink to her tonight; it was Gray Eagle. He handed her a water skin and wooden tray without meeting her gaze. His aura was cool, punishing. "I go to council. Sleep when you are weary." He collected his prayer pipe, informing her never to touch it or other tabu items. He left before she could thank him or speak.

Her appetite lagging, she only nibbled at the food. The silence in the tepee was taunting; loneliness and despair kept her company. The resolution to her problem wasn't simple or easy. It seemed her only peaceful recourse was to become his wife in all ways, but how could she? Why was he being so selfish? Why had Leah tarnished his bronze image?

The happy sounds outside the tepee called out to her, but she couldn't bring herself to entice more rejection and anguish. She wept in dejection, feeling she was as much a white prisoner here as Leah was. Leah . . . why did her thoughts keep returning to her? She knew why. Leah had widened the breach that had been steadily closing between her and Gray Eagle. But he was as much a distressing stranger as Leah was! If only she knew who to trust. . . .

The hour grew late. Night owls called to their mates. A gentle breeze played at the ventilation opening. When she could resist the weariness of her mind and body no longer, sleep came to her.

By midafternoon the next day, the only person she had seen was Shining Light when she brought her meals. The loneliness increased after the genial woman's departure and Shalee faced another lengthy span until nightfall. If her sullen husband had returned last night, he had departed before she had awakened. Was he avoiding her and their problem? Afraid of touching a ritual object, she resisted the curiosity to investigate their possessions. Did female contact actually cancel magic or power?

When the silence and solitude seemed unbearable for a moment longer, Gray Eagle entered. He looked at her, his expression unreadable and stoic. "I go for a walk, Shalee. Do you wish exercise and fresh air?" He impassively invited her for a walk.

She brightened immediately. "Yes, please." She quickly accepted his offer before he could withdraw it or disappear again.

"Come, the day is warm and refreshing." He held out

215

his hand to her, testing her responsive mood. She looked at it only a moment before taking it. He smiled and relaxed. "The Great Spirit told me your anger had cooled and you needed me."

He led her outside. As they walked through the camp, her eager eyes darted here and there. They encountered only a few people; all smiled or waved to them. Her spirits rising, she smiled and waved back. "Where is everyone? There are many tepees, but so few people."

"My people rest this time of day," he reminded her.

She caught herself before saying she had forgotten. That one word could rapidly dampen this sunny day. They walked into the forest. When they reached the riverbank, he headed to his right, gently pulling her along. She gazed at the birthing beauty and serenity that surrounded them. "It's so lovely and peaceful here," she remarked absently.

"*Sha*," he concurred in a vital tone, steadily mellowing.

Reluctant to cloud their sunny aura, she did not apologize for their misunderstanding yesterday. Upon reflection, she was as much at fault as he had been. He stopped and sat down. "*Yanka*," he instructed, patting the ground beside him.

She obeyed without thinking twice. "Soon, we must return to the Plains. The work is hard, Shalee, and you are still weak. Will the journey be too hard for you?"

"I don't think so. I'm getting stronger every day. How far is it to your summer camp? Do we walk or ride?"

"Such a journey tires even the strong and healthy. You must be careful. The journey will take eight or ten moons. We halt only for heavy rains or to defend against enemies. Most walk while the horses pull the possessions.

216

You will ride with me."

"I'll be fine, Gray Eagle. What about our son?"

"He will ride upon the *tipi*. Other times, he will walk with the others. He is strong; he has made this journey many times."

"Is it . . . too soon to see him again? I know I upset him last time, but . . . we can't get to know each other again if we stay apart."

"He will eat in our *tipi* this moon. You must . . ."

"I must what?" she asked when he halted.

"I was going to say lie upon the mat and let him think you are still weak and his visit must be short and happy. This is wrong. He is our son. We must not deceive him. We must try hard to look happy and relaxed."

"You do not like deception, do you?" she abruptly asked.

"No, Shalee. But such teases at my mind when I see how the truth hurts those I love. His mind and the mind of his mother are keen; they would know of such tricks and resent them. It must be the truth, even if it hurts."

"What will we eat? We can't ask Shining Light to cook for us every day. I know!" she exclaimed in excitement. "If you could kill a rabbit, I know how to cook it over an open fire. I can also cook bread upon stones. I could fix our meal."

He grinned in pleasure. "Come, I must hunt, wife. I will take you to our *tipi* to cook for your family. Gray Eagle must search the forest for a fat rabbit," he teased.

She laughed in elation. At last she was needed for something important. He pulled her to her feet, quelling the temptation to kiss her. She noted the desire in his eyes and the tautness that stiffened his body. She smiled and stated softly, "You can kiss me if you wish."

217

That provocative invitation widened his gaze. His eyes fused with hers. His hand caressed her cheek and slipped into her silky hair. His groin tightened in warning. "I dare not. A kiss would enflame me to desire more. Come, Shalee. We must prepare to eat with our son."

Shalee was miffed and disappointed at his rejection, then recalled how his kisses could spark wildfires in her body. She suddenly giggled. He was right again! The confession that she could dangerously enflame him as he enflamed her was a heady and thrilling feeling.

"You taunt me, woman?" he jested, eyeing her roguishly.

"No, Wanmdi Hota. I was thinking how true your words were."

He was about to say something, but mastered the urge to tease her. He must walk lightly upon this new truce. He must tempt her to desire him beyond her control; she must reach out to him in great need. He would become like the *pizuta yuta*, the drugging peyote buttons; he would ensnare her mind until she could not resist or defy him. If he was patient and cunning, his prowess would call out to her.

The evening went exceptionally well as Gray Eagle unobtrusively translated his son's words and aided Shalee with replying in Sioux. The rabbit was roasted to perfection and relished with the wild greens cooked and offered by Shining Light for this joyous occasion. To hold Bright Arrow's attention, Gray Eagle wittingly entertained him with exciting tales of his past coups, winking at Shalee to let her know where to laugh or nudging her when to sigh in awe. The ploy worked beautifully. Gray Eagle bragged with Shalee's help, allowing Bright Arrow to relax and enjoy this family event.

Later, he sat calmly in his mother's lap while Gray Eagle offered a prayer to the Great Spirit to help them teach Shalee all she needed to learn. When the child added his compliments to her keen and quick mind, she smiled and stated, *"Pidamaye."*

He beamed with contentment and hugged her.

Gray Eagle said, "Listen, Bright Arrow; the night owls say it is late. Soon, you will return to our *tipi.* It is time for your mother to sleep now. She used much energy to care for us tonight."

Bright Arrow happily kissed her and bid her goodnight this time. At the entrance, he whirled and ran back to her to hug her once more. She laughed and squeezed him tightly. When Gray Eagle returned, he was grinning from ear to ear. "Bright Arrow's tongue moves as swiftly as the river, Shalee. By morning, all in camp will know of the rabbit and the happy time."

She giggled in satisfaction. "It did go excellently, didn't it? Thank you, Gray Eagle. You made our son very happy tonight."

"My heart sings with love and pride. We have shared many such moons. Soon, many more will join them. Sleep, Little One." He spread a buffalo mat near hers and lay down. He sighed in pleasure and closed his eyes. There was only one way better to end such an evening, but that was impossible tonight.

"Goodnight, Wanmdi Hota," she called across the short distance, her voice soft.

"Goodnight, Grass Eyes," he replied cheerfully.

A tickling sensation teased at her nose. She brushed at it several times. As she opened her eyes to greet a new day, she discovered the source of the mischief. Gray Eagle was propped upon his elbows and trailing a feather over her nose. He laughed as their eyes met and fused.

"You must open your eyes, Little One. Your father has arrived and wishes to see you," he stated as casually as possible.

"My father? You mean Black Cloud?" she asked in suspense. "What will I say to him?"

He smiled. "He knows of your injury. He will speak and I will tell you his words. Do not worry; I will remain at your side."

"I have to freshen up first," she said, instantly seeking to delay this event.

"All is ready. I will wait outside," he offered before she could ask.

Within a half an hour, they were approaching Running Wolf's tepee to eat and talk with Chief Black Cloud. Gray Eagle grasped her hand and affectionately pressed it. He smiled encouragingly. She smiled in return and tightened her grip upon his comforting hand. They entered the tepee.

Black Cloud rushed forward and embraced her. She smiled and spoke his name, "Mahpiya Sapa," as Gray Eagle had taught her. When he paused in the rapid flow of his words, Gray Eagle translated them: words of love, concern, and apology for not coming to her sooner.

She smiled and asked her husband to tell him she understood the mix-up with the messages. She sat down beside Gray Eagle to be served by Leah, along with the men. She ate slowly as the men talked. Ever so often, the virile warrior near her would explain their words and offer her comments to the two chiefs. When they burst into hearty laughter at something Running Wolf had said, she curiously asked what was so amusing.

His roguish grin nagged at her heart as he replied, "Running Wolf told your father we behave as we did

220

after our joining and his eyes hardly touch upon us. He claims we spend all our days and nights in my *tipi*." It was not a literal translation, for the joke was rather risqué and he didn't wish to offend her. After all, she couldn't recall the events following their wedding in the Blackfoot camp. How could she know she had been kidnapped by a love-blinded half-breed scout two days after their joining and been lost to him for many months? But when she had been found, they had spent all their days and nights in his *tipi!* Powchutu had stolen many moons and happiness from them. He forced vexing memories of his past rival aside.

She pinkened and lowered her lashes, concealing both her shyness and her wayward thoughts. "The way the sun sets upon your face, Grass Eyes, they will think us guilty of such play," he teased.

She risked a glance at him, then smiled at his mischievous expression. Every clever quip she could think of had provocative undertones, so she remained silent. He laughed, whispering into her ear, "Knowing you, Grass Eyes, your wit is strained to remain silent."

Their gazes locked. "Have I no secrets from you, husband?" she teased merrily.

"Many moons ago, none. But this moon, I think yes," he mysteriously concluded.

"If you could know and read me as easily as the lines upon your hand, I would become dull and boring," she seductively murmured.

"For as long as I have known you, you have always come to me fresh and different each time. You are a challenge that I shall never fully win. But I will keep trying," he warned playfully.

She was sorely tempted to ask, what would happen if I

221

allowed you to win? She did not, for Leah's glacial and mocking attention seemed focused upon them. Without appearing overly quizzical or suspicious, Shalee furtively observed both Gray Eagle and Leah. By the time the meal was over and they were leaving to sit in the sun to continue their visit, Shalee knew two facts: one, if Leah held any interest or intrigue for her husband, he concealed it totally; two, Leah was definitely attracted to her intrepid husband!

The morning was long and demanding. When they retired to their tepee to rest, she slept deeply. That night, another lengthy visit was enhanced by a celebration, giving the people their first real glimpses at Princess Shalee and her troublesome injury. Still, she was treated with great respect and affection.

By nightfall, she was so enraptured by her warm reception that she allowed Gray Eagle to entice her to dance with him. Music came from kettle drums, eagle-bone whistles, and an assortment of gourd rattles. Many couples moved around the large campfire in a mixture of steps that were easy to pick up and follow. She laughed at herself as she attempted to follow his instructions, soon moving as gracefully as he did. When the music halted briefly, they collapsed in merriment upon the same buffalo skin.

"If I did not know of the cloud over your mind, Shalee, I would say you have not forgotten the Dance of Lovers."

"Dance of Lovers?" she entreated him to expound.

"You danced with me, telling others I am your chosen one," he elucidated mirthfully.

"Since you are my husband, should that surprise anyone?" she saucily retorted, smiling up into his relaxed gaze.

"They would only be surprised if you had refused to dance with me or selected another to dance with," he nonchalantly murmured.

"What if you had selected another partner?" she continued their jest.

"With both Chief Running Wolf and Chief Black Cloud watching me?" he exclaimed in feigned terror.

She placed her hand over her mouth to suppress her giggles. "That would have been difficult to explain. I would have urged my father to whisk me away from a man who cared so little for his daughter."

"He knows the Eagle's eyes light only upon the Bird of his Heart."

"That's lovely. The Bird of the Eagle's Heart, very nice."

"Do you wish to leave my nest and return to your father's?"

She hesitated but a flash before saying, "No."

His smoldering gaze engulfed her. She promptly added, "Unless the sharp talons of the Eagle harm his little bird."

His hand touched her face and stroked it tenderly. "Do my claws injure you, Little Bird of my Heart?"

"No, they do not," she answered honestly, unable to pull her gaze from his.

"Do not look at me this way, Grass Eyes, or I will forget other eyes are upon us. I will taste your lips, then hear the laughter of my warriors at such weakness."

"Perhaps they would not laugh if I did the tasting," she boldly hinted.

"If you bravely claimed my lips, they would laugh even more. For I would pick you up and race to our tepee before your lips left mine."

223

"Perhaps I'll test your weakness for me one day soon. . . ."

"When you do, you will become my wife again," he vowed confidently.

"I am already your wife," she parried, wondering why she was continuing this heady conversation in public.

"In name only, Grass Eyes. Not so, if you tempt me beyond my power of control. I warn you now, so it will be."

She laughed and remarked, "I stand warned, my husband."

Later, he walked her to their tepee. "The warriors meet to talk in the ceremonial lodge. Sleep, for I will return near the time for Wi to show his face," he stated reluctantly.

Somehow, relief didn't flood her as she imagined it would. When he behaved as he had today, he was most appealing and compelling company. She smiled, allowing him to kiss her goodnight. As she entered their tepee, she chuckled to herself, feeling like a common girl being courted by a prince.

Chief Black Cloud left early the next day, permitting only enough time to visit for a brief period. Gray Eagle left shortly afterwards to hunt. She tried to summon the courage to stroll around the encampment, but thought it best to wait for his return. When Leah called out to enter, Shalee remained silent and still until she was forced to leave. For some inexplicable reason, she didn't wish to see or to talk with Leah, not after the way she had watched Gray Eagle yesterday!

Shalee was furtively peeking through a slender parting in the flap of their tepee to lessen her boredom when the towering, well-developed physique of Gray Eagle arrested her line of vision and captured her attention. His keen mind dealing with other pressing matters of their imminent departure, he was unaware of her eyes following his every move. There was such a vivid aura of energy and agility about him, of brute strength and self-assurance, of animal magnetism, of sensual prowess and subtle mystique. She warmed.

His masterful air and commanding stance compelled respect and obedience, as did his stirring voice. Here was a vital man who reeked of power and passion, of tenderness and ruthless potency. In countless ways he was like a king: He spoke and men obeyed; he went and others followed; he acted and others trembled. Her body tingled and her pulse raced. This awesome, magnificent creature was her husband. She was consumed with wonder at his choice of her as wife, for it was abundantly clear he could have any female he so desired.

Her mind alert and enthusiastic, she was gradually learning his language. Soon, they would be able to communicate with ease. Then, she could be taught his ways and her chores. Their son could return to his rightful home. Eventually, life would be as it had been before her attack.

Shalee's eyes sparked to life as she watched Leah brazenly approach him. Too far away to hear the words between them, Shalee intensely observed their movements and expressions. At first, Gray Eagle's indicated annoyance and leashed fury. Whatever Leah was saying to him, he began to stare at her and to relax! His mood altered drastically and he suddenly laughed at one of the white girl's statements. Leah smiled and nodded several times. Gray Eagle turned and walked to his father's tepee. Leah's gaze devouring his retreating frame, she followed him inside! Shalee had not seen the older man return. She angrily wondered why her husband lingered in the tepee alone with a girl he claimed to despise! There had been no mistaking the invitation in Leah's eyes. Shalee fumed at the images that stormed her mind. She stomped her foot in rising irritation as time passed snailishly and he remained with Leah. What business with a white slave could possibly take this long?

The chief and his illustrious son sat together discussing the plans for their imminent migration to the Plains near Fort Pierre. They decided on the groupings and alignment of their tribe as they made their trek across the vast stretch of land between their summer and winter camps. The date of their impending departure was settled. Bands of warriors were selected to protect the column along its journey. It was concluded that Leah must help Shalee with the dismantling of their tepee and the packing of their possessions. Until she regained her strength and knowledge, others must assist her. With everyone so busy at this critical time, Leah was the best and perhaps the only choice for this task.

Her back to them, they missed the pleased smirk upon her face at the several mentions of her name. Besides, she could make out many of their words after the length of time in their camp. After all, you couldn't give a slave orders if you didn't teach her your tongue! So, she was to help Princess Shalee . . . how very generous and thoughtful of them to present her with countless opportunities to undermine her budding relationship with the impressive and irresistible Gray Eagle! But she had already offered her help to the stalwart warrior when she told him his father wanted to speak with him. She had even guilefully promised to remain mute so as not to offend the injured princess, the very remark that had drawn a mocking chuckle from him. She had vowed respect and friendship toward his wife, inspiring several taunting remarks from him. The seeking couple would pay dearly as she devastated their path back to each other!

When each matter was settled, Gray Eagle left the tepee. His mood was cheerful and his spirit elated at their decisions and plans. He was smiling and sighing in contentment as he entered his tepee. Her chilling glare lifted his brow quizzically. He came over and sat down beside her, preparing to relate those plans.

She stiffened and turned her back to him. "Shalee? What troubles you this sun? Where did the smile and joy of my little bird fly to?" he jested.

"Did you want to talk to me about something?" she frostily asked, her eyes and tone withering.

Perplexed, he nodded. "We will leave here in seven moons. Leah will help you. . . ."

She icily cut him off, a rudeness which stunned him. "Leah! I thought you didn't like her! Until now, you've insisted she keep her distance from me."

"The others are busy with their own families and possessions. Leah is the only one who can help you with ours," he explained moodily.

She was an Indian princess, an injured one, and no one could spare any time or effort to assist her! Leah was responsible for Running Wolf's chores and possessions; yet, she would be forced to work twice as hard and long to help them! Slave was an accurate term to describe her! As she listened to the tasks involved in dismantling and moving the camp, resentment and vexation chewed at her.

"How can Leah take care of your father's chores and then help me with ours?"

"Leah is strong. She does as she is told."

"But that's twice the time and work. That isn't fair, Gray Eagle. Just because she's a white captive, you don't have to work her into exhaustion!"

"Is there some reason you do not wish her help or to have her at your side?" he questioned.

"Her company and assistance aren't the issues. Demanding so much from her because she is a vulnerable slave is!" she angrily blurted out.

"Issues means problems?" he queried the unfamiliar English word.

"No: the point!" she snapped irritably. "Why can't some of the others lend me a hand until I learn what's to be done and how to do it? Surely Princess Shalee deserves help and kindness from her own people!" she scoffed bitterly.

"Are you ill this sun, Shalee?" he asked in concern.

"No, why?" she panted.

"You speak and act strangely. Leah has no family or husband. Her work is light and swift. The others must tend children while making ready to leave. Running Wolf is but one man; the others have many in their families to care for. Leah can help you. Why allow others to do so? But many have offered. I saw no need for their help."

The news that they had offered to help her softened her anger. Still, it hadn't required over an hour for him and Leah to decide she was to become Shalee's helper!

Gray Eagle captured her face and kissed her soundly. He teased, "Allow Shalee to send Alisha away. You speak and think as white, my love, but you are now Indian. What new fear eats at your mind and steals your joy from

228

last moon? I have been patient as you asked; I have not forced you to become my wife. I wait for the time when love burns within you as it does within me."

That was the crux of her torment! Was he burning inside, or was he secretly cooling his passion and gaining this unselfish patience with the eager Leah? "The light in your eyes is unknown to me, Shalee. What brings it to life?" His words rifled through her warring thoughts.

"Perhaps I'm just bored and restless," she deceitfully excused her actions. "All this pressure and uncertainty is nerve-racking. I'm kept in here like some prisoner. I can't talk to anyone! I have nothing to do because I don't know how to do anything here! It's either avoid my son or torment him! How can I adjust or learn anything when you won't let me? You're so afraid I'll offend your people with my white tongue you keep me here alone for hours on end like some prisoner. I'll go crazy if I don't get out of this confining tepee and find something to occupy my time and energy!"

"You are only restless?" he asked, suspecting there was more to her mood.

"I don't know," she astutely answered. "I feel like this tepee is pressing down upon me, as if there isn't enough air in here to breathe. My mind searches for any topic to distract it. My hands quiver with the need to be busy. How long must I sit here trying to force myself to remember things I can't?"

"You were weak and afraid. You needed time to learn things slowly. Are you ready to face new challenges?"

"Yes! Anything to prevent this silence and solitude," she rashly panted.

"Anything?" he cleverly caught her slip. "You wish to become wife and mother again?"

Frustration seared into his mind as she stiffened and paled. "No, Shalee, not anything. As with me, your tongue is faster than your wits."

"Let me become a mother and an Indian first and learn all the things I have forgotten. In time, surely the love and being your wife will return."

"Time," he sneered disdainfully. "How much time do you need to love me again? How many moons will you resist me? How long do you punish me for your injury? How long must I pay for not protecting you? How can you know what we shared if you refuse to see and feel it? It is not your way to be cold and selfish. You do not desire me, so you refuse me your touch. What of my love and needs, Shalee? Desire not shared brings pains to my body. Does my suffering mean nothing to you?"

"You expect me to sleep with you to ease your physical needs? What is sex without love?" she debated in apprehension.

"I love you and desire you. Mating is the sharing of love."

"What about me-and my feelings?"

"You have no love or desire for me?" he demanded a little too harshly, fearing her answer.

"I am trying to . . ."

He severed her sentence, "Trying! Love is not a chore to be done, Shalee. Love comes to a heart and body, or it does not," he stated in a tone she found distressing. "Do you feel such things for me?" he demanded.

Trapped, she murmured, "I don't know."

"Then we shall find the answer," he threatened huskily, pulling her into his arms, putting his lips over hers.

Fires leaped dangerously within her. Her small world

reeled precariously. How could he desire her if he had just mated, as he called it, with Leah? Was he determined to end this physical standoff? Was he resolved to show his rank as husband? She trembled in need and dread.

His deft hands began to unlace her dress. "I will show you what it is to share love and desire," he coaxed in a strained voice. His hand moved to her breast and cupped it. He pressed her to the mat and glued his mouth to hers, sensuously stealing her breath. His hand slipped up her thigh, stroking the fiery flesh as he sought her most private domain. The masterful movements of his fingers made her weak with desire. For a time, she allowed her emotions to run wild and free. He made a terrible mistake when he took her hand and placed it to his enlarged manhood, vowing, "See how it craves a union with you. It is starving to be fed with the sweetness of your body. Let him go home and pleasure us."

Unable to recall such feelings or the intimate contact that he urged upon her innocent mind, she jerked her hand away from the alarming member, which he seemed determined to plunge into her innocent body. As if some skittish virgin about to be brutally ravished, she was petrified by his fierce passion and the immense size of the manhood. "No," she cried out in alarm. If it happened between them, it should not be like this! As she frantically mistook his intentions, he was not tenderly seducing her, he was demanding his rights as a husband. "Please don't, Wanmdi Hota. I can't," she whispered in terror.

He leaned back and stared down at his wife, reading the horror in her eyes and witnessing the tremors of her body. "Why do you fear me and our love so deeply, Shalee? We have made love countless times."

231

"As far as I remember, I've never made love to any man."

"Let your mind see this as our joining day. Let me teach you of love."

"On our joining day, we had known each other for a long time; today, you are a stranger to me. I cannot give myself to a stranger."

His frustration was replaced by vivid annoyance. "If you were not going to love me, why did you stir my body to such fires? That is cruel."

"I didn't mean to excite you! I thought I might — could . . . I can't."

It was either retreat or force the issue. He recognized the danger of his second alternative. He jumped up, dressed hastily, and left without another word or glance. Shalee had no choice but to view herself as partly to blame for this chilling misunderstanding. She cried for a long time.

Endeavoring to lessen the strain between them, she gathered firewood and fetched water later that day. When he returned from the forest, she would cook his supper and seek a genial evening. Somehow, she had to make him comprehend her worries and fears.

But her good intentions were harassed by Leah when they met at the stream. The baneful girl sneered, "I see you're falling prey to his charms and cunning mind after all. Since he despises whites so much, I wonder why he married a half-white girl. I bet he wouldn't look at you twice if you weren't a chief's bastard daughter. Why do you refuse my friendship and help, Shalee?" she absurdly asked, her expression mocking and her voice insulting.

"My life doesn't concern you, Leah Winston. Besides,

what better man to fall prey to than your own husband?" Shalee snapped, then left hastily, her agitated emotions in no condition to banter with that venomous girl. In her tepee, she scolded herself for allowing Leah to vex her so easily. That white witch was like quicksilver!

That night, Gray Eagle slyly called upon another method to relieve the tensions and reservations in his wife; he calmly shared two cups of buffalo berry wine with the unsuspecting Shalee. The strong wine, combined with her warring emotions, appeared to have the desired effect upon her. He grinned to himself, eagerly anticipating a successful seduction.

"Come, Shalee. It is time to sleep," he suggested innocently.

Once stretched out upon the mats, he pretended to kiss her goodnight. But the heady kiss lingered and warmed her, as the potent wine did. His kisses and caresses had the needed effect until she suddenly realized he was probing her womanhood with some hard object. She tensed and pushed against his chest, crying out, "No! You tricked me! You got me drunk so you could have your way with me," she angrily accused.

"I only wished to relax you to explore your feelings and needs!" he said, subtly admitting she was correct in her wild assumptions.

"It is you who desires to explore, explore my body! You are crafty and deceitful! You know I am not ready to become your wife yet. Please don't trick me like some dim-witted fool. When the time is right, we will love," she promised, needing to soften the blow of her new rejection.

"Right time," he sneered, fighting to master his thwarted passions. "I doubt it ever will come, Shalee. Go to sleep," he commanded, seeking another mat to sleep on, one placed two feet from hers.

Was she relieved or disappointed? She honestly didn't know. All she experienced was unbidden fear of the unknown, the awesome move of yielding her all to this mercurial creature who pressured her, taunted her. She wanted to apologize, but she knew her words counted little at present. It was a lengthy time before either found fitful slumber.

Gray Eagle was away most of the following day. When Shalee joined the other women to gather wood and pick berries, she discovered herself in Leah's company much too frequently. As usual, the white captive continually sent stinging barbs and rash innuendos her way. But a new and disquieting fact came to light during the day, Leah was doing her best to delude her son with conniving overtures and extremely genial conduct. What alarmed Shalee the most were the snide remarks about his altered mother who seemed content to be separated from him, tactless statements veiled by laughter and feigned innocence. She became greatly concerned when she sensed her son was responding to Leah's love and attentions and was watching her oddly, as if actually doubting her identity and love! It was abundantly clear they had grown too close during her absence. To his childish mind and heart, Leah was behaving more like his adoring mother than she was! To avoid a nasty scene that might unwisely entice Bright Arrow to side with Leah, Shalee kept this staggering theory to herself. She would deal with Leah later!

Following supper, Shalee gingerly broached this nettling problem with her sullen mate, sullen because she had rebuffed his amorous attempts once more. "Why is

234

Leah so friendly with y . . . our son?"

He glanced over at her, then asked her to explain. When she related scenes she had witnessed since returning home, he laughed mockingly and asked, "Why should he not be drawn to a woman who cared for him during a time of suffering and loss? Even now, he seeks from her what his own mother denies him, part of herself. He is a child; he needs love and attention. Your time and energy should work on Shalee, not Leah."

Incensed, she panted, "You are the one who hesitates to give me more time with my son. Perhaps you overprotect both of us. It is clear Leah is trying to entice his love from me. Why do you defend her?"

"I do not. She is no threat to you. I grow weary of her name upon your lips," he snarled tersely, this topic obviously a precarious one.

"Then why is she constantly intruding here?" she peevishly quizzed, riled by his defensive mood.

"Such envy and doubts are beneath you, Shalee. Forget her."

"How can I when she pursues my son and husband?" she pressed.

"If you gave your son and husband as much time and thought as she does, you would have no reason to fear her presence," he alleged.

Unintentionally provoked to recklessness, she stated, "You have me in all but one way."

"You withhold yourself from us; you behave like a white slave. But you are wife and mother; you are Indian!" he curtly rebuked.

"Why do you say such cruel words to me? I am trying."

"No, Shalee, you are not. You resist the return to wife

235

and mother. You coldly reject us. I do not understand."

"That isn't true!" she sharply disputed.

"Then prove you are my wife," he challenged, meeting her gaze.

"Does sex prove love, Gray Eagle?" she parried in anguish.

"The rejection of it proves many things to me, wife," he countered.

"It does not prove I lack love and desire for you, only that I need time to adjust to this life I have forgotten."

Their gazes fused and mutely battled. "How can I reach you, Shalee?"

"You have reached me, Gray Eagle. Just a little more time to understand what it is to be a wife in all ways. My whole existence is new and strange. I have been forced to accept so much since awakening without the last five years. You expect me to feel, act, and think the way I did before the accident. But such emotions and behavior required years, now you wish them to return instantly. I wish I could comply, but it isn't that simple. Why do you not woo me and win me again? Why do you insist upon all or nothing so soon?"

He stared at her. "I have been patient and loving. I have inspired fires in your heart and body, fires you quickly put out. I can only enflame you so much without creating dangerous and demanding fires within me. I burn for you, for my mind recalls what it is to possess all."

"That is my point, Gray Eagle; I do not. Your pressures and insistence frighten me. I do not recall passion."

"No, Shalee; the point is you refuse to learn passion again."

She wretchedly stated, "We could talk all night and you would still refuse to see my side of this matter. I'm sorry, Gray Eagle. All I can promise and give for now is my vow to try very hard."

"It is easier to learn new things than to forget old ones. When icy winds steadily attack a warm fire, often the flames are put out forever," he ominously warned, wanting to compel her to him.

The underlying meaning of his words struck her the wrong way. "Perhaps if your patience and love are so small, that is best," she concluded, wishing she could take those words back the moment they were spoken.

"Perhaps you are right," he glacially agreed, going to his mat.

Although she was distressed and alarmed, her pride refused to allow her to yield or to debate his claim, to be compelled by duty to love him. Patience and compassion? The selfish brute had none! In light of her injury, she had known him for a short time!

The next day offered little comfort or warmth for either person. Shalee busied herself with small chores hopefully to keep her mind off the breach between them. Just as she was about to fetch water with Turtle Woman, she glanced up to observe Gray Eagle and Leah Winston leaving the dense forest: together! She stiffened in suspicion as she noted the way Leah was smiling at him and the way he swaggered forward as though he was at peace with the entire world! How so when a war raged between him and his wife? Leah was becoming more and more like an infuriating chigger!

Having witnessed Shalee's irate gaze upon them, Leah laughed and chatted as if sharing some jovial time with Gray Eagle, who ignored her completely, unaware of her

237

devious and taunting ploy to vex Shalee. Leah grinned in pleasure, for there was no way Shalee could know he was just fetching her for his father! No doubt the insecure princess wondered what they had been doing alone in the forest. Suddenly Leah was delighted she had left her wood sling behind to answer Running Wolf's summons, guilefully using this innocent event to her advantage.

Shalee could barely contain her jealousy and temper when Leah, strolling past her later on her way to retrieve her wood sling, smiled provocatively and whispered, "Thank you, Shalee."

"For what, Leah?" she responded in confusion.

"For coldly rejecting your husband so many times that his eyes now seek another female to fulfill his desires and to renew his male pride. He is such a splendid man," she sighed dreamily.

Shalee paled, then drew in a deep breath to steady her nerves. "If you wish to cast doubts over my husband's fidelity, Leah, it won't work."

"Are you so naive, my Indian Princess? He has needs that compel him to seek relief elsewhere when his own wife coldly and humiliatingly rejects his touch. If you only knew what you selfishly deny yourself . . . he is such a proud and virile man. He possesses the most beautiful body alive. Why does it repulse you? Why do you punish him by denying him his rights? I'm surprised he hasn't taken you by force for teasing him. One night you'll tease him past control and he'll rape you. After all, you are his property."

"How dare you speak such vulgar words to me!" Shalee spat.

"Passion is a wildfire, Shalee, one not always controlled. He burns with desires and must find another

238

place to cool himself."

"Not with you!" Shalee angrily sneered.

"Many things can happen in a forest when you're alone," Leah sultrily intimated, seductively swaying her rounded hips.

"Stay away from my husband, you vile witch!"

"Why should I? You obviously don't want him. You've given his pride and manhood a fierce beating. He wishes to soothe them elsewhere. Can you blame him?" Leah sweetly taunted.

"Get away from me, you slattern!" Shalee shrieked.

"You think you're so damn special! I hope you do resist him forever, then he'll be mine. I can satisfy him as your naive mind could never imagine."

Shocked, Shalee stared at her. "He's mine," she faintly stated.

"Is he?" Leah sarcastically sneered. "If you had caught us together earlier, you wouldn't be so smug with your false claim. Keep pushing, Shalee, pushing him right into my open arms and onto my mat."

Before Shalee could reply, Leah was gone. Was there any truth to her brazen insinuations? Was she gradually losing her husband to that vixen?

That next midday when the time for rest arrived, Gray Eagle was in a curious mood. He was relaxed and cheerful. He smiled and chatted freely. She wondered what had brought on this geniality and tenderness. He acted as if he was actually courting her!

When she remained quiet and guarded, he jested merrily with a roguish smile, "You watch me closely, Grass Eyes. Tear away the fort around you. I will not attack my own wife. Perhaps we should become friends before lovers."

"Friends?" she echoed in bewilderment.

"How else can you come to know me again?" he jested mischievously.

Sensing an offer of compromise, she relaxed and smiled. Leah had lied! Yes, she was hotly pursuing this vital man, but she would never win him. He was making a new effort to reach her; she must assist him.

They talked for a time, cautiously avoiding any disturbing topics. Later, he smiled tenderly and said, "We must sleep. Soon we must work."

This time, he joined her upon her sleeping mat. He lay upon his back with his eyes closed. Yet he made no move to pressure her. After Leah's taunting conduct, she fearfully wondered if he was losing interest in her. She turned this way and that, too cognizant of his close proximity.

"You are restless, Little One," he commented, propping himself upon his elbow to gaze down at her. "Friends do not hurt other friends," he lazily remarked, caressing her cheek before placing a light kiss to her brow.

His tone was mellow and rich; his look was arresting. He held her gaze with his potent one. A beguiling smile tugged upon her wayward heart. She smiled at him. He leaned forward slowly and kissed her upon the mouth, leisurely, thoroughly pervading her senses. Disarmed, she responded to his rapturous invitation, losing herself briefly to his masterful control.

He worked slowly and skillfully so as to enflame her and to avoid alarming her. Savoring this blissful moment and the exquisite sensations, she surrendered to his arms and his advances. Her body warmed as the molten liquid of passion flowed within her veins. She felt heady and serene. Surely it was not wanton to respond to her own husband? She fought to restrain her fears and doubts. Her arms slipped around his neck and held his mouth to hers.

Their garments were cast aside. The contact between their naked flesh was intoxicating. His mouth left hers to feast gently upon her taut breasts. She watched this provocative action, feeling strangely wicked. Her gaze widened as he shifted to lie upon her nude body, poising briefly before entering her womanhood. She stared at the swollen shaft about to plunge into her helpless body, appearing enormous and threatening to her small recess. If night had concealed such a petrifying view, his battle would have been won.

"No!" she suddenly shrieked, twisting to pull free of her impending peril. "Don't! You'll hurt me."

"It will not hurt, Shalee. You have loved many times before," he coaxed.

"Please, don't. It's too soon," she pleaded, fearing his state.

"It is not too soon. Does your body not burn as mine does?" he negligently discounted her belated withdrawal and hesitation.

"I need more time. You offered friendship first," she reminded him.

"I need my wife," he vowed raggedly, his manhood throbbing.

"You are being selfish," she ridiculously charged.

"When it is done, you will learn there is no need for fear or refusal."

To her, his slightly harsh words sounded like a threat. Would he actually ravish her as Leah had warned? He didn't own her! How could he force himself upon her if he truly loved her and was concerned about her?

"It is too late to stop now, Shalee. I must open your eyes to the truth. If I do not, you will continue to waver in fear."

Sheer terror washed over her. He was going to ravish her if she refused to give in willingly, or so she mistakenly thought. She did not realize he meant he was going to lovingly seduce her, slowly and feverishly until she could not summon the will to resist him. "If you force yourself on me, I will hate you forever," she vowed, her chest rising and falling rapidly as she struggled to breathe and to free herself from his grasp.

Astounded, he could not believe what he was hearing and witnessing. "You would hate me for making love to you?" he probed incredulously.

"You attack me like some animal in heat, not like a loving husband. It is not love you want from me; it's sex."

Her insults stunned him. "Look at me and swear you do not want me."

Pressed either to lie or submit, she panted, "Do not touch me. If you must have a woman so badly, Leah is more than willing to cool your hot blood!" she declared before thinking, shaking violently.

"You wish me to take another woman in your place?" he demanded.

"Evidently you cannot wait for me, so do as you please," she snapped, deceiving both of them. After all, from the looks of things, he was already enjoying Leah on the side! Why did he try to make her feel obligated to sate his needs? Why couldn't he be understanding and loving?

He jerked away from her, moving as quickly as if she

were searing his flesh. He stood up and stared down at her. Yanking on his breechcloth only, he snarled angrily before he stormed out, his heart ravaged and his body tormented, "Then keep your love and your resentment to yourself, Alisha! I will not force my savage body upon your selfish one!"

Whatever had possessed her to offer Leah in her rightful place? What could she be feeling and thinking to order him to take another woman and to leave her alone! He was wondering the same.

She stared after him. Her own body quivered with desire and anxiety. He had called her Alisha! Such tenderness and desire had exchanged places with anger and bitterness in his eyes. She had brutally rejected him. Why? It wasn't because she didn't want him! God, how she did. She was simply consumed with apprehension and jealousy. She must have hurt him deeply. If she continued to treat him in this glacial way, he would turn away from her . . . a new kind of panic seized her. Why did she resist the truth: She wanted and needed him! What a silly and frightened fool she was!

Leah wisely concealed herself to the side of the tepee as the rage-taut frame of Gray Eagle exited and headed for the forest. She grinned at the foolishness of Shalee. Was she blind or stupid? No modesty or feminine games should prevent a union with that virile animal. Was he going to cool his passions in the stream or in his own hand? Her blood boiled as molten lava in a turbulent volcano. There was no need for either action! Shalee had given her blessing to their union! She daringly trailed the figure that had vanished into the trees.

Chapter Eleven

His mind spinning in a mental whirlpool, Gray Eagle walked to where he normally bathed. He stripped off his garments, angrily casting them aside. He stood rigid and erect in his moody world, facing the stream with his manhood boldly announcing his rampant desire to the green eyes that furtively and lecherously ogled it.

Leah glanced around to make certain no other presence could be detected by ear or eye. The camp was enjoying its ritual of rest. Her timing must be perfect. Had he reached a necessary point of sexual frustration and vengeful defiance? His body had been denied release for weeks now. Shalee was behaving like some icy stranger. His pride was attacked and bruised. His body ached for solace. Yes, the setting and atmosphere were perfect. Now, she must tempt him swiftly before he could master his warring emotions or recall his resentment toward her! Surely his pride and manhood seethed with a fire that would dull his mind!

Leah was accurate in one assumption; his keen senses were dulled by the fierce battle which tormented his mind and the intense cravings which wracked his aroused body. Shalee obviously didn't want him or need him. She didn't even care if he took another woman! Unnatural spite filled him; he wanted to hurt her as she was hurting him. Maybe he should feign interest in another female to awaken her jealousy! How else could he reach her? How could he tear down the barrier she was placing between them?

Leah traveled the distance between them, her feet noiselessly vanquishing the space. The drama before her line of vision so intense that Leah never saw Shalee as she halted her frantic pursuit of her husband to witness in shock the scene unfolding before her ... Why Shalee dropped to her knees to conceal her presence behind the cluster of bushes, she never understood. Unless it was to observe this heart-stopping event; once and for all time, she would know what strange sensations passed between the audacious white girl and her complex husband.

She held her breath as Leah quietly moved forward. She was brazenly approaching Gray Eagle in his state of undress! Surely he would be furious! Her anguish and tension increased as the episode revealed a much different light. Had she pushed too far?

His face pointing upwards, Gray Eagle's first awareness of Leah's arrival entered his mind the moment she revealed her intention. His gut tightened and he inhaled sharply as his head jerked downwards to stare at this torturous intrusion upon his privacy and pain. Leah's warm, stimulating hand had furtively and defiantly encircled his swollen and aching manhood. Determined to sway him during this highly emotional upheaval, she enticingly stroked the eager member. Taken off guard and in such a distraught mood, he gaped at her as his shaft greedily and selfishly responded to her tempting task. Had Shalee sent her to him? Was she placing this girl between them? Should he teach his wife a painful lesson? How he wished it was Shalee here with him!

"What madness seizes you, Leah?" he hoarsely demanded, his body refusing to instantly rebuff her entreating hands. So distressed was he by his mental turmoil, he recklessly and unwittingly spoke to Leah in fluent English!

Leah astutely caught this rash error, but made no comment which would alert him to his careless slip. As Leah trailed her stirring hands over his sensitive groin, she seductively whispered, "I am starving for you, Gray Eagle. He is aflame; let me cool him for you. Shalee does not care. She does not desire you. She wants me to take her place. She said I was to cool your hot blood for her," she lied to confuse him.

"No! What would I say if others viewed this shameful act?" he demanded, not meaning his words the way they sounded to his wife. "Another moon you placed your greedy hands upon me and tempted me to evil weakness. I desire only Shalee. Be gone from my sight, white whore," he snarled, failing to deter her resolve.

"Does Shalee ease his pains? No! He is filled with seed. I will please him as she never has. She rejects you, but I don't. I want you and need you. Even if you don't desire me, see how he loves my touch. She tempts you, then cruelly rejects you. She wants me to become your slave and serve this need. She can't stand for you to touch her." Her hand circled the flaming shaft, provocatively teasing its full length.

She wantonly caressed his firm buttocks and eased her playful hands up his strong back to roam over his brawny chest.

Gray Eagle tried to control his response. He closed his eyes and swallowed, then said, "No, Leah; this is wrong and wicked. I want only Shalee. My seeds belong in her body, not in the body of a white slave who tempts me when I am weak in mind and body. Go!" Yet, his instinctive longings reacted to those wild and wonderful sensations which his wife was denying him.

"I can't. She doesn't want your seeds; I do! I don't

246

torment your manhood; I can bring sweet pleasures and relief to him. Can you deny this feels wonderful? Can you honestly say you want me to stop? Who will ease your needs then? Shalee? She hates you; she'll never let him enter her white body! You can have anything you need or want from me. I must have him if only once! Please, make love to me. If you must punish me for this, do it after I have pleased you." She leaned forward to place kisses upon his bronze chest.

"You are evil, Leah. Shalee is my wife. She will learn to love me and trust me again. Go, before I punish you greatly," he warned, wondering how to do so without giving some incriminating explanation.

All the while he talked, Leah continued her heady assault upon his senses. "I don't care if you punish me. But first let me end this torment which eats at me every day. You are irresistible, Wanmdi Hota. There is no other man like you. I would do anything to lay beneath you upon your mat. I won't tell anyone about us. Until Shalee comes to you, you need a woman to sate your fiery passions. Why should he ache this cruel way? Why should your own wife refuse him and you? She is selfish and foolish, Wanmdi Hota. I can love him as she never has," she smugly vowed. "She is repulsed by him, but I crave him."

Gray Eagle pushed her away. "No, Leah!"

"Yes, Wanmdi Hota," she seductively murmured, grasping his shaft and moving her hand as if it were mating with him. "If you wish, pretend I am Shalee. Pretend I am your Shalee and it is her willing body you are driving into. She said I could have you."

Gray Eagle stared at her, then at the sensual sight of his manhood slipping in and out of her hand. Could he possibly allow her to ease his pains? Could he pretend she was Shalee? Why did her wickedness feel so good? Why did his traitorous manhood plead to empty its fullness, even into this repulsive slave? Had Shalee sent Leah after him? Had his body grown so weak he could not master it?

He slapped her away and spat, "You prey upon me as a cunning fox upon a weak and helpless rabbit. You freely offer what you know my body burns to enjoy. Yes, Leah, my manhood enjoys such wild pleasure. But I cannot allow you to take what is Shalee's alone. I love and desire to mate only with her. Go!" he sternly commanded.

Leah finally realized he was serious! "You can refuse the pleasures I generously offer you? What if Shalee never lets you touch her? She said it was all right for us to mate!"

"I will earn her love and desire again. She is injured and afraid. Soon, she will not feel this way. She spoke in anger, but she does not hand me over to you."

"What if she suspects we are lovers?" she hinted.

"We are not lovers! We will never be lovers! Not once have I sought your touch! Not once have I gazed upon you with desire! You are no rival to her! No female is! Return to camp and never come to me again!"

"You're a proud and stubborn man, Wanmdi Hota! I'll be patient. The day will come when your body will force your mind to agree to my offer! How long can he suffer like this?" she challenged, reaching up and brushing her hand against the tip of his member, instantly renewing its instinctive interest and size.

Leah laughed seductively. "See, Wanmdi Hota. You do not want me, but he does," she boasted.

"Halt, Leah, or I will beat you this moment," he harshly commanded, wondering how to explain such a harsh punishment.

As she stubbornly caressed it, she cunningly challenged, "Do you really want me to stop this?"

Agilely and swiftly placing his foot to her abdomen, he shoved with all his might and sent her tumbling backwards. *"Wasichu witkowin! Hiya!"*

Upon calling her a white whore, he seized his garments and yanked them on, tying his breechcloth hurriedly. He glared at her and sneered, "You will never take her place! I will not be tempted to betray her!"

"What if she learns of our contact?"

"If you speak one lie to her, I will slay you," he growled.

"Lie? What about the other times when she was gone?"

"Silence your tongue before you lose it!" He whirled and left.

The moment he was out of sight, Leah sat up and stared straight ahead. "You will pay for this, you savage! It will be only a matter of time before you're begging me to sate your needs. I'll fill Shalee's ears with so many lies she'll never let you touch her! I'll have you yet!" Eerie laughter left the curled lips of Leah. "Shalee is a fool. She really thinks we were friends. I wonder how you'd feel, my envious princess, if you knew the truth about me and that virile animal. Too bad you can't recall our last argument. If you thought for one minute your warning to forget Gray Eagle bothered me in the least, you're wrong. Like I told you that day before your accident, I will worm my way into his tepee, then into his life! Too bad those soldiers didn't get rid of you for me. No matter what, I will replace you, somehow and some way. If I'm patient, you'll hand me my victory with your coldness and rejections. How long do you think a man can ignore such fires when I'm dangling before him like a fat worm before a starving bird?"

Laughing happily and feeling not the least defeated, Leah hummed in confidence as she returned to camp. Shalee was distraught. What should she do? She couldn't tell Gray Eagle Leah was hotly pursuing him; he was well aware of that fact! Leah couldn't be dissuaded from her goal easily. What would happen if she carelessly pushed him into the arms of that scheming, immoral woman?

Suddenly another fact came to light: Leah was surely spying on them! She had deviously driven a wedge between them. What a fool she had been! She was gradually shoving the man she loved and desired into that predaceous spider's web! Her hot and cold behavior was confusing him, preventing his understanding, filling him with frustration and insecurity! She had offered her bronze treasure to Leah on a silver platter! She was allowing her fears of the unknown to defeat her. After all, she wasn't a virgin; she was his wife!

As Shalee returned to camp in a dejected and apprehensive daze, she met Shining Light. She forced a warm smile to her quivering lips. The perceptive Indian woman sensed how distressed the princess was. Surely such a tragedy was frightening and confusing. She knew how she would feel under such trying circumstances. She smiled and asked, *"Yuzaza?"*

Shalee glanced at the objects in the young woman's grasp and nodded in delight. Perhaps a cool and refreshing bath was exactly what she needed. *"Sha. Pidamaye,"* she thanked her new, and yet old, friend. She promptly went to her tepee and gathered the necessary clothing and a blanket to dry herself. She returned to Shining Light's side and they headed to the stream.

As they leisurely strolled along, Shining Light pointed out objects and said their names to Shalee, who readily accepted this assistance and jovial encouragement. The

250

tricky words inspired shared laughter. When they halted, Shalee looked around and decided the selected area for bathing presented enough privacy.

They splashed and enjoyed the invigorating exercise and relaxation. When Shining Light reluctantly signed it was time to return to camp, she left the water first. A vivacious female, she was fully dressed in moments. She sat down to lace her moccasins while she waited patiently for Shalee to follow her lead. She wondered what was plaguing her friend and making her so unhappy and tense.

A mellow voice teased, "You are far from camp, Shining Light."

She glanced up and replied, "Yes, Wanmdi Hota. Your wife is shy and desired a private place to bathe."

Gray Eagle glanced around. The spot had been chosen wisely, for large bushes sheltered the river from sight on this side and tall rushes blocked the view from the other. A narrow path left just enough of an opening to find the deep stream. He smiled. "Yes, Shalee is timid like the deer. If you must return to camp, I will wait for her," he politely offered, knowing the hour was growing late and Shining Light had family responsibilities. Besides, his temper had cooled and he needed to apologize for his previous harshness. Shalee was only afraid of the feelings that he stirred within her, feelings new to her clouded mind.

The romantic Shining Light assumed he wished her to leave them alone for other reasons. She grinned and remarked, "Things will soon be good again, Wanmdi Hota. She is trying to conquer this terrible injury. She is much like our old Shalee. We practiced many words today and she smiled with her eyes this time. Yet, she is sad and doubtful. It must be frightening to remember nothing, to find herself among strangers, to learn she has a child and a husband. No doubt I would cry every hour in fear and panic."

"Would you fear this man who claimed to be a husband you did not remember?" he abruptly asked.

"Yes," she vowed incredulously. "It would take many moons to trust him. But it is not so with Shalee. When she speaks your name, her eyes glow and her face reflects the fire. Her eyes linger upon you when you do not see her. I see such tenderness and longing upon her face. This new Shalee also loves the son of our chief. But she is troubled and afraid."

"You think she loves me?" he asked in amazement.

She looked at him in vivid surprise. "Does she also hide such feelings from you as she does from herself? I am a woman; I see and know the feelings beneath such looks. But you are a powerful man, known to her people as enemy. It is only natural for her to walk slowly and cautiously toward a man she does not know. You are eager to possess her again; she fears such eagerness she does not understand. Her mind has returned to the days before she knew the love and touch of a man, of you. It is not easy to yield yourself to a man the first time; for her, this will be a first time to experience love and passion. But love and desire burn within her and she will soon surrender to them."

"You are kind, Shining Light. Shalee is blessed to have your understanding and friendship. You have helped me understand many things. I feared she would not come to love me again," he confessed ruefully.

"Do not fear such things, Wanmdi Hota. Her heart belongs to you even now. For a woman, sex is like walking into a dark cave; not so for a man. Show her patience and love," she advised.

252

"I will do as you say," he happily vowed, her news stirring his heart.

The woman left him to wait for Shalee alone. He was about to sit down when Shalee came through the bushes, clad only in a blanket. Damp curls clung to her forehead and wet locks to her back and neck. She looked at him, then glanced around for her friend. She appeared dismayed to find him there in her state of undress.

She stammered, "I . . . my clothes . . . are there. Where . . . is Shining Light?"

"Wi nears his time to sleep. I told Shining Light I would wait for you and protect you. Your dress." He leaned over and picked it up, holding it out to her. "Do you wish me to leave?" he asked.

His ebony eyes had darted to her half-exposed chest before he could fuse his gaze with hers. His respiration had quickened and his body had stiffened as he sought to control her unsettling effect upon him. His words to Leah about desiring her from only seeing her flickered through her mind. He loved her and wanted her. He absently lifted a dripping curl and placed it behind her creamy shoulder, his warm fingers trailing across the cool flesh.

He shuddered and inhaled. He leaned forward and kissed her lightly, but even the light touch of his lips impassioned her. "I'll wait . . . there," he stated huskily, pointing to a large tree not far away.

"Don't leave me," she urged without thinking twice, knowing now of his innocence of betrayal and of the danger Leah's temptation presented, knowing it was time to challenge her fears and desires.

"I'll be near, Shalee. No harm will come to you. I cannot remain so close and not touch you," he claimed unsteadily.

"Then kiss me again," she entreated, her own

respiration erratic.

"It is not safe to kiss you. I must leave before I forget myself and frighten you again. Passion cannot always be controlled."

"But I'm not afraid of you," she informed him.

"But you fear the things I make you feel," he reasoned hoarsely.

"I do, but you can show me why. Teach me to understand such feelings, not fear or reject them," she unexpectedly enticed him.

"Do you hear your own words, Shalee?" he inquired, his passion rising to a perilous level.

"*Sha, Wanmdi Hota,*" she calmly replied, strangely relieved that the time had arrived to settle this stirring matter.

"There is only one way to understand them," he hinted.

"I know," she agreed. "Do you love me and want me?" she asked.

"More than my own life, more than the breath of Wakantanka that fills my body, more than the food that gives it life," he vowed earnestly.

"Then show me what it is to share love," she bravely entreated.

"You speak the truth?" he queried, hoping she wasn't innocently or cruelly tempting him.

"Do you want me as your wife again?" she answered his question with another one.

"Yes, Shalee," he confessed, his gaze seeking the meaning of hers.

"Then make me your wife in more than words. . . ."

"What if you become afraid and pull away when my passion flames brightly?" he worriedly asked, wondering how he could retreat at such a point.

Her eyes scanned his handsome face and upper torso. She eased up to kiss him. "It is too late to hear the callings of fear."

He smiled as he lifted her shapely body and headed into the cover of the trees. He laid her down upon the grass and gazed longingly at her. "Shouldn't we go to our tepee?" she asked modestly.

"It is too late to hear the callings of shyness," he teased in return.

His spirits soared when she smiled and relaxed. He lay down half across her and covered her lips with his. After several intoxicating kisses, he leaned back and pressed, "Do I dare make you my wife?"

Her arms encircled his neck and pulled his face back to hers. She provocatively asked, "Do you dare not to claim what is yours?"

"Are you mine, Grass Eyes?" he asked gravely.

"I will be soon, if you halt these twenty questions and make love to me," she laughingly replied, kissing him soundly.

New life and hope surged through him. His mouth tenderly ravished hers. He kissed her eyes, her nose, her chin, and her mouth. As mirthful laughter filled her ears, so did his warm breath as he nibbled at her lobe. A finger wandered over her collarbone and down her chest, hesitating momentarily at the blanket. His hungry lips claimed hers once more as he loosened the last barrier between them.

His lips trailed down her throat and brushed across her breasts. She inhaled as his tongue teased at each one in turn. Her body tingled and glowed with wondrous feelings. He returned to kiss her deeply and pervasively as his hand slipped lower and lower, stroking the silky flesh along its enticing journey. He stirred her to life and fierce yearning. His control was strained, but he determined to arouse her to mindless bliss before entering her. This first union must be unique.

She moaned as her body called out to his; her head rolled from side to side as he masterfully explored regions he had missed. At last, he mounted her and rode his powerful stallion into the moist canyon that was no longer guarded against his loving invasion. He gently charged down the dark passage in search of brazen and blissful ecstasy. His stallion reared and prodded, prancing happily along its path.

Back and forth he rode the distance of her womanhood, encouraging her to follow his guide. He reclaimed the territory that was once the Eagle's domain, that was eagerly yielding to his control again. His stallion would bravely charge forward, to reluctantly retreat for another successful charge. When their passions reached the point of no retreat or compromise, he galloped to possess his love. The summit of rapture came in sight. With confidence and daring, he raced happily toward it. He set his pace to allow her to arrive at their mutual destination first.

A muffled cry of victory left her throat as she topped the blissful peak, hesitating there before racing down the other side into the peaceful valley that compelled her forward. Her quivering body was a signal for his hasty pursuit. He smiled as his mouth took hers and followed her direction. His body shuddered with his triumph, then eased into the tranquil valley to rest with her snuggled into his arms.

Never had she known, that she could recall, such stimulating and intoxicating sensations. How could such feelings be so torturously sweet? Aglow with love and serenity, she looked over at him and smiled. "I am your wife now, truly your wife."

"Do you now understand the fires that burned for this union?" he asked tenderly, smiling into her softened eyes.

"Yes, my love. If I had known it would be like this, I would have offered myself to you that first night," she confessed, for once not blushing.

"It was always this way between us, Shalee. Do you understand now how hard it was to recall such feelings and to halt them?"

"Yes. It must have been difficult for you. I'm sorry I hurt you so deeply. I'll never reject you again," she promised. "You're mine."

"*Sha*, Little One, you are mine," he agreed, his happiness flowing around them. He nibbled at her lips, bringing a new fire to her.

She grinned, "I starved you for so long that you're still hungry for me?"

"I shall never have enough of you." His mouth tasted the sweetness of hers. His hands roamed his newly conquered territory. He slid his manhood into her, moving slowly and deliberately. Her passion increased with each stroke; she pulled him tightly against her. She watched as his tongue circled a protruding nipple, the sight stirring her. His smoldering ebony eyes drilled into her liquid green ones. Her hands moved up and down his back, reveling in the rippling of his muscles as he moved to stimulate her. His flesh was firm and smooth. She bit him lightly upon his shoulder. He laughed. His mouth captured hers as his manhood worked deftly and exquisitely to heighten her fervor. Suddenly the ecstatic spiral loomed before them, challenging them to scale its heights.

Upward they began to climb, slowly at first, then more

rapidly as their needs cried out for appeasement. The molten lava within them exploded, spewing forth to flow and to mingle and to carry them along in its calming aftermath. He rested upon his back with her head lying upon his left shoulder. His powerful arms lovingly protected her, refusing to release her. He sighed in contentment. She was his. . . .

His eyes looked upwards, watching fluffy clouds playing in the ever darkening heavens. The leaves upon the trees stirred and rustled. Cicadas and tree frogs began to serenade them. The birds were lessening their cheerful songs as the night birds sang out for their turn to lull the peaceful world to sleep. The air was cooling, but not chilly. This was such a tranquil spot. What more could a man desire? He was one with the Great Spirit, with Nature, and with his woman.

He cocked his head and looked down at her. A tender smile played upon his sensual lips. She was fast asleep in his arms, as it should be. At last she felt and shared love. She was at peace with him and with herself. Even if she never recalled their past, this new love would become as strong and passionate as their lost love. Great tenderness washed over him. He would protect her from all future harm. She was his. . . .

As darkness descended upon them, she stirred and nestled into the warmth he radiated. She stretched and yawned. She met his gaze the moment her eyes opened. She smiled as exquisite memories filled her mind, bringing a softened glow to her eyes.

"You are happy now, wife?"

"As much as you are, my love," she whispered meaningfully.

"The night air chills your skin. Come, let us return to

our tepee."

A reluctant and teasing smile touched her lips and eyes. "*Sha*, my love, let's go home."

The heady emotion that tinged her voice and eyes brought happiness to him. "Home . . ." he wistfully repeated. "You are home at last."

They dressed quickly. Taking her hand in his, he led her along the grassy bank toward camp. How strange life was: he had lost her and then found her again in the same spot . . .

As she glanced up at him, he grinned knowingly. "Many times our thoughts are the same," he hinted subtly, caressing her cheek.

She giggled and whispered, "I hope so, Wanmdi Hota, I certainly hope so."

He chuckled in unsuppressed amusement, his ebony eyes sparkling. Not wanting anything to dampen his elation, he suppressed worries over his confrontation with Leah. He had been furious with himself for permitting his closely guarded secret to slip out while arguing with her. Knowing there was no way to recall spoken words or actions, he rationalized his careless mistake. What could Leah do? Nothing, for she was a captive! Still, it was not good for her to know of his ability to speak English. But his life and secret were not in peril at her discovery! She would never be allowed the opportunity to reveal it to the unsuspecting whites. Besides, she would probably overhear him speaking with his wife, if she hadn't already! Vexed, he contemptuously dismissed this deed and the audacious Leah from mind. He was too happy with the return of his love to allow any trouble to dismay him.

Chapter Twelve

For the next three days, Shalee worked and studied with enthusiasm and concentration. Since her husband spoke such fluent English, her lessons in Oglala went swiftly and enjoyably. Between their own chores and obligations, Shining Light and Turtle Woman taught Shalee many things. Even Bright Arrow was as busy and constructive as a beaver. Her new friendships flourished and strengthened, as did her love for Gray Eagle and her son.

Although this sport was serious and this season an active one, this growing process took on an air of heady challenge and pleasure for all who became involved with it. Shalee's vocabulary and skills increased with each day that passed. Her elation rising and her knowledge expanding, soon it was as if Princess Shalee had fully recovered, but she had not.

Possessions were gradually sorted and packed, encased in large buffalo skins, and secured with leather strips. On the third day following her blissful truce with her husband, the inevitable happened: the tepee must be dismantled and packed upon the travois that her deft lover had constructed from slender and sturdy cottonwood saplings. Gray Eagle had not argued against Shalee's firm demand to perform these many chores without the assistance of Leah Winston. It was obvious Shalee didn't like the white captive, but her reasons remained locked in her now happy heart.

Shalee spent a great many hours observing this process among the other women, beginning with Shining Light and finishing with Turtle Woman. Perhaps Turtle Woman was the most helpful and enlightening because of her sluggish accuracy. Shalee smiled as she realized this Indian woman had been named correctly. But there was a reason for Turtle Woman's excessive leisure: one of her hands was oddly twisted from some accident before birth. But Turtle Woman skillfully and cheerfully did everything expected of her, perhaps more. She was a gentle and impressive female; she was stimulating and inspiring. If her disability disheartened her in any way, she concealed it well beneath her spirited and buoyant nature.

By midafternoon when the others were fatigued from their labors and had halted to rest, Shalee bravely and confidently attacked the job of dismantling their tepee. She loosened the knot near the bottom of the skin-abode. She began to unlace the two sides as far up as she could reach. Then, she picked up the Y-tipped stick and used it to complete the chore to the very top of the conical dwelling. The most difficult part, freeing the lengthy, thick strip was made easier as her son held the two sides together at the base.

She pushed and struggled for nearly twenty minutes before the edges left the last two holes and fell triumphantly to the ground, allowing the connected skins to slide down the poles and pile upon the ground. She shrieked excitedly, gathering her son into her arms and swinging him around as merry laughter came forth. Bright Arrow giggled as she stroked his arms and complimented him upon his strength and thanked him for his help.

The small boy reveled in this affection and in his pride. Between bursts of laughter, he told her he was a warrior, but he would help her since she had no daughter to do so. Knowing he had told some amusing tale, she laughed and kissed his cheek as if she understood his every word. The two cheerful people then worked diligently to roll and secure the large bundle that represented their home. When that task was completed, they began carefully to shove the poles together near the center of what was once their home. Checking to make certain no one was in the line of danger, she let her son give the collection of poles that were still secured together near the top a last shove to send them crashing to the earth.

Shining Light had told her new poles must be cut before the tepee was put up again; the old ones would be used for firewood to cook the supplies for their imminent journey, as Indians wasted nothing from Nature and the Great Spirit. The lively woman also explained how new buffalo skins must be tanned to replace those worn by time and weather. As Shalee gazed at the poles and connecting hides, a sense of wonder and confidence filled her as she realized she had actually constructed this strange home. If she had acquired such skills before, she could do it again!

This laborious event had taken many hours, but now it was done. As Bright Arrow replaced the circle of rocks that had been disturbed by their task, she realized it was time to prepare something to eat. As if hearing her mental question, Gray Eagle appeared with a hunk of meat from a freshly slain deer that had been divided among the ten hunters.

When she saw what burden he was carrying, she

smiled in relief. He halted and gazed around at her progress. Their eyes met and locked. He grinned and caressed her cheek. She nestled her face into his open hand as she smiled at him. He nipped playfully at her ear. She whispered, "I did it, Wanmdi Hota. Bright Arrow helped me; no one else," she proudly informed him, his astonishment matching hers.

Loving pride and amusement filled his ebony eyes. She quickly related the events of her day, savoring the telling of such feats. He laughed as he listened to her suspenseful deeds and victory. "Now, all I have to do is cook food for our journey and figure out how to pack all this stuff on that funny wagon," she exclaimed in doubtful assurance.

"The cooking is a wife's task, but I will help you load the 'wagon,'" he mirthfully teased, bringing happy giggles from her.

For a moment, she was tempted to tell him of her strange feeling of familiarity with these chores; she quickly changed her mind, thinking it would inspire false hopes of her returning memory in him, and telling herself those twinges came from observing the process many times before attempting it. She watched the muscles flex in his arms and back as he forcefully broke the poles into lengths of firewood. She sat down to build a fire, thankful this was a chore learned long ago along the trail with her people.

She brushed an unbidden tear away as she forced such thoughts from her mind. Uncle Thad had been dead and buried for many years. Her life and happiness were here now. Still, her grief and loss seemed recent.

She cut the meat into ragged squares and skewered them, hanging the sticks upon the two Y-shaped holders

263

on either side of her eager fire. Soon the meat was sending delightful odors into the air as it cooked. Ever so often she would rotate the meal as she mixed and cooked pones of *aguyapi* upon the hot rocks. She eventually discovered that she and Bright Arrow had consumed the water from the skin while doing their mutual chore of love.

She held up the skin and called to her son, "*Mni, Wiyakpa Wanhinpe?*"

He smiled and accepted the water skin, trudging toward the stream as if she had given him some critical mission to perform. She glanced at her husband and suppressed her giggles behind her hand. Her smile vanished as a thought came to mind. She hurriedly questioned, "Was it wrong to send our son for water, Gray Eagle? I was busy and didn't realize we were out. Will the others make fun of him for helping me?"

"He is a small boy, Shalee. This time is busy. Many do chores to help their mothers and fathers. See how proud and eager he is to help you?"

"*Sha, Wanmdi Hota.* Do you know how happy I am?" she asked.

"*Sha, Shalee.* I see it in your eyes and hear it singing upon your lips."

They exchanged looks of yearning, a crackling from the fire pulling her gaze from his. "Oh-h-h," she cried in distress. "I better pay attention to my supper or we'll be eating burned meat," she jested.

He laughed. "If you must burn something, wife, best it be the meat."

"You're impossible!" she playfully chided him, laughing herself.

"With you in my life-circle, all things are possible," he

remarked, drawing her softened gaze back to his igneous one.

"That is true, my valiant husband," she readily concurred.

"I must speak with Running Wolf. I will return quickly," he promised, heading off to greet the chief not far away.

"I see you're doing just fine without my help," a surly voice commented, handing her the water skin.

Shalee glanced up, highly intrigued by Leah's hostility under the circumstances. But of course, Leah didn't know she had discovered the truth about her! The brassy witch was surely aware of the new intimacy between herself and her husband; no doubt envy and defeat vexed her greatly! Her gaze widened as she viewed Leah's hold upon her son's hand, a smile playing upon his lips.

Leah brashly reprimanded her, "It is not a man's place to do a woman's chores, Shalee. Since you can't recall that fact, I'm reminding you. To spare your son ridicule from other boys, I fetched the water for him. It would be better for everyone if you didn't resent my help and refuse it. Surely you can lay aside your spite and jealousy long enough to get us moved?"

"How dare you speak to me in such a rude and forward manner, Leah!" Shalee snapped in irritation. "You forget your place!" she warned, shaking her head as the words rang with inexplicable clarity in her mind, paling her face with the eerie sensation.

Her odd reaction wasn't lost on the observant Leah. "Does your head still pain you?" she sullenly asked, the inquiry laced with sadistic pleasure instead of real concern.

"Do not fret over me and my problems. I daresay you

have enough chores and troubles to occupy your time and energy," Shalee snipped.

"I don't think so," Leah brazenly retorted. "I can think of better ways to spend my energy and time," she added, her wanton gaze wandering to the virile frame of Gray Eagle.

Fury and bitterness crashed against Shalee's body like violent waves upon a stormy sea. "Remove your lecherous eyes and wanton thoughts from *my* husband," she demanded coldly, emphasizing her claim upon the robust warrior.

"My, my," Leah clucked annoyingly. "Aren't we the touchy one today? If you're so confident in your hold upon him, why are you so upset? He's a very handsome man, a powerful one. Surely a mere look doesn't threaten him?" she sneered. "Are you still mad about our unforgivable conduct while you were gone?"

"If a mere look would satisfy your whorish mind and body, I would permit it," Shalee said, consciously insulting her with clarity and resentment. "He is mine, Leah. Mine . . ."

"For how long, Shalee? Your confidence escapes me," Leah dauntlessly taunted. "A man can only accept so much rejection and abuse. Soon he'll tire of his futile wooing. Besides, he knows what I have to offer, naturally from experience."

Shalee actually laughed at her. "I would be a fool to reject such a handsome and virile *husband*, Leah, and I'm certainly no fool," she murmured silkily, again stressing her legal claim.

Leah's eyes widened, her animosity and dismay revealed before she could prevent it. "You mean you're sleeping with him?" she snapped harshly, as if she had

266

some right to such intimate information!

"My life is no affair of a white slave, Leah. But such naivete, under the circumstances, is absurd for a woman like you," she retorted.

"What do you mean?" Leah asked in dread, suspecting this innocent-eyed female had guessed her ruse.

Shalee laughed tauntingly. "Though your face is unpainted and your dress isn't gaudy red, Leah, a harlot can be recognized from her aura." She went for blood, wanting to punish this vile creature and her ruthless attempt to ensnare her lover.

"How dare you call me such names," Leah exclaimed, cautiously holding her voice low, wanting to slap the lovely creature before her.

"If a name fits you like your skin, then you wear it," Shalee calmly announced, focusing her attention upon her impending meal as if dismissing the woman from mind.

"You sleep with an unknown savage, then call me a whore?" Leah scoffed.

"I sleep with *my husband*, Leah. He is not a savage. I daresay he would find your insult dangerous," Shalee threatened in a silky voice.

"Then tell him, if you dare. Considering what has taken place between me and *your husband*, he would think you mad from that blow to your head," she vowed acidly, mocking Shalee's confidence and claim.

"Your total lack of honor does not tarnish his, Leah. He has never slept with you, and we both know it," she smugly announced.

"A woman doesn't have to *sleep* with a man to pleasure him, my foolish girl!" Leah recklessly implied.

Knowing it was best to withhold her knowledge of

Leah's lewd conduct from both Leah and her husband, Shalee approached the quarrel in another way. *"Iyasni, Witkowin!* If you speak again, whore, I will reveal your wild claims to Wanmdi Hota and see how he views them."

In the heat of the moment, neither woman realized Shalee had spoken Oglala words she shouldn't know in her state of amnesia. "Go, Leah."

Leah gaped at the Indian princess, then whirled to walk away. Shalee exhaled slowly, releasing her pent-up tension. When Gray Eagle came back to her, he questioned her about the scene he had witnessed from a distance too great to comprehend it.

"Leah was scolding me for letting our son do a woman's chores. I reminded her I am Indian and she is white. You were right all along, Wanmdi Hota; it isn't possible to be *kodas* with white slaves. If I behave white, she loses her respect and fear of me."

"She spoke bold words to you?" he asked incredulously.

"Do not fret, my wonderful husband; Leah won't bother me anymore," she stated with blind certainty.

"I will punish her," he declared angrily. Surely Leah wouldn't dare reveal her wicked temptations to his wife! But if she did, what would Shalee think and feel? Dread and panic attacked him, for their loving truce was still new and fragile. Not one to accept such intimidating and perilous threats to his happiness and pride, he bitterly resented them.

"No, Wanmdi Hota," she softly disagreed. "Punishment with words or actions would only call attention to the trouble with Leah. To respond to the evil and weaknesses of others only casts shadows upon us. Let me deal with Leah in my own time and way. Please," she entreated sweetly.

He gazed at her thoughtfully. Already her words and wisdom were sounding like his old Shalee. This perception warmed and calmed him. "As you say, wife. But I will not allow her to shame or to hurt you."

She smiled. "Leah is no threat to our happiness; I will make sure of it. *Ku-wa, wa unyun tinkte.*" She invited him to begin their tasty meal.

He called to Bright Arrow. He sat down, waiting to be served. "You learn much quickly, Shalee. My heart is filled with pride and love."

Much later, they lay side by side upon the buffalo mat under the twinkling stars and quarter moon. She sighed contentedly as she snuggled into his arms. He murmured into her ear, "Lie still, woman, or I will forget our tepee does not surround us."

She laughed as she whispered, "I wish it did."

His hold tightened and he pressed a kiss to her forehead. "*Istimna, Shalee;* this moon has taken much from your strength."

"Not that much . . . if we still had our tepee," she seductively replied.

His senses flamed at the invitation in her voice. "Perhaps we should stroll in the forest on the new sun," he slyly suggested.

She hugged him fiercely. "Perhaps we should," she agreed, thrilling to the idea, vividly recalling their last day in the forest. Shalee lifted her head to look at the small boy sleeping deeply beside Gray Eagle. "He looks so much like you. It amazes me that we created such a perfect child."

He chuckled. "When the fox and otter play in his

269

mind, you do not think him so perfect," he hinted mischievously.

"No matter what he does, he's still perfect, just like his father."

"I am not perfect, Shalee," he solemnly corrected her.

She kissed him and vowed, "Yes, you are."

"Your eyes are clouded with love, Grass Eyes. Only Wakantanka is perfect."

"Then I pray my eyes and wits will always be clouded this way. I love you," she tenderly declared, bringing an instant reaction to her words.

"Do my ears hear what my heart desires?" he asked.

"I love you," she stated again.

His hands captured her face and kissed her thoroughly. *Waste cedake, Pi-Zi Ista,*" he murmured time and time again between heady kisses.

Soon, he reluctantly halted this siege upon their senses. "Tomorrow," he promised.

"Tomorrow, my love." She readily accepted the intoxicating pledge.

By the time her chores were done, Bright Arrow was playing a game with several other restive boys. She observed them for a time, pleased by his manner. She tensed slightly, then relaxed against the towering body of her husband as he came up behind her and stole a kiss from her neck. "Soon, the others will rest," he roguishly reminded her.

She turned to face him, her hands resting upon his narrow waist. She smiled and answered his unspoken question. "I have not forgotten." Her expression revealed no lingering distress at the portentous word.

Later, Gray Eagle took Shalee's hand in his and

sensuously ventured, "Walk, Little One?"

Her reply was a tremor of anticipation. Gray Eagle waved to Shining Light to let her know they were leaving camp for a time. Shining Light surged with delight, having agreed to watch their son while the distance between her two friends steadily lessened.

For a time, they strolled hand in hand in peaceful silence. Not wanting to rush this precious moment, he halted to sit upon a large rock. Before he could place her upon his lap, she sat upon the grass between his spread legs. Resting her arms upon one muscled thigh, she placed her chin upon them. She felt so at ease in his company and at his touch, as if it were the most natural thing in the world to say or do as she wished.

He stroked her hair as he observed her lack of hesitation or modesty with him. As he began to loosen her braids, she glanced up and inquired, "What are you doing?"

He laughed and remarked nonchalantly, "Your hair shines like Wi and feels like the hide of a newborn fawn. My hands wish to play in it."

He spread the auburn tresses around her shoulders, savoring the silky texture. He leaned over and kissed her. Her arms encircled his neck to hold him there for another one. As his lips left hers, he slid to the ground to lie upon his side facing her. She promptly reclined upon her back with only a few inches between them. He folded his elbow and placed his open palm against his head. She instantly moved upwards to rest her head upon his powerful biceps, so that there need be little distance or effort between them.

He grinned. His hand touseled her hair as his head came downward to lock their lips. Her hand moved slowly

271

over his jawline, noting its planes. When he pulled back to pleasure his eyes with the sight before them, she ran a finger over his lips. The enticing finger eased over his chin, down his throat, and lingered upon his chest. He absently wondered why she didn't question the two scars from the Sun Dance upon his bare flesh, and she never realized herself why she knew what they were and how he had gotten them. A look of pride and respect filled her gaze at this proof of his courage and stamina. But Gray Eagle merely thought she was responding to his strength and appeal of body.

He placed feathery kisses over her eyes and nose. She giggled at the tingly sensations his actions inspired. As her hand wandered over his brawny torso, she realized he was beautiful and exceptionally strong. His flesh was cool and healthy. Her smoldering gaze fused with his. "You are the most beautiful man alive," she murmured.

He chuckled in good humor. "Does not the English word 'beautiful' speak of females?" he taunted devilishly.

She laughed mirthfully. "It applies to anything complex and unique. You are a work of art, my love."

For the next few minutes, she hilariously attempted to explain her words and their meaning. He summed up her hazy explanation with, "To you, I am appealing and exciting?"

"Yes, yes, yes," she elatedly answered, kissing him between each word.

"I please you?" he asked unnecessarily, but jovially.

"That you do, my love. More than I dreamed possible," she added.

Without asking permission, he pulled her to a sitting position and unlaced her dress, then lifted it over her head. His gaze shifted to her breasts before she lay down again, placing her hands over her head upon the cool earth to permit his unhindered view of her. She smiled provocatively, inviting him to feast his eyes upon a sensual body clad only in a breechcloth.

He reclaimed his prior position, his smoldering gaze leisurely traveling her shapely frame from auburn head to bare feet. As if he was physically caressing her, each place his gaze lingered warmed and tingled. "Does this also please you?" he hinted, gently biting her lower lip.

She laughed. "Does this also please you?" he probed again, his moist tongue sharing its warmth with her breasts.

This time she moaned softly and murmured weakly, *"Sha . . ."*

Following several minutes of this stimulating sport, he questioned against her lips as their gazes fused, "Does this also please you?" He had deftly removed her breechcloth and was presently exploring the taut peak located there.

Her stomach tensed, then relaxed. Fires glittered brightly in her eyes. *"Sha,"* she agreed as her respiration grew swift and erratic.

"And this?" he further tested, a finger entering her with agonizingly exquisite skill.

As his lips sought the sweet nectar of her breasts and his hands masterfully explored her most fiery region, her head rolled from side to side as moans of pleasure answered for her. Her body taut with heady suspense and her pulse racing wildly with fierce cravings, she mutely pleaded for this intoxicating sport to continue. Enraptured, she willingly allowed him free rein upon her body.

A hard and fiery object touched her bare hip. She

reached for it, pulling a moan from his lips at her breasts. She artfully fondled the torrid shaft, relishing the power and smoothness of it. She was sorely tempted to brazenly taste its sweetness as Leah had done. Soon, she would find the courage to sate that wanton desire. For now, she patiently and greedily surrendered herself to his tantalizing actions.

He moved between her parted and pleading thighs, gently driving his manhood into her receptive body. He halted but a moment as he mastered the urge to ride her wildly. Gradually he set a rhythm that provoked her to writhe beneath him. Tremors came to her as her tension and delight mounted.

The weight of his body left her as he knelt between her legs. He slightly lifted them, sealing his gaze upon the sight of his shaft seeking and finding its target many times in rapid succession. Her gaze followed his. She wondered at the intensity of her passion as she couldn't remove her glazed eyes from that sensually erotic vision, which seared her body with pleasure, but she was too entrapped by her mesmerized state to question such a feeling. It was a beautiful and stirring sight to observe. She hypnotically watched the damp manhood disappear from sight, only to return and repeat the movement that enflamed and thrilled her heart and body.

Seeing the effect of his intoxicating skills mirrored upon her face, his manhood threatened to end this blissful torture. He quickly lay upon her and drove her mindless with his prowess. His mouth went from breast to breast as he plundered her womanhood. She cried out with pleasure as a liquid warmth caressed his throbbing shaft, telling him his restraint was no longer necessary. With her needs sated, he worked upon satisfying his own.

Spasm after spasm shook his body as he released his passion into her, his fluids mingling with hers. He continued his movements until every drop was expelled. His mouth left her softened mounds to kiss her with vivid love and tenderness. When he lifted his head, she wiped the sheen of perspiration from his upper lip and forehead. She smiled and vowed, "You are utterly magnificent, my love."

He chuckled and advised, "Fill yourself this sun, Grass Eyes, for the journey will allow few feedings along the way. Once we enter the grasslands, there is no privacy for such unions."

Her look of dismay touched him, as did her words: "How shall I endure many days without you? Perhaps I should have waited until we made our new camp to so brazenly tempt you in your weakened state."

"Would you have missed what we just shared?" he taunted.

A look of blissful guilt told him so, as did her verbal answer. "You said our journey would take eight to ten days?" she inquired.

"*Sha*. But you will be so weary by the time Wi sleeps that you will also sleep easily and quickly."

"With you lying beside me and being unable to touch you?" she playfully scoffed, then giggled at his feigned wounded expression.

"Then I will sleep with the other warriors to avoid such painful temptation," he roguishly suggested.

"Oh, no, you won't. At least I can enjoy your company if not . . ."

His hearty laughter halted her words. "Don't laugh yet, my noble warrior; you will suffer right along with me," she pertly reminded him.

He groaned dramatically at that statement. "Surely I will die of starvation."

"Right beside me," she saucily added, caressing his cheek.

"Perhaps if I feed before we leave. . . ."

"Does food last for more than a few hours?" she taunted impishly.

"I fear it does not," he murmured, sighing heavily.

"And fear is not good in a warrior." She echoed words spoken many times in their past.

He looked at her strangely, then dismissed the twinge of hope that her innocent words had inspired. It was a common jest, no more, he decided.

In her own inexplicable state, she didn't notice his reaction as those words curiously echoed through her mind several times, but in his stirring voice . . . strange . . .

The romantic setting and their imminent physical separation teasing at their minds, they made love again. This time, it was a leisurely and serene union. With much to do and the hour growing late, there was little time to savor the final aftermath to an afternoon of rapturous enjoyment.

"We must go, Grass Eyes," he stated reluctantly.

"I know, Wanmdi Hota," she acquiesced in that same mood.

They went to the stream and bathed before returning to camp. The others were now stirring about, picking up with their tasks where they had left off. When the travois was loaded with all except the last minute items, Shining Light came to invite them to share a delicious stew. Shalee and Gray Eagle thanked her, then completed their work and joined them for a relaxing and genial evening.

She watched the two men talk as the children played nearby. She helped Shining Light clear away the remains of their meal. They joined the two warriors at the small fire. Gray Eagle's gaze passed over her warmly before turning back to continue his discussion with Moon Gazer.

Allowing her gaze to wander around this peaceful group, she smiled as she realized how different this day was from her first ones since regaining consciousness. Life was good here. She was happy, as happy as she could be with five years missing. As she permitted her softened gaze to linger upon her husband at the rock-enclosed fire, strange images flashed briefly before her mind's eye.

For a flicker of an instant, he was doing something with his hands: He was winding a slender strip of rawhide around a strong shaft. A pointed white rock was being attached to the end; a bright yellow feather tinged with black decorated the other end. She shook her head and the curious illusion vanished.

What was happening to her? Why did these mysterious thoughts, images, and dreams flash before her mind's eye, sometimes during sleep and sometimes while she was wide awake? Perhaps it was the rapid accumulation of sights and sounds converging to form illusions? Perhaps there was some injury inside her head that caused these uncanny fantasies? Was her mind damaged? Was she going crazy? For these reasons, she kept these dismaying and confusing episodes to herself.

Very early the next day, the packing finished, the columns were ordered into alignment, the warriors sent ahead to scout the approaching area, and the journey was a fact. At first, Shalee insisted on walking with Shining

277

Light and their children beside the horses bearing the travois. By midmorning, she was fatigued beyond belief and her dress was soaked with perspiration. She hadn't known it was possible to hurt everywhere at once. Her lungs fussed at the strain upon them as she struggled for fresh air during her exertions. Her face was flushed and exhibited a moist sheen. The pace was steady, but the walking seemed endless. She wondered how long she could keep up, but forced herself to take step after step.

She caught herself wishing the spring air was as cool as that of the fall. She laughed, knowing she couldn't recall what autumn was like here. Riding in a covered wagon was a dream-come-true compared to this arduous foot-journey. An annoying stitch in her right side caused her to halt for a moment.

Shining Light glanced over her shoulder and asked if she were ill. Having been asked that question many times since being here, she smiled in comprehension and shook her head. She pointed to her side and twisted her hands, signing a muscle cramp. She motioned for them to continue and she would catch up soon. Shining Light smiled and nodded her understanding of the accurate signing and Oglala words. . . .

Shalee leaned forward to remove the strain from her waist. She inhaled and exhaled several times. She ached in every spot of her slender frame. Even the bottoms of her feet argued against this demand of them. As she looked up, summoning the willpower and obstinance to press on, her gaze touched upon her husband. She went rigid as she stared at him.

She couldn't move or take her eyes from the stunning vision. Was it real or imaginary? As the sun lifted itself into the heavens, the fingers of pink from sunrise had given way to rays of bold yellow, outlining the indomitable warrior against an azure skyline. Why weren't the bunch and buffalo grass set aflame by the sun? Silly girl, they are newborn and vivid green! Where had the winds come from? It should be motionless and deathly still; why, she didn't know. He sat before the advancing group like the leader he should be, and was. Odd, his face was not painted and Chula was unadorned. True, he sat proud and erect upon the mottled horse, but something was wrong, different. He didn't present the pagan God of War!

He motioned to her to come to him, guessing her exhaustion and reoccuring weakness. She remained still and silent. Why did she hesitate? Why did it seem she was waiting for someone or something to take her to him? Who was missing from her side? She trembled in fear and uncertainty, but she didn't understand why. She shook her head to clear away this eerie and frightful vision. She sank to the ground upon her knees. She would not go to him! If he desired her return, he could come to her! The moment these resentful thoughts came to her, she rejected them. Why should she think such ridiculous things? Why was she suddenly cold when the day was daring to become hot and sultry?

Gray Eagle urged his horse forward as he witnessed her curious distress, something more than physical. He leaped off Chula's back and raced toward her, panic filling him. Kiowa and Waubay had gone to her aid the moment she collapsed to the dry earth. Her senses spinning in confusion, she was trying to tell them she was all right. Kiowa offered her water, which she accepted to moisten her dry throat and lips. Waubay seized a piece of hide from his waist and wet it, offering it to her to freshen her ashen face. *"Pidamaye, pidamaye,"* she repeated her gratitude at each show of kindness and assistance.

"Shalee, are you ill?" Gray Eagle inquired anxiously as he dropped to his knees before her.

Distressed by her weird thoughts and feelings and weakened by her emotional stress and the physical demands of this trip, she burst into tears and flung herself into his protective embrace. "I'm sorry to be so much trouble, Wanmdi Hota," she wailed in dismay. "I don't mean to act like such a baby or a silly weakling."

"Do not excite yourself, Shalee. You are still weak; you have done much work and walking. Come, you must ride with me," he coaxed.

"The other women and children are walking. What will they think if your wife rides? Just let me rest a little while, then I'll be fine. My side was hurting; now, my head aches. It must be the sun and the heat," she offered apologetically.

"Is it the injury to your head that troubles you?" he asked worriedly, fearing another lapse in memory.

"I don't think so. I was a little dizzy for a few minutes, but it's passed. Was I this awful on all our other journeys?" she teased, hoping to lighten the tension.

"Hiya. You traveled easy the other times, even when you carried our son. But you are still suffering from the wound. Come, ride with me."

She met his entreating gaze and smiled. "Only for a little while," she finally agreed.

He laughed. "You are a proud and stubborn woman, Shalee."

"And you are a proud and stubborn man," she retorted fondly.

He quickly explained her lingering weakness from her

attack. The others smiled and nodded agreement that she should ride with her husband for a while. He mounted up and reached down for her. He started to question the strange look that filled her eyes at his action, but didn't.

She rested her head against his chest, her arms encircling his narrow waist. She speculated upon her feeling of having done this before. She moved her hands at his back. Why had she imagined for a moment they were bound?

They rode thus for two more hours. Shalee dozed several times, fighting the intangible sensations that plagued her mind. Later, they halted to eat and to rest. Within moments, she was asleep in his arms. He worried over the paleness of her face and the rosy splotches upon her cheeks. He tested her forehead for a fever, but found none. Perhaps she had done too much too quickly, he assumed.

But the next day upon the trail was vastly different. Shalee grinned at him each time he came to check on her progress and condition. This time, she traveled without any problems until they halted for rest. As they sat together upon a buffalo mat, she remarked happily, "See, I did just fine today."

"*Sha.* You did just fine." They slept for two hours before beginning their seasonal trek again.

The days and nights blurred into one seemingly endless episode of walking, eating, walking, resting, walking, sleeping, and more walking in her sleep. The tribe was spread out over such a lengthy distance, there was little chance for socializing. During their periods of rest, most families spent their time together. The days were long and taxing; the nights, too short and demanding.

She found herself wanting and needing Gray Eagle, but unable to have more than a kiss or a light touch. Most nights, their son slept between them or on one side of them. During the day, he would burst with energy and vitality, running here and there to chat or visit as they steadily moved along. Shalee felt as if this trek would never end.

On the fifth day of their journey, they camped for one full day at this halfway point. They had reached a spot where trees and lofty hills surrounded them. They halted near a wide stream to fill their water skins, play in the refreshing water, and enjoy this brief respite in their rigorous schedule. When the horses were secured to a lengthy rawhide rope near the riverbank where they could drink and nibble at the lush grass, an air of elation filled the area.

They ate from the swiftly dwindling supply of *wasna* and *aguyapi*. Soon, the men would need to hunt for fresh game and the women for wild vegetables and berries. Friends and families visited amongst themselves, relating tales of past adventures or discussing the new season of life on the Plains. Many bathed and splashed in the cool stream. Others strolled around to relieve taut muscles and excessive suspense.

Shalee glanced up to see Leah heading for the stream to fill Running Wolf's water skins. She suddenly realized how wonderful these past days of avoidance had been; she had almost forgotten Leah's existence!

Gray Eagle came back from his meeting with a group of warriors who were chosen to guard the camp during the night. He dropped to the earth and assumed his normal cross-legged position. Soon, it would be time to call Bright Arrow from his revelry with the other boys.

Having been told they would sleep on this same spot, Shalee was busy stretching out their sleeping mats as she had done each night since this trip began. She glanced over at her husband. A scowl lined his handsome features. She followed his line of vision to where Leah was making her way from the stream to where Running Wolf was sitting upon his own sleeping mat and conversing with two other warriors.

Her inquisitive gaze shifted from Gray Eagle's frown to Leah's inviting smile. Wouldn't she ever learn her lessons! How dare she openly flirt with the future chief of this awesome tribe, her husband! Was she blind or simply brazenly daring? Didn't she think others would notice and wonder at her wantonness and boldness? Didn't he? Why did he permit her unforgivable conduct and actions? She had practically ravished him that day, and perhaps other days? Why was he so tolerant and lenient with her? She was just like Chela! She was vindictive and conniving! Both had resented her presence in Gray Eagle's life and wanted to replace her.

Chela, vindictive and conniving? Resented her and wanted to replace her? Why would she make such a comparison? She shrugged in puzzlement. It must have been the things he had told her about Chela and their past relationship, she surmised casually and dismissed her insight. Perhaps her imagination was playing tricks on her, but she couldn't forget Leah's past insinuations or her suspicions about them.

Shalee drilled her stormy gaze into her husband's profile, her irritation mounting as he continued to observe that white witch. What was his fascination with her? If there was nothing between them, why did they behave so oddly? As if sensing the power of her intense

283

gaze upon him, Gray Eagle's head slowly turned. Shalee was glaring at him! Her eyes went to Leah's retreating back and swaying hips, then back to his now stoic face. A chill walked over him as he viewed the anger and accusation exposed in those green pools of ice. He lifted a quizzical brow. Her eyes froze as he pretended not to know the source of her vexation.

"Do you wish to take a walk?" he asked, governing the strain in his tone.

"No, I do not, Gray Eagle. Perhaps you can find another *friend* to keep you company. Perhaps you have been rudely ignoring some *special friend* since my unexpected return," she sneered sarcastically, her gaze drilling into Leah's back and then his face once more. She sat down upon the mat and presented her rigid back to him.

Irrational and erroneous suspicions filled her heart and mind anew. What if Gray Eagle had known of her presence near the stream that formidable day? What if his actions and words had been a deceitful ploy to convince her of his loyalty and love? What if there had been something between him and Leah while she was presumed dead, or even before that time? Were Leah's fury and bitterness those of a woman scorned? Was she actually in love with Gray Eagle? Was she desperately attempting any measure to regain him? Was there any truth to her prior claims? Did some brutal rejection following a torrid and secret affair explain her arrogance and bold intimacy? Had her husband given Leah reasons to desire him, to brazenly pursue him? Why did he accept her actions so calmly? Perhaps she had been a blind fool to trust him so completely, so swiftly, so romantically!

Gray Eagle speculated upon her sudden change in

mood and behavior. Why had she glared at him and Leah in that curious manner? Why had she suddenly turned against Leah? Why was she furious with him right now? As deadly and quickly as lightning strikes a tree, the truth dawned upon him. He had been staring at Leah; Leah had been smiling enticingly at him; he had done nothing about her audacious behavior; Shalee had been watching their interaction all the time. What was his wife thinking and feeling? The look in her eyes was not one of simple jealousy or mild irritation. There had been tacit accusation and fury in her snowy expression! Why?

"Shalee?" he called softly to her. She stiffened and refused to turn or to answer him. Dread escaped his mind and ravaged his body. Something was going on inside her lovely head, something that alarmed him.

"Let's go for a walk, Shalee," he stated more firmly, making his words sound like an order rather than a genial request.

"I do not hold you captive, Gray Eagle. If you wish to visit friends, you are free to do so. I wish to remain here . . . alone."

Why did she keep emphasizing certain words, peculiar words? "Are you ill? Do you wish to sleep this early?" he solicitously inquired.

"It isn't necessary to trouble yourself about my health and safety. I'm fine. I wish to think for a time," she added in a curious tone.

"Think about what?" he asked, a quiver in his voice.

"You and me and all the things you told me about us. Before, I merely accepted your words as truth and fact. Perhaps I did so too hastily," she sassily informed the startled warrior.

"What do you mean?" he probed unsteadily.

285

"I think you know exactly what I mean," she sneered. She jumped up and headed for the stream. She sat down upon the bank and dangled her sore, bare feet in the refreshing water. Such a disturbing collage of rapidly appearing and disappearing images darted through her mind to haunt her and befuddle her. What was the matter with her? Why did her head pain her so during these fanciful moments? Why was she so curt and jumpy?

He came and sat down beside her, watching her intently. "You think I spoke falsely about us?" He bravely came to the point.

"Did you?" she challenged just as boldly.

"No, Shalee; I did not," he stated honestly.

"You're saying you've never lied to me?" she charged heatedly.

"I spoke the words of truth to you," he vowed, piqued and insulted.

Even when you let me believe you couldn't speak English for months, she clearly heard her warring mind debate. Her mental deliberation continued. I do not understand. He spoke English to me that first day, her logic countered in bewilderment of her implausible insinuation. Why did she think it was months before he told her the truth? She struggled to recall his exact words concerning their first meeting and those following weeks.

I must have meant days, she reasoned anxiously. It was days before he finally came to Brave Bear's camp to find her. Had he been too busy with Leah to even realize she was missing? No, he had explained about the messages gone awry. Why did this white girl spark such suspicions and self-doubts within her? Gray Eagle had given her no reason to mistrust him.

He studied her for a time. Had she meant she was

doubting him? It was unlike Shalee to question and mistrust him. But this female wasn't Shalee, not in mind, only in body; that fact plagued him.

Shalee remained ominously silent and thoughtful. This wasn't the first time she had been harassed by strange remarks and moody behavior. Could it be possible she was recalling bits of her past? Was it possible she didn't even realize it? That first day on the trail when she became ill, why had she stared at him so strangely? Why was she frequently haunted by feelings of *déja vu?* If she truly had amnesia, why did some events seem so real?

Stunned by her change of mood, he stared at her. "What has Leah got to do with our life?" she quizzed seriously. "What powerful force passes between you and her? Why do you allow her open flirtation?"

"Do you doubt me? Answer me and I will explain," he stated mysteriously. "If you think my words false, speaking is useless."

"Why," she pressed, feeling uneasy, mildly threatened.

"Tell me," he sternly commanded, the sheer force of his voice compelling her to reply before thinking. "Do you think I lie to you?"

It would sound silly, she feared. For a moment she had thought that same event had taken place before, as with others she had witnessed or dreamed. How could she logically explain her weird feelings, and those intimidating illusions of him dressed or acting differently, again waiting for her to come to him or to be brought to him?

Guilt flushed her cheeks, but for another reason he would never suspect. "Why would you ask me that? Do you think I'm crazy? That would supply a good reason to replace me with Leah."

287

"No, Shalee, madness does not touch your mind. Perhaps doubts about me and your past do," he suggested, his expression wistful and grave.

She longed to question him about her illusions, to learn if they had some factual basis; but she couldn't bring herself to do so, not yet. She turned to face him fully, her gaze wide and seeking. "Why?"

"You have lived with me many moons. The Bluecoats raided our camp, injuring you badly. They thought you a white captive and saw no worth in your life. You awakened to learn your people were your enemies and I am your husband. Such words are hurtful and confusing. You compare me to the white man and his ways. I am a warrior, an Oglala. You think because I thought you dead I would take another woman. I did not. You are my love."

"But . . ." she faltered in uncertainty.

Perhaps the past was slowly returning to her? When she reviewed the other episodes, she smiled and prayed it was. Still, they were such a few events in a five-year span. "Leah troubles you deeply. Soon, it will not be so. When the summer camp is ready, Running Wolf is to sell her. She will leave our camp forever. There is nothing between us; this I swear to you."

"She wants you, Gray Eagle," she declared angrily.

"Wanting and possessing are not the same, Shalee. I want and need only you. When your thoughts return, you will know this truth."

"Why can't I remember everything now?" she panted in exasperation.

"Perhaps there is some lesson or test in this matter."

"For me or for you?" she asked seriously.

"Perhaps for both," he candidly replied.

"You swear you have no love or desire for Leah?"

she insisted.

"*Sha*. Only for you, Grass Eyes."

How could she deny the love and lucidness in his compelling eyes? How could she take her insecurities and uncertainty out on him? It wasn't fair. "Perhaps I am only troubled and foolish, but I believe you. I was just angry and upset when I saw her looking at you. You did nothing! Why?"

"You asked me to leave the matter alone, to keep the eyes and ears of others from the offensive matter," he reminded her.

"That's going to be difficult with you and her exchanging those curious looks! I'll be glad when she's gone; I don't like her or trust her."

"You never did," he stated casually. "You did not understand my expression. Leah has been too friendly with our son these past moons. She shows her face as boldly as Wi. I do not understand her reckless courage. Does she not fear for her safety and position with us? She is strange."

Surprised by his deductions, she looked up at him. "But Leah said we were friends, that we worked together. She said I protected her from abuse. She said . . ." Shalee's eyes widened with enlightenment. "She lied to me. She was only trying to cause trouble and to ensnare you. She was playing upon my loss of memory. She tricked me! Why, that little tart!"

"Leah claimed you two were once friends?" he pressed in disbelief.

"Yes. She said because I was white that I befriended and helped her."

"What other lies did she tell you?" he suspiciously demanded.

289

Shalee blushed. "It doesn't matter now. I know she lied."

Afraid he couldn't convince her of his innocence in their repulsive conflict if Leah had dared to relate it, he didn't press her for answers in her highly agitated state of mind. "You never were *kodas*, Shalee. Many times you said you did not trust her. You said she was too obedient and respectful for a captive, our enemy."

"She isn't respectful and obedient; it's just a wily pretense! She called you a savage. She said she wanted to replace me," she blurted out before thinking clearly.

He threw back his head and laughed. "To Leah, I am a savage, Little One. But she could never replace you; no female could," he assured her.

"If you forgot me, would you come to love me again?"

"Yes, as I love you now."

She lowered her head in shame. "I'm sorry, Wanmdi Hota. I've been acting terrible. I won't do it again, I promise."

"If other eyes were not upon us, I would make you prove your shame and love," he teased, relieved their problem was settled for the present.

She smiled ruefully. "When we get home, I will."

"That is one promise I will not allow you to forget."

He pulled her close to him and placed his arm around her shoulder. She rested her head against him. For a long time, they sat there watching the full moon and savoring their renewed closeness. She mentally vowed she would never permit Leah to come between them again, especially not while they were still seeking each other. He, too, made a mental promise; Leah would be gone as quickly as possible. For some reason she had fiercely displeased his father; now, he was determined to be rid of

290

her. Soon, they would enjoy a peaceful life again. . . .

Their journey had begun near a place that would one day be called Rapid City, to progress through a vast territory later to be named the Badlands, over flat prairies and lush grasslands, past lofty buttes and picturesque bluffs, over areas of arid, desertlike terrain, along the Bad River to where it joined forces with the mighty Missouri River, near a place then and now called Pierre, to head southward for several miles to their intended campsite. All the lands they traversed comprised the massive Dakota Territory.

The warriors often left the group to ride out and talk with other tribes who passed within visual range of the Oglala: the Sisseton, heading northward now; the Cheyenne, steadily heading northeastward; the Brule, calmly heading southwestward; and the Yankton, leisurely heading southeastward. Each tribe recognized the proclaimed sites of their allies and member tribes. From Gray Eagle's instructive talks, Shalee knew there were other tribes living not too far away: the Crow, Santee, and Winnebago. She was relieved to learn that many formerly hostile tribes had made truce to fight a more deadly, mutual foe in the white man. For a time, warfare among the neighboring tribes was halted, and Indian truce reigned in the opulent Dakota Territory, the largest portion of which comprised the Eagle's domain.

Chapter Thirteen

The remainder of their seasonal trek passed uneventfully. After nine taxing days, they arrived at their final destination. No orders were necessary to begin the flurry of activity. Locations were selected for each tepee. Travois were unloaded, the possessions of each family placed near its chosen campsite. Horses were rubbed down, watered, and tethered in the lush grassland by a group of teenage boys. Youthful girls collected large rocks to form cookfires, then wood and water was gathered. A band of hunters headed into the dense forest soon after their arrival. Tonight, they would celebrate their homecoming with a joint feast and merriment before new labors began.

Tepees were gradually taking their conical shapes once more, standing like pointed mounds against the cobalt skyline. This area was beautiful and tranquil. Grass and wildflowers were plentiful, generously offering their beauty and abundance to anyone who needed or appreciated them. A variety of trees and scrub-bushes dotted the landscape and cluttered the nearby forest. Countless shades of green revealed the harmony and artistry of Mother Nature. The sky was intensely blue, traveling far beyond where the eye could see. Lofty plateaus and craggy peaks could be noted in the distance. Other rocky slopes colored the vista with their blacks, browns, tans, and an unusual blood-red.

They were setting up camp in an immense clearing about eight hundred feet from a wide and untroubled river. In several spots, small streams ran off in various directions, two forming small, round pools that would be perfect for bathing and swimming. The water in those natural pools was so calm and clear it reflected the harmonious beauty above them like two mirrors.

Insects and butterflies abounded amongst the wildflowers, stealing their sweet nectar while sharing their music and beauty with those who observed them. Birds perched in the trees, singing heartily as they furtively watched for opportunities to swoop down and devour careless insects. Shalee inhaled the fresh and invigorating air, then slowly expelled it once its essence had been savored. She walked over to the site chosen by Shining Light to observe the task of putting up the tepee, hoping to learn something.

Later, she watched others before seeking out Turtle Woman. She smiled fondly as she approached the genial woman, who was steadily making progress without complaints or bitterness. Turtle Woman grinned in pleasure as Shalee asked if she could assist her to learn how this task was done. The gentle-spirited woman nodded, smiling cheerfully, knowing Shalee was sincere in her request.

Together, they finally had the poles attached and standing. They positioned them to form a wooden pyramid. Looping a heavy rawhide rope through the thick strip that secured one side of the attached skins, Turtle Woman tossed the rope over the top of the poles where they separated to point in different directions. It required several throws before she passed the rope through the center of the poles. She laughed in satisfaction as she headed around the cluster of cottonwood saplings to seize the rope. With her twisted hand, this task was the most difficult and strenuous. Shalee grabbed the rope and helped her pull the heavy weight near the top of the poles. As she held tightly to the burden, Turtle Woman reached for the two dangling strips and yanked upon them with all her might to close the opening around the junction of poles. As Turtle Woman used a stick to straighten the laces, she continually pulled upon them to secure the two sides. When this task was completed at the ground, she knotted the two strips and tucked the raw edges beneath the skins.

She smiled at Shalee as she took one end of the rope and yanked upon it until it fell free of its duty. They headed around the conical dwelling in opposite directions securing the joined hides to the bottoms of the poles. When they met again, they laughed joyfully as they eyed their success. Shalee thanked the woman for her instructions and patience. To her pleasure and appreciation, Turtle Woman insisted upon helping her assemble her tepee. She smiled in gratitude, telling the unselfish woman it wasn't necessary to repay her, for she had needed those lessons.

Still, Turtle Woman insisted. Within two hours, the larger and more colorfully decorated tepee of Wanmdi Hota was positioned upon his chosen spot like some proud warrior watching over the camp. Shalee hugged Turtle Woman and thanked her. The older woman smiled and walked away. Shalee hastily began carrying their possessions inside their new home, except Gray Eagle's weapons and other tabu items. She beamed in satisfaction, knowing how surprised and pleased her husband would be when he returned. More, she warmed to the thought of the long-missed privacy that this tepee represented. Then, she recalled their son. She scolded herself for wistfully thinking she yearned for solitude with her husband. She sighed in resignation. Tepees certainly didn't offer any privacy for couples! Her body ached to taste those heady delights again. But how could they make love when their son was sleeping within feet of them? Since the others had also been denied closeness with their mates, she couldn't expect one of them to allow Bright Arrow to spend the night in their new tepee. Besides, their son should be in his new home with his parents.

She sat upon the ground to dig a small pit for their fire, then lined it with flat rocks. She shoveled the dirt upon a square of tanned hide to take outside and dump. As she stood up and brushed off her clothes and legs, she was startled to find her husband standing behind her. "I didn't hear you come in," she remarked in surprise.

His ebony eyes locked upon her flushed face, filled with life and spent energy. He reached out to lovingly push aside a lock of hair that had strayed from her braid during her work. His contact with her face was wonderful; she nestled her cheek against his palm. The hand slipped around her neck and drew her head toward his. His lips captured hers and stole their nectar as the bees did to the black-eyed Susans and the Pasqueflowers. His other arm went around her back and pulled her tightly against his lean and lithe frame.

She groaned in need of him and this intoxicating blending of love. Her arms encircled his waist and she pressed even closer to him. Their passions flamed to an incredible and overwhelming level. Her hands wandered over his back and shoulders, delighting in the feel of him. Lips burned sweet and tormenting messages over her closed eyes, satiny face, and creamy neck. Enflamed beyond reality or reason, she pleaded for him to vanquish this hunger that raged within her. When he cupped her breast, the protruding nipple loudly shouted her need to his roaming hand. In wild abandonment, her hands dove into the midnight mane and held his mouth against hers as she almost savagely responded to his kisses.

Adrift upon this turbulent sea of emotions, no sound reached her spinning head and no will remained within her submissive body. Enthralled by him and his passionate siege, only Gray Eagle and her urgent needs existed. Lost to reality himself and drugged by his desire for her, he whet her love-starved appetite with fever and skill. Beyond fearing an intrusion or caring what anyone would think about her wantonness, she struggled with the ties at his sides to loosen his breechcloth. When it fell free of his virile body, her hand encircled the flaming shaft that could end her torment.

At her touch upon his manhood, he shuddered and groaned in irrepressible need. Her garments were nearly ripped from her body, but neither cared nor minded their destruction. His mouth devoured the strained tip of her bosom. Flames seared through her womanhood that even the moisture flowing there could not douse. When his hand sought out her throbbing peak, she trembled and opened her thighs to permit his easy entrance to the place that brazenly pleaded for the ecstasy that only he could grant. The gentle stroking of his deft hand was tantalizing, and his feasting at her breasts feverishly blissful.

"Make love to me now or I shall surely die of pain,"

she urged.

Her voice sparked a brief return to reality. He groaned in fierce need and the thought of an untimely intrusion. Still, it was too late to halt the fires that threatened to consume them. He left her to lace the flap, an indication of privacy. He had sighted their son playing with the other boys. He hurriedly returned to her and carried her to their sleeping mat. He resumed where he'd left off. Dazed with desire, she hadn't moved or spoken, noting his actions and their insinuation.

"There is little time for teasing you, my love. We must sate our needs before our son returns. Another moon and I will pleasure you slowly."

She smiled, her eyes limpid with fiery longings. "I want you too much to wait. Enter me now," she coaxed him. "You don't need to entice me; I feel like my body is afire with need for you."

He gently plunged his manhood into her body. Stimulated to boldness, she arched to meet his entry and moved seductively beneath him. Her legs crossed his to hold him tightly within her. She pressed his mouth to her swollen, taut bosom. She matched the rhythm he set as her head thrashed upon the mat. Her eyes closed dreamily, and her quickened breathing passed through parted lips.

It was a terrible strain upon Gray Eagle's control to plunder her body without taking any booty until she had claimed her first prize. His mouth closed over hers to prevent the cry of shattering release from leaving her throat as she ground her body against his to extract every ounce of pleasure and relief he was offering to her. As her fires burned at their brightest, she opened her glazed eyes and entreated, "Come ride with me, my love."

Her provocative words had the desired effect. He swiftly and feverishly strove to simultaneously match her climax, claiming his treasure as his body shook with the forceful release of many moons of pent-up cravings. As he had done to her many times, she savagely ravished his mouth and held him tightly against her, nearly driving him wild with the increased intensity caused by her unbridled actions. He exploded as a dam bursting after a deluge of water had weakened and overpowered it, crashing against it and destroying it with great power and determination.

Wave after wave pounded against her womanhood until only a calmed river remained behind. Spent and breathless, he could only roll half off of her. Tenderness and confidence flowed over her, for she had pleasured him well. When his respiration slowed and his thundering heart relaxed, he lifted his head to gaze down at her in wonder and tenderness. She smiled up at him, then kissed him soundly.

"You demand much, woman, but you give much," he complimented her efforts. "It is never the same with you. Each time we join, it is new and exciting. How can my heart hold so much love or my body accept such pleasures? Surely I will burst with fullness," he teased in a mellow voice.

"If you do, I will gather the pieces and put you together again. Then I will fill you until you burst again." She hugged him possessively. "I love you so much," she suddenly exclaimed.

"Shalee, Shalee, my beautiful and desirable wife, how I love you," he vowed in a husky tone.

Her breath caught in her throat at the look in his eyes and the stirring quality in his voice. "My God, how is it

298

possible to want you again right now? Yet, I do. Surely I am wicked to feel such things," she concluded playfully, pulling his head down to take another kiss from his lips.

They kissed longingly several times, until he unwillingly pulled away and advised seriously, "We must not build a fire we cannot light."

She giggled and mischievously replied, "The fire is already built, my love. What we cannot do is put it out in the best manner. It must smolder until another time. Perhaps my people have one definite advantage over yours; they build many rooms in their wooden tepees to allow such fires to burn freely at will," she playfully jested.

"At dark when little eyes cannot see clearly, such does not matter. Only the fires that burn when Wi fills the sky must be carefully tended," he smiled, adding his two cents.

"You have taught me to build such fires and to enjoy them, but you have failed to show me how to tend or douse them," she chided him, laughing merrily.

"And I never shall, wife. Then, you will not be tempted to tease me with a fire that consumes only me."

"Ah lass, you would allow me to suffer from such pains?"

"If I share such suffering, then you must endure only your half."

"You are too wise and cunning, my noble warrior. I fear I cannot match wits and words with you."

"Then match only my love and desire," he suggested beguilingly.

"Impossible. Mine already exceeds yours."

"Impossible. Mine has lived longer than yours."

"Impossible. Time has nothing to do with the depth or

299

power of such feelings."

He chuckled in amusement. "You match my wits and words too well, wife. I accept this because you also match my love and desire."

"Just as it should be. Your prowess is matchless, for it has conquered me twice. I love you with all my heart."

He embraced her, then kissed her. "To leave your side is harder than fighting a fierce battle with enemies. Have mercy and help me find the strength of mind and body to do so."

She pursed her lips in thoughtful consideration. "If I say no?"

He fell backwards upon his back, throwing his arms above his head. "Then do with me as you desire," he stated, as if resigned to defeat.

Her eyes gleamed with mischief and anticipation. She tapped each wrist and ankle, saying seductively, "You are tightly bound, warrior. You are my captive and I will sate my lust upon your helpless body."

She laughed at the smoldering gaze that glowed within his obsidian eyes. "What manner of captive are you?" she playfully scolded him. "I see no fear and respect in your eyes for your master. You will obey me or I shall punish you."

"What is your command, Princess Shalee?" he inquired, forcing a grave expression to his face, a beguiling grin threatening to shatter it.

"I command you to love me, to please me with every skill you possess, to come to me whenever I have need of you," she listed her orders.

"I love you now, Princess. I will answer your call each time. To please you, you must free my bonds," he said, playing along with her stirring game.

When she pretended to loosen those imaginary bonds,

he seized her and imprisoned her body beneath his, pinning her wrists to the ground on either side of her chestnut braids. "Your lust is so great it steals your wits, my beautiful enemy. Now, you are my captive. Never trust a cunning foe. I will hold you captive forever. You will come to me when I call and you will obey my commands. You will please me greatly, or I will punish you like this," he intimated, his tongue circling her breasts to tantalize them.

"And I will torment you like this," he added, ravishing her mouth until she was breathless. "Then I will torture you like this," he roguishly warned, slowly entering her and slowly withdrawing. Each time he withdrew, he grinned at her as he hesitated before gently plunging into her again. When his sport became serious, he withdrew and demanded, "Do you promise to obey me in all words and ways? If you do not speak wisely, I will torture you by leaving your side."

"I will do anything you say," she responded hoarsely.

He slipped within her again, pulling a moan of exquisite pleasure from her lips. Yet he began his deliberately intoxicating game once more. Each time he faltered before returning his manhood into her, she arched upwards to seek it. When it skillfully drove into her, she sighed in rapture. His teeth worked gently upon her breasts between frequent savorings of the whole tip. When she reached a frenzied state, he knew it was time to halt his loving torment and sate her needs, which he did, then his own.

Exhausted, she curled into his arms and sighed contentedly. "If that is how you torture and torment a disobedient captive, I shall be defiant and bad every day."

"If you obey me, my sweet slave, I will reward you

better than I can torment you."

"What could be better than this?" she asked incredulously.

He chuckled. "There are many sides to love. I will teach them to you."

Without shame or modesty, she asked, "Like we shared that day in the forest?"

He nodded. "But there are others too, if you are truly brave and obedient to my commands."

She locked her gaze with his. "I am brave and submissive to you."

He warmed and grinned. "Soon, you will enjoy new lessons," he ventured.

"How soon?" she probed in excitement and abandonment.

"Two more moons and I will take you into the forest for a walk."

"For only a walk?" she impishly teased.

"A lover's walk. I will walk upon you, and you will walk upon me."

She trembled with suspense and intrigue. "Two moons."

He nodded and grinned. "You must learn patience, wife."

"Impossible with you as my husband," she informed him.

His finger trailed over her chest, around each breast, then up to dance upon one erect point. "If you don't stop that, your walk will begin right now," she threatened, half in jest and half in utter seriousness.

"Then I will stop until later," he readily agreed, kissing her before getting up. "We must find a place to bathe. Soon we must join the feast."

302

"Bathe in the forest?" she murmured suggestively.

"Bathing only, woman, no walking today," he stated, grinning.

"If I am to obey your every command, then bathing only."

They dressed, then headed for a place to bathe, walking hand in hand. He called to Bright Arrow to let him know their plans. The boy waved and smiled, then returned to his game.

The feasting and merriment lasted until midnight. Despite the fatigue of everyone, an air of elation and expectancy filled the crisp air and the joyful hearts of the Oglala. Small children, exhausted from their games, had gone to bed earlier. Other youths sat in groups talking excitedly about the days when they would become either wives or warriors. Unwed braves clung together as some social clic, discussing wars and adventures and great hunts, past and future. Couples sat with mates, making plans and rehashing the good times they had shared or the bad times they had endured. Others swayed or moved to the rhythm of the music supplied by several older Indians. It was a good moment to be alive and free, to have no worries or perils to trouble their cheerful minds.

Shalee sat between Gray Eagle and Running Wolf near a large campfire, enjoying the tranquil sights and sounds of her people; for that was how she viewed them now. The strangeness had worn off; she felt an intricate part of this impressive group. Gone were the feelings of loneliness and insecurity; gone were the doubts and suspicions. She was Shalee, wife to Gray Eagle, half-breed daughter to Black Cloud, member of the Oglala Tribe of the mighty Sioux Nation: the Dakota Oceti Sakawin, "Seven Council Fires of the Sioux." Life was wonderful. Only the return of her memory could make things better and happier for her . . . and them.

She glanced over at her husband, his attention upon the dancers with colorful shields. "I must go to sleep now, Wanmdi Hota. There is much work to do tomorrow," she teased, slightly serious.

"Do you wish me to come with you?" he asked, his gaze mellow.

"Stay here and enjoy the fun if you aren't tired," she encouraged. "But I need some rest. Under your Eagle eye and wing, I will be safe and happy," she added meaningfully.

"In the shadow of that smile and warmth, I must remain," he teased, lightly stroking her silky hair.

"Perhaps you should for both our sakes," she saucily agreed.

He helped her to her feet, then watched her walk to their new tepee to join their slumbering son. Running Wolf remarked, "You love her much, my son. It is good she was returned to us. Soon, all will be good again. I had a dream; Shalee will return. Watch over her closely; some dark shadow fell over her before she could see your face clearly. It was not the wing of my son," he warned, that eerie sensation haunting him again.

The warrior's expression waxed grave. "Her life is in danger, Father?"

"*Sha.* But the evil did not show its face in my vision."

Gray Eagle's somber gaze flickered to the tepee that held his wife and lingered there. "The Bird of Death feels cheated, but he will not fly away with my woman. I will challenge him myself. She is mine," he vowed, angered by this new and intangible threat to his love.

A firm believer in dreams, Gray Eagle readily accepted

his father's dismaying words of caution. Many times his worried gaze shifted to their sleeping tepee, wondering from where this new peril would come, praying he would be present to defeat it.

Gray Eagle reverently observed the Shaman as he chanted before the Medicine Wheel, that sacred object that represented the forces and influences of life and the entire world. The center exhibited a buffalo bull's skull, which exposed the imagery of the "blue tails" design. Brain-tanned hide was stretched taut over a willow hoop. The surface displayed attachments of hair, heart beads, fur, feathers, and trade cloth, all colorfully tinted with earth paints. There was significance to the four directions upon its face: south, the innocence of mind and body at birth; east, enlightenment; north, wisdom gained during life; and west, meditation for self-examination and understanding. All spokes radiated toward the center of the design: the heart and meaning of life itself, total harmony with self and nature.

Gray Eagle fingered his war shield. Pride and self-assurance flooded him. All knew the meaning of the "shooting star" design emblazoned upon his shield, a design that conveyed his superior strength, speed, cunning, and valor. A warrior must earn the right to paint his shield with this particular pattern; naturally, he had.

His concentration returned to the climax of this ritual. The celebration soon ended and the others gradually retired. The night passed swiftly and a glorious new day of adventure and promise began. . . .

Chapter Fourteen

Shalee's command of the Sioux language expanded and sharpened every day with the assistance of her husband and good friends. Under the gentle hand and genial eyes of Turtle Woman and Shining Light, her skills and knowledge of their daily chores also increased and were honed. Within two weeks after their arrival in the summer camp, she moved and lived amongst the Oglala easily and serenely. Soon, it was as if that fateful accident had never taken place. Bright Arrow's vivacious mother had returned, as had Gray Eagle's adoring wife. Others found delight and joy in the happiness that surrounded the life of their greatest warrior and future leader.

This season was a busy and vital one, and none realized how quickly and easily Shalee recaptured her lost knowledge and deft talents. She had been known for her keen mind, the apparent reason for her swift progress. Even Shalee did not realize she was working so accurately, because the tasks seemed natural to her. Yet, the strange dreams and haunting images frequently plagued her mind.

She allowed herself to believe her inexplicable experiences were the results of learning so much so hastily, inspiring daydreams or fanciful conclusions to things told to her. She hesitated to question her husband about such weird thoughts, for she did not wish to inspire false hopes in him. She also feared to learn that these things were illusions, hinting at some irreparable damage to her mind. So, she kept her unproven flashes of her past to herself, dreading to test them for accuracy and verity.

The warriors and braves were preparing for the spring buffalo hunt. It was decided who would go on the critical hunt and who would guard the camp. The women who would accompany the men were selected and told to make ready for this task. Children were informed of where to stay while those mothers were away. The ever impending threat of lethal conflict with the whites and Bluecoats was gravely debated. An aging chief, Running Wolf would remain in the camp to be responsible for his people. Gray Eagle and White Arrow were chosen as leaders of the two groups of hunters.

All plans made, the hunters met in the ceremonial lodge to ask for the guidance and protection of the Great Spirit for their vital venture. Prayers and chants were sung in stirring voices. Prayer pipes were smoked to entice the breath of Wakantanka to speak with them. Peyote buttons were ingested to invoke the spiritual presence of the Great Spirit and to allow Him to instill His messages within the Indians by way of hallucinatory visions. Bodies and hearts were purified through prayers and sweatings from the tightly enclosed lodge, which steamed from the large fire in its center over which a soaked skin of water was positioned. Following their purification ritual of fasting, praying, and sweating, the warriors and braves returned to their tepees to refresh their spirits and bodies before their departure early the next sun.

Unknown to Gray Eagle, Shalee was presently enduring a demanding and weighty experience of her

307

own. Having leisurely enjoyed the weather and beauty of nature before starting her chores of gathering firewood, fetching water in the skins, and washing clothes in the river—the others had completed their daily tasks and returned to the camp—Shalee was humming a song she recalled from childhood as she worked.

Suddenly a spleenish voice snarled accusingly, "You did it, didn't you? They think you're so sweet and innocent, but you're vindictive and hateful! You just can't stand having me around, can you?"

Shalee glanced up at the antagonistic face of Leah Winston in total bewilderment, then flushed with anger at her nasty and perplexing remarks. "I haven't the vaguest idea what you're talking about, Leah. But I suggest you calm yourself and guard your vile tongue. Aren't you forgetting I'm not a white slave; I'm the wife of Wanmdi Hota," she crisply rebuked the sullen and aggressive Leah.

"No, I'm not forgetting anything! You're the one who doesn't know anything," Leah mysteriously hinted, reeking of animosity.

"I know enough to tell me you had better watch your step here."

"You don't say! Or what, Princess Shalee?" Leah snapped contemptuously.

"Or you won't be here much longer," Shalee threatened.

"I think you've already taken care of that problem, haven't you?" the other woman purred sarcastically. "I must really have you worried. What's the matter? Afraid I might steal your man after all?"

"I've heard enough, Leah. Shut up and return to your chores."

"You've heard enough?" Leah taunted disdainfully. "Before Running Wolf sells me today, you'll hear plenty more."

"Sells you today?" Shalee echoed in astonishment.

"Don't play innocent with me! You're behind this malicious sale and we both know it!" An air of sinister malice exuded from her.

"You're wrong, Leah. It's true I want you gone, but the decision was Running Wolf's. Considering your behavior and hatefulness, your surprise at his action escapes me."

Irrationally driven to enmity and desperation, Leah scoffed, "You know why he wants me gone, don't you?"

"I presume it's because of your malicious attitude and possibly your unforgivable flirtation with his son."

"Flirtation? You're teasing or just plain crazy! He wants me gone before I'm showing! Damn their concern for their bloody honor!"

"Showing what?" the naive Shalee inquired.

Leah's chilling laughter distressed her. Was the girl going insane? Was she dangerous? "Showing with the son of Gray Eagle. Hasn't he told you yet? You can't give him another child, but he doesn't want my half-breed bastard either! I told you he was a savage! What civilized man would sell his own child? I suppose he also withheld the news you're unable to give him another child. Didn't you wonder how it was possible to mate with him every day for four years after Bright Arrow's birth and have no more children? You're barren now, Shalee!" she shrieked at the stunned, white-faced Shalee. "One day he'll want more children and take another wife."

Shocked speechless, Shalee gaped at the baneful creature making such horrible accusations. At last, her

309

speech returned. "You're a liar! I might be naive, Leah, but not that dumb! You've never slept with Gray Eagle! How dare you speak such terrible lies! Get out of my sight!"

"How dare you force him to sell me just because you can't stand the idea of another woman giving him a child when you can't! You're afraid he'll want me and the child, aren't you?" Leah challenged deceptively, knowing Shalee lacked the knowledge to refute her claims.

"There isn't any child!" Shalee debated confidently.

"When my belly grows fat and round, will you still deny its presence?" Leah gloated cheerfully.

"If you are pregnant, the child isn't Gray Eagle's!" Shalee shouted.

"I'm a captive here, Shalee. How could I possibly sleep with anyone in secret? I live with Running Wolf, an old man. Gray Eagle is the only man I've spent any time with. In light of my condition, I don't need to relate what happened while we were alone!" she spitefully contended, a shade of mocking reproach in her scathing tone.

Shalee's gaze automatically and uncontrollably slipped to Leah's stomach. The loose garment prevented a hint of what was beneath it. "Why don't you ask your faithful and honorable husband what we were doing when the message arrived of your miraculous survival? Ask him what happened another night in his tepee while Bright Arrow was sleeping at Talking Rock's! Ask him what happened near the river the day you coldly rejected him! Ask him why he visits Running Wolf's tepee when the old man isn't there!" she boldly and wickedly insinuated.

Leah's guileful charges were ignored in light of a slip she had recklessly made. "How do you know I rejected him that afternoon? Is that why you followed him to tempt him with your whorish ways?" Shalee dropped a brazen hint of her own.

Leah's face showed her shock before she could quickly conceal it. "What did you expect after he had me in his power? You know how irresistible and persuasive he can be! How can any woman ignore him after having him? He addicts you like some potent drug. I won't deny I want him. I've desired him since the first minute I laid eyes on him! But now that you've come back, he doesn't need my body anymore! But I still crave his! I can't help myself!" she wantonly confessed. "I'm carrying his child, and there's nothing you can do about it! At least wait until the child's born, then take him to live with you and his father," Leah cunningly entreated, softening her words.

"I don't believe a word you're saying," Shalee argued, dread helplessly washing over her, a flicker of doubt revealed in her eyes.

"It will be easy to prove no other Indian has touched me! Hate me if you must, Shalee, but think of the innocent child. He deserves to be free, to live with his father." Leah feigned concern for the illusionary child.

Shalee rubbed her aching temples. Her mouth felt like cotton. Tremors raced over her chilled body. Gray Eagle hadn't lied to her about Leah; he hadn't! Without her awareness, she twisted her hands over and over in her lap as her respiration became erratic and beads of moisture dotted her upper lip and forehead. But how else could Leah be pregnant? Why would she speak such claims if she couldn't prove them?

"If you doubt me, Shalee, ask him," Leah challenged, viewing the wavering of Shalee's confidence. "What kind of man would deny his own flesh and blood? Even if

311

he tries, the truth will be revealed in his look of guilt. No matter, the truth will show itself very soon," she remarked, caressing her stomach as she smiled dreamily, wishing her words were true.

Such a lie would be easy to disprove, so why was Leah so confident and bold in her daring and dangerous assertion? It couldn't be true; it couldn't! But what of those strange currents between them? What of the way he had allowed Leah to taste his flesh? "You've been after him all along, haven't you? Even before I disappeared, weren't you? We've never been friends! You lied to me! You've done everything you could to cause trouble between us! You're despicable, Leah! While he was grieving for me, you tempted him and taunted him with your likeness to me and with your sluttish skills! If he yielded in a moment of weakness and agony, you are to blame, not him."

"No matter who is to blame, Shalee, an innocent child shouldn't suffer for our lust for each other! Can you honestly be so cruel and selfish? Please don't send me away until the child is born and you accept him as your own," she coaxed the wide-eyed girl.

"You expect me to take your child as mine?" Shalee shrieked in disbelief.

"Why not? You're married to his father! If I keep him, he'll be a despised slave like me. Irregardless of who his mother is, the son of Gray Eagle should have his rightful place at his father's side! Besides, you're half-white; Bright Arrow is also a half-breed."

"How dare you insult my son! Tell me, Leah; who did you cunningly seduce in order to pull this repulsive trick? You may have tempted my husband, but you never seduced him. I'm certain you tried many times, tried anything no matter how despicable; but it never worked. I know," she suddenly and smugly claimed.

"You know nothing! You're afraid he'll want me to replace you once he looks into the face of his newborn son. You're afraid he'll want more sons, and you can't give them to the noble warrior." Leah didn't need much to formulate her assumption, for Shalee hadn't given birth to another child in four years.

Shalee sought to end this nightmare with a bluff of her own. "Even if there was any truth to your claims, which there isn't, why would Gray Eagle be tempted to keep your son when I'm carrying his child? What man in his right mind would permit his wife and his whorish mistress to give birth simultaneously?"

"My child would be born before yours, seeing as I became pregnant first."

"Still, would he allow the birth of your bastard to overshadow the imminent birth of his second heir? You see, dear Leah, I'm not barren after all."

"I don't believe you," Leah shrieked, her fury rising at this defeat. In the heat of her hatred, Leah had birthed a tragic ploy.

"Ask him, if you dare," Shalee challenged, smiling triumphantly.

"I won't let them send me away! I won't be treated like some animal! You know how slaves are abused! How can you let them do this thing?"

"You bring it upon yourself! You had a good life with us. You chose to throw it away. You chose lies and hostility. Blame yourself!"

"If I must, I'll kill you first," Leah threatened wildly. "When you're gone, he'll turn to me again."

"Get out of my sight!" Shalee screamed at her, then

delivered a stunning slap across her face, sending the unprepared Leah backwards to fall to her seat.

Leah sprang up and crouched like a tiger about to spring upon its victim. "You'll pay for that!" she warned. Just as she was about to lunge at Shalee, White Arrow grabbed her arms and painfully imprisoned them behind her back.

Both women looked at him in astonishment, wondering from where he had come. *"Wanhinkpe Ska?"*

He spewed forth wrathful words upon Leah, then asked Shalee if she was all right. Shalee smiled and nodded, then thanked him. *"Pidamaye."*

He smiled at her, intensifying his hold upon Leah until she grimaced and cried out in pain. He suddenly flung her to the ground and kicked her, calling her names. Leah appealed to Shalee for mercy and help. Shalee glared at her, then turned and walked toward camp, leaving her to the furious warrior's mercy and punishment.

Shalee had gone only a short distance when she recalled her possessions. She halted and went back to fetch them, without even glancing at the whining Leah. Leah had threatened to kill her; perhaps a harsh punishment would make her think twice before attempting another vile ruse or thinking lethal dreams. Besides, something was going on inside her head. She needed to be alone. . . .

Shalee carelessly deposited her burdens in the middle of the tepee and went to sit upon her mat. She covered her face with her hands, rocking to and fro. She must relax her body and mind to allow it to roam where it willed. So many images were crashing into the dark barrier of her mind, images that demanded to destroy it, images that demanded to be seen clearly for the first time

314

since her injury. A crack had appeared in the dam of her memory the moment Leah had mentioned children; it had widened with every word she spoke afterwards. There was no doubt in her mind at all now; Gray Eagle had not and would not sleep with Leah.

"Shalee?" Gray Eagle called to her, dreading her state of mind. White Arrow had brought Leah to him and his father; he had related part of their argument near the river. Leah would be punished, but what damaging lies had she told to his beloved wife? Why was Shalee acting so strangely? What had that wicked girl said and done to his love? "Shalee?" he tried to capture her attention once more.

"*Iyasni, Wanmdi Hota,*" she commanded sternly. "*Iyotanka!*"

He stared at her bowed head and hidden face. She had ordered him to silence, to sit down! "Hear my words, Shalee. Leah speaks falsely. Do not allow her words to trouble you," he gravely entreated.

"*Iyasni, Wanmdi Hota!*" she shrieked angrily, fearing he would vanquish her train of thought and halt her progress. "*Shalee iwaktaya. Iyotanka o-winza. Wastay pezuta. Wakantanka wayaketo. Wilhanmna ku-wa. Shalee wayaketo, wohdate. Wiyakpa wowanyake. Shalee htani si. Shalee wookiye wocin,*" she hurriedly related.

Gray Eagle was bewildered and alarmed. Why was she babbling about coming dreams, about wanting peace, about the Great Spirit seeing, about Shalee seeing, about good medicine, and about bright visions? Why did she want him to sit down on the mat and keep silent?

Suddenly she was crying! "Shalee?" he hinted in panic.

She looked up at him and took his hand, pulling him

down beside her. *"Kokipi sni, Wanmdi Hota. Waste cedake. Leah kaskapi. Leah witkowin. Leah hiya wastay. Shalee Wanmdi Hota winyan."*

He stared in greater confusion. She was telling him not to fear! Leah was a captive, a whore! Leah was bad! Then, she found it necessary to claim herself as his woman, to say she loved him! What was the meaning of her words and actions? Abruptly, he realized she was speaking only Oglala! In private, they still spoke English, for it seemed easier for her. Was she trying to make some point? What? Why?

"You're speaking Oglala," he remarked, his voice strained with warring emotions.

Shalee laughed merrily. "And you, my husband, are speaking *wasichu*."

He shook his head to clear this web of mystery and alarm. "What did Leah say to you to upset you this way? You talk and act unlike Shalee."

She scanned his worried expression. "My love, my one and only true love . . ." She caressed his cheek and smiled radiantly. *"Kokipi sni, Wanmdi Hota. Shalee Oglala; Shalee ia Oglala. Wanmdi Hota hiya wasichu; Wanmdi Hota ia wasichu,"* she mirthfully teased, savoring the telling of her wonderful news.

"I do fear, Shalee. You are Oglala and my woman. I speak *wasichu* to understand you," he panted in exasperation.

She covered her mouth to suppress her happy giggles. His brow lifted inquisitively. *"Ia Oglala,"* she coaxed, wishing him to communicate in Sioux.

"This is not the time to practice your new skills," he chided her.

"I need no practice, dear husband. I have spoken your

316

tongue for many years," she stated lightly, wondering how long it would take before he comprehended the truth of her recovery. She grinned mischievously.

Perplexed by her odd behavior, he decided it was best to humor her, to avoid upsetting her further. He asked her to tell him what Leah had said to her.

She shrugged her shoulders and stated calmly that it didn't matter, for it was all lies. She said she agreed with Running Wolf's decision to sell her since she was trying to cause so much trouble. She casually told him Leah loved and desired him, but she wouldn't ever have him! But he was struck speechless for a time when she related Leah's daring scheme about the baby. She sighed ruefully when she informed him she had slapped Leah and ordered her to silence!

"She lied! She does not carry my child! I have never mated with her!" he shouted his denials.

She laughed happily. For the first time, she spoke in English, "I know, Gray Eagle. You have never desired or loved any woman since meeting me. I trust you and love you with all my heart. I know Leah tempted you many times. But I also know you never betrayed me or our love, not even when you thought I was dead."

He lowered his head to shield the guilt that must be shining in his ebony eyes, guilt she was acquainted with and understood. "Look at me, Gray Eagle," she softly commanded. "Didn't you hear me? I trust you. Nothing happened between you and Leah."

He mopped the beads of sweat from his upper lip. "How can you believe me and trust me when you cannot recall our love?"

"That's why I can believe you and trust you; I do remember. Haven't you realized by now that I'm

317

speaking fluent Sioux? Don't you wonder why?" she teased.

His head jerked upwards and he stared at her. "Yes, my love; I remember everything," she answered his unspoken question. "You forgot to tell me that after my people lashed you, you bit my hand to punish them through me. You forgot to tell me I was wearing a beautiful white dress the night we were joined, the night I foolishly tried to escape your love. You forgot to tell me how you teased me with the feathers the day you fought for me. You forgot to tell me we made love for hours by a stream at sunset after you bluffed my release at Fort Pierre. You forgot to tell me how I got the white eagle *wanapin*. Or how I made your first buckskin shirt. Or how you stayed at my side during Bright Arrow's birth. Or how you chose the name Sun Cloud for our next son. You also forgot many important things, my adorable husband."

"You recall everything?" he asked in amazement.

"Everything, the good and the bad, the happy and the sad," she jested.

Elation filled him. He seized her and hugged her fiercely. "It is true?"

"Sha, it is true," she vowed between giggles and kisses.

He captured her face between his hands and gazed longingly into her sparkling eyes. "I feared you would never recall our life," he confessed.

"Didn't you once tell me that the Great Spirit would return my mind when the time came? The time came today. When Leah threatened our love, Wakantanka revealed the truth to me."

"Leah threatened our love?" he repeated in puzzlement. "How so?"

318

"When she claimed she was carrying your child. When she said I was barren."

"Barren?" he echoed.

"That means I can't have any more children, but I can. When the Great Spirit sees it is time, He will also answer that prayer. Sun Cloud will ride at your side one day," she vowed confidently.

"Why would Leah speak such lies?" he pondered aloud.

"She wanted to destroy our love. What better way than to bear your son? To prove you had betrayed me with her?" she hinted tenderly.

Gray Eagle shuddered, thinking how close he had come to making her lie a possible fact. If he had yielded to her, there would be no way he could positively deny he was the father. He sighed in relief and thanked Wakantanka for preventing such a cruel punishment for his weakness. "My seed has entered no body except yours; this I swear to you."

"It isn't necessary, my love. I know you love only me, as I love only you."

Fury suddenly washed over him. "Leah must be punished and sold!" he fiercely declared, recognizing the damage she could have caused.

"No, my love, not yet. Leah wouldn't have made such a claim if she couldn't prove it," she reasoned aloud.

"But she cannot! I did not mate with her!" he proclaimed.

"Not you, but someone else. Such a claim could too easily be disproved. She must be pregnant. If so, we can't endanger the life of an innocent child by lashing her," she argued, her gentle nature showing vividly.

He smiled and caressed her cheek. "It will take many

moons to seek such a truth. If we cannot punish her, what will we do with her?"

"First, find out who the father is; then, decide whether to sell her before or after the baby's birth. If we sold her now, some other warrior or wife could harm the child by punishing her harshly. Leah does have a way of infuriating people beyond control," she hinted contritely.

"How is it possible? She is slave to my father. I have seen her cast her eyes upon no other warrior except . . ."

When he apprehensively halted, she laughed and remarked gaily, "Except Wanmdi Hota. Still, a woman doesn't get with child alone."

"Come, we will force the truth from her lips," he decided, getting up and pulling her to her feet.

"Yes, perhaps that would be best," she agreed.

They left their tepee to confront Leah. They walked to Running Wolf's tepee to find Leah in tears, shaking in fear before the withering words of White Arrow and the dauntless Sioux chief. The moment they entered the tepee, heavy with an air of hostility, Leah ran to her and fell to her knees, throwing her arms around Shalee's thighs and pleading for help.

"Please, Shalee, you must help me!" she cried in panic, honestly terrified for the first time. "They're going to lash me! They're sending me away! Help me, please. I promise never to hurt you again. Please . . ."

Shalee gazed down at the distraught girl, annoying sympathy pulling at her. Leah had been wrong, even wicked and cruel. But did any woman deserve such harsh torture? She knew the demand of the lash. Once she had received five lashes for attempting to escape, for humiliating her captor and now husband. She cringed at the thought of witnessing another white woman undergo such a savage torture. She quelled her anger and resentment to make a decision she would live to regret. . . .

"Listen to me closely, Leah Winston. Are you truly pregnant? If so, who is the father? I have regained my memory, so I know without a shadow of doubt it cannot be Gray Eagle. I know of your past sins," she hinted meaningfully. She hadn't dared tell Gray Eagle of her suspicions. She prayed she was doing the right thing. If it was possible she had guessed who the father was, she couldn't allow his son to become a lowly slave. Yet, she feared the revelation and confirmation of her suspicion.

Before Shalee could change her mind, Leah caught her insinuation and grasped another daring and deceptive ploy. "You know about us? Did you tell his son the truth? He'll kill me! A powerful and proud man like that would never accept a half-breed child!" she craftily debated, fooling Shalee completely.

"Then it's true? You were sleeping with him?" she probed, their English lost to all ears except those of the warrior at her side.

"How did you know?" Leah asked, watching her closely as she struggled for time to think and to plan this daring scheme. Would it work?

Knowing her husband could understand every word, Shalee wisely replied, "I suspected the truth the day before my attack near the stream. Since I lost my memory that day, I didn't remember those suspicions until moments ago. Is he the child's father?" she boldly demanded.

Leah dropped her head to conceal her face as she lied, "Yes. . . ."

"Then why did you tell me the child was Gray Eagle's?" Shalee angrily probed, as the others witnessed some critical drama taking place, one they didn't understand yet.

"Because I love him and want him. I thought if I drove you apart, he would turn to me. I hoped I could convince him the child was his. I didn't think you would have the nerve to tell him what I said," she replied, calling upon her perceptions of Shalee's character and nature to say the right things to win her trust and assistance.

"If I hadn't regained my memory, perhaps your vile scheme might have worked on me, but never on Gray Eagle. You underestimate his intelligence and cunning. You also underestimate his love and loyalty to me."

"I was crazy with love and desire for him. You have him! Can't you understand my feelings? It was wrong, and I'm sorry. I was terrified and desperate. I didn't have much time to trick him. I knew he would keep me and protect me if he thought I was carrying his second son."

"Why didn't you tell the father?" she challenged.

"Tell him?" she echoed in disbelief. "He would kill me! Do you think he would allow anyone to learn what happened between us? He only used me for a short time, then cast me aside. How could I tell him I was pregnant?" she debated incredulously, cunningly.

This information staggering, the enraged warrior briefly forgot Shalee's memory had returned. Gray Eagle demanded in English, "What man does she speak of, Shalee? Who would dishonor himself in this manner? She is a white whore; no Oglala warrior would place his seeds within her to grow," he sneered contemptuously.

"See!" she exclaimed in horror. "The only thing they guard with their lives is their bloody honor! He'll never

322

confess to such a cruel deed!"

"Who?" Gray Eagle harshly repeated.

"I can't tell you," Leah fearfully refused.

Gray Eagle seized her arm and yanked her to her feet. He painfully twisted upon it, extracting a scream of agony. "Speak his name, *Witkowin!*"

When Leah shook her head, he applied more pressure. Shalee started to interfere, but didn't. She would later berate herself for her silence. She was savagely torn between right and wrong, between justice and punishment. If the child was his son, didn't he have the right to know, to claim him, to keep him, to prevent his enslavement and abuse?

"Running Wolf!" the name left Leah's lips as Shalee wavered in doubt.

Gray Eagle's face grew livid with rage at her insult. His fury was unleashed. He forcefully shoved the offensive slave from him. For an instant he was tempted to kill her. When he menacingly started toward her, Leah scrambled to her feet and sought refuge behind the chief. She was shaking in terror. Never had she seen such a look of sheer hatred or murderous intent upon that handsome face.

"It's true; I swear it," Leah shouted in panic.

"I shall cut out your lying tongue!" he shouted at her, drawing his knife. He was suddenly aware of speaking English, but the truth demanded he continue this infuriating discussion. No matter now, Leah knew of his secret talent! She would die for this unforgivable insult!

Shalee seized his arm and cried out in alarm, "No, Wanmdi Hota. She might speak the truth."

When Gray Eagle focused his astounded gaze upon her pale face, she quickly added, "I think they were . . . I think they did . . . sleep together several times. Ask Running Wolf if she lies," she softly coaxed.

"Ask my father, our chief, to defend himself against such lies?" he exclaimed disbelievingly. "Does your white blood betray you, wife? You take a white slave's side against my father's?" he charged unwittingly amidst his anguish and turmoil, cutting her deeply.

Her face drained of what little color was left in it. "No, Gray Eagle, it does not. I'm not taking Leah's side, but I saw and heard things long ago that tell me she speaks the truth."

"Then your ears and eyes deceive you, wife! My father would never touch a white slave! No Oglala warrior would mate with a white slave!"

"Not even you?" she sent her stinging barb home.

Stunned, he gazed at her. "You are my wife," he coldly snapped.

"When you took me, I was not your wife," she reminded him, pained by his hurtful words, temporarily forgetting Leah's presence and keen ears.

"That was different!" he argued.

"Was it? You saw and took a white woman you desired. Did it matter at the time that I was your lowly slave?" she challenged artfully and boldly.

"If you recall your life here, Shalee, then why do you speak to you husband in such a disrespectful manner? It is not our way."

"I speak back to the cruelty of my husband's words," she replied.

"You do so to defend a white whore over my father?" he probed.

"No. If the child is his, doesn't he have the right to know, to prevent its enslavement and cruel treatment?"

324

she reasoned sadly.

"She lies! Running Wolf's seeds are old; he has not placed them in the body of a white slave. He would not," he stubbornly argued.

"Older men than Running Wolf have sired children. Ask him and end these cruel words between us," she pleaded.

"To ask him would reveal my lack of trust in him. It would shame him and me to show I wonder at such a repulsive act. I cannot!"

Shalee deliberated this brutal and weighty scene. "Then say only that Leah is with child. See what he feels and says to that news," she suggested.

"I play no false games with my own father," he blatantly refused.

"Please, Wanmdi Hota. I promise to say nothing more if you just tell him she's with child," she compromised.

"You will say nothing more?" he asked wistfully.

"Not one word," she vowed, suddenly reserved.

He gave her offer of truce some thought. What harm could it do? It seemed the only way to convince her Leah was lying and to prevent further words between them. He met his father's baffled look and casually announced that Leah said she was with child. He was about to ask if they should sell her quickly, but the startled expression upon Running Wolf's face prevented another word from him.

The chief shuddered, then whirled to gape at Leah. His eyes flew to her stomach as he demanded if she was pregnant. Leah lowered her lashes in mock shame and nodded. His gaze fused with White Arrow's and some intangible message passed between them. He looked as if he didn't know what to say or to do, alarming Gray Eagle. Running Wolf had no way of knowing if Leah had

325

proclaimed him the father, but he assumed from the scene he had just witnessed that she had. His child?

Running Wolf faced Leah and demanded if she was telling the truth. She voiced a shaky, *"Sha."* Running Wolf paled and trembled.

Gray Eagle approached his father and stared into his face, a face lined with shame and anguish. He couldn't believe what he was viewing and thinking. *"A'ta?"* he hinted.

"Sha, michenkshe?" he replied, his tone empty and sad.

Before he could control himself, he blurted out, "Leah claims the child is yours. What punishment do you command for her lies?"

The old man's shoulders slumped. He could not lie to his son, not again. Once before he had denied another son, and many had paid dearly for his selfish denial, including Gray Eagle and Shalee. Could he declare innocence? Could he hide the shame that flooded his body? Could he even look his son in the eye with such dishonor staining his face?

At his self-incriminating silence and shameful behavior, Gray Eagle scathingly challenged, "Did you place your seeds within her?"

"I am not worthy to be chief, my son," he subtly answered.

Gray Eagle's heart was seared with pain and disillusionment. How could such a thing be possible? "Leah slept upon your mat?" He demanded a clear answer.

"For five moons when the mating fever was upon me. My body and mind were weakened by her temptations," the chief raggedly confessed.

Those words told Gray Eagle more than he cared to hear. He, too, had been tempted by Leah in a moment of weakness and distress. He had resisted her skills, but his father was older and weaker. Shame washed over him again at the recall of Leah's evil magic. Yet, he could not reveal such evil to his father. As painful as it was to admit, he realized the old man was just as proud and tormented. Could he sell a child of his own seed? Shalee was right; a man must learn of his own child. Shalee . . .

He turned to apologize for his harsh words and glacial challenge to her honesty. Shalee was gone. Why had she left? Perhaps to allow them to settle this offensive matter? Perhaps to spare Running Wolf the added shame of her knowledge of this deed? He would seek her out soon and talk with her. Now, there was another pressing matter to decide. . . .

But Leah's senses were reeling with the curious facts she had overheard between Shalee and Gray Eagle. What was the meaning of such wild claims and accusations? During her first talk with Shalee, the princess had alluded to being a white pioneer, to coming here from the East. The princess had curiously asked what an Indian was! How could the daughter of Chief Black Cloud not know of the awesome legend that ruled the Indian territory? Why had the loss of five previous years made her appear and behave white, all white? Why had she reverted to English? Shouldn't she at least know Blackfoot? Something didn't add up here! Shalee, ravished as an enemy? Shalee, captured by this intrepid warrior? Shalee, once his white slave? Could this mysterious information be deciphered and used against them somehow? Perhaps . . .

Chapter Fifteen

The discussion in Running Wolf's tepee was exacting and cumbersome. The crux of the agonizing problem boiled down to the question of which was more important: the pride of Running Wolf or the life of his unborn child, a child who existed only in the treacherous mind of Leah Winston. The three warriors argued, debated, talked, and reasoned. What was the best decision for all concerned—excluding the white girl who had brazenly and willfully instigated this disastrous matter.

White Arrow and Gray Eagle noted a critical and distressing fact as the grave conversation continued for a lengthy time; Running Wolf's male ego, inflated at the idea of having sired another child at his age, severely clouded his logic in regard to the dissenting troubles such a horrific birth could bring to him and to his people. Shalee was the proclaimed daughter of a Blackfoot chief and his white captive Jenny; yet, she was now an honored and loved princess, wife to the Oglala chief's own son. Running Wolf pondered aloud if it could be so different for his child. Which blood was stronger, the Oglala or the *wasichu?* Could he condemn his own child to a life of hardships and hatred, to embittering and perilous enslavement? Could he bear to envision his child suffering at the hands of another warrior of a distant tribe? His masculine pride and parental instincts played

328

havoc with his logic. Too, he had made this tragic mistake once before.... Yet, he could never reveal the antecedent motive for his present seditious behavior.

The other two warriors recognized his emotional dilemma and appealed to his wisdom and courage. They tried to show the chief the precarious conflicts this situation could inspire. The birth of his child by this particular girl could cause dissension and resentment among his warriors and people. How would his followers feel if their chief took a woman who was not of their kind, especially since his own son had already chosen a woman who was half-white? It was an implicit law to marry among your own kind. Besides, Leah was already a disgusting predicament. If she bore the son of the chief, she would become impossible to deal with or to handle. They touched a sensitive nerve when they reminded Running Wolf of the dark stain this episode would place upon his honor, not only here in this camp but also in others.

In frustration and anxiety, Running Wolf roared, "Why did the Great Spirit allow this evil to touch me and my tepee? Can I slay the woman who carries my seed? Can I send her away to never place my eyes upon it? Surely you must see my grief and confusion, my son? What if this girl was Shalee, when she was Alisha? What if the child in question was Bright Arrow? What if you stood in my tracks now?" he challenged wretchedly.

"I see and feel both your shame and sadness, Father. But Shalee is the daughter of Black Cloud. Leah is a white slave, one with cunning evil in her heart and blood. Do you wish to pass such evil to your seed? Even when Shalee was Alisha, she was unlike Leah. She was born good, with an Indian heart. The blood of Black Cloud flows stronger than her *wasichu* mother's in her body. Such is not true with Leah. My life and yours do not match," he rebutted patiently and lovingly.

White Arrow made a vital point previously ignored, "What if the white girl lies? You slept upon her mat only a few times, Running Wolf. What if she uses such times to trick us? What if she does not carry a child?" he politely contended, without hinting at the old man's likely inability to produce a child at his advanced age.

Both men, father and son, focused their concentration and gazes upon their friend. White Arrow continued, "We must watch her closely. If she does not come in the woman's way soon, we will know she speaks true. If she does, we know she lies. A new moon will clear this matter. We must be patient. We must tell no one of our suspicions. If Leah does not carry your child, we will punish her and sell her. I think she lies. She is evil."

White Arrow's suggestions and assumptions filled them with excitement and relief, especially Gray Eagle. Leah had lied to him many times before; she had attempted to destroy his relationship with Shalee; she had tried to seduce him. She had first claimed the unborn child was his. Was no evil too great to challenge her? Perhaps this was another brazen lie! Even if she was pregnant, Running Wolf might not be the father!

"You speak wise and cunning, White Arrow. We must hold this deed hidden in our hearts. A new moon will reveal the truth. If Leah lies, I say she is sold that day. No, Father," Gray Eagle instantly changed his mind, eyes glowing with vengeful justice. "Do not sell Leah. She is evil and her magic great to cloud your eyes. Find a warrior whose strength and cunning are greater than hers, one who hates the whites and will not be tempted to

330

fall prey to her dark evil. Give her to him as a gift. A man does not hesitate to punish a prize he has not traded for. If she is free, her value to him will be less."

"Will they not wonder why I give away a strong slave? Will they think I am too weak to control her?" the chief pressed apprehensively.

Gray Eagle laughed cynically. "Many times our enemies the Comanche and Apache have hinted at truce with us. If we offer them truce and many presents, they will not question our deed. We will send fine horses, gifts, and the white girl to Night Rider or Thundering Wind. They live far to where Wi ends his day. Leah will trouble us no more," he concluded.

"Our enemies cannot be trusted to keep their truce," Running Wolf stated truthfully.

"It does not matter. We are stronger than the Comanche or the Apache. Is your face not worth the sacrifice of many presents and the doing of this false deed?" Gray Eagle slyly hinted, grinning devilishly.

"Only a trick to be rid of the white girl?" White Arrow probed.

"Yes," Gray Eagle casually informed them. "The offer of truce will cover the deed from all eyes."

"Yes," Running Wolf quickly concurred, his eyes brightening and his shoulders coming erect. "We will wait for the moon to reveal her words, then we will send her to . . . Thundering Wind," he made his decision, knowing there was no way Leah could entrap that puissant warrior who was known to slay whites for simply gazing at him too long or too boldly.

"It will be so. We must tell no one of this matter."

"You have saved my face and revealed much love and forgiveness," the chief remarked to both men. "My heart

331

will not forget such deeds."

Leah picked up the last water skin to head back to camp. All her plans were ruined now. How long could she conceal the truth? It was only a matter of time before they would know she had lied. What would they do to her then? Terror filled her. Such a trick would surely bring deadly reprisals, tortures too horrible to imagine. What a fool she had been! Shalee, it was all her fault. If she hadn't returned from the dead, things would have eventually worked out for her. Removing her now would be impossible, for she would be on guard against any threat or danger. There was only one thing left to try; she must tempt Running Wolf beyond his control; she must get herself pregnant!

After all, if he believed she was already carrying his child, there would be no reason to deny his carnal desires. The arrogant savage! He was so damn proud of his prowess! His pride must become the weapon to bring him down! Surely he would alter his lowly opinion of her since she was accepting his aging seeds? Surely affection, or at least tolerance, would result from his excessive conceit and joy? She must plan this matter carefully. If she could entice him to lie with her each night, surely she would become pregnant! Time was short, for her monthly was approaching; its heavy flow would be impossible to hide from his astute mind and keen eyes. Time, why was it always against her? If her desperate ploy failed, she must plan to escape the day her monthly began. And on that eventful day, she would kill Shalee before she left! Shalee had destroyed all her dreams, and she would pay, as promised. . . .

Too bad that splendid savage had managed to clear his wits that critical night in time to prevent her seduction!

At first, he had been too drugged to resist her. If only she had enjoyed him to the fullest that night, then he could not be positive the child wasn't his! Vengeful lights flowed in her emerald eyes as another brazen scheme hastily formulated in her devious mind: What if Gray Eagle couldn't recall what happened between them that first night before his mind cleared? After all, he was heavily dazed on some drug. Could she convince him they had actually made love before he regained his senses? If he couldn't recall that night clearly . . . visions of Shalee's anguish at such a betrayal glimmered in her mind's eye. Even if she lost her tolerant life here, she could have her revenge upon all of them, especially Shalee and Gray Eagle. She could easily cast doubts over Gray Eagle simply by revealing their intimate contact! Running Wolf and White Arrow would be stunned by their warrior's conduct, not to mention the staggering blow to Shalee's trust and love! Did she dare to make one final attempt to seek this brazen ecstasy? Yes . . .

It was very late when Gray Eagle returned to his tepee. Shalee was sitting near the fire, absently endeavoring to keep his meal warm without ruining it. Bright Arrow had eaten long ago and was fast asleep. A gloomy aura hung depressingly heavy in the still air of their tepee. When he came forward and sat down beside her, she did not look at him. Instead, she quietly served him his food.

His heart plagued by her reticent constraint, he accepted the food offered by his wife. He ate mechanically, without awareness of what he was consuming, his appetite gone. This should be a happy day for them, but Leah had spoiled it. Antipathy and malice sat down to eat with him.

When the remains were cleared away, he watched her

through anxious eyes, trying to find the words to break this oppressive silence. "Shalee," he hesitantly began.

Shalee stood up, her heart in a vicious turmoil. "I need fresh air. I will return soon," she stated in a voice tight with the fierce emotions that churned turbulently within her. She left him sitting there, pondering whether to leave her alone or rush after her.

She slowly walked through the camp, which was preparing for the night. She strolled a short distance from camp, heading for a cluster of boulders not far away, the massive rocks looming dark against the indigo heavens. Rays of moonlight danced among the wildflowers, scrub trees, and wavering grasses. A gentle breeze played in her auburn hair, blowing wisps across her face. She automatically pushed them aside as she continued her purging trek into the welcoming arms of darkness.

Night birds sent forth their soulful notes to their mates, their mates answering in like fashion. As if to not be outdone, several owls began their matching game of hide-and-seek. Nocturnal insects joined in this musical salute to the freedom of life here on the Plains, the cicadas easily claiming the loudest voice. The mournful howl of a coyote traveled across the shadowy terrain, also seeking his mate. What a soothing and tranquil place this was! Even the sooty night could not conceal the untamed beauty of untouched Nature.

As her gaze roamed over the vista left behind and the one entreating her to come forward, she was amazed by the vivid difference between the two landscapes so close together. The ground became sandier the further she walked. Vegetation grew scant and offered a lucid contrast to that left behind. How strange that the earth would suddenly crave to become barren and harsh. It was like a comparison of life and death; yet, this area was far from dead. Other creatures and growth populated it. She halted to allow her eyes to visually walk for the length of their ability. Despite its wildness, it was captivatingly beautiful and demandingly perilous.

In a mystical way, the two vistas alluded to the striking contrasts between Gray Eagle and herself, the unconquerable warrior and the gentle English girl. Like the complexion of the verdant forest, hers was ever changing and ever maturing. A promise of a serene aura and a sheer delight in being were revealed in both. As with the river, her flow of life was willingly constrained by her surrounding banks. She was alive and green, offering freely of her gifts. She made very few demands, but gave much. She could be as carefree and colorful as the wildflowers or as stoic and strong as the tall trees. She could be as tranquil as the mirror-surfaces of the small ponds or as mischievous as the animals that came to drink there.

But Gray Eagle was reflected in the presentation of life before her. He was demanding and often unrelenting. He was complex and resolute, no matter the passage of time or the seasonal requirements. He was mysterious and mercurial, his shifting moods as drastic as the temperature changes during the frigid nights and fiery days upon that perilous land. He could be prickly like the cactus and bramble bush; he could be as deadly and secretive as the vipers and scorpions that lived out there. An awesome aura pervaded each of them, the invincible warrior and the aggressive desert. His body was as hard as the massive boulders out there, his heart often as immovable. Like the panorama before her, he wanted things to remain as they were forever. But life would not permit that course. As this rugged land was unwelcoming to strangers, so did Gray Eagle deal harshly with anyone or anything who dared to enter his domain and try to change him. Why did he fight against the scant beauty offered freely to him, as the desert resisted nearly all floral beauty except the stubborn and tenacious cacti and yuccas? Was it so difficult to harnass his exacting power, to generously yield to new life?

"Shalee," he spoke softly from her side, startling her. "Why do you wish to be alone on this great day?" he worriedly asked, knowing her reasons only too clearly.

"I needed to think. Even after all this time together, some things never change, Gray Eagle, just like that desert," she sadly stated, pointing to the view before them.

"Your words confuse me," he remarked, eyeing her intently.

"Our life is like that desert out there. You allowed me to enter your fierce domain, but you never forget I am an intruder here. You tolerate my presence as long as I offer no threat of change to you. But when the winds of evil blow over your lands, you punish me for their damage. I am as much a vulnerable trespasser in your life as I would be out there. As long as I conform to your needs, you tolerate me. But if I briefly step from the shadow of your awesome wing, you see me as a betrayer, as white. As you seize me and return me to your shadow, your talons are sharp and painful. Many times you have lacerated my heart with them, but I had thought such days of danger were past," she dejectedly stated.

She sighed heavily, then continued, "But when it came to a choice between accepting shame upon the face of your Oglala father or listening to the tormenting words of your white wife, you would rather think me a wicked liar and viciously attack me rather than believe he was capable of giving himself to a white woman. Perhaps it was your lingering resentment of me that stirred your lips to attack me. One thing for certain, you have never forgotten or forgiven my white heritage. I saw it in your eyes and heard it in your voice. My heart is heavy, for I fear you never will. No matter how long we are together, something always seems to come along to remind you of our differences. The white barrier will always be there to plague us; for even the awesome power of Gray Eagle can never destroy it. Yet, you are compelled to try, for my sake."

"Your words trouble me, Grass Eyes. I do not mean to hurt you."

Tears stung her forest-green eyes. She swallowed the constricting lump in her throat. She inhaled several times to master her warring emotions. "But you have hurt me, my husband," she quietly informed the tense warrior. "These past moons have been difficult for us. Only through the love and kindness of the Great Spirit was I spared and returned to your life-circle. I have lived in your tepee and loved you for many winters; I have borne our son. I have become Indian in all ways, except for my skin color. I have changed and adjusted to you and your people, to your way of life. I have asked little from you, only your love and acceptance. Yet, some part of you is withheld from me. When trouble touches our life, you become a stranger to me; you see and treat me differently. You close your wings around your body and deny me their comfort. It strikes fear and sadness in my heart and mind when you become Indian rather than my husband. Is Running Wolf more important to you than your own wife?" she painfully flung at him. "Is his honor greater than mine, his words more acceptable? If our words differ, must I be viewed the liar and he the unquestionable truth-teller? Am I capable of such treachery, but he is not? How many pains and winters will it take before you trust and love me as I do you, before I am Indian?"

"I cannot call back my harsh words, but I ask you to understand their reasons," he tenderly entreated, pulling her around to face him. When her head remained lowered, he lifted her chin to fuse their gazes. "I love you, Shalee, more than my life or my father. When I heard such traitorous words, it was not you I attacked, but the words. They sliced into my heart and my mind brutally rejected them. He is my father!" he stressed in anguish. "How could I believe such evil of him, even when the truth came from my love? I fiercely resisted them, thinking my rage would make them false. Even now when Running Wolf speaks them, my heart rebels. My heart wars with my mind. Do I persuade him to slay my own brother or to sell him to another warrior? Do I deny my own anguish and advise him to keep Leah and the child? Do I ignore the warning signs of conflict within our tribe? Do I offer him love and understanding? Do I scold him and dishonor him? Since I left my mother's body, I have been taught to think of my laws and people first, then myself. I have battled and hated our white enemies. Yet, you entered my life and I have never been the same again. I denied all I was and believed to take you and love you. Only White Arrow knows you are white. I have kept your secret from my own father's ears. When I argued against his desire for a white woman, guilt filled my heart and battled me. Once you told me, 'Words say we are enemies, but hearts do not.' It is so, for I love only you. Still, the words of my people and laws challenge me to prove your place in my life-circle. Surely the Great Spirit agrees, for He allows you to remain with me. Evil and trouble brew here, Shalee. Leah is not like you. It was not wrong for me to take you, but it is wrong for Running Wolf to claim Leah. Spirits warn me to fight against her, but do I have the right to do so loving you?"

"I understand how deeply this matter hurts you, Gray Eagle. Leah does not belong with us. But it is too late to halt the damage she can do. I had hoped to spare you this agony and shame, but I could not. Who has the right to force a man to deny his own child? Does it matter if Leah tricked your father? Does his brief weakness or humiliation count more than his child? Perhaps I shouldn't have said anything, but I felt the truth should be revealed. If things had been different long ago, it could have been me and our son in a similar position. Even as your white captive, could you have denied us and sold me? I think not. Which pride is greater: to father a son or to prevent any small stain upon your face? Honor can be regained; a lost child cannot. Which guilt is larger: guilt over the mating or guilt over denying a child and endangering his life? There are no simple answers. Such deeds demand high prices. It is Running Wolf's place to decide which price to meet, not yours or mine or our people's. Leah is not important, only the child. He will be your brother, an innocent child; could I hold such secrets within me? Would you not suspect them? To withhold the truth would be the same as lying and deceiving. I want no such things between us. You must come to terms with this lingering resentment of my white

339

blood. We cannot change it. You must open the wound, cleanse it, and permit it to heal. If not, the festering will always be painful and destructive to us. Your people believe I am half-Indian; why must you continue to feel guilty that I am not? The Great Spirit allowed the trick and has guarded it well. Throw away your guilt and resentment before they destroy our love," she urged him, eyes misty and entreating.

"You speak wisely, Little One. Love sees no shame. No matter the price, I could never lose you. Perhaps the illness that claimed your memory and made you white for a time also caused me to view you as white again. I did not mean to do so. For many winters, you have been only Indian to me. It will be so again. I will pray to Wakantanka for strength and wisdom never to hurt you again. Return the light of happiness and forgiveness to your eyes, and I will try never to remove it again," he huskily promised.

His stirring words made her realize a point she had not considered; she had been acting white for weeks. He was right about another point; he had denied all he was to claim her. Too, Leah's successful ploy gnawed at his pride, defeat being an unwelcome stranger to him. What a precarious predicament! Thank God her love had not submitted to Leah's cunning schemes! How would she ever accept another woman's child as his? If only she could comprehend a woman like Leah . . . she could not.

She smiled up at him. "I believe you, my love; you battled my words and not me. I was simply too hurt and stunned to realize this before. What happens now?" she sighed in frustration and dread, hugging him tightly.

His strong arms eased around her slender body and held her possessively against his stalwart frame. "Wa-

340

kantanka must solve this riddle for us. White Arrow thinks Leah lies; he thinks a coming moon will reveal her treachery," he said, submitting new hope.

She leaned back and looked up at him. "What do you mean?" she pressed, suspense edging into her voice and relief flooding her sea-green eyes.

"Perhaps Leah's daring was not in tricking my father to her mat, but in claiming a child from their joinings. When it is time for her woman's way, the truth will shine brightly like Wi. We must wait and watch."

"You mean she might not be pregnant?" she exploded in astonishment.

"White Arrow thinks she is cunning and terrified. He thinks she lies."

Shalee contemplated this new suggestion. What if Leah was lying? If so, all of their problems were solved. But why would she tell a lie that could be so easily unmasked? If she wasn't pregnant now, there was no way she . . . "Warn your father to be on guard for her tricks!" she hastily advised.

When his brow lifted inquisitively, she hurriedly explained, "If she is desperate and tempts him to sleep with her again, he might fall prey to her spell again. If he thinks her already carrying his child, what harm could another joining do? An aging man's pride in his prowess is great, and Leah is very desirable," she conjectured meaningfully.

A scowl darkened his handsome features. "You speak wise again. If his guard is down and his pride great, her evil magic might make her lie true. I must speak with him. Even if she bears his son, she will be sent away after his birth. We will help him raise his child, my brother."

Shalee laughed and quipped to lighten the aura around

them. "What if it is a sister? Even noble chiefs have daughters, too."

He chuckled and caressed her cheek. "A girl child would be more acceptable than a boy," he promptly announced.

"Why?" she curiously inquired.

"A chief's son follows his path; he stands above others. If the Great Spirit called me to join him, Running Wolf's second son would become chief. A half-breed could not. This would not be true of a girl child."

"I see," she murmured in mock annoyance. "A female is not as valuable as a man?" she teased impishly. "Surely the intrepid Gray Eagle does not worry that a mere half-breed brother will outshine his many coups?"

He laughed heartily. "Your tongue dares much, wife. Gray Eagle fears and cowers to no man, only one cunning white girl," he playfully confessed. "But a sister would cause less conflict than a brother. Even a chief's son born of an Indian maiden of another warring tribe must fight to earn his place as chief. Half-breeds are filled with resentment in such matters. Often tribes are torn apart by those who side with and against such a leader. In my heart and mind, I know the Oglala would never follow Leah's son. We must pray for a girl child," he stated gravely.

Unintentionally recalling the half-breed scout who had once befriended, protected, loved, and tragically betrayed her, she knew his words were accurate. To live as a despicable half-breed was worse than to exist as a lowly white slave. How very demanding and destructive were prejudice and excessive pride. It was distressing to realize what marvelous destinies such people were cruelly denied. She didn't need to ask about their son's half-white heritage, for Bright Arrow was viewed as Indian, as she was. How fortunate for both of them. . . .

"You are right, my love; a half-breed woman is more tolerable than a half-breed chief's son," she astutely concurred. "I am grateful the Great Spirit chose not to stain our son with such an existence. I will do nothing to remind your people I am white."

"Our people," he mildly chided her.

She smiled radiantly and nodded. "I am Princess Shalee, nothing more or less," she happily concluded.

"You are far more, my love," he corrected her again, his tone resonant and caressing. His words were tender and comforting. She became lost in his mellow tone and hypnotic gaze, as if peacefully floating upon a tranquil black sea.

"Come, let us return to our tepee," he encouraged, his passion gleaming in those mesmeric jet eyes.

She snuggled into his arms and rested her cheek against the smooth, firm chest of coppery flesh. She sighed contentedly. He lifted her chin and provocatively devoured her lips, enticing them to respond heatedly to his. His hands moved up and down her back, savoring the feel of her warmth and nearness. His lips traveled down her neck, then back to her eager mouth. Her respiration quickened to match his erratic breathing. A glow suffused her body, causing her to tremble.

"Oh, how I love you, Gray Eagle," she murmured in a voice laced with mounting desire and feverish emotion. When he gazed into those lucid pools of green, her eyes said more than her words.

Enraptured and enflamed, he playfully seized her in his arms and headed for their tepee. She laughed merrily and taunted, "The camp is far away; do you have enough

343

strength to carry me there?"

"You are but a feather and I am a strong arrow. I can carry you anywhere," he roguishly retorted, bending forward to kiss her soundly.

"But passion steals your breath, my love," she seductively replied.

"How so when you are the air I breathe?" he instantly and cunningly parried, chuckling in amusement.

"I also steal your keen eyes. What if you stumble in the darkness and injure us?" she wittingly fenced, relishing this merry game.

"If so, we will make love where we fall," he murmured.

"I think not, for who has keener senses than my Wanmdi Hota? You are matchless in all ways. My heart swells with pride and love to know you are mine alone."

"As you are mine alone," he vowed in a compelling tone that settled around her like a warm blanket. "How did I exist without you?"

"Because you did not know the heights of passion or depths of love before me, as I did not before you. The moment our eyes touched, we knew and felt such things. The moment we joined our bodies, our hearts and lives were joined for all time. There is no power that can separate us, for no power is greater than yours."

"You forget the Great Spirit," he reminded her.

"You have found favor in His eyes and heart. He gave you the one woman who could love you and fulfill you as no other, not even Indian. You cannot be defeated, for He shares his power with you."

He halted and placed her feet upon the ground. He cupped her face between his hands and kissed her tenderly and pervasively before saying, "Yes, Shalee, you are the only woman who touches my heart and claims it."

She hungrily meshed her lips with his, holding a jaw between her hands that represented so much strength and beauty. After several fiery kisses, he grasped her hand and led her toward camp. "If we do not put out this fire soon, my body will burn to ashes," he jested.

"Patience and anticipation will increase your desires, my love."

"What patience can I find when you are near and I cannot touch you?"

"Shall I share mine with you?" she saucily came back at him.

He eyed her suspiciously, then chuckled. "You cannot, for you lack enough for yourself."

"You are to blame," she mirthfully accused. "Your teaching lacked one thing; you taught me to build fires, but only to put them out in one way."

"Shall we race to our tepee and test who has the greater fire?"

"It would only prove who has the greater speed and skills: you. We will forget all problems and think only of our fires." She unwittingly reminded him of Leah and her schemes.

He halted abruptly and stiffened. "I must see my father. Return to our tepee and wait for me. I will return to your side soon, Little One. I cannot rest until I warn my father. Do not be angry," he coaxed her, smiling ruefully.

If she hadn't witnessed Gray Eagle's rejection of Leah, she might mistrust him. Perhaps he was right. Perhaps Leah was too tempting for an aging man, even a proud Indian chief. Besides, Gray Eagle wasn't himself when Leah had boldly conspired to seduce her husband. She

345

smiled and nodded, "Do not be long, my love," she hinted sweetly, then kissed him.

"Before you can ease yourself down upon our mat, I will be at your side," he promised huskily, tugging upon a lock of chestnut hair.

She walked away as he headed for Running Wolf's tepee. When Running Wolf called out permission for him to enter, his voice was strained. Gray Eagle ducked and went forward with several agile strides. His gaze moved from his father's furious expression to Leah's embarrassed one. He didn't have to ask what had angered him. In a low voice he stated, "I came to warn you she might attempt her magic once more, my father. You must guard against her tricks," he needlessly offered.

Running Wolf's narrowed eyes glared at the white girl kneeling upon her mat, vainly trying to hide her humiliation. Gray Eagle shook his head in irritation and disbelief. He went to tower over Leah, his stance and aura menacing. Her head jerked upwards and her gaze widened in shock as he spoke to her through clenched teeth, his tone glacial and distinct, his words thundering at her in fluent English.

"If you wish to live to see Wi's face again, white whore, do not tempt my father to betray his honor. If you lie about the child, you will die," he warned ominously without mercy or feeling. "You have dared much here. Soon, you will pay for such evil deeds. If there is a child, you will be sent away when it is born. If not . . ." He left his threat hanging in midair, his meaning clear.

Fury and bitterness stormed her spiteful body. She determined to fix him! She would make him squirm and notice her! "There is a child, but it is not Running Wolf's!" she sneered coldly, instigating her vindictive ploy sooner than she had expected to do, if at all. "I dared not tell the truth before your loving wife's ears; you would have slain me where I stood! Can you be so blind and ignorant? Have you forgotten the night I slept upon your mat when you thought Shalee was dead? Running Wolf did not take me first, you did! Running Wolf is too old to father a son; the child I carry is yours!"

"Your evil has stolen your mind, Leah! I have never taken you!" he declared fiercely.

"Where is your honor, Great Warrior? Do you deny I made love to you that night after you left the ceremonial lodge? Was your mind so dazed you cannot recall the fiery joining of our bodies? When your head cleared and you threw me aside, we had already made love. You refused our second mating, but not our first! You cast a magic spell over me that night. Since that time you took me, I have desired and loved no man but you. Why did you think I pursued you so boldly? Because I knew what it was to make love to you! The memory of that wonderful night has tormented me. Your father took me by force; I did not seduce him. He came to my mat; I did not go to his. If you doubt me, ask him!" she challenged. "I only wanted you; I could not forget you or the fiery night we shared. What did it matter you called me Shalee? What did it matter your heart was making love to your dead wife? Your body made love to mine. It is *your* son I carry, Gray Eagle, the son she cannot give you," she cunningly and cruelly alleged.

"You lie, white whore!" he shouted in outrage.

"Do I?" she charged. "Have you truly forgotten taking me, or do you only claim you do not remember? Look me in the eye and swear you did not make love to me that night. I gave you great pleasure that night. My mouth feasted upon him until I drove you wild with desire. You drank from my breasts and teased my womanhood until I burned to have you. Your head was dazed and would not allow you to ride me. So I climbed upon your body and rode you until he spewed his seeds into me. While we rested and my hands caressed him to new life, your head cleared and you rejected another mating. You wanted Shalee, but I was the one at your side. If she had not returned, I would still be at your side," she smugly announced. "You have refused me other times, but you wanted me. Are you too proud to confess the truth? Were you honestly too drunk to recall that wonderful night? Do you remember any of it?" she asked, forcing her expression to somber gravity.

His moody silence handed her victory number one. His warring expression, which exposed his indecision and horror, handed her victory number two. Before he could vividly recall that night, she sought victory number three, "Have you forgotten how I touched you? How I comforted you while you grieved for her? How I sated the urgent needs of your body? Later when your mind cleared, your pride returned and you shoved me aside. But my heart and body craved other nights upon your mats. I love you, Gray Eagle; I have since the first moment I looked upon you. That is why I shamelessly chase you and tempt you. Why did you awaken me to such desires, then reject me? Why do you force your father to claim your son? If Shalee had not returned, you would have taken me to your tepee and mat. If you do not believe me, ask your father if I was a virgin the night he brutally forced himself upon me. I said nothing because I love you and feared your hatred and revenge if I told the truth. Can you deny your own son? Can you raise him as

348

your brother? Can you place unjust guilt upon your father's head? He is not strong enough to protect our son. What will happen to him when Running Wolf dies? You are a virile man; surely one woman is not enough for you. I could love you as much as Shalee does. I can give you sons and pleasures she cannot. Try to remember that night. If you do, you will recall I pleased you as she never can."

"I have never taken you, Leah," he weakly argued. His shaky voice and doubtful air presented her with victory number four.

"Only you have touched my heart, Gray Eagle; I shall never forget you or that night. If I did not love you so much, I would have told Shalee about us. I have not mentioned that night or the other times when you were tempted to take me. Perhaps the darkness of your tepee allowed you to forget I am white when the light of day refused. Perhaps you were drunk and honestly thought I was Shalee. No matter, the child is yours; my love is yours."

"If you speak such lies to my father or Shalee, I will kill you with my bare hands," he threatened icily, haunted by his loss of memory, abruptly realizing how terrible this same ailment must have been for his precious Shalee.

"I will tell no one, my love. Not because I fear for my life, but because you would hate me even more. Besides, my life will end when our child is born and you send me away. How can I live without you?"

Gray Eagle's body was taut with rage and dismay. Was the guilt his to bear? Was the child his responsibility? Was there even a child at all? "I do not believe you carry a child, Leah. Your body will soon reveal the truth."

"Your power is great, Wanmdi Hota, but you cannot order or wish our child away. If you wish to claim him as brother, I cannot stop you. You can deny we made love that night, but it will be a lie. Your pride is larger than your father's. Where was your pride when the heat of lust consumed you? You wanted me and needed me that one night, but Shalee returned and took you from me. Have I not been punished and hurt enough? I will lose you and our son. How can I ever forget what it was like to taste your kisses and body, to feel your manhood driving wildly into my body until I could think of only you and having you again? You enslave not only my body, but my heart and passions as well. Go away and stop tormenting me. Deny our child if you must, but he is still from your seed."

Gray Eagle did not realize Leah had just won her victory, but she did. She was only too aware of Shalee standing in the entrance, staring at her husband's broad back in agonizing disbelief. "You call me evil and wicked, but you are the evil and cruel one! I did not cast a spell of love over you; you cast yours over me. How can I deny these feelings that haunt me each night? How can I forget what it was like to love you, to feel your arms around me, to taste your lips, to know the smell and touch of your body? How can I forget what it was like when you drove him into me time and time again until I cried out with pleasure? Even now I want you," she fiercely and boldly admitted.

"I should cut out your lying tongue, white whore. I desire and love no woman but Shalee. I did not join with you that night."

"Perhaps not in heart or mind, but you did in body. What would Shalee think and feel if she knew about that

350

night?" she mildly hinted.

"You dare to threaten me!" he exploded angrily.

Running Wolf hastily questioned the turbulent argument that he could not comprehend. Gray Eagle glanced over at his concerned, probing stare. It was time to confess the truth and expose the depth of Leah's evil and treachery. Perhaps his own wavering would assuage some of his father's guilt. He sighed heavily and began his astonishing tale.

He told his father about the night Leah came to his tepee to seduce him while he was drugged on the peyote buttons. He went on to relate the two times she had attempted to entrap and to lure him with her skills. He spoke of how he had refused her, even amidst his grief and pain. "Now, she claims I made love to her that first night and the child is mine. She lies, Father; I did not touch her."

A point previously ignored came rushing back to Running Wolf. To Gray Eagle's alarm, he hesitantly informed his son, "She was not pure the night I took her." He went on to explain how Leah's sensual actions had enticed him to take her. "The mating fever came over me and I took her before I could master my fiery body. But she did not fight me, my son; she yielded to me. Other nights, she provoked me while I was held in her powers. If you cannot recall that night, are you certain she did not also provoke you beyond reason or control?" he asked fretfully, their conversation in rapid Oglala, denying Leah most of their words, but not the distraught Shalee.

Leah smothered her pleased smile, knowing whatever they were discussing was playing havoc upon her rival. Was Gray Eagle confessing his deeds? Was he admitting

351

to a blank void on that all-important night? Still, her scheme couldn't work if she didn't get pregnant soon! How? Who?

"What should we do, my son? Your loss of memory is as deadly as Shalee's was. Can you swear the child is not yours?" he pressed worriedly, knowing the damage Leah's claims would inspire.

"I do not recall such things, Father." Gray Eagle spoke honestly and reluctantly. "She did come to me and try to lie with me. But I do not think I touched her, not in that way. I was dreaming she was Shalee. I held her and kissed her, but I do not recall entering her body."

"Then we must say nothing to Shalee," his father vainly concluded. "I will accept the blame if she carries a child. If not, the matter will end."

"I will ask the Great Spirit to return my memory as He did Shalee's. I must know the truth. If she bears my child, I cannot stain your face with my dishonor."

Her world torn assunder now by the new possibilities, Shalee could listen no longer. Anguish violently rocked her world of trust and love. How could she look into the face of his child by another woman? How could she ever allow him to touch her again, knowing he had claimed Leah's purity and placed his seeds within her sinful body? How could it ever be good and right between them again? Leah had lusted after her husband; in a way, she had won her demonic battle for him. How could he deny himself the sons she obviously couldn't give him? How could he truthfully claim she was enough for him? Within days of her alleged tragic loss, he had been surrendering to that greedy succubus! Not just another woman, but Leah Winston! Her heart ravaged, she walked through camp toward the stream.

White Arrow passed her near the edge of camp. When he spoke to her, she never even heard him or replied. He swiftly pursued her and grasped her arm. "Shalee? Does something trouble you?" he asked.

The eyes of his longtime friend that met his were glazed with agony and sadness. "I wish I had never remembered our life together," she mysteriously stated, baffling him. "If not for my son, I would also wish I had not escaped that raging river to fight a more traitorous force."

"I do not understand," he said in confusion.

Shalee laughed, a wintry and disturbing sound. "Neither do I, White Arrow. Neither do I . . . sometimes it is best to forget good in order to forget evil. The whites have won, for I have been defeated and punished. For once, I wish I did not know English. God, how I wish I were deaf," she wailed in anguish.

"Come, I will take you to your tepee. Some new fever clouds your mind," he speculated aloud, fretting over her agitated mental state.

"No, my friend. Do you realize we were friends long before Gray Eagle accepted me? I've often wondered what my life would be like if my people had captured you instead of him or if he had sold me to you long ago."

What wild words was she speaking and thinking? Why would she recall such things from the past? Her mood was bewildering, haunting. Dread washed over him. Something was terribly wrong. What?

"You must explain your cloudy words to me, Grass Eyes," he coaxed.

She smiled sadly. "Do you remember the day you gave me that name? Remember how I teased you about naming you Black Eyes, Sapa Ista? So many times you

353

befriended me and helped me. How could I have survived this long without you? So many times you reasoned with Gray Eagle when he fiercely rejected me or harshly punished me. How different things would be today if Matu hadn't . . ."

In horror he clamped his hand over her mouth. "Silence, Shalee!" he hastily warned. "To reveal her ruse would endanger your life and happiness. Why do you speak of such treachery and peril? You are Indian now. No one must learn the truth!" he sternly ordered. How he wished these feelings of desire and affection would cease to torment him. If not for his best friend, Shalee would be his woman. He could not forget that Gray Eagle's pride had almost compelled his friend to sell Alisha to him long ago. If things hadn't worked out for them, she would now be his woman, perhaps his wife. He shook his head to clear it of such dangerous and traitorous thoughts. Shalee would never be his; she loved his best friend, as he loved her.

"What does it matter, White Arrow? Will their love and respect halt if they learned the truth after all this time? Can't they finally accept me for who and what I am?" she irrationally theorized.

"Think of Gray Eagle and Bright Arrow, Shalee. They would also suffer for your careless words. Why do you speak them tonight?" he probed.

"My son . . ." she murmured thoughtfully. "Yes, I must think of my son. A son is vital to a man, White Arrow. No man could deny his own flesh and blood."

White Arrow gently seized her shoulders and shook her. "Tell me what hurts you so deeply, Grass Eyes," he encouraged.

"The child Leah carries," she softly responded, her

hazy words telling him nothing.

"Why does Running Wolf's trouble torture you this way? Perhaps Leah lies. Perhaps there is no child," he wistfully alluded.

"If only the child was Running Wolf's," she cried out in distress.

When she began to sob, White Arrow pulled her into his arms and offered her solace to a crisis he did not comprehend yet. "What disturbs you so greatly, Little One?" he asked in rising concern.

"Don't you understand, White Arrow? The child Leah carries is not Running Wolf's; it's Gray Eagle's," she incredulously declared between ragged sobs. "It's my husband's," she repeated near a ragged whisper.

"What? This cannot be!" he said, firmly refuting her illogical statements.

"Ask him. When he thought I was dead, he took Leah. It is his son she carries. He has betrayed our love; he has destroyed it. I heard it from his own lips just now. She lay with him upon his mat while I struggled for life. While mine was slipping away, Leah was beginning a new life, his son's! When she said the child was his, he could not deny it. Running Wolf is old; Gray Eagle is young. If both have taken her, what chance did the old man's seeds have over my traitorous husband's? He lied to me and deceived me. He said he never touched her or any other woman. But he did."

White Arrow staggered under this news. "It cannot be! He would never take another woman. He loves and desires only you, Grass Eyes."

"Perhaps his heart did not desire her, but his body did. Running Wolf asked him to swear the child was not his, that he had not taken her. He could not, White Arrow.

355

While I lay dying, he lay mating with another woman. I will never forgive him, White Arrow; I will never forgive him."

White Arrow was disturbed by the bitterness and accusations against his best friend, a man who was like his own brother, a man he had ridden with since youth. "Come, we must speak with Gray Eagle and settle this matter."

"No. I cannot face him again. I would die if he ever touched me again. If he desires Leah, then he can have her! I cannot remain here now; I must leave," she suddenly and unexpectedly announced.

He exploded in shock. "You cannot! He did not take the white whore!"

"He says differently, White Arrow. Whose words should I accept, yours or his? I cannot remain here while he desires her, not while she grows heavy with his child. I cannot." He raged at her immense suffering.

"But you love him," he argued, at a loss for wit and words.

"No, White Arrow; he has cruelly slain my love and trust in him. Even a powerful love as we once shared cannot survive such wicked betrayal. Leah will always be there between us now, for he carelessly placed her there. I have loved, forgiven, and suffered too many times to win his love and acceptance. The time has come when I possess no more understanding, when I can accept no more torment. I have given, shared, adjusted, and sacrificed until I have nothing left. How much can love endure before its demands outweigh its rewards? You know our past well, my friend. Have I not denied myself and my people to give him my all? Was he required to do the same to earn my love? Don't you understand, White

Arrow? This situation is grave. I was missing for only twelve moons when he yielded to Leah's temptation, more than once. How can he expect me to understand and forgive such cruelty? If I had betrayed him like that, he would slay me! It is over between us and I must go away. Will you take me to Black Cloud's camp?" she asked, startling him with her request, knowing that was the only safe place she could flee to in this treacherous wilderness.

"Gray Eagle will not let you go," he stated confidently.

"This time he will, White Arrow. There is no way he can stop me. Who would side with a traitorous husband against a wronged wife?"

"He could not betray you!" White Arrow stormed in frustration.

"He already has, my friend. I heard it from his own lips. How could he do this to us, to me? I thought there was no power strong enough to separate us, but there is: his lust for Leah. He has placed a barrier between us that can never be removed. I could never love or trust him again."

"We must go to your tepee and end this treachery now, Shalee. Leah carries no man's child; I know this within my heart. She lies."

"Even if she lies about the child, White Arrow, Gray Eagle still betrayed me with her. How great is his love when he yielded to another woman only a few moons after my death? I cannot forgive him, for his betrayal will always come between us."

She laughed cynically. "It's funny, isn't it? It isn't my white blood that will finally destroy our love; it is a white woman. Leah warned me long ago she would take him from me and claim my place. I didn't believe it was

357

possible for any woman to do that. She's won, White Arrow. The magic of the son she carries is too great for me to battle. I lost him the day the Bluecoats attacked me and Leah was given the chance to reveal her magic. Even mine dulls in the light of hers."

"No, Shalee, you have not lost him. Leah is no threat to your love. He would never trade you for her. You are hurt and distressed. Think."

"The child, White Arrow, he will defeat me. I haven't been able to give him another son. If Leah does, all is lost."

"Then I will slay her," he heatedly offered.

"No, you cannot. To do so would also slay the son of Gray Eagle. Don't you see? If I had not recalled our love and happiness, this betrayal would mean nothing to me. How can I remain here and watch her grow fat?"

Before he could summon some answer, Gray Eagle hurried forward to join them. "I could not find you, Shalee. Why are you here with White Arrow? I spoke with my father; all is settled."

"Is it?" she glacially challenged.

Her look and tone hinted at trouble. Gray Eagle eyed one person, then the other. "Yes. Running Wolf will have her guarded until the truth is revealed," he stated, wondering at her inexplicable mood and coldness.

"Which truth, my faithful husband?" she sneered angrily.

"The truth of the child," he replied, his tension mounting steadily.

"Whose child, my traitorous husband," she lucidly intimated.

"Why do you speak so strangely, Shalee?" he inquired in dread.

"Do I?" she fenced, vexing him.

White Arrow ended the sparring when he casually announced, "Shalee knows about you and Leah, Gray Eagle."

Gray Eagle's eyes widened in shock before he could master his surprise. "What does she know?" he demanded softly, controlling his words and tone carefully.

"When will Leah have your second son, my deceitful love?" She clarified the matter quickly and scornfully.

"My son?" he echoed in disbelief, sheer panic attacking him.

"Even now the truth escapes you! You lied to me and betrayed me. I will never forgive you. Never!"

"The child is not mine, Shalee," he argued desperately.

"How can you be certain? You did take her to your mat while I lay dying in Black Cloud's camp, didn't you?" she furiously challenged.

Before he could conceal it, a look of uncertainty flickered in his obsidian eyes. "Don't bother to confess aloud again. I heard your words of guilt in Running Wolf's tepee. It is over between us. I will leave in the morning."

"Leave! You cannot!" His arguments matched White Arrow's.

"I will never forgive you. You have betrayed me! You have killed our love as lethally as you slay your enemies."

"I must explain," he hastily began.

"No!" she quickly interrupted him. "Tell me nothing about my dishonored husband and his white slut! If you desire her so greatly, take her; I do not care! I will never remain here while she carries your son."

"It is not my child!" he growled in rising exasperation.

"Look at me and swear you never mated with her in our tepee while the peyote dazed your wits. Tell me she did not tempt you only a few days after my loss," she cornered him.

Their gazes fused and clashed. "I do not recall ever taking her." He tried to extricate himself without lying.

Tears filled her eyes at his crafty and desperate ploy. "Your loss of memory serves you well, my false love. Even if the child is not yours, your betrayal is. It is over, Wanmdi Hota; you have brutally ended our love."

"If I took her, I do not know it! I was drugged with the peyote buttons. I thought she was you. I do not want Leah; I want only you. Forgive me if I have hurt you or shamed myself. My grief stole my senses. Do not take your love from me," he pleaded hoarsely.

"I have not taken it from you; you have destroyed it. Leave me alone. I must think and plan. I will go to the Blackfoot camp tomorrow. I will never return while Leah or the child is here, if I ever return at all."

"I will not let you go, Shalee. You are my wife, my love."

"You cannot stop me. I am viewed as Princess Shalee, daughter to Chief Black Cloud. You would not dare to reveal my true identity and endanger your face and our son's life. How else could you stop me from leaving? You have betrayed our love with a white whore. Who would blame me or halt me from returning to my father's *tipi?*"

"I will not let you go," he repeated firmly.

"We shall see," she snapped, then left the two warriors standing there.

"Will you stop her?" White Arrow asked. Gray Eagle nodded moodily.

360

Chapter Sixteen

As the uncommonly agitated warrior whirled to go after his wife, White Arrow forcefully seized his arm and prevented his hasty flight. "She must have time for her heart to overrule her pain, my brother. To speak now would only widen the break between you. She is hurt and will not hear your words. Only a denial of her charge could change matters, and you cannot give her such a denial. She must reason upon this deed and find forgiveness in her heart," he sincerely counseled.

"I must tell her the truth, White Arrow," Gray Eagle exclaimed in astonishment.

"What is the truth, my brother? If there is a child, can it truly be yours?" White Arrow asked solemnly, praying the warrior would deny any blame.

"I do not know, White Arrow; only the Great Spirit knows," he answered candidly. He went on to expound upon his dazed condition that fateful night and what he actually recalled of it. "Leah claims I thought she was Shalee and made love to her in the darkness of my tepee while my mind reeled with the peyote. My father says she was not pure when he took her. I only recall kissing her and touching her. When I knew she was not Shalee, I rejected her and sent her away. How could I join her and not remember it? But how can I swear I did not when my memory fails me? Why can Shalee not understand this matter? I did not take another woman to love. I did not

361

betray her. If she loves me, can she not listen and forgive a weakness during my sufferings?"

He was contrite and yet resentful. How could she throw away their love and happiness over a mistake he could not even recall making? She was his heart and life. How could she possibly feel threatened by a despicable woman like Leah? Perhaps her pride was greater than his! Perhaps she sought to punish him! Didn't she realize the toll this action would take on their love and serene existence? Did she even care? He was not guilty! At least not intentionally! Didn't that matter to her?

"It is more the child than Leah, my brother. She could not bear to see another give you the son that she has not. How can she forget and forgive this vile deed when the child will always be there to refresh her memory? But how could she demand you sacrifice your own son? Making love is something very special to her, something you shared with another. You belonged to her, but you gave a vital part of yourself to another female: your seeds and your next son. Much has happened to her lately, and her mind swirls like the raging river. Give it time to calm. Pray there is no child, my brother. For if there is, you have lost her," he stated somberly.

"Does it not matter I am innocent? Leah tricked me and my father with her whorish skills! I was not myself when she came to me. Does a man pay for a wicked deed he did not commit?" he impatiently snarled, his lithe body shuddering with rising fury and irritation.

"Long ago, you taught her others often pay for wicked deeds not their own. Did she not suffer at your own hands because she was white, for her people's evil? If you cannot prove your innocence, the battle is lost."

"How can I, White Arrow?" he entreated in dismay.

362

"Leah is more cunning and daring than we realized. I still say she lies."

"If she does not, how can I prove the child is not mine? Even a brother could reflect me like a son! How did Shalee learn of this matter?" he suddenly demanded, comprehending the short span of time.

"She was at Running Wolf's tepee when you and the white girl spoke; she heard all."

"She spied on me!" Gray Eagle stormed apprehensively, instantly flashing the scene before his mind's eye for study.

"When she heard your shouts in English, she came to investigate. She did not enter when she learned of your betrayal. When you could not deny Leah's claims, she judged you guilty."

Why had he wavered? Why hadn't he declared his innocence? When Leah accused him of such a deed, he should have slain her where she sat! Leah! "Leah was facing the entrance! She must have seen Shalee! I will strangle her! She led me into her trap and captured me, White Arrow. In my hesitation, I was thinking on her words, trying to recall that night. I cannot believe I touched her! She lies! I know she lies! How can I prove it?" he pleaded for White Arrow's help.

In self-recrimination and boundless wrath, Gray Eagle forcefully struck his chest with his fist. "Am I blind and mindless!" he exploded like dynamite.

"Did you recall something?" his friend anxiously asked.

"Yes!" he cheerfully declared, beginning to pace in rapid thought.

"What?" the second warrior demanded in suspense and elation.

363

"If a man enters a woman's body in fiery passion, would there not be some trace of it later? I have made love countless times; why did I forget such a hint of her deception. Before I went to sleep, I touched my manhood to test my loss of control. I never entered her body!" he decided, vividly recalling the lack of moisture and stickiness before drifting off to sleep.

"Why would she dare such a lie?" White Arrow pressed suspiciously.

"Perhaps she does carry Running Wolf's child. Perhaps she hoped I could not recall that night. She desires me and tries to pass the blame to me. Is it me she wants or revenge upon each of us?" he speculated aloud.

"The darkness in her heart is great, my friend and brother. She battles viciously for what she cannot win. Her treachery cannot go unpunished. The child must not carry her evil blood and hatred."

"If there is a child," Gray Eagle sneered skeptically. "I must go to Shalee and tell her these things. Surely she cannot doubt me now!"

As he hurried away with pantherlike strides, White Arrow shook his head, fearing she was too hurt and humiliated to listen yet.

Gray Eagle had gone to his tepee, picked up his wife, and taken her to the same place they had left earlier before this fiendish nightmare began. Shalee had fiercely resisted his gentle force and determination, to no avail. Cognizant of the effect of a fight before their son's eyes, she was compelled to be swept off in his powerful arms. Without speaking along the way, he purposely stalked to the same spot before setting her feet upon the barren ground. He was forced to grip her forearms in a restraining and painless hold to prevent her from fleeing.

His jaw twitched and set in vivid determination. His arresting stare exposed his naked obstinance and ire. He stood tall and erect, his body tense and his mind alert.

She glared at him, half in anger and half in challenge. "Take your filthy hands off of me, you betrayer! We have nothing to say! I will be gone tomorrow!" she shrieked, her body trembling as she sought to govern her warring emotions. The man she loved had brutally trampled her heart and now he demanded to explain how this crime was committed! Did he expect her to act as if nothing was wrong? Did he think she would fall into his traitorous arms and drop the entire perilous episode? Damn him for being so utterly irresistible! Damn him for his magical pull upon her heart and body!

To her astonishment, he threw back his head and actually sent forth amused laughter, his sooty mane dancing in the night breeze! The jet eyes that were glued to her startled green ones shouted of roguish mischief and vitality! His virile body of warmest cinnamon relaxed, muscles rippling with each movement. His confidence and pride filled the crisp air like a floral scent. A beguiling grin played upon his wide, sensual lips. A noticeable tenderness and delight glimmered in those ebony eyes. A pinnacle of brawn and good looks. She simply watched him in curiosity and vexing appreciation.

When he noted her calmed air, he smiled lovingly and stated in a clear and mellow tone that stirred her heart to race rapidly, "I remember that night, Little One. I swear to you I have never touched Leah. If she carries a child, it is not mine. Upon my life and honor, I did not take her."

Stunned by his declaration, she gaped at him. Was he beguiling her or telling the truth? Her doubts registered brightly in her eyes. His jaw grew taut and his eyes narrowed. "You do not believe me?" he demanded irritably.

"How can I when you 'swear' you have never touched her?" she panted sarcastically, emphasizing the word "swear." "You can swear you have never taken her, if that is the truth. But you cannot swear you have never touched her; neither can you honestly swear she has never touched you in fiery passion," she sublty insinuated.

"I have not taken her! The child, if one exists, is not mine!" He forcefully reiterated his stand, choosing to ignore the other charges.

"Look at me, my husband. Swear upon the Great Spirit and all you hold dear that your seeds have never entered her body . . . anywhere," she abruptly and frightfully challenged, telling him something he dreaded to discover.

He inhaled sharply, unwittingly offering her a torturous and erroneous conclusion of her own. Tears eased down her cheeks as she miserably shook her head. "You cannot," she whispered in a choked voice. Her heart devastated, she tried to pull free.

"Shalee, hear me," he hoarsely entreated, refusing to release her.

"No! I can hear no more," she screamed in dejection and disillusionment. "How could you do this to us? To me? Our son? White blood has torn us asunder, but not mine or your resentment of it!"

"I swear I have not placed my seeds within Leah, anywhere!" he thundered honestly. "It is true she tempted me several times, but I did not yield! Even when my heart suffered at your loss and my body craved yours in the night, I did not betray you. I love you. Please trust me," he pleaded.

"When you rushed to your father's side tonight, it was because you knew of her whorish skills and magic. You knew because she practiced them on you! Is that not true?" she recklessly dared him to confess.

"She tried many times, but I did not allow it. My heart and mind are stronger than my loins. Why do you say such words?"

"Because I saw you with her that day by the river," she helplessly alerted him to her knowledge. "That was why I yielded to you! I feared I would lose you to her if I continued to resist you. But when my memory returned, I believed you could never betray me with any woman. I was wrong, for there were other times. You kept the truth from me. You lied and deluded me. You wanted her, but your pride stood between you and your lust! I wonder how long you would have rejected her if I hadn't surrendered to you or returned to your life!"

"What madness is this! Perhaps my body craved a female's, but I have never desired another woman! Is your faith and love so small, Grass Eyes?" he defensively assailed her. "If you saw Leah's actions that day at the river, then you know I did not yield! I did not weaken that night in my tepee or the other time she pounced upon me like a wolf on an injured rabbit! Your words and doubts pain me deeply."

"And you have not pained me deeply! You have not shamed me and yourself! Do you recall how long it took for you to resist her? If you did not desire her, why did you hesitate to kick her aside? How could you allow her to touch you in a place that is mine alone?"

"I did not tell you because I was ashamed. My body was weakened by the battle that raged in my heart and mind. I feared I had found you again, only to lose you forever to the blackness of your mind. Do you not see how much she looks like you? I thought you dead, and she cunningly came to me with your likeness and manner. It was you within her that caused me to waver for a moment. I do not desire her, Shalee. I swear I love and want only you. Do you forget you told me to take her!"

"Perhaps that could explain what happened while you thought me dead. But not what I witnessed by the river that day!"

"Have you forgotten the state I was in? You had enflamed me and coldly rejected me! Yes, I was tempted to ease the pains of my manhood and to cool my anger upon her. But I did not; I could not! She could never take your place, never! The fires of passion are dangerous and powerful; I but needed time to conquer them. You know such ways of love; you know their power! I am not some all-powerful, unmovable man. I was tempted, but I did not surrender. Do not punish us for a brief moment of weakness and confusion," he urged.

When she remained stiff and silent, he dropped his hands to his side in exasperation and despair. He walked to a large rock and put his right foot upon it, propping his elbow upon his knee and placing his chin upon his balled fist. He sank into deep thought. There was no way to reach her, to adequately defend and justify his rashness.

Shalee stood with her back to him, her mind in a violent turmoil. This short distance between them was cold and relentless. If she wished, she could simply walk away and end this devastating conversation. She wavered between love and hate, between repulsion and attraction. Her imminent decision would be monumental; her eventual response irretractable. Their entire future hinged upon her next move and words. God, if she only knew what they should be. . . .

Was his conduct so impossible to comprehend, to accept, to forgive? She could not find it in her heart or mind to doubt his claim of never making love to the devious Leah. From her own observation, she knew Leah was the crafty temptress. Could her pride and anguish reject his apology for temporarily wavering? He was a man, a virile one. She had practically ordered him to use Leah to sate his desires.

At that time, she hadn't realized the power of unbridled passion; she had enflamed his body, then rejected him. Surely his throbbing loins had craved the release and pleasure that Leah's mouth had offered after she snuck up on him. Was she so naive and selfish that she couldn't admit to his brief and natural wavering?

Most women were controlled by their hearts and love where sex was concerned; men were not. Men were physical beings, where women were emotional and romantic creatures. Were her faith and love so shallow and selfish that she would destroy their love and life together? Once the deed was done and he lost face, the damage would be irreparable. Could she live without him? Was his crime that great? Under those unusual circumstances, could she blame him for being tempted?

Irrational jealousy and bruised pride splashed obliterating tarnish over his previously golden image. No matter how fiercely she tried to blot out his past deceptions, she could not. Images of times when he had guilefully, often justly, tricked her returned to haunt her, to accuse him anew. Could she place her total trust in him, even now, after all these years of love? If only he had not vacillated that day by the river. Why did his indecision wound her so deeply? Was a mental crime as immense as a physical one?

She slowly turned and scanned his broad back, touched by the suffering displayed there. How complicated and expensive life could be. Their love was too special to recklessly vanquish; their struggles to find each other had been long, costly, and difficult. They had finally overcome all barriers between them. Could she selfishly place another one between them or refuse to tear down the one he had carelessly and innocently constructed? He was probably hurting as badly as she was. But why shouldn't he endure shame, guilt, and anguish? The ravaging battle offered no truce or cessation. She must settle upon what compromise was best for all concerned.

She soundlessly crossed the length of ground that separated them. She summoned her courage and strength to defeat her own qualms and fears. She could not let Leah win this vital battle with her own rash aid! He belonged to her, and she would fight to defend her territory and to foil Leah's brazen schemes. It would be foolish to sacrifice this vital creature whom she loved, her very reason for existing, to that cunning and malicious witch.

"Wanmdi Hota," she softly began, noting the instant tensing of his body, dreading her coming words. "I am trying to understand. I believe the child is not yours. I also believe you are mostly innocent in Leah's schemes. But I must have time to forgive you and to learn to trust you again. In time I will forget you were tempted to yield to her. Until I can blot the scene by the river from my mind, you will sleep on another mat. If you refuse this

370

truce, I will return to the camp of Black Cloud tomorrow. If you go near Leah again, it will end that very moment between us."

He straightened and whirled to confront her. As if doubting his own keen ears, he asked, "Did I hear you? Do you threaten me or warn me?"

She sighed and shook her head. "You are mine; and I will fight all powers, including Leah's, to keep you. My life is here with you. But you have hurt me and deceived me. Time must heal such wounds. Prove you desire only me and not Leah; do not go near her dangerous magic."

A shout of gleeful relief split the still air. He seized her and swung her around, laughing in carefree abandonment. Her arms went against his muscled chest as he cupped her face and gazed intently into it. "You are my life and heart, Shalee. Life is empty and meaningless without you. I did not think I could survive even for our son when I thought you were dead. I love you, Grass Eyes, with all I am or can be. I will do as you ask. I cannot lose you again." For her, he denied all pride and even resentment at her tacit blackmail. He must prove himself to her again. His brief weakness had inspired a loss of confidence in herself and in him. She must be made to see Leah was no threat to her or to their love.

His mouth closed over hers and attempted to reveal his great love and desire for her. Visions of Leah enjoying such feelings tore at her reason and pleasure. She pulled away from him. "It is too soon. Too much has happened this night. First, Leah's ghost must be removed."

He was stunned by her chilling rejection. "You do not want me now?"

"I cannot pretend all is well when it is not. The mood is not right to touch as lovers. My heart is bruised and must

371

heal," she explained softly.

"But I love you and need your closeness," he argued.

"Not when my thoughts see Leah in your arms," she refused hoarsely.

"But you have known such things for a long time. Why do they trouble you now? I do not understand," he stated in utter bewilderment.

"After I saw you with her, I was afraid. I desired you and feared to lose you. I was too upset to reason on the depth of your weakness; tonight when I heard your words of doubt, I realized how close I had come to truly losing you to her. I also learned of other times. How do you know the child cannot be yours?" she abruptly asked, eyeing him closely.

"While I talked with White Arrow, a suspicion entered my mind. When I make love to you, are the signs not visible upon your body, upon mine? Can you make love without lingering evidence? There were no traces of betrayal upon my body that night or the next sun. I could not have taken her. She lied. She seeks to entrap me with my loss of memory. If I had not been drugged that night, I would never have envisioned her as you. But the Great Spirit guarded over our love and my honor; He cleared my mind before I could commit such an unforgivable and offensive deed. If she carries a child, it is my father's," he finished, feeling that he had unraveled the puzzle for her.

Bitterness tinged his voice and hostility gleamed in his dark eyes as he voiced aloud Leah's near victory at his expense. Like some intrepid badger, he was cunning and utterly fearless. He attacked any enemy without heed of its size or power. He was confident and relentless. An animalistic and sensual wildness pervaded Shalee's emotions. He was as skilled in battle and as aggressive as nature's counterpart in the awesome and defiant badger. He was alert and agile, his body attuned to danger and triumph. He wisely tolerated the presence and existence of those who did not challenge his life or territory. He was proud and self-assured. But he could be just as ruthless and deadly as that furry, four-legged, solid warrior of the forest.

Yet, he could be as gentle and protective with his own as that dauntless creature of Nature. Unlike the badger, whose sole interest was in its survival, Gray Eagle was complex and compelling. Even after all these years, an intangible aura of dark and provocative mystery cloaked him. Would she ever totally understand this magnificent creature who had stolen her heart on first sight, who had given her life such meaning and happiness? His very essence offered vivid perceptions of warning and matchless prowess. His truculent equal in the animal kingdom did not possess any edge over him. His stance and air boldly announced his invincibility and obstinance. His potent stare exposed cunning and control. She doubted it was possible for either to be defeated but once, for only death could end such a reign of indisputable strength.

As if by some godly power, he seemed to reach into the heavens and snatch Leah's ominous cloud from over his head. Shalee absently wondered if this was the first occasion when he had exhibited himself to her as a mortal man, one with flaws and weaknesses. During this episode with amnesia and Leah, Shalee had glimpsed a facet of him that she had never viewed before. He was not perfect or all-powerful. He was as human as all other men. Was that the crux of her dilemma? Had she been holding him upon some irrational pedestal? Was she judging and treating him unfairly for this one slip? Perhaps that was it; she hadn't believed him capable of an error.

"Why do you remain so silent, Shalee?" He finally questioned her moody reflections and lack of response.

She inexplicably smiled. The fever of brief weakness had passed; he was himself again. She could feel it and witness it. God, how she loved and desired this vibrant creature. She must deal with her jealousy and resentment quickly. "I am a woman, my husband, and women are often foolish creatures. Perhaps you are innocent in this matter. But a careless or accidental mistake hurts none the less. Soon, all will be good between us again. But the matter of Leah must be settled first."

"Leah means nothing to me, Grass Eyes. Why do you fear her and let her come between us?" he inquired in frustration, stung by her lingering doubts. He captured her hand and brought it to his lips to kiss its tips.

The unconscious action sent tremors over her body. "I did not place her between us, my love," she softly accused.

"*I* did not, Shalee." He tenderly declared his innocence.

"Whether you intentionally allowed it or Leah's cunning forced herself between us, she is there all the same. Not just once did she almost tempt you to replace me, but three times. After the first time why did you not see her lusty sport and prevent the next two incidents? That is what I cannot understand and accept. Do you even realize how long you wavered in her power by the river? How difficult it was to resist her? That hesitation haunts me."

"But I did not yield!" he stormed in rising annoyance.

"Do you recall a day long ago when I was your captive

374

and two white trappers tried to rape me in the forest?" she mysteriously asked.

Her meaning lost on him, he nodded, but queried, "What does that day have to do with this one?"

"You were away from camp, as I was when Leah began her sport. White Arrow was the one who rescued me and comforted me, as Leah offered you devious comfort when you were suffering. When White Arrow carried me to your tepee in his arms, do you recall the mistrust and jealousy that flooded your heart when you witnessed our innocent contact? For a long time you watched us and suspected more than friendship between us. If you could suspect your best friend and brother of such treachery, why are my doubts about Leah so hard to comprehend? White Arrow but touched me in protection and affection, but your contact with Leah was so much more. If that time had been like this one and you were believed dead and then returned without memory of me, how would you feel if the scene by the river had taken place between me and White Arrow? How would you feel to learn there were other times when he pursued me and touched me in such an intimate manner? What if I had wavered and hesitated before refusing him? Would you have no suspicions about me in your mind? Would my brief weakness deny any wounds to your heart? If you stood in my place, how would you feel?" she softly challenged, sending her points home like tiny arrows.

In frankness, he replied quietly, "I had not reasoned in such a way. You are right, Shalee; my jealousy would be limitless where you are concerned. If you but wavered for the flicker of your grass eyes, I would be tormented. I wish you had not viewed my shame and weakness. I have proven unworthy of your love and trust," he unexpectedly admitted, his tone and gaze odd and alarming. "My body is soiled and cannot touch yours until I purify it. I must seek a vision from Wakantanka to learn what must be done to remove the stain from my face. If I cannot prove worthy of the return of your love and trust and remove Leah's evil from between us, you will be free to leave me. Once I held you by force and then by love; now, I do neither."

Shalee was frightened and perplexed by his sudden change of mood, a drastic and ominous one. Until her explanation, he had held Leah to blame for his weakness. Now, he was faced with the realization that he had dishonored himself and her. He was a stranger to defeat and weakness; to learn that he was actually capable of both tortured him in a way that she dreaded to analyze. The ensuing silence was staggering. She jumped as some mystical door slammed loudly and perilously between them. He knew, as well as she, that he had tumbled from his lofty pedestal. Perhaps for the first time ever, he was comprehending that he was a mere man, after all. It was oppressively clear he did not like the image he was perceiving of himself, a tarnished image that she had exposed to him. He was mentally struggling to accept the heavy weight of his guilt and diluted prowess. Her words had savagely flogged his immense pride. Did he resent her for revealing the extent of his injury, his careless downfall?

An eerie sensation tingled over her body. Why had she trampled upon his manly ego to appease her own pains? She had ripped at his self-respect, practically telling him he was truly unworthy of her and her love. Why? That wasn't true at all! The glacial reserve and stoic stare before her sent ripples of sheer terror through her. She had cruelly rejected him and denied him forgiveness. The blow was awesome and destructive.

He had dropped her hand from his grasp. He was standing legs apart, hands on hips, head bent forward, and shoulders defiantly erect. An intense scowl furrowed his brow and squinted his eyes; his body was rigid, moonlight caressing the bronze frame. His jaw was set and his teeth clenched. She wondered what he was thinking and feeling.

She laid her cold hand upon his bulging upper arm and she whispered, "Wanmdi Hota, I'm sorry. I didn't mean to hurt you this way."

"I earned such punishment, Shalee. Your revenge was deserved," he remarked in a controlled tone of ice, his mind far away.

"Revenge?" she echoed in disbelief. "I was not seeking revenge. I was only trying to explain my feelings, to make you understand," she apprehensively vowed.

"You have done so, Shalee. Your thoughts and feelings are clear. I must go now," he suddenly stated, turning to leave her standing there with a dazed mind and an aching heart.

Fear raced through her; her stomach knotted. "Wait! Where are you going?" she quizzed in panic, grabbing his arm to halt his departure.

Without meaning to do so, he jerked his arm free and snarled harshly, "I must seek a place to cleanse my mind and body of this evil and defeat. I will not return until I succeed," he indifferently announced, to her dismay.

"Leave? You cannot! How can we settle this matter if you go away?"

"How can we settle any matter until I free myself of this shame?" he parried in a tight voice.

"You don't understand! I don't want to leave you or lose you! I only need time. Please. Where will you go? What will you do? For how long?" she anxiously demanded.

"For the first time since your attack by the Bluecoats, I understand many things. I had thought our love pure and safe. It is not so. I also need time. I will go into the mountains and cleanse myself. I cannot seek you again until I find myself. I will remain there until such time as I do. You said you did not desire me now. Do you want me to stay because you only fear to lose your husband and life here?" he asked, his gaze accusing and piercing.

Tears sparkled in her eyes. She gaped at him. What was happening to him, to them? "How can you speak such cruel and false words? I love you," she vowed in an anguish-riddled tone.

As if unmoved by her claim and sadness, he stated, "Love is more than words, Shalee. To speak them is not enough when actions disagree. Love offers understanding and forgiveness, not revenge and rejection. You once said I loved you and accepted you only when it was easy and peaceful, that my love and acceptance wavered in times of trouble. Is that not true of you this moon? When I need your love and help the most, you refuse it. Is your love so great after all?"

Stunned, she simply stared at him for what seemed an endless and racking span of time. "Why are you doing this to me? Why are you making me the villain in this deed? I did not inspire this situation, but I'm trying to understand it. Are you blaming me for your moments of weakness because I pointed them out to you? You speak of revenge when none exists in my heart. You claim I am rejecting you just because I need time to heal? Why do

378

men always think sharing sex solves all problems, that it magically proves love? After all that has taken place, I'm to swoon upon your mats because you desire me and want to prove your prowess over me? What about my feelings and desires? Do I yield to prove some point when my heart is not in it? The joining of bodies is not a physical thing for me; it is the total giving of myself. To do so when my heart is ravaged would be a lie. Must I prove my love with a deception? It is you who seek punishment and revenge, my husband, for what I foolishly revealed to you! Your resentment is so great you cannot bear to look at me or be near me; you run away as some coward to avoid me," she shouted angrily, not meaning half of what she was saying in her distraught state.

The moment she uttered the word "coward," the tormenting conversation went awry. It didn't help matters that Shalee had converted to English somewhere along the path of her verbal tirade. His ego already sorely bruised, her unwitting word struck him like a physical blow. He painfully seized her forearms and shook her. "You dare to call Wanmdi Hota a coward! I do not run from any danger or problem. I go to cleanse my body and heart."

My God, what was she saying? Why were they shouting such terrible words at each other? Instead of talking, they were hurling stinging and false insults at each other! "I didn't mean it like it sounded," she said hurriedly, attempting to halt the flow of this raging conversation. "Coward doesn't mean the same to me in this case as to you. I only meant you were leaving when we needed to be together to talk."

Her explanation only slightly softened the sting of her barb. "It is best I leave soon, before we fire more painful arrows at each other which will be impossible to remove or to heal," he stated stoically.

She flung herself into his arms. "Do not go away, Wanmdi Hota. Please, not now. I'm so afraid I will lose you if this trouble brews within you."

His own mind in a vicious turmoil, he couldn't offer her the solace and encouragement she begged for. They both needed time alone. "I will return as quickly as possible, Shalee, but I must go for both our sakes. If we continue to rip at each other this way, we will destroy our love and peace."

She was surprised to suddenly realize she desperately wanted to make passionate love to him here and now. How absurd, after just telling him sex was not a panacea! But her words did not match her feelings! Could it be that joining their bodies somehow joined their hearts and souls, somehow soothed their troubled waters, forged them in some magical and special way?

She looked up at him. "I promise not to speak another cruel word to you. It was wrong of me to salve my wounds by giving you injury. I love you, Wanmdi Hota. I swear it with all my heart."

"This matter has revealed many unknown things to us, Shalee. Our love has been blind and selfish. We must think upon these things that threaten our love, which cause us to fear its loss. Fear is not good. We must conquer it and our mistrust. A separation will open our eyes and minds to the truth."

"Do you love me?" she helplessly asked.

His eyes went upwards, his silence searing her soul. His fathomless gaze returned to her pale face and misty eyes. "Yes, Shalee, but all is not right between us."

"If we love each other, isn't that the most important thing?"

"You spoke of time alone and I think it best for now. It troubles me our love is not strong enough to conquer this evil that has entered our life."

Was it his pride or guilt speaking through his sensual lips? Why couldn't he take her into his arms and make everything right again? Was the breach widening steadily and uncontrollably between them? He was right; something was terribly wrong. "My love is strong enough to forgive and to forget these past moons, my husband. Are you saying yours is not?"

"You confuse me, Shalee. When our talk began, you turned away from me and asked for time. Now, you act betrayed because I agree. There was no forgiveness earlier. Where did it suddenly come from? You claimed Leah was between us and our love was weak. Now, you say it is strong and safe. It cannot be both ways, nor change so quickly."

"I was upset and hurt; I was jealous and angry. As I talked with you, many things were revealed to me. I was wrong about many of them. I lashed out to hurt you as you hurt me. I don't want it to be like this."

"When I accused you of desiring revenge, you were angry and denied it. Yet, you now say you wished to punish me. It is wrong for us to spite each other."

Her gaze walked over his unyielding expression. "You don't want to understand my side, do you? You want to cleanse yourself, but what of me? To punish yourself also punishes me. Let it be over now, Wanmdi Hota," she entreated earnestly.

"The trouble between us or our love?" he asked for some strange reason.

"If you must ask such a question, the distance between us is greater than either of us realizes. I freely offer you my love, my forgiveness, and understanding. If that is

381

not enough to remove the wedge between us, then seek your answers and needs where you must," she surrendered in a ragged voice, her lips and chin trembling. "Go and find your answers alone since I cannot supply them." She turned away, unable to gaze into his face.

How could he offer himself to her when he was stained? First, he must purify himself. Then, he must find her again. "I will return when it is done, Shalee," he quietly stated, hardly able to resist seizing her and crushing her in his arms. The matter must be resolved, not buried. Such hidden deeds had ways of unearthing themselves and returning to haunt a person. "I will ask White Arrow to watch over you and our son until my return. You must also search and cleanse your heart."

"If you go away at this time, Wanmdi Hota, things might never be right between us again. We must remain together to solve this problem," she coaxed just above a whisper. She remained with her back to him, tears easing down her cheeks to drop unchecked upon her dress.

"Things are not right between us now, Shalee. Time and distance will help us to see things clearly and to heal our wounds. I must go," he declared in determination.

Why was he refusing to open the door that separated them? His ways were still strange to her. How could a sweating and praying ritual solve these types of emotional problems? Could guilt and shame be drawn from a body as easily as perspiration? How could he believe it was truly possible to cleanse his soul with such a physical ceremony? But he did, as was his custom. He would go and find some secret and dark place to entrap himself with steam from hot rocks and clear water. He would sit and chant under the influence of the *pezuta yutas* as sweat oozed from his stalwart frame. He would think, and reason, and pray. But all the while, she would be here alone, suffering and dying inside. She felt so vulnerable and powerless, for she could say and do nothing to change who and what he was.

"I go tonight, Shalee," he cut into her thoughts when she remained quiescent. "I will prepare to ride." He made no attempt to touch her or to bid her a reluctant farewell. He feared if their bodies made contact, he would not be able to do what he must. Why did she not say goodbye to him? Why did she remain so quiet and still? Did she understand him and his ways at all? Why was she acting as if he was deserting her? In many ways, they were as different as night and day, as the green forest and the barren desert. "Do you wish to speak before I leave?" he politely asked.

Without turning aorund, she slowly shook her head, not trusting herself to speak or to look at him. There was nothing more to say, and any overtures would be painfully rejected. No, let him leave hastily and halt this racking agony. She drew in a ragged breath of air, which tore at his heart. She sniffled to master her loss of control. But the tears refused to stop coming forth; they burned a salty trail down her cool face.

He turned and headed for camp, his muffled footsteps seeming to thunder into her ears as he walked away from her. She was tempted to run after him, to beg him to stay or to take her with him. It required all of her strength and willpower not to do so. He was Wanmdi Hota, fierce and legendary Sioux warrior. He was Indian first and man second; he was Gray Eagle first and her husband next. He was her whole world; yet, her beautiful world was spinning away and she was helpless to prevent it or to recall it.

She sank to the sandy earth. She rested her arms upon a large rock and laid her damp cheek on it, the tears now moistening her arm and the rock instead of her dress, the same rock upon which Gray Eagle had propped his foot to sort out his worries and fears. She curled against the rock, as if it could protect her from the emotional enemies that assailed her without mercy. Had so little time passed since he had lifted her and carried her to this spot? Why did it seem eons of time had passed? Where had things gone wrong? If only she could return to the moment she approached him as he stood in moody thought. If she had spoken and acted differently at that vital moment, she would not be here alone while her love prepared to ride away. When he laughed with joy and swung her around in his arms, she should not have spoiled that imminent truce.

She was oblivious to the passage of time and to the melodious songs of nature. She rested her forehead upon her tightly clasped fingers. Her sobbing had ceased, for her well of tears had been drained. She felt numb, as if grieving for some permanently lost love. Gradually she became aware of the steady lifts and falls of a horse's hooves. She knew without looking up who was approaching her. She steeled herself to allow him to ride away with her lagging pride intact.

He reined in his striking Appaloosa. He gazed down at the beautiful woman who was his meaning in life. She appeared so vulnerable, so small, so tormented . . . so close and so far from him. He must not weaken. To dismount and to embrace her would prevent what must be.

He hoped and feared she would defy his necessary action, but she did not. He was plagued by relief and sadness when she did not. "You must return to camp, Shalee. It is not safe to be here alone." He wondered why she would not look at him or bid him farewell, unaware she could not risk either without severing her heart completely.

She failed to respond in any fashion. He wondered if she had fallen asleep from sheer exhaustion. "Do you hear my words, Shalee? Do you sleep? You must return to camp before I go."

"Go if you must; I will be safe. Who would dare to hurt the wife of the Gray Eagle, except Gray Eagle himself?" she said in a small voice that echoed her anguish, a voice nearly smothered by her lowered head.

"I do not wish to hurt you, Shalee. You must understand why I do this for us."

"For us, Wanmdi Hota? Or for yourself?" she corrected him sadly.

"I cannot offer you half a man, Shalee. I must become whole and strong again."

Pride! Always his damn pride! It stood between them as stubbornly as her white heritage! "I will be fine here; do not concern yourself with me."

"Why do you not tell me goodbye? Is that not the white man's custom?" he plausibly asked, attempting to draw her out.

"Because I am not the one leaving. Why should I follow the *wasichu* customs when I am Indian now? Or have you forgotten that?"

"No more than you have forgotten my customs. Do not resist my leaving," he suddenly entreated, his tone soft and compelling.

"I am not begging you to stay, nor am I trying to halt your departure. What is it you wish me to say? Your

385

decision is made; I will not defy it."

"Goodbye, Shalee," he murmured in English, the word unknown in Sioux.

Where was the "I love you and I will miss you"? Where were her farewell kiss and embrace? Where were the words of comfort and encouragement? She had previously used hers to no avail. To repeat them would matter little since he was riding away. "Goodbye, Wanmdi Hota," she finally stated, the word ringing with an ominous tone that haunted him.

Neither moved for a time, each waiting and hoping for the other to demolish the door between them. At last, he kneed his horse into a swift gallop to leave the torturous scene, never glancing back. She lifted her head and watched the dust and dark shadow until both vanished from sight, then gave in to the sobs that conquered her remaining strength.

Within moments, she was being held tightly in White Arrow's comforting embrace as he spoke softly to her. She wept for a long time; he allowed her this necessary release. She was like a hurt and frightened child. Why had the Great Spirit summoned Gray Eagle to leave her side at this terrible time?

When Shalee regained control of herself, she looked up into his worried eyes so full of affection and concern. "Leah did not win her victory, White Arrow; but she has her revenge. She has not replaced me, but she has driven us apart. It will never be the same again. He cannot even bear to look at me, or to touch me, or to stay at my side when I need him so much."

"When the Great Spirit calls, Grass Eyes, a warrior must follow. He feared to touch you and to weaken. I will care for you and Bright Arrow until his return."

Her somber gaze fused with his warm and sincere one. "He does not seek a vision from Wakantanka, my friend; he goes to seek his pride and to vanquish his guilt. He wishes to punish me for revealing to him that he must share the blame with Leah over this trouble. Since my accident, we have been drifting apart; soon we will be too far away to find each other again. I am losing him, White Arrow, and I don't know how to prevent it."

"No, Shalee. It is not so. He loves you, and you love him. This is but a rock in your path; he will remove it and all will be happy again."

"What will the others say when they learn he has left me?"

"Warriors are often called to seek visions. Have you forgotten this? He is a leader and these times are dangerous. It is natural for him to seek guidance and to purify himself. He will return soon. Do not permit Leah's victory, Shalee. If you love him, fight for him."

"I used every skill I know and possess, White Arrow. I failed. He would not remain here to settle our troubles. He would not even kiss me farewell and hold me in his arms for but a moment. He did not even say he loved me."

"Did *you* do and say such things?" he astutely asked, knowing she hadn't, since he had been watching.

"I couldn't. It took all my strength to keep silent and to let him ride off."

"It was the same with him, Shalee. He is Gray Eagle and much is expected of him. It is hard for him to view any weakness in himself."

"Does a farewell kiss and embrace reveal weakness? I am his wife!"

"He could never touch you, then ride away. You are

387

the only woman ever to reach his heart or to earn his love."

"If that is true, why are we both suffering this way?" she cried out.

"Love such as you share is special and rare, Shalee. Evil cannot bear the sight of such love and happiness. Evil uses Leah to end it. Do not yield, Shalee. Pride and resentment are its cunning weapons. Defeat your enemy, not your husband," he tenderly advised. "Come, let us return."

He helped her to her feet. She smiled up at him, then placed her arm around his narrow waist. "What would I do without you, White Arrow? How many times have you saved my life, or my happiness, or my sanity? I love you, dear friend," she exclaimed, hugging him tightly.

He held her possessively, rebelling against the wish that she was his woman. He dropped a light kiss upon her forehead, then gently grasped her hand to lead her back to camp. He prayed Gray Eagle would return quickly for two reasons: one, the buffalo hunt was near; two, it was not wise or safe for him to share such closeness with Shalee. Would his longing for her never cease? Would the dangerous love never alter to simple affection? For years he had concealed this lingering love and desire for his best friend's woman. If the day ever came and Gray Eagle was slain, he would take Shalee to wife. Was that why he hadn't taken a wife yet? Gray Eagle's life was in constant jeopardy; was he foolishly waiting to . . . no! he angrily scolded himself. He would never desire his friend's death to possess the woman they both loved. He must find a wife and end this obsession for Shalee. Only then could he find peace and love. . . .

Chapter Seventeen

Two days passed with such sluggishness that Shalee grew tense with the insufferable waiting. How long would this purification require? She missed him terribly. White Arrow was constantly at her side, lifting her spirits when they sank, teasing her when she was close to tears, playing with Bright Arrow while she fretted over her husband's absence, sharing meals and talks with them, hunting for them, protecting them, loving and caring for them: everything a devoted husband and father should do.

She and White Arrow had been friends since shortly after she had met Gray Eagle. Because of Gray Eagle's rank, he had been unable to offer her the genial friendship and easy acceptance that White Arrow had from the beginning. They had spent many times together; their rapport was immense. They could laugh and share easily. Like kindred spirits attuned to each other, they had a full and happy relationship. And it was tranquil and safe, for Shalee was unaware of White Arrow's great love for her.

During those early days years ago, she had sensed that he was physically attracted to her. But his love and respect for Gray Eagle had prevented real love, or so she thought. As time had passed, their friendship had mellowed and deepened. He had become adjusted to concealing his love, to displaying it only as fondness and pleasure. A few times when she had been Gray Eagle's white captive, White Arrow had spared her many punishments and given her much assistance and encouragement. But in ravaging times like this one, his protective role plagued him. He wanted to comfort her in ways a friend should not.

They had discussed many topics during these past two days alone. Facts she had ignored about her husband and his ways were refreshed for her by his friend. She searched her heart during the long and lonely nights, coming to know that nothing was more important than their love. Leah's ploy took on newer and clearer dimensions. She flushed as White Arrow explained many intimate things about men and women. She wondered how she could still remain so naive after being married for so long. Perhaps because there had been no need for her husband to tell her such things.

Fortunately, she had avoided Leah during these two trying days of discovery, partially because of White Arrow's companionship and nearness. Regardless, Shalee watched Leah from a distance. Evidently Leah didn't realize that none of them accepted her claims against Gray Eagle. Her speech was cocky and her manner insolent. She strutted like some vain peahen or regal queen. It galled Shalee to watch her infuriating smugness. It was time to bring Leah back down to reality! She wasn't some defenseless victim; she had willingly played the whore! She assumed they believed her vicious lies about Gray Eagle. How dare she prance around pretending to carry her husband's child! How dare she slander him! How dare she cause this rift between them!

About to rush out and set the lecherous girl straight, Shalee cautioned herself to patience and control. Leah would thrill at the sight and sounds of her anger and insecurity. No, my wily vixen, you will not dance with joy over my body!

Late on the third afternoon, Shalee was watching her son as he played with other boys his size and age. She contained her bubbly laughter as he appeared to better each one in the hoop game. Not once did his hoop-net miss a cone, while others steadily dropped out one by one as theirs did. Finally, Bright Arrow lifted his arms in triumph and shrieked with elation. He raced to Shalee and threw his arms around her thighs.

"I won, Mother!" he squealed excitedly.

"Yes, my son; I saw. You are as strong and swift as your father. Your eyes are alert and your mind keen. Soon, you will be a great warrior like he is. I am so proud of you, Bright Arrow. I love you so much," she whispered softly, kneeling to hug him.

"Before many moons, I will seek a vision as my father does."

She smiled and nodded. "Just like your father. The Great Spirit will guide him and make him strong and wise to lead his people. One day you will be chief of the Oglala. But first, you must work to become stronger and quicker. A chief must have keen eyes and ears and his legs must run swiftly. But you must also learn patience and kindness to others. Lose as well as you win," she advised, smiling.

"You are as wise and cunning as my father," he mischievously stated, then raced off to join a new sport.

Shalee stood up, watching his retreating back. He was a good child, and he would become a good man. Each day he resembled his father more and more, in manner as well as in looks. She had so much to be grateful for and to give her happiness. She must allow nothing and no one to spoil such special feelings again.

391

"He will be chief if my son allows it. But I will teach my son to be more cunning and more powerful. I think I will name my son Eagle Star. He will soar with his father and shine brighter than a tiny arrow. When they are both grown warriors, the Oglala will name my son chief over yours. You make him too soft and gentle. A chief must be cold and ruthless," Leah sneered, eyes glowing with hostility and arrogance.

In the flash of an instant, Shalee had balled her fist and slammed it across Leah's jaw. Leah reeled backwards from the stunning blow and crumbled to the ground. The two women glared at each other. Leah regained her footing and stood, arms akimbo.

"You dare to strike me and endanger the child of Gray Eagle," she scoffed contemptuously. "He will slay you if you harm his son."

"You are a fool, Leah. No one accepts your vile lies. Gray Eagle knows he never touched you that night. He was playing along with your game to test the depth of your evil and daring. You are such a harlot. Besides, there isn't any child. All will know that soon, won't they?" Shalee nonchalantly sneered, laughing in Leah's hostile face, which was red with rage and hatred. "I wonder how many days it is before your monthly declares you the witch you truly are."

"There were other times we touched!" Leah snapped acidly.

"If you mean by the river, when you tempted him with your treacherous hands, what man wouldn't enjoy such treatment? Are you so naive, or simply stupid? Or perhaps the other time when he went to bathe and you 'accidentally' presented your naked body as offering to a savage god? We have no secrets, *witkowin*. I know each time you went near him and all that happened

392

between you."

As Leah's face paled at the reality in Shalee's scornful claims, Shalee went for her finishing blow, "I also know about you and Running Wolf. What do they call a woman who craves brutal joinings? How sick your mind must be to enjoy pain at such a special moment."

"You're lying. You think you know everything, but you don't! A little guessing or adding to facts you were told! Gray Eagle will soon be mine!" Leah confidently vowed.

Shalee burst into laughter. Speaking just low enough to avoid being overheard, Shalee began to describe Leah's adventures with both Running Wolf and Gray Eagle. She went on to inform the stunned girl of her knowledge of Leah's interference on certain occasions. "You see, Leah, you are not so cunning after all. You are merely a brazen woman without morals or conscience. All laugh at you. All plan your punishment the moment it is certain you do not carry Running Wolf's child," she hinted, relishing Leah's fear and humiliation.

"You are the fool if you believed his claims about never touching me!" Leah panted in anxiety.

"I would be a fool if I did. Gray Eagle will always love and desire only me. Long ago I warned you of failure and punishment if you sought to pursue him. Now, you are trapped. You are safe only until your lie reveals itself. You could never win Gray Eagle's heart; it is mine alone for all time."

Shalee dramatically withdrew her small knife and pointed it at Leah. She ominously warned, "If you speak such lies again, I will cut out your sinful tongue. A tongue isn't necessary to carry a child, if one exists. I am Princess Shalee and I have the power to carve you into little pieces if I so desire."

Leah actually backed up several steps. Shalee was serious! Soon, the scheme would come to light. She had rashly alienated the only person who could have helped her. Shalee! Always Shalee! Damn her! A pox on her beauty!

"I will give you one chance to confess the truth, Leah. If you refuse, I will be the first in line when your punishment starts. With the help of the other women, who will rage at your defilement of our chief, we will leave nothing for Gray Eagle and Running Wolf to punish. I warn you now; if your story does not match Gray Eagle's, your lying tongue will be missing before nightfall."

"You wouldn't dare harm me! Running Wolf will not allow it!"

"Running Wolf says you are mine until the truth is out. If there is no child, you are still mine. It was my husband you set your evil eye to taking. Look around you, Leah; no one will come to your aid."

As the terrified girl glanced around, any eye she caught was hostile, knowing the white girl was up to some wickedness or the gentle Shalee would not have assaulted her and would not be holding a knife upon her. Her wide gaze halted briefly upon the leering face of White Arrow.

"You see, Leah, no one can save you from me. Like a loosened rock, you are swiftly rolling down a dangerous hill. Only I possess the power to save you. If you speak the truth, I will spare your life. I will send you to live in another camp, even if you do not carry Running Wolf's child. Only your honesty can inspire kindness and mercy within me."

Leah studied Shalee for a time. "If you know the truth, why do you demand that I tell you everything? You aren't so bloody sure of yourself or your lover, are you? You're afraid! You're jealous! You do think I have the power to entice him from you," she exclaimed, bubbling with false hopes and assurance.

Shalee laughed, then called White Arrow over to her side. She spoke to him in Oglala; they both laughed. In English, she said to Leah, "White Arrow thinks we should place you in the *Tipi Sa* as punishment for your lies and wickedness. If you refuse to speak the truth, I will suggest this to Running Wolf."

Shalee couldn't believe she herself was actually making such malicious threats, but she wanted to terrify Leah into a confession to end her lies and to prevent others. But the gentle-spirited Shalee had been pushed to desperation. She burned to know the truth and to force Leah to voice it aloud. She was outraged by this girl who possessed no conscience, morals, or wisdom.

"What about the child? Such treatment would kill it! You are not that savage or cruel!" Leah confidently announced.

"You have declared bloody war, Leah. In battle, one must fight as fiercely and dirty as one's enemy. I merely follow your lead."

"I suppose White Arrow wishes to enjoy my skills first," she hatefully charged.

"No, Leah. White Arrow would never touch a filthy woman like you. He is much too proud." Shalee smiled up at White Arrow, who had been her close friend for years.

"Are you and White Arrow only friends?" she scoffed insultingly, enviously eyeing the man at her side.

"Don't be absurd, Leah!" Shalee admonished the baneful girl. "White Arrow and I have been *kodas* for many winters," she unnecessarily explained.

"The truth, Leah?" Shalee refreshed her prior demand.

"No. I think I'll let you squirm with doubts and suspicions."

Shalee spoke to White Arrow again, relating her plans to force the truth from Leah and to bring her down. White Arrow nodded agreement, then seized Leah's arms to drag her into the forest. Leah kicked and screamed, but no one came to her aid, as Shalee had vowed. It was clear the girl was being taken away from camp for some just punishment. Each person calmly returned to his duties.

White Arrow halted to pin Leah to the hard ground before binding her hands and feet to prevent her thrashings. He didn't bother to gag her, for no one would listen to her words in English and she didn't know enough Sioux to reveal their plans. They walked a long way off, then stopped. White Arrow dropped Leah to the ground none-too-gently.

"You could harm the child!" she shrieked in rising fear.

"There is no child, Witch!" Shalee shouted back at Leah, her temper unleashed by now.

To White Arrow, Leah appealed about the child's safety. White Arrow hissed in her face.

"He doesn't believe you either," Shalee said. "In fact, he was the first to suggest you were lying. He despises you. He blames himself for giving you to Running Wolf. Nothing would suit him better than to kill you with his bare hands." Leah glared belligerently at her, fighting to conceal her fear and anxiety.

"Now, Leah, tell me everything you did and plotted."

"You wouldn't believe me!" she insolently snorted.

"If you speak the truth I will."

"You mean if my words agree with your husband's!"

"They do not have to agree with his, but they will if you tell the truth."

"I cannot! Gray Eagle and Running Wolf will kill me!"

"If you do not, I will kill you. You have until ten to confess, then your evil tongue will lay in my hand to speak no more lies and inspire no more troubles. One . . . Two . . ."

"You can't do this! They won't allow it!"

"Who won't, Leah?"

"Running Wolf and Gray Eagle!"

"But they are not here, are they? Others witnessed your attack upon me. Will I be blamed for protecting myself?" she bluffed the white girl who had nearly devastated her life.

"I wish Sergeant Starnes had stuck his saber into you rather than bash your skull with that rifle! Too bad those two soldiers didn't have time to rape you like they wanted to do!" she blurted out rashly.

Shalee went rigid. "How do you know he was a sergeant or that there were two of them?" she demanded.

Leah clammed up instantly, then defensively sneered, "I was just babbling! I must have heard someone say it!"

"My God, you actually witnessed my attack and said nothing! You were close enough to hear them speak their names and lethal plans! What if they had slain Bright Arrow? You didn't even go for help! Just how long did you wait before pouncing upon my husband when you presumed I was dead!" Shalee's fury mounted.

Leah's face became defiant. Shalee related the girl's slips to White Arrow. His deadly rage alarmed Leah as he snatched his knife from the leather sheath at his waist and would have slain her if Shalee hadn't stopped him. Leah cringed in terror. Had these two gone mad? Would they really do such terrible things to her? Why had she recklessly blurted out the truth? She hastily cautioned herself to guile.

"If you had summoned help, they could have rescued me that day. You wanted me to die, didn't you? You are worse than even I imagined. Now I see why you were so shocked by my return. You really believed they had killed me that day. Did you cover the evidence? Is that why my trail couldn't be found? Are there no limits to your hatred and evil? So, my crafty witch, you want me dead . . ." she murmured thoughtfully, reassessing this perilously devious white captive.

"All right! I saw them attack you and I didn't run for help! I was afraid they would kill me just because I was white. I pretended to know nothing. I looked after your son. I thought they had killed you."

"You mean you hoped they had! You are a demon from Hell, Leah Winston, and I will enjoy sending you back again! But first, you will speak the truth for once. Three . . . Four . . . Five . . . Six . . ."

The rebellious white girl quivered, but held her silence. "Seven . . . Eight . . . Nine . . . Ten . . . White Arrow hold her tightly. I will do this deed myself," she bluffed one last time, wondering what course to take if Leah called it, suspecting she might.

Leah did not. Through gritted teeth with hatred burning in her emerald eyes, she told Shalee nearly everything. But she made certain to insinuate how much each man enjoyed her for a time. The only thing Leah left out was the fact she was not pregnant; that was her final hope for survival. She must find some way to escape, but after she killed this rival in front of her.

Shalee smiled triumphantly, then sneered disdainfully, "Any man would thrill to such pleasures. I will not demand the truth about the child, Leah. I wish to watch you quiver in fear waiting for your monthly to challenge your life and dispel it. You will be watched closely each day for the first sign," she stated, as if reading Leah's mind.

"You said you would send me away if I told you everything. Did you lie, too? It is not unknown to be wrong about pregnancy."

"Wrong, yes; but not intentionally. I know you carry no child, but I will keep my word. If you wish to confess to Running Wolf this very day, I will convince him to send you to another camp. He will do so for me. Perhaps it would be safer and wiser to end this matter before Gray Eagle returns. His hand of vengeance will be harder to control. I don't care to see you dead, Leah, just banished from our camp."

"Your kindness astounds me, Princess Shalee," Leah bitterly noted. "But of course you are in a position to be all-powerful. You have won. What more do you want of me? I love him as much as you do! I only wanted to win him from you and to share his life."

"But you battled for a prize you could never attain, Leah. I warned you long ago of the consequences of such foolish and lustful dreams. I hold no power here, only the love and respect of my people. You had a good life here, better than any other slave. Why did you throw it away? I have won, but you have caused much pain and trouble in our camp. You rant of uncontrollable love, but I do not think you know how to really love someone. Your heart is evil and your mind black." To White Arrow she said to cut Leah's bonds free. "Do you carry Running Wolf's child, Leah?"

"Yes," she proclaimed, fearing to trust this new Shalee.

"If you do not, I will still try to save your life. But if

you do, you will remain here until the child is born. When you are sold, I will care for the child for Running Wolf. You need not fear for his safety or happiness."

Astonished, Leah irrationally screamed, "You would take a child from its mother's breast! What kind of a monster are you?" A brief glimpse of imminent madness was exposed, but carelessly ignored.

"They will never permit you to stay here. I wished you to know the child will be taken care of by us. If they but learned of your part in my attack, they would lash you until dead. After all you have said and done, I pray you speak the truth about the child. If not, I pray I can halt their deadly hands against such wickedness. Go, Leah, return to your chores. Speak no more lies, or my help will be withdrawn," she cautioned Leah, wondering if she could ever give aid to this girl.

Leah turned and raced for camp as if some demon chased her. Shalee leaned against a large tree and sighed heavily, this episode draining her. Gray Eagle was innocent. By Leah's admission, he had mistaken Leah for her that portentous night. What a tangled and perilous web of lies that feminine spider had woven! How could she have doubted Gray Eagle for even a moment? What would they do to Leah?

"I wish he would return today, White Arrow. It has been three days. How much longer will this matter take? There is so much I must tell him. I love him and need him so much. I must have hurt him deeply with my doubts."

"He could return this sun or be away for many more, Shalee."

"Then I must go to him and tell him the things in my heart. We have both suffered too much. It is time to settle this matter once and for all time," she exclaimed happily.

"You cannot, Shalee. It is not permitted," he quickly debated.

"Surely he has prayed and cleansed himself sufficiently by now, White Arrow. He is probably just sitting there unhappy and anxious like I am. Please, I must go to him. Where is he?"

Knowing there was but one way to halt her, he smiled and shook his head. "There are many places to look for the Great Spirit. He could be nearby or he might have gone to the Sacred Mountains near the winter camp. If he failed to contact Wakantanka in one location, he could move to another. To find him is impossible. We must wait for his return." He unwillingly deceived her.

"But when will that be?" she said in annoyance.

"I do not know, Shalee," he replied, honestly this time.

"I must tell him of Leah's confession. Surely those words will ease his mind and heart. Are you sure we couldn't find him?"

"He would be like a grain of sand upon the desert, Grass Eyes."

"But the spring buffalo hunt begins tomorrow. Why would he not return for it? What will the others say about his absence?"

"Nothing. A man answers to the Great Spirit first. I have been chosen to take his place until his return."

That news nettled her. "The buffalo hunt lasts for weeks, White Arrow. Who will take care of me and Bright Arrow?"

"Shalee," he softly chided her, "the braves will see to the hunting for all families while the others trail the buffalo. Where is your keen mind hiding?" he playfully teased.

"Wherever my stubborn and proud husband is hiding," she laughingly replied.

"While I am gone, you must watch Leah closely. She is dangerous and crafty," he cautioned Shalee.

"I know," she absently concurred. "Come, join me for late meal," she lightheartedly offered.

"If you would help me find a good woman to join, life would be easier for me," he roguishly suggested, to change the conversation.

"Are you serious?" she exclaimed in suspense, eagerly grasping his casual statement.

"It is past time, do you not agree?" he smiled, finally yielding to a destiny he could not alter. Perhaps another woman was the answer.

Amused laughter filled the air. "Do you have someone special in mind?" she hinted, intrigued.

"You can help me pick one." He artfully dodged her query.

"A man should select his own wife, White Arrow. Is there no one who steals your eye and breath?" she romantically inquired.

"Only Grass Eyes, and she is wed to a fierce and jealous warrior. Perhaps I should steal her from his mats while he is away," he teased lightly, his honesty lost amidst his chuckles.

"Perhaps he would hurry back to defend his property if he knew another pined for me," she joined the merry banter, giggling.

"It is a great coup to steal the woman of a chief or noted warrior. But to steal the most beautiful one alive must surely be worth ten coups."

"You honor me greatly, Sir Warrior. How lucky can a simple maiden be than to catch the eye of another powerful and handsome warrior? No doubt many females scheme to catch your attention. You are strong and cunning; you will make a valuable husband. Most warriors cannot boast of your looks and prowess. We must search the entire land for a woman worthy of you."

He smiled. "What do you think of Tasia?" he quizzed.

"Tasia . . . she is very pretty. She has a gentle air and soft tongue. She is skilled in her chores and glows with cheer. She often sings while we work. Tasia could be carefully considered," she replied without any enthusiasm. She irresistibly jested, "What about Little Moon or Piala?"

He inhaled in mock dismay. "Little Moon is as round as a full moon and Piala is invisible behind the slenderest blade of grass. I desire a wife, not a curse," he genially remarked, grinning.

"There is a lovely and delicate female whose husband lies near death," she hesitantly implied, wondering if he preferred a chaste wife.

His eyes gleamed most noticeably. "Yes, I have watched her many times since Leaning Bush fell to his mat. But Leaning bush holds to life like a trap to a fox. It is not good to wish for another's wife while he still lives. He could meet the Great Spirit this moon or not for many winters."

Observing his restrained interest, she casually asked, "If you have waited this long, White Arrow, what is a little more time? Surely Leaning Bush will not see the fall buffalo hunt. He is weak and old. It is no secret she did not wish to join him. They have no children and she is younger than you. She is a very special female. Is she not worth lingering for a while longer? She is a woman to cause a man's heart and body to sing happily."

"What if she desires another warrior when Leaning Bush walks the Ghost Trail?" he asked seriously.

"How could she look at another if she knew of your

eyes upon her? There is no better mate in camp," she declared sincerely.

"What if I am gone when Leaning Bush dies? What if she joins another before my return?" he pressed, leashing his anxiety.

"Perhaps some playful Grass could whisper hints into her ears. If she should 'accidentally' learn of your interest, she would refuse all others until your return. By the winter snows, she could be warming your mats," she teased, then blushed.

He laughed heartily. "Others would laugh and think evil of me if I spoke for another warrior's woman while she still warms his mats."

"Not if only Grass Eyes and your future mate know of such plans. I will cunningly seek her feelings and thoughts of you first. If her eyes glow, I will drop a clue for her to wait for your return."

"It can be so," he concluded cheerfully.

They talked for a while longer before returning to camp. White Arrow left soon after their meal to prepare himself for the morning ride. With Shalee's help, he might gain the second best woman in camp. . . .

The hunting parties had been divided into three groups of men and women. The men would shoot the racing hunks of massive beast and the women would follow behind to skin and carve the dead animals. Several braves would return the laden travois to camp when loaded, only to return for another trek. It was a dangerous, bloody, exhausting, stimulating, and necessary chore, which took place each spring and fall. But it was an efficient and rewarding task, which occupied half of the tribes' women in the spring and the other half in the fall.

Braves were left behind to guard the camp and to hunt for all the families. The warriors and imminent warriors would stalk the thundering hooves of countless hairy beasts who covered the Plains like an endless black carpet, their rumbling approach or retreat heard from miles away. Younger braves were chosen to transport the hides and meat to camp to avoid spoiling or tempting the ravenous appetites of vultures and coyotes. Each assigned duty was carried out with skill and resignation, for such was the Indian way.

This was a busy time for everyone, but not too busy for Shalee to miss her errant husband. Another three days passed as she worked herself into exhaustion to inspire deep sleep and to prevent worry. She made certain Leah worked within sight of her, denying her any chance of another deception. Yet, with each passing day, a greater sense of foreboding plagued her.

If she lived here one hundred years, she would never get used to this bloody and odorous chore. She struggled to keep her mind elsewhere as she labored with the other women, this being a joint venture that profited the entire tribe. The heat inspired insects to pester them and to heighten the stench of drying flesh and untanned hides. Often it took every ounce of control she could muster to avoid retching.

She diverted her attention with various chores, for there was no favorite one. Not once did she ever try to avoid her part in this vital matter of life on the open Plains. She pulled and struggled with a stubborn hide to secure it tightly to a rack for curing. She deftly scraped the bits of flesh and fat from the underside. The difficult part came later, when the brains would be rubbed over the inner surface to oil and soften it. At night, she frequently feared the smell would linger upon her hands forever, awakening her each time they drifted too close to her sensitive nose.

She was more than delighted on the third day of this ritual when it was her turn to gather wood, wild vegetables, berries, and water to prepare the evening meal for the entire tribe. During her work, she furtively observed two other females: Tasia and the lovely Wandering Doe, who had caused that bright and warm glint in White Arrow's eyes. If privacy permitted, she would promptly check out that particular female. Tasia was all right, but not for White Arrow. Wandering Doe was the perfect choice!

Shalee was only too conscious of the lengthy passage of time since Leah had declared herself pregnant. Could it be true after all? Had Leah told the truth just once? Since the women bathed together, it was clear to her probing eyes that Leah's time had not come yet. . . .

Leah was also cognizant of this curious situation, aware and relieved. There had been no brief moment to attempt escape yet. She had hoped to sneak away while everyone was busy and distracted. But she had been carefully watched at every turn, no doubt on Shalee's orders! Shalee . . . it was obvious Shalee had tricked her into a confession by terrorizing her. Why had she weakened? What if she were pregnant? How would that change matters for her?

Leah's back ached from the arduous labor, as did Shalee's. Often each caught the other's probing eyes upon her. A silent clash would result until one or the other looked away. If only the old chief would leave camp and grant her some respite from his intimidating glare! Her nerves were as taut as his bowstring from this constant observation as they eagerly anticipated her downfall. Her hands trembled. How much longer could she endure this maddening period?

Another matter also occupied Leah's concentration.

How could she discover the facts behind that strange conversation between Shalee and Gray Eagle that eventful night? Something terrible had taken place between them long ago, something she needed to explore. They had actually alluded to meeting as enemies! How had he captured and enslaved an Indian Princess, mistaken her for a white thrall? What horrible events took place before the truth was revealed? Had the noble Eagle been forced to marry Shalee after such vile treatment, possibly brutality and rape? Were there suppressed feelings of hostility to be craftily brought to the surface? Very odd indeed . . .

Shortly before dusk, the chores were put away for the day and the evening meal was served. In spite of their fatigue, many laughed and chatted as they relaxed. Shalee leaned against a tree near the edge of the stream, relishing this serene location and time of day. The birds were gradually quietening and settling down for the night. Vital leaves rustled softly above her head, almost too softly to be heard. A gurgle was heard from the nearby stream as the water swirled around rocks or debris. The sky was muting its lovely periwinkle shade to lively grays and the vibrant colors of an impending sunset.

Her lids drooped several times. She was so weary, but her mind continued its busy schedule. She arched her body and stretched to relieve the tautness near her lower waist. She slipped her hands to that area and massaged the nagging muscles. She sighed heavily and yawned.

Please hurry home, my love. I miss you so much. Why do you stay away so long? My heart longs for you and my body craves to be near you. Is there so much to ponder to keep you from our tepee this many days? Do you not ache for me as I do you?

A new thought came to mind. She suddenly straightened and stiffened. Surely he would not join the hunt before coming home first? The hunt required many weeks. Could he keep her waiting around this way before telling her the secrets of his heart and allowing her to reveal hers? Surely he would send some message?

But he had left so coldly and angrily. Was he afraid she was still in that same mood? Was he staying away intentionally? Had this trouble changed his feelings about her, about them? How long did it take for bruised pride to heal? Each of them had been given ample time to sort out their feelings. How could he continue to ignore her in this cruel manner?

In spite of her loneliness and love, annoyance forced its way into her mind. He wasn't being fair to her. How could he simply ride off, then stay away without sending word home? Was he laughing and talking with his friends in the buffalo camp this very moment while she fretted over their separation? Was he digesting the excitement and freedom of the great hunt while she starved for his touch and voice?

Another worry joined that one; what if some accident had befallen him? His enemies were many, including the aggressive soldiers. What if he was injured, or captured, or slain? No! she mentally defied those speculations. He was invincible. He was Gray Eagle!

Didn't he realize how worried she was? Why didn't he come home? At least send some word to her? This waiting was gnawing viciously upon her. Too, Leah's inexplicable and piercing gaze upon her disquieted her nerves. What was that girl plotting and thinking now? Was she only trying to decide if she could trust her? Was she summoning the words and courage to confess all?

The still air was severed by the loud clattering of

horses' hooves. She whirled and looked toward camp. Riders were coming in. Who? Why?

Her heart lurched wildly. Shivers passed over her body. She raced for camp. Breathlessly she approached where the men were dismounting. In confusion, she went to White Arrow's side. He was wounded! A long gash marked the coppery flesh of his upper arm. It was bleeding profusely.

"White Arrow! What happened?" she cried out in alarm.

"The Bluecoats attacked the camp. Most were slain. I arrived just in time to battle two soldiers who had lingered behind to rob the bodies of fallen warriors and women," he managed, trembling from weakness and unleashed fury.

"Here, sit down and I will dress your wound. Which camp did they attack?" she fearfully asked.

"Moon Gazer's. He is dead, Shalee. Many long knives pierced his body, but he fought well. The Great Spirit will be honored to greet him. I came too late; I could not save them," he stated dejectedly.

"Moon Gazer's camp . . ." she repeated, mentally going over who had been in his party. "Turtle Woman! Little Flower! Did you see them?" she demanded in panic.

He lowered his head as if the shame and defeat were all his own. "Dead, Grass Eyes. I am sorry. The white-eyes took them by surprise; they had no chance to flee or fight."

"But they are women! How many did they slay?" she was compelled to ask, dreading his answer. "What about the other two camps?"

"Bluecoats slay any Indian, Shalee. Ten women and three warriors gave their blood to Mother Earth and the

Great Spirit. The other camps have been warned. I came to warn Running Wolf to guard the village against a sneak attack."

They had murdered innocent women? Slaughtered them? Why? So many families torn apart. What about the children and their mates? At least no two from the same family had been present. My God, she thought, and they call Indians savages! "Do you think they will come here next?" she asked, shuddering in fear and anger.

"I would not be surprised, Shalee," he answered as she completed the tight binding upon his left arm to staunch the flow of blood. She carefully washed the reddish-brown liquid from his lower arm and hand, searching for other injuries.

Running Wolf had joined them, pressing the fatigued and wounded warrior with many frantic questions. Before she could ask about her husband, White Arrow recklessly murmured, "Running Wolf, we must send a brave to the Whispering Caves to alert Gray Eagle. He must return to battle our enemies and avenge those who have fallen. All parties must return to camp until we settle this deed. We must go for the bodies of our people and bring them home. The Bluecoats are on the warpath once more. They could be waiting in ambush for us anywhere."

"I will send Ten Days to fetch him," the furious chief announced. "Even we do not massacre innocent white women!"

Shalee stared at her friend, then asked, "You know where he is? All this time, you knew and didn't tell me? Why?"

A sheepish face lifted to look at her. "It is not permitted to disturb such times. I feared you would go to him if I told you where he was. He said no one was to come to him, not even you."

"Have you seen him since he left here? Is he in one of the camps now? Why hasn't he sent me a message?" she quizzed, her tone strangely calm and her gaze unreadable.

"No, Shalee; I have not spoken to him or seen him. He was not in any camp I visited today. When the time is right, he will return home. But we cannot wait for that time now; he must return tonight."

Her gaze revealed her skepticism. "Are you telling the truth this time?" she panted. "Why do so many lies fill the air this season?"

"I ask forgiveness for my false words. He will return tonight, Shalee. Have you lived with us so long and still do not grasp our ways?"

"He will return for his people, White Arrow, not because of me. Have you eaten?" she inexplicably asked, needing to change the topic.

He shook his dark head sadly. "I will get you something. You must have strength to battle such evil foes. Rest, and I will bring you food and water." She hurriedly left.

White Arrow glanced up in astonishment, for it was not Shalee who assisted him. A timid smile flickered upon a lovely face with shining chocolate eyes. He returned the smile before slowly devouring his first meal of this awesome day.

Shalee watched Ten Days mount up and ride away. White Arrow had said her husband would return tonight; that meant he could not be far away. So near, my love; and yet, so very far away . . .

Shalee quelled her own stormy state to look for her son. She quickly and carefully issued instructions for his survival in case of an attack here. When he puffed out his chest and declared he would battle the white-eyes with

411

the warriors, she pulled him into her arms and said, "No, my son, you must seek the safety of the forest. One day you will be chief; your life must be guarded until you are tall and strong like . . . your father. You must train to battle such fierce enemies. It is unwise to endanger your life at this time. You must promise me you will hide in the forest if they ride into our camp."

"But, Mother, all warriors must fight them," he idealistically and childishly reasoned.

"But you are not yet a warrior, Bright Arrow. You must think of your people first. Who would lead them after your father if you foolishly lose your life before you are ready to battle? Do you not recall how the white-eyes stole you to trade for your father? They could do so again. You must protect his life and yours. It is difficult to watch and wait, but it is sometimes necessary. You have much to learn, little son. No matter what happens when they come, you must flee. Even if my life is in danger, you must not look back or return to camp until it is safe. Do you understand? Promise me," she firmly demanded. "You are strong and swift; there are old ones and sick ones who I must help escape."

"Yes, Mother, I will obey," he reluctantly answered.

"You are a good boy, Bright Arrow. You will be a great leader one day, but you must first live to see that day. You are very brave. If other children cry in fear, silence and comfort them."

With that grave responsibility, he beamed and raced off to tell his friends of his new role. She was apprehensive about allowing him out of her sight, but one could not live in fear and hiding every moment. Why couldn't they live in peace? Why did the battles seem endless?

412

The moon was directly overhead; Shalee caught glimpses of it through the ventilation shaft. Too tense to sleep, she paced the confines of the tepee that she and Turtle Woman had constructed. Memories of days spent with Little Flower and Moon Gazer flashed before her mind's eye. Tears slipped down her cheeks. Such a tragic waste of life. Such cruelty and hatred. Times like this made her wish she was still in England.

She went to kneel by her son, gently stroking his hair as he slept so peacefully. How wonderful to be so young and innocent, so unknowing of the tragedies of life. Again she arched her aching back to ease the cramps playing there. She stood up and turned, needing some fresh air from the open flap. She halted and stared.

He had entered like a shadow, silent and nimble. He didn't move; he simply returned her gaze. How tall and handsome he was. How could six days seem like forever; and yet, only a brief moment when they were gone? His stalwart body reeked of brute strength and pride, revealing no trace of denial of food or weakness from his ordeal. He radiated robust health and compelling masculinity. His expression was impassive, his gaze guarded. Should she fly at him in a fit of anger and resentment? Should she throw herself into his arms and cover his face with kisses? How long would he have stayed gone if they had not sent for him? What response did he expect from her, want from her?

The stirring voice calmly announced, "I must ride with the warriors at first light. Protect our son until I return with the bodies of our slain people. When the other hunting parties are safely returned to camp and the bodies of our people sleep upon their scaffolds, I must avenge their murders."

She waited. Was that all he had to say after their tormenting separation? No warm greeting? No words of love? He would ride away once more, this time to confront peril and death, and nothing? He hadn't missed her or ached for her? No apology or plea for understanding and forgiveness? He had been close enough to reach and to return within a few hours, and nothing for six torturous days?

"White Arrow was wounded. Have you spoken with him?" she asked, wondering what to say or do, feeling like some polite stranger to this vital and arresting creature.

"We spoke in the Warrior Lodge. He will ride with me."

The lodge? He had been here long enough to have a meeting with his warriors? He had come home for his people, for his duty, for his pride and revenge . . . but not for her. "I see. . . ." she murmured.

If she had forgiven him, why did she not rush into his arms and declare her love? Had their separation touched her in no way? He had been unable to question White Arrow about her in the presence of others. Why was she still so withdrawn and alarmingly quiet? Could she still reject him now that his body and mind were clean again? He yearned to hold her, to kiss her, to make love to her. Why did she not run to him and say all was good again? He was strong and pure once more. Didn't she long for him as he longed for her? Didn't she realize he would soon challenge the Bird of Death? Had he found her body only to lose her love? Loneliness and desire chewed at him. Perhaps time and distance had not favorably assisted him. . . .

Chapter Eighteen

Perhaps his beautiful Shalee was only proud and stubborn, or still hurt deeply. Once he had felt he knew her better than himself. If that was true, there was only one way to discover it: make the first overture. He had been the one to create this gulf; he must be the one to breach it. He couldn't imagine what he would do if he was wrong.

He slowly and purposefully strode forward, his movements fluid and determined. His muscular body had been honed and tempered over the years as some deadly and potent weapon, but it was magnificent and smooth. The bronze flesh gleamed as if oiled for quickness and shine. That old masterful, self-assured aura permeated her senses. His dark eyes glittered like two brittle chips of precious obsidian. His well-defined, noble features presented an exceptionally handsome visage. His massive ego was rigidly governed, his prior insolence noticeably missing. Combining these traits and appearance, he was the epitome of manhood and superiority.

He halted within three inches of her, keenly aware of her quickened respiration and tremors, of his delightfully disturbing effect upon her. Her gaze had leisurely traveled his body to lock upon his face. His jet eyes scanned the face that had haunted him day and night during his purification rite. In that fiery cave, his desire and love had increased as the evil and weakness had poured from his body. At last, he felt whole and alive again, clean and strong. Eager to hurry home, his ritually weakened frame had recovered in just one day from his mandatory ordeal. But the winds of war were ruffling his powerful wings again.

"Shalee," he spoke tenderly, then halted instantly. How did he begin? What to say or do first?

Panicked by his mysterious mood, she hoarsely probed, "You wish to tell me something?"

To test her emotional waters, he stated, "You do not seem happy to see me home."

"This is a sad time, Wanmdi Hota. Many of our people were brutally murdered. The Bluecoats are calling you to challenge again. Your people need your guidance and power. Only you can right this terrible deed," she softly replied, revealing only her vivid sadness and her confidence in his prowess.

"Do you also need me?" he asked pointedly, watching her.

"I am your wife. A wife always needs her husband," she cautiously responded near a whisper, her eyes never leaving his.

"That is not my meaning. Do you need me? Me, Wanmdi Hota?" he huskily clarified, knowing she was guarded and uncertain.

She needed a question of her own answered before she exposed her aching heart and soul to him. "Do you need me? You have been away for many days without sending any word to me. Did it require so many moons to decide if you wanted or needed me? Tonight, you return only because your people sent for you. All these many days, they knew of your hiding place, but I did not." Her voice was laced with anguish and her eyes were naked with warring emotions.

Could it be possible she actually believed he had not missed her? Had not ached for her nearness and touch?

416

Had not battled evil for his very soul to return to her a whole man? Did not love her? Had his absence created more anguish and insecurity? She knew his ways and customs, yet she did not comprehend their importance or meaning. His departure appeared a desertion to her, a tormenting separation when she needed him. Her dejected aura said she honestly thought he was returning for the sake of his people, not her! But that wasn't true.

He shook his head of flowing, sooty hair. After her ragged words, she had lowered her head and focused her gaze upon his *wanapin*. He gently grasped her chin and lifted her head, pulling her gaze back to his. "No, Shalee, it is not so. I was riding for home when I encountered Ten Days. Once more I am Gray Eagle, warrior and man worthy of the love of my people and the Great Spirit. My body and mind are cleansed of evil and defeat. Before all others, I return to you."

She had reacted with astonishment to his first two statements. "You were coming back tonight?" she probed suspensefully, praying she had heard him correctly. His last statement warmed her very soul.

"Yes, Little One. The days and nights have been empty and long without you," he murmured in that low, hypnotic voice of his.

Tears of joy and relief welled in her green eyes. "So very long and lonely, Gray Eagle," she readily agreed. "I missed you more than words can say. Each day I prayed for your quick and safe return to me. Each night I became more and more afraid of the meaning of your delay. But you have never been defeated or possessed with evil. We have all made mistakes and suffered from brief moments of weakness. If you were perfect and pure, you would be Wakantanka and not Gray Eagle. I love you and need you. You judged yourself much too harshly, and I loved

417

you so much I also weakened in fear of losing you. Perhaps my illness placed a strain upon both of us, a strain that caused us to react as we should not. Those weeks of not knowing you shone brighter than I realized and confused my mind as the memories returned. I hurt you deeply and I am sorry. This time has been difficult for us, but it cannot destroy our love. There are no ghosts between us now."

A smile captured his sensual mouth, a dazzling one that seemed to drive every shadow from the dim tepee and her heart. He pulled her into his embrace and held her possessively and lovingly. She could feel and hear the thundering of his heart. "Tonight, I was coming home to you, my one love above all others. I have hungered for you each moment I was away. I feared the Great Spirit would rage at my lack of attention. As I prayed and chanted, I would hear your name slip from my lips. As I dreamed, your face would float before me. Even as I weakened, my needs for you grew stronger. Never has patience tested me more. Many times I had to force myself from the entrance to the cave as my heart was drawn to leave, to return to your side. But I was not yet Gray Eagle, and I could offer you no less. What is my life without you? From the moment you stepped before me at your fortress when I was the captive of your people, I have loved and desired you, Little One, only you with all my heart and body. You fill me as my body fills my skin; there is room for no other."

She leaned back and looked up into his smoldering eyes, reading the love and passion blazing there. "We were so foolish, my love. We must never allow anyone or anything ever to spoil or endanger our love and joy. Only we have the power to destroy or protect it. For me, there will never be a man to take the place of Gray Eagle, for you are my place in life. I would cease without you."

His mouth came down upon hers, exploring and tasting the sweet nectar there. He crushed her so tightly to his chest that she could hardly breathe, but she did not care. Eagerly seeking the treasures she possessed, he plundered her mouth with skill and resolve. Her arms encircled his waist and slipped up his back. How intoxicating it was to touch him. Her mind reeled with the fiery sensations that they shared. His nearness was like an aphrodisiac, she was drugged by it.

Surely there was no spot upon her face which did not tingle from his searing kisses. Her body surged with life and desire, as did his. Never was she more alive or elated than when in his arms. He controlled the very essence of her being. His warm breath sent tremors over her flesh as he nibbled at her ear and whispered tender words into it. His insistent hands roamed her sensitive body, each area responding hastily to them. They moved leisurely as if refreshing each inch within his mind, enflaming her with their gentleness and fire.

There was no spot upon her that did not cry out for him to invade it, to conquer it, to claim it as his own domain. As his lips and tongue played upon her palms, she shivered with excitement. "My body burns like a fiery torch for you, Little One. My needs are as tight as the beaver's dam. I almost fear to take you so soon, for surely the dam will explode the moment I enter you."

Her voice was sensually husky as she vowed, "I am a careless beaver, my love. The dam is so weak that it will require little to tear it away." Thus she revealed her own desperate need for him.

Flames licked greedily at his smoldering body and igneous eyes as he removed her garments and enticingly roved the shapely body before him. He bent forward to capture an inviting breast with his lips. As his tongue circled the point, she watched with a mesmerized gaze. Wild and wonderful feelings played havoc with her control. She wanted to savor this long-awaited and special moment, but her needs were too great to wait.

Her hand went to his head and wandered into the sleek midnight mane. Each time he left one breast to tease the other, it would mutely plead for his return. His lips began to move upwards until they locked fiercely with hers. His hand provocatively slipped down her hips and over her taut stomach to seek out the secret place that summoned his attention and deft movements. A moan escaped her lips between kisses.

"This fire that rages within me will surely consume me to ashes if you do not feed it soon," she declared hungrily.

Her shaky hands sought and loosened the ties to his breechcloth. It was a difficult task, but eventually a successful one. As it fell away, her hand claimed the prize that possessed the power to drive her mindless with ecstatic pleasure and blissful torture. It was sleek and warm. It reared proudly like some wild and carefree stallion. Her daring hand stroked it gently, causing its spirit to heighten. His body shuddered as a groan came from deep within his brawny chest.

Her hand was forced to slip away as he lifted her and carried her to their mat. He lay her down, instantly joining her and fusing his mouth to hers as his hand returned to taunt her breasts and womanhood, to seductively anticipate what was in store for them.

Dazed with heady desire, she pleaded, "Love me, Wanmdi Hota . . . love me now or I shall surely die of need. . . ."

This joining so long-denied and her body so eager for his, he swiftly entered her, the contact nearly causing her to swoon and to cry out with exquisite rapture. Her face imprisoned between his hands, he artfully ravished her mouth, his manhood striving to sate her great need. She was trapped in his power. All restraint and resentment torn away, she heatedly surrendered her will and body to his loving assault, seeking the sublime fulfillment that only he could grant.

Her hands moved up and down his back, reveling in the strength of the rippling muscles. As he probed her body, his lips could not leave hers, for her passion was so great that she could not constrain her moans, which could awaken their son and disrupt this victorious moment. More and more he realized the advantage of the white man's wooden tepee with its offer of privacy that could shut out the world in times like this. In the heat of the moment, that amusing thought was discarded.

When the raging waters of passion crashed forcefully against her weakened dam, it was torn asunder. She was blissfully swept away with its powerful currents, helpless to do anything but allow herself to be carried along with its savage surge for freedom and release. He continued his control of her mouth, suspecting the muffled cry of pleasure could have been heard throughout the entire camp if he had not prevented it. He was heady with the knowledge of the way he could please her.

As her flood of passion began to subside, he quickly pursued her before she could reach the tranquil pond. Giving free rein to his manhood, he plunged forward to join her. His release was so potent, his body shuddered violently as he exploded within her. So ensnared was he by her magic that he almost lost control of his own tongue. He rode the intense waves until every spasm ceased and he was peacefully drifting to join her in the quiet waters that lapped serenely at them.

His respiration erratic and his heart pounding fiercely, he whispered against her lips, "*Waste cedake, Cinstinna. Waste cedake.*"

He rolled to his left side, carrying her along with him, unwilling to break their contact. Her hand caressed his cheek, then pushed the raven-black hair over his bronze shoulder. It lingered there to caress the flawless and smooth surface, to slowly trace over his chest, to ease up his throat, and to play over his lips. As her eyes met his, she vowed, "As I love you."

She smiled mischievously and teased softly, "You have much strength, control, and prowess for a weakened eagle, my warrior of the sky."

"I needed you more than food or air, Little One. You nourish me as they never can. With such a prize in sight even a weakened eagle can soar like the wind and claim it. But if your passion had not matched mine this night, Grass Eyes, only I would be smiling happily this moment. My control vanishes when I but look at you or touch you. Surely you recall the last day of purification includes refreshing the body with food and rest?" he jovially reminded her.

"If I am your food and peace, you could not refresh yourself until now," she saucily mocked, grinning at him, leaning forward to playfully nibble upon his lower lip.

"Why do you think I rode like the wind for home near darkness?" he parried, as his beguiling and amused smile stirred her heart.

"Because the Eagle needed to protect and enjoy his territory."

"And you are my territory?" he seductively jested, pushing aside a straying auburn tendril that blocked his total view of her body.

She lifted a shiny joining necklace and smiled. "This

tells the whole world I am yours forever."

"Would it do so if I had not challenged for your hand and forced you to marry me?" he said, slyly continuing this stimulating game they frequently shared.

"If it was not around my neck, surely my eyes and heart would shine more brightly than it does. I belonged to you long before you demanded to marry me. No doubt if you had not come for me, I would have stolen a horse one night and abducted you. I would have taken you to some secret place and held you as my captive. I would have driven you wild with desire until you could not resist me."

"How so, when I have never been able to resist you, Grass Eyes?"

"I would have weakened your mind as your body."

He chuckled softly. "Do you not prefer me strong and cunning?"

"I prefer you as you are. No other man compares to you."

"In what way am I matchless?" he pressed in pleasure.

"In all ways, my love. In all ways. . . ."

"All?" he gravely questioned, his meaning clear.

She smiled. "Each is a part of you. If not, you would not be Gray Eagle. If not Gray Eagle, then not the man I love."

"As I love you in all ways," he replied passionately.

"All?" she seized his challenge, grinning.

"I love all that was once Alisha Williams, all that is now Princess Shalee. I love all that is you."

She smiled contentedly. "It is true, my love; I am Princess Shalee. Alisha was but a name, not a woman."

"Alisha did not die, Little One. She only became Princess Shalee, my woman, my wife. It was but a white name, and now you are Indian."

423

She gazed into his eyes. "In the cave, you accepted this, did you not?"

"The Great Spirit showed me many things, Shalee. Your blood is red like mine. Only life is carried there, not the white man's evil. Evil lives in hearts and minds. They do not in yours. You are Indian. When I look at you and touch you, that is all I see and feel."

Her heart soared as free and light as a feather in the wind. "I love you," she declared.

His gaze caressed her enchanting face. "I know, Little One." His lips claimed hers as they rekindled the smoldering fire that would never cease to burn within them.

Later, as they lay entwined in the afterglow of lovemaking, they talked about many things. "When Wi shows his face, Grass Eyes, I must leave your . . ."

She pressed her finger to his lips. "Say no more of partings, my love. For tonight, there is only us. But you must promise me to guard your life with all your cunning and strength, for without you I am nothing."

"I will claim the bodies of our people. But I will return to your side before I avenge their deaths. Do not fear, Grass Eyes, for it is not the season for me to join Wakantanka. He revealed many things to me. Our people will know a greatness other nations will not. The white man will fear the power of the Sioux Nation. It will be many winters, Little One, but Sun Cloud will come to us."

She glanced up at him and grinned. "What did the Great Spirit reveal to you about our next son?"

"We must be patient. When the vision came to me, I saw Bright Arrow riding at my side. Long before we join the Great Spirit, our sons will ride against the white man together. Both will be great leaders." Dreams and visions were powerful magic they did not doubt.

A haunted look clouded his eyes. She questioned it and

his abrupt change in mood. "Wakantanka revealed some trouble to you?"

"There were many visions I did not understand. Running Wolf was dying upon his mat. A warrior stepped from the nearby shadows. It was Gray Eagle; yet, it was not. Who but my son could reflect my face? I pray this means Running Wolf will live to see my son grown."

He glanced at her curiously as some imperceptible chill passed over her. He pulled her against his body to draw comfort from its warmth. "Many times a knife gleamed before your face. Perhaps I only dreamed of the night Chela tried to slay you long ago. Still, you must be careful. Promise me this."

She could see he was deadly serious, so she smiled and promised. Their firm belief in dreams often confused her. Yet, so many times he had spoken of things that had come to pass. Was it only keen perception and logic, or was he the receiver of some mystical premonitions? Who could explain the mysteries of life? Regardless, they believed in such signs; therefore, she had to take them seriously.

He truly believed they would have another son one day. Now, his dream filled him with patience and contentment. But why had she reacted so oddly to his first revelation? Why did she also sense there was some foreboding message there? Knowing how frequently his visions were accurate, she listened intently.

Gray Eagle glanced over at the sleeping form of their first son. His eyes revealed a sadness she dreaded. "The seed of Gray Eagle will not pass through our first son, Shalee; the greatness of the Oglala will live within Sun Cloud and his children."

She paled and trembled. "Are you saying he will be slain?"

"No, Little One. But Sun Cloud will ride as chief

425

before Bright Arrow is old enough to pass it to his son. Sun Cloud will show a greatness few warriors ever know. His coups will outnumber even mine. Many winters after we join the Great Spirit, the line of Sun Cloud will rival the power of all white-eyes. The white man's words will speak of the greatness of one who takes the name of the buffalo bull who sits in council with wisdom and who rides with courage and skill unmatched."

"I do not understand. How will Sun Cloud take the chief's bonnet from his older brother?" she worriedly asked, imagining some fierce struggle for power between her two sons.

"A woman will enter his life; her love will defeat his power."

Bitterness edged into his tone and his eyes chilled. "A woman? But who? How can a woman's love remove his war bonnet?"

"I do not know. But he will choose her love over his duty. Her face was not clear to me, but she carried some guarded and persistent enemy within her."

"Perhaps it is Wakantanka's way to move the line to Sun Cloud. If the greatness will pass through him, he must first become chief. Perhaps the Great Spirit gives this special woman to our son to appease his loss and to grant him peace and love. Can such a powerful love be wrong, my husband? Can he not be a great warrior?"

"He will become a great warrior. But her love will cost him much."

"You are saying he must step aside to claim her?"

"Yes."

"It troubles you to know such things?" she pressed.

"I am confused. How could the son of Gray Eagle chose a woman over his duty?"

"Perhaps his love will rival ours. Do you not recall

426

how much my love once cost you? Do you not recall how you refused to give me up, even at the cost of much honor and suffering?"

He smiled ruefully. "It is so. I thank the Great Spirit I was not forced to chose between you and my duty. I cannot think of what such a decision would be," he stated quietly.

She smiled and caressed his cheek. "I understand, my love. To sacrifice all for a love must knife the very soul. To live without either would be tragic. How cruel and demanding life can be. If the vision is true, we must not interfere," she cautioned him.

"You say I must not step between him and this woman?"

"Yes, my love. His destiny lies in the hands of Wakantanka. As with many times before, we do not always see or know the workings of the Great Spirit's mind. We must learn to trust him and to halt defying His plans, even when we do not comprehend them or agree. Perhaps He will find some way for Bright Arrow to have both, as you do. Until this day presents itself, we must forget such knowledge. Do not allow such confusing visions to come between you and your son. Perhaps it was only a warning, nothing more," she hinted cheerfully.

He grinned. "Perhaps. As it was with us, she would not enter his life and heart if it is not the will of the Great Spirit."

"With so many visions sent to you, how did you have time to think of me or to miss me?" she jested, to lighten their grave moods.

"You are wily, Little One. You are also right; we have spoken enough of such matters. It will be many winters before we see such things. Bright Arrow will make us proud to call him son."

"He brings pride and joy now, my love. Each day he is more like you."

"Perhaps too much like me?" he teased lightly.

"Never. You are perfect."

"Love blinds your eyes to my flaws, Little One."

"You have none. Perhaps only very tiny ones," she altered her claim as he chuckled, and his gaze mocked her.

"Since I am not the Great Spirit, I cannot be perfect." He used her prior words.

"Alas if it must be so, I accept you as you are."

"We must sleep, Little One. The new sun will show its face soon."

"You will be careful," she repeated apprehensively.

"How can I be harmed when we have another son to make?"

"If it will be many, many winters before he comes, need we work so hard for him now?" she merrily jested, eyes sparkling.

"We must practice our skills to hone them for the right moment." He ran his finger over her lips and grinned.

"Your body needs to regain its strength from the visions. How can you practice more than two times in this weakened state?"

He pinned her to her back and teased at her breasts. She giggled softly. "Such stamina, my noble Eagle," she whispered tenderly.

He slipped easily into her receptive body. He moved slowly and provocatively. When she was aroused to fiery passion, he withdrew and asked, "Have I practiced enough this moon?"

"If you do not practice more, I will cut out your

cruel heart."

They both laughed, then made love feverishly. As she lay sleeping in his arms, he moodily reflected upon something he had not told her about a certain vision, something he could not. He lifted his head to gaze at Bright Arrow. An aura of imminent prowess surrounded him even now. He laid his head near Shalee's and closed his eyes.

Within moments, they opened again. He longingly studied her lovely and serene face. Her reality challenged his selfish future plans. She was his life; yet, she was white. Their son carried her blood as well as his: white blood. Much as he loved her and challenged all to keep her, could he allow his son to follow in his steps? Could he deny him a love to rival his own? Could he interfere with the destiny of either son?

The vision returned to plague him. He was standing with Bright Arrow when a woman stepped between them, her back to him. Bright Arrow did not halt her when she removed his feathers and let them float silently to the earth. She grasped his hand, he smiled at her with a love pure and strong. As they walked away into the shadows, she glanced over her shoulder at Chief Gray Eagle. He could not move or speak. Her eyes were those of a doe, her hair the color of Shalee's, her skin white. . . .

At last his troubled mind gave in to much needed sleep. It was only three hours before he was called to join his band of warriors to fetch the bodies of his people upon the open Plain: lands that were theirs and would remain theirs.

He kissed Shalee soundly and hugged his son. "I will return."

She smiled radiantly. "Yes, my love, I know." They parted.

Chapter Nineteen

The other two hunting parties and the bodies of the slain Oglala people were soberly returned to camp without any hostile incidents. Shalee rushed to greet her husband as he slowly rode into camp, his burdens a gruesome sight. Tears washed down her cheeks as she viewed the mangled bodies of Turtle Woman, Little Flower, and Shining Light's beloved Moon Gazer. The others also brought grief and anger to her mind, but those three people were special to her.

The atmosphere in the camp was solemn and oppressive as the slain were placed upon their death scaffolds, their bodies to be absorbed by the elements of nature, allowing their souls to be delivered to the Great Spirit. The weapons of the slain warriors rested with them, as was their custom. The chants were sung in mournful tones to send their souls along their journey. Children wept for fallen parents; mates grieved over their own losses; friends prayed for those they had known since birth.

Shalee watched her husband as he covered the distance between the place of burial and the camp, the weight of his responsibilities heavy upon his broad shoulders, the peril of revenge charging the still air with ominous currents. She could not wholly agree with vengeance, for it bore a high price. Yet, how could she argue against just payment for such a brutal slaughtering of innocent women, against a way of life they had known since birth? In exacting times like these, she was compelled to hold her tongue and reluctantly accept what must be.

He joined her, but remained silent for a time. His strong arm slipped around her to comfort her loss of her good friends. "Why must it be so, Shalee? Why must they come and war with us? They have their lands where Wi awakens. These are our lands and forests. We do not enter theirs and war to possess them. Why must they invade ours and take away our peace and lives? Before they came, joy and peace ruled the Sioux domain; for others feared to challenge us. The white man has no fear or wisdom. When all are slain, more come. When those are slain, even more come. The whites are many. One day it will come to the destruction of one side."

"It grieves my heart, my love, but your words are true. No matter how much land they have, they always want more and more. But many are not so. Many only seek freedom and peace from the cruelty of other whites. To you, all appear white. But like the many Indian nations, the whites are divided amongst themselves. Many groups of whites are tormented by others. Some do not know about the Indians. They are given lies about this land. They come with good in their hearts, then are forced to take sides against us, for we refuse all whites. It saddens my heart to know the good will die because of the evil deeds of the bad. Is truce so impossible? We cannot stop them from coming. They are like a swollen river that cannot be damned. Should we not try for peace before they are many and strong?" she reasoned.

"To yield truce to some would encourage others to think we yield from weakness and fear. If we allow many to come and remain, soon others will follow. How long before the Plains and forests are filled with them? Once they are many and strong, their defeat will be difficult. We must not allow such dangerous numbers to enter here."

How could she argue with the course of history? Once this entire country had belonged to the Indians. Now, the eastern coast was nearly all white. At first they had come in small numbers, then steadily increased until there was no room left for the Indians. As more and more whites came to America, they gradually pushed westward with their abundance of people and with their desires for more land and goods. Already the gold and furs enticed evil men here. The future looked dim. She dreaded to think of the days when her sons would battle large numbers of whites.

She determined to teach them English and all she knew about the white man. If this land became white one day, they must be given the tools for survival. But what of her husband? He was a thorn in the side of the whites, one they fiercely struggled to remove. How long could he avoid their probings, their resolve to end his powerful reign? It was too clear that a strike at him was a deadly blow to the entire Indian nation. The life of a legend was perilous!

That next day was spent in hunting to supply the camp with fresh meat while the warriors were away. In order for everyone to remain near camp, a large supply of wood, water, and wild fruits and vegetables were gathered during the tiring day. When dusk came, the dreaded ceremony began.

Shalee tensed the instant the battle drums sent forth their awesome notes. Her gaze flew to her husband. He smiled knowingly. She rushed into his arms. "I wish you did not have to go after them, my love," she exclaimed in panic, knowing she could not beg him to stay. He was Gray Eagle, their leader, their spirit, their essence.

He covered her face with kisses. "If we allow this deed to go unpunished, the whites will gather deadly pride and joy. They must learn we will retaliate in kind. They must be taught to hesitate before doing such evil deeds. Do not hate me for what I must do to your kind, Shalee."

"I could never hate you, my love. They are no longer my kind, for I am Indian now. I will pray for your safe return to me. They sealed their fates when they slaughtered innocent people. I will not defy our ways."

He hugged her fiercely. "You are truly Indian, Shalee."

Considered bad medicine for a woman to touch a man's ceremonial garments, she could not assist him as he dressed. His body was clad in chamois-colored buckskins, his *wanapin* dangling from his neck. She stared at the white eagle, knowing what the whites would pay to hold it in their hands. The upper portion of a deer's head with hide still intact was placed over his flowing black mane. His forehead was concealed, as were the sides of his face to his ebony eyes. The hide was rich chestnut, tipped with white around his bronze face. The empty forelegs hung over his chest, as if the animal were merely resting over his broad back. Twelve points upon its head revealed its age and its cunning in evading the hunters for many years.

The headdress was maintained in excellent condition, only its mouth and entrails missing. Even in its lifeless state, it was a magnificent sight to behold. The black eyes appeared tranquil, as if revealing no animosity toward its slayer or terror at the moment of death. The ears stood erect; the nose was a shiny ebony shade. As if reflecting the traits of its new owner, both hinted at cunning, speed, gentleness, and strength.

Taking a small pouch, Gray Eagle artistically used his forefinger to smear three yellow slashes over the bridge of his nose and across both cheeks, the sunny shade loud against his deep bronze flesh. Just beneath his lower lashes, he added a small line of jet black on either side, carrying them past the ends of his ebony eyes to drift beneath the deerskin. What was meant to inspire fear in enemies only gave him a wild and sensual appearance, at least to a woman.

He glanced up to note the way she was looking at him, his effect upon her clear. "Your eyes betray your thoughts, Little One," he teased happily.

"I wish it were not forbidden to touch you now, for you sorely tempt me to ravish you. How can a man be so bewitching and irresistible?" she wondered aloud, aching to love him wildly and freely.

He chuckled roguishly. "If you do not change your look and voice, Grass Eyes, I will be sorely tempted to permit such an exciting deed," he quickly retorted, grinning broadly.

"If you but weakened for a brief moment, the cause is lost to us," she seductively warned, smiling at him.

"Then come, let us share the company of others for safety. Later, I will sorely tempt you once more," he remarked casually.

He ducked to exit from the tepee without dislodging his headdress. They walked toward the center of camp where a large fire was burning brightly, meaningfully. She urged her rebellious legs to move forward. It was

434

time. She dreaded this portentous moment; for once begun, there was no turning back. . . .

Gray Eagle sat upon a buffalo hide before the campfire with the other noted warriors and their aging chief. The aspiring warriors and younger braves sat on the other side. The women stood behind either group at a respectful distance. The children were inside their tepees under the watchful eyes of older youths, elders, or white captives. It was nearly dark. A grave silence filled the air, which was highly charged with ominous emotions. Each person was alert.

The Pezuta Wapiye Wicasta Itancan, their medicine chief, arose and took his place amidst this circle of people. His voice was resonant and spellbinding as he sang the mournful chants for those who had fallen before their enemy. Afterwards, he chanted of the coups of the deceased warriors, pride and grief filling the hearts of the Oglala at such terrible losses. Shalee tensed uncontrollably as his clear voice sent forth the strains of the chants for guidance and protection as his people prepared to seek justice and revenge for those deadly events upon the Plains. When his meaningful part in this vital ceremony was completed, he reclaimed his seat near Gray Eagle.

The Token-pi-i-ceyapi Itancan, the ceremonial chief, arose next to fulfill his duty. *"Hiya wookiye Oglala wasichu,"* he stated, voicing the known fact that there was no peace between the white man and his tribe. He spoke of their *yuonihansni,* their shame and dishonor, if this lethal crime was not avenged. The Oyate Omniciye, the Tribal Council, had met and voted for retaliation. Their tribe boasted of a powerful warrior society, the O-zu-ye Wicasta, which would carry out this act of justice. His voice revealed respect as he announced the names

435

of those warriors selected as *tiospaya itancans:* band leaders for the raids. The people listened intently. "Capa Cistinna," he revealed the name of Little Beaver. "Mahpiya Luta," he added Red Cloud's name. "Wanhinpe Ska," came White Arrow's name, to be followed by Talking Rock's as the last man. Nods from the others indicated their concurrence in the choices of those intrepid warriors.

Tautness seized Shalee's body and fear her heart. "*Akicita-heyake-to ki-ci-e-conape Oglala,*" the ceremonial chief declared the Bluecoats' challenge to the Oglala. "*Ku-wa, wohdake, Akicita Itancan,*" he solemnly invited the chosen war chief to speak to his four bands of warriors.

It did not surprise anyone when Gray Eagle arose to accept this great honor. It was unnecessary for Shalee to listen to his imminent words to know what he was about to say. He spoke of the seemingly endless warfare between the Indians and the whites. He listed the many grievances against their aggressive foe, the hostile Bluecoats. He talked of days long past when peace and joy ruled their lands, that time before the whites had boldly invaded this territory. He smiled encouragingly at his father as he related the aging chief's inability to lead such a fierce and deadly charge against them. Everyone agreed the elderly chief should remain here to guard the camp against a surprise attack while the warrior society pursued the soldiers who had slain his people.

He did not risk a glance at his wife as he announced they would ride at first light the following morning, to return only after their impending victory. The assigned band leaders were given their orders, stirring and crafty ones, which only Gray Eagle could envision and carry

436

out. When all was said and settled, Gray Eagle sat down.

For a time, all was still and quiet; the portentous aura of this moment was etched upon each face around the campfire. Running Wolf stood up to dismiss the meeting, suggesting all retire for rest and farewells: many goodbyes to be said possibly for a last time. The group gradually dispersed.

Gray Eagle's ceremonial garments were carefully returned to their proper place, then he joined his exceptionally quiet wife upon their sleeping mat. He observed her for a long time, neither speaking. Finally, he reached out to caress her pale cheek, inspiring her to fling herself into his waiting arms.

"Forgive my weakness and fear, my love," she murmured raggedly as she wept. "I do not doubt your prowess, but my heart suffers to think of what you must face before you can return to my side. I cannot think upon who will not be riding at your side when you come home. I hate this endless war! If they even harm one hair upon your head, I will fight them myself!"

He hugged her and kissed her. "Do not worry, Little One. Soon I will be with you again," he tenderly promised.

"I know. But my heart pains for those who will not return. I share the anguish of Shining Light over her loss of Moon Gazer. I ache to know Red Cloud can no longer share the love of Turtle Woman, or Talking Rock the love of Little Flower. You must caution him to clear his head of her loss, or he might not return to their children. War is such a useless waste of life."

"We must accept it, Shalee, for peace will never fill our lands and hearts again."

"We must train our sons well, my love. Their powers

437

must be matchless against their future enemies. It saddens me to know they will never experience life as you once knew it here."

"Time is short, Little One. We should speak of other things," he insisted, needing to forget the demands of tomorrow at this time.

Her gaze locked with his as she desperately implored, "Love me as if there is no tomorrow, only tonight."

He needed no further encouragement to make passionate love to her. His mouth plundered hers with breath-stealing kisses. His lips taunted her yearning breasts until she moaned with overwhelming desire. His deft hands explored and pleased her shapely body. They loved as if this moment was eternal bliss and another day was only a dream. As ecstasy claimed them, over and over he whispered his love for her between intoxicating kisses.

Spent, still they did not release each other. Her head nestled at the curve of his shoulder where it joined his neck, his cheek resting against her auburn head. Ever so lightly his hand stroked her silky back as her finger wandered over the smooth flesh upon his chest. Her arms encircled his body as she lifted her face to entreat another heady kiss from his full and sensual mouth.

After their second and feverish joining, she beseeched him to get some much needed sleep so as to offer keen and alert senses to the coming day. He smiled at her, dropping a playful kiss upon her nose. "I love you, Little One," he murmured tenderly.

She smiled happily as she replied, "I love you." Sleep came to the two lovers, whose bodies remained together all night.

At his first movement, her leaf-green eyes opened. In spite of her confidence in his prowess, dread and anxiety filled her eyes and body. A knowing and mocking grin eased over his compelling features. "It is time, Little One," he stated soberly.

Undaunted, she smiled and added, "Time to make love before you must leave."

He laughed heartily and retorted, "It is so." Their emotions unbridled, they made love with carefree and heady abandonment.

Afterwards, they slipped to the stream to bathe. When he was dressed and prepared, he left to join his warriors.

She lingered outside the entrance to their tepee. It was not the time or place for her to be near him. The warriors mounted up. She smiled as Gray Eagle seized one last look at her, such possessive and intense love written in his eyes. Regardless of the countless eyes trained upon him, he touched his balled fist to his heart, then extended his outstretched hand toward her, the palm open and looking skyward, signing for all creation to witness that he freely offered his heart and love to her.

Joyous tears clouded her enraptured gaze. Mesmerized by him, she shamelessly repeated his action for all the world to see and to know she loved this man above all else. He smiled and nodded, slowly pulling his igneous gaze and enchanted senses from her.

He checked to make certain all was ready. A deadly calm and lucid confidence surrounded him. *"Ku-wa, Oglala; hiyupo,"* he called to his warriors to ride.

Numberless hooves thundered upon the hard ground as the large band raced from the Oglala camp to search for their enemies, not one man glancing back at the loved ones who witnessed this critical departure. Not a single person moved or spoke until the dust cleared and the warriors were completely out of visual range.

Shalee allowed her gaze to slip over the dispersing group, halting upon the worried expression of Wandering Doe. She walked toward the delicate creature who was inspiring White Arrow to ponder marriage. She stopped before her, inviting the lovely young woman's inquisitive gaze to meet hers.

They exchanged amiable smiles. Shalee asked if she could speak with her for a few moments in private. Wandering Doe speculated upon Shalee's mischievous expression. She nodded agreement, then followed Shalee to her tepee.

Shalee politely invited the hesitant girl to sit down. Wandering Doe complied uneasily, asking, "What do you wish, Shalee?"

"How is Leaning Bush?" she inquired casually.

"He grows weaker every sun. His eyes will not view the coming season when Wi reflects his face upon the grasslands," Wandering Doe said, softly hinting at his imminent death.

Shalee nodded understanding. "Do you love Leaning Bush, Wandering Doe?" She asked an unexpected question, astonishing the young woman.

"Why do you ask such things?" Wandering Doe responded in a guarded manner.

"It is known Leaning Bush traded for your hand in joining, that you did not choose him to mate. He will walk the Ghost Trail soon. Does your heart soften yet for another warrior?" she boldly inquired, yet gently.

"It is not wise to think of such things while he still enjoys the breath of life, Shalee," the other answered.

"Perhaps if you loved him. You have no children and soon you will be alone. It is natural to think upon your new life, for it is near. Is there no other man who warms your heart? For you have the power to select your new mate," Shalee probed, her air one of idle curiosity.

Wandering Doe actually blushed and lowered her

lashes. "Why do you ask me this?" she pressed.

"There is a warrior whose heart you have touched. While Leaning Bush lives, he cannot approach you or let his desire be known. He will not speak until Leaning Bush rests upon the death scaffold, but he fears you will select another to join while he is not here."

Wandering Doe's alert mind flickered over the unmarried men who had left camp earlier. "Who is this warrior?" she entreated, suspense flooding her.

"He has never taken a mate before. He is handsome and brave. Others follow him in battle. He is kind and generous. He is a man who stands above others," she hinted.

Excitement and happiness were vividly exposed in the chocolate eyes. She trembled with anticipation and delight. Yet, she almost feared her guess would be wrong. "Is it bad to pray the warrior you speak of is . . . White Arrow?" she helplessly asked, holding her breath.

Shalee smiled at her reaction. "I speak of the man who rides at my husband's side, the man who is our good friend and brother. His heart is touched and warmed by you. If you also feel this way, he will wait for you to be free to join him."

It was nearly impossible for the Indian woman to contain her exhilaration. "I feared the Great Spirit would punish me for desiring him while joined to Leaning Bush," she confessed openly to Shalee. "No other man causes my heart to race with love or my body to warm with desire as White Arrow does. Can it be true he also desires me?" she asked, challenging her good fortune.

"It is true, Wandering Doe. We must keep this news between us. Be patient, my friend. When the Great Spirit calls Leaning Bush to him, White Arrow will ask you to join with him. If others come to you while he is away, wait for his return."

"My heart will surely burst with this joy and love. I will mate with him when the time comes. I will pray for strength to guide me. And for forgiveness," she added mysteriously.

"Forgiveness?" Shalee questioned her strange word.

"Forgiveness for wishing Leaning Bush's illness to end quickly," she admitted contritely.

Shalee stroked her dark head. "Wakantanka understands all. You have sacrificed much to be a good wife. He rewards you and White Arrow by opening your eyes to each other and by joining your hearts in love. You both deserve this love and happiness, and you will share them."

Wandering Doe affectionately embraced Shalee. "I shall love him and give him the happiness you share with Gray Eagle. I will soar with joy if he returns only half the love your husband gives to you."

Shalee smiled cheerfully. "White Arrow is as my brother. I am happy he has chosen you, Wandering Doe. You are suited to him. You will be as happy as we are."

They talked for a while, like two young girls plotting their first romantic conquests. It was good to share such feelings during this demanding time.

The truculent band of Sioux warriors roamed the expanse of their territory for two days, always finding themselves one step behind the hostile troop of soldiers from Fort Henry. Each time the aggressive Bluecoats' trail was fresh and inviting, they would trespass upon a neighboring tribe's domain, as if mystically warned of the hot pursuit of their most feared enemy, the Oglala. It would require hours of patient and determined exploration to discover where the cavalry had sneaked onto their lands once more. This lethal game of hide-and-seek nettled Gray Eagle and his bands, for it appeared the soldiers were continuously invading their territory in hopes of finding another unsuspecting and vulnerable group of hunters to attack and slaughter.

As they made camp at twilight on the second day out of camp, Gray Eagle speculated upon the daring and cunning of his avowed foes. All five war parties rendezvoused at the edge of the splendid grassland that entered the vast territory one day to be known as the Badlands. The location of the soldiers' exit each time suggested which tribe they were presently harrying. It was obvious it was a waste of valuable time to await their reentry at that same point, for the crafty Bluecoats never retraced their paths. Did they suspect the intrepid Eagle was closing in on them? Did they arrogantly believe they could run the valiant warriors around in circles, to somehow instigate a surprise attack upon the defenseless village to the east? It would be foolish and deadly to underestimate the resolve and recklessness of the soldiers!

Wisely remaining in their own territory, the Oglala warriors could forestall an attack upon their camp. When questioned why they did not chase the Bluecoats and destroy them no matter whose territory they invaded, Gray Eagle informed them of his belief that the soldiers were guilefully enticing them to follow a false trail.

Red Cloud asked warily, "You think they draw us from our camp to attack there?"

"*Sha, Mahpiya Luta,*" Gray Eagle replied with assurance. "Have you not realized the tracks we view here and there do not match? There are several bands of Bluecoats teasing us. Do you not see how each new trail pulls us further and further away from our camp? My

443

instincts warn of danger and deceit. As we track one group of Bluecoats, I say the others are secretly working their way to band together near our camp. Each trail that returns to our territory does not reflect the one that left it before. When each band leaves, I think they join the others. Soon, we will be far away, while all but one group of Bluecoats gather near our camp to attack. The last band hopes to entice us into the badlands where they can hide and taunt us for days while the larger band invades our camp. I say we head for camp at first light; that is where we will find our enemies," he concluded.

"Surely they know the cunning of Gray Eagle would guess their trick? That they would then be riding into a trap of ours, not us into theirs," Little Beaver politely debated.

"They think us consumed with grief and fury, which should dull our keen wits. Each band that rejoins the others laughs and tells of how we are being pulled further and further from our camp. We now follow but ten crafty foxes. The tracks of the other twenty horses do not bear the weights of riders."

White Arrow inhaled sharply and his eyes widened in suspicion and alarm. "He is right! Our senses have been dulled and tricked! They advance upon our camp at this very moment. Once it is razed, they will wait in ambush for us to tire and return, to boldly slay us!"

"Your thoughts join mine, White Arrow," Gray Eagle complimented his deductions. "They are sly, but I see their game."

"When Turtle Woman and Moon Gazer were slain, I accepted the care of Shining Light and their children with mine. The Bluecoats must not destroy other families as they did ours," Red Cloud sneered angrily, the pain of his recent loss gnawing upon his heart and mind.

Talking Rock added, "Our people think we chase the enemy and protect them. It is not so. They would not think of a sudden attack upon them. We chase only a black shadow of evil. Wandering Doe watches over my children; perhaps when Leaning Bush walks the Ghost Trail, I should take her to mate."

No one noticed White Arrow's reaction to that last comment as the war chief stood up and paced in moody thought. "We must rest our horses and bodies for a short time, then head for camp."

The other band leaders concurred with Gray Eagle. "The cover of night will hide our wisdom from their eyes," remarked Little Beaver. "They will unknowingly ride into our waiting lances and arrows."

"White Arrow," Gray Eagle began, "you seek out the Bluecoats who vainly lead us astray. When you return home, bring only their horses as prizes of victory," he ordered, clearly saying he wanted no prisoners or survivors.

Fretting over Talking Rock's amorous intentions toward Wandering Doe and worrying over her safety, White Arrow commented, "I have always ridden at your side, my *koda* and brother. Why do you select me to stay behind during this great moment of revenge?"

"The others have families in camp to defend. You have no one to distract your wits, and the foxes who lead us astray must also be punished," Gray Eagle said, explaining his logic.

White Arrow couldn't voice his disagreement without revealing his feelings and plans for the wife of another warrior, one also desired by his friend and fellow band leader. He reluctantly nodded, accepting his assignment.

"There is another side to consider," Gray Eagle went on. "If the foxes nearby realize we have given up their

445

pursuit to return home, they will send messengers to warn the others. This must not be. After we rest, Red Cloud and Little Beaver will ride from the north to our camp; Talking Rock and Gray Eagle will enter from the south. If I see the Great Spirit's guidance clearly, the Bluecoats will be trapped between us. We will ride between them and our camp, then head westward to meet them face first. If you conquer the others quickly and head for us, they will then be trapped between us and you if they attempt to flee. When they are slain, the place they call Fort Henry will be conquered. Then, only Fort Meade will offer resistance to us."

The warriors and leaders pondered these words. It was known the new leader of the Bluecoats at Fort Meade was unlike all others who had come here. The white-eyes who ruled the camp of Fort Meade did not war against them unwisely or rashly. Sturgis had already earned the reputation of a man who defended rather than attacked. This particular white man was a mystery to the intelligent Gray Eagle. . . . The legendary warrior was baffled by Sturgis' refusal to join forces with the offensive Hodges. Perhaps Sturgis was only biding his time until the rash Hodges defeated himself to allow Sturgis the chance and right to gain command of both forces. As with weaker tribes, a stronger and superior chief often assumed another's rank through cunning and force, or through the self-defeat of his rival.

Three hours later, the two bands mounted up and left White Arrow's behind. Within a short distance, one large war party headed northeast and the other southeast, Gray Eagle's ploy clear in their minds. They rode at a pace that would plant them securely before their camp near dawn, yet a pace that would not overly tire man or beast.

446

As Gray Eagle's group rode along, he smiled to himself as he reflected upon the secret words from his best friend. At last, White Arrow's eyes and heart had settled upon a woman. Calling Wandering Doe to mind, he grinned in pleasure and agreement. It was time for his friend to enjoy a love and passion such as he and Shalee had discovered. He made it his duty to also protect the life of White Arrow's choice. Hopefully Talking Rock and White Arrow would not harshly disagree over the possession of the same female. . . .

Miles apart, the two bands of Sioux warriors halted near sunrise and concealed themselves. If not for the rocky formations between them and the Oglala camp, the village could have been seen from where they were situated, awaiting their elusive foes. The Bluecoats were known to attack unsuspecting camps near dawn or late at night, and Gray Eagle knew the attack upon his people would come shortly, or late tonight.

As if the sky had suddenly caught fire and was burning brightly out of control, fiery pinks seared the horizon. The dull grays hastily retreated before the powerful demands of dawn's roseate shades, hinting at a glorious day for victory. Soon, the leadish sky above altered to hues of intense blue with periwinkle edges. All was in readiness. . . .

Far away to the west, White Arrow and his band of twenty-two warriors were challenging the ensnared group of white soldiers, a decoy band of ten men, as Gray Eagle had surmised. Endowed with superior skills and consumed with a desire for justice, the warriors would eventually claim their triumph at the incredible price of only two minor injuries. Not so for the white men. For when this tragic battle finally ended, the only survivors from their group would be thirty horses and two men who barely managed to sneak away to escape the Indians' lethal retaliation.

Hidden amidst towering rocks of intermingled blood-red and bluish-black, the Indians settled themselves at the crucial points that would prevent the soldiers from entering this terrain, which was now a guardian to their camp. Their horses, well-trained in such furtive maneuvers, stood silent and still in the canyonlike location that would prevent any sighting of them.

His body rigidly controlled, his keen eyes alert, his mind perceptive, and his instincts matchless, Gray Eagle patiently anticipated and envisioned this awesome victory. His body was agile and strong, his reflexes and muscles honed and developed for such an event. This was a critical moment such as he had trained for, since birth, such as he had successfully challenged many times before, and such as had previously tempered his skills and prowess. Since the coming of the white man, this was an episode he had expected repeatedly, had lived and witnessed many times, and had come through victoriously each time.

Both his destiny and that of his people hinged upon this event in time, and upon his leadership. He refused to consider a mistake in his conclusions. The Bluecoats would come today. He felt this deduction with all his being. Soon, all he was and possessed would be challenged.

The waiting was torturous; the atmosphere charged with awesome tension. The Oglala destiny rode with the winds. When the treacherous breezes swept down with body-racking force, would he once again experience brazen ecstasy—or stunning and unfamiliar defeat? He was Gray Eagle; he could accept nothing less than mighty triumph over his foes. . . .

Confident in his personal skills and those of his puissant warriors, he smiled and leaned against a weather-pitted carnelian boulder to watch for the time when he must go into action. Hours passed without a sign of anything. The sun climbed higher and higher in the heaven until Wi poised directly overhead, flooding his dazzling light and heat upon the warriors below. If the warriors doubted his assessment, none revealed his doubt. If tension or stress assailed them, these were also suppressed.

Gray Eagle's eyes scanned the azure horizon for the hundredth time, detecting nothing unusual. He passed the word along for the men to rest between watches, but to hold themselves in readiness. In his opinion, the Bluecoats wouldn't attack during daylight. Since they had not shown themselves at dawn, he vowed they would after dusk. He hoped the soldiers had not become aware of their return and ambush. At least their hesitation would enable White Arrow to flank them! They would come today; he was positive of that fact. Still, the waiting inspired vexing anxiety, which was rigidly held in check.

Two hours eastward, a husky white man was shouting furiously at a large troop of men in navy blue and sunny yellow uniforms. "My God!" he thundered in his booming voice, "Is Hodges insane? Only a bloody fool would attack a Sioux camp after dark! And of all camps to challenge! Riding into the arms of Running Wolf and Gray Eagle doesn't call for courage; it demands stupidity!"

The scarlet-faced sergeant replied, "I've already told you Gray Eagle and nearly all of the warriors are miles away from here. That camp is as helpless as a baby. Trent's men will lead them a merry chase in those hills, then strike out for the fort from the other side. While they have those redskins hounding them, we can strike a deadly blow at their heart and strength. Hodges is smart; he knows the effect a massacre will have on those warriors. Without a camp and family, they'll be devastated. If they don't band up with another tribe, they'll be powerless against us. With luck, we can ambush them on their return and wipe 'em all out."

The stalwart soldier shook his head and sighed contemptuously. "Collins, you're as big a fool as Hodges is. If you ride into the Oglala camp, you're all dead men. You'll never defeat Gray Eagle. If you know what's best, you'll make a truce with him."

"Truce with that savage?" Collins snarled in disbelief. "He ain't as invincible as you think, sir. Didn't you hear Hodges captured him not long ago? If it hadn't been for that slimy Spaniard, he would be dead now," the rosy-eyed Collins boasted.

"You think slaughtering innocent women, children, and old people will defeat him? Nothing justifies such brutality, sergeant! If you recall, Gray Eagle retaliates in like manner for such crimes. When the American government settles down, they'll refuse such measures to attain this wilderness. Mark my words, son; this war will end soon."

"Any means of acquired victory over mindless savages is fair play, major. I take my orders from Hodges, not you, sir. Your rank matches his, but he's been here longer and he knows these redskins better. I can't ignore or refuse his direct order to attack the Oglala camp tonight. If you disagree with my orders, I suggest you head for Fort Henry and discuss them with my commanding officer."

The arrogance and nettling obstinacy of Collins

enflamed Sturgis. "By the time I can reach Fort Henry, you will be carrying out this reckless attack. Give me two days to change his mind," he coaxed, knowing his request was futile.

"Can't do that, sir. The attack comes tonight, the minute they're asleep. We can't risk sitting around waiting for Gray Eagle to suspect our trick and hurry home. Before midnight, not a soul will be alive in his camp."

"You best pray you either succeed or die alongside Hodges when Gray Eagle avenges this crime. I doubt you'll care to fall under my command later, which you assuredly will if you survive," Sturgis ominously warned.

"What kind of soldier would I be, sir, if I balked a direct order?" Collins inserted uneasily, aware of the sincerity of Sturgis' threat.

"I would question the rank and sanity of any leader who blindly ordered the butchery he has, sergeant," Sturgis scoffed acidly.

"We didn't start this bloodbath, sir. They did."

Their gazes clashed mutely before Sturgis alleged smugly, "Did they, sergeant? Whose land are we presently standing upon? Did we invade their territory? Or did they trespass upon ours? What did we expect? Are they supposed to calmly step aside and allow us to take over? Truce is the only answer, Collins. You attack that camp, and you're all dead men."

"Maybe so, sir, but we're riding in after dark."

Sturgis sighed heavily. There was no way to change Collins' mind or to alter Hodges' commands. Worse, his detail was vastly outnumbered by the combined details of Collins' troop. Hodges had planned this reprehensible annihilation well. His hands were tied; there was no way to prevent a raid upon the camp of the Oglala. He wondered if he should brazenly ride into the camp and give warning there. That would be foolish, idealistic. He wouldn't make it past the first tepee before braves filled his blue-clad body with arrows. They would never accept his words of warning and truce under such contradictory circumstances. If only he could parlay with the Eagle himself . . . it was impossible at present; it would be more impossible after the wanton destruction of his camp. Damnit! Was there no end to this madness and bloodshed, no answer that could bring peace?

"I'll ask you one last time, Collins, don't invade that camp tonight," Sturgis made a final appeal to the man with icy blood.

"Sorry, sir, but it's too late to stop it. Our plans have all fallen into place. The warriors are two days' ride from here by now. What few braves were left behind won't stand a chance against my armed outfit. It's defeat him now or never. We ride in tonight."

"Don't say I didn't warn you, sergeant," were the last words ever spoken between them.

Tragically, while the Oglala warriors anticipated and awaited confrontation with the cavalry from the western face of their village, Collins and his large troop were moving in from the eastern side! Gray Eagle had assumed the soldiers would merely ride directly toward the camp, but they had furtively skirted it to cunningly approach from the opposite direction. Within miles of each other, one group's destiny would fiercely challenge that of the other. . . .

But other fates were being simultaneously tested and decided in the Oglala camp itself. . . .

452

Chapter Twenty

A desperate frenzy filled Leah as she arose from her sleeping mat to feel the sudden rush of scarlet liquid down her thighs that vividly exposed her many lies and treachery. Sheer panic flooded her limp frame. It seemed as if all the forces of nature were against her. Thankfully, she was alone. For a time, her deadly secret was known only to her. There was but one path of action and survival left open to her: escape. But first, she owed several people revenge: Shalee for destroying all her dreams and desires; Gray Eagle for coldly and brutally rejecting her; White Arrow for assisting in her defeat; and Running Wolf for using her and then discarding her. A lethal blow at Shalee would accomplish all of these!

Lingering behind until she observed the other women returning from their morning bath at the river, she fingered the lethal blade in her sweaty grasp as she mentally plotted her malice and flight. She concealed the knife beneath her dress. Packing a few supplies, she hid them in her bundle of laundry. She placed the evidence of her exposed deceit beneath her sleeping mat, for Running Wolf would never discover the bloodstained cloths in time to expose her trickery. She would be long gone before anyone suspected her plans or could foil them. She headed for the stream, knowing Shalee had not returned to camp yet.

A malicious sneer crossed her face as she noted the

three women completing their baths. When she joined them and apologized for her tardiness, Wandering Doe and Tasia ignored her to leave Shalee alone with the offensive slave, no one imagining the danger the Indian princess was about to confront.

Leah's monthly was terribly late, and Shalee was beginning to believe Leah was pregnant with Running Wolf's child. With so much on her mind, Shalee's guard was dangerously lowered. How she longed for this weighty matter to be settled one way or other.

"You needn't fret over my tardy arrival or fear I'll be too sick to do my chores," she viciously snapped at the unsuspecting Shalee.

"Frankly I try not to think about you at all, Leah! Just do as you're told or these next months will be extremely hard for you as your time approaches."

Time approaches? Leah excitedly pondered, recognizing that Shalee was finally accepting her word about the baby. In just a short time, she would alter the fates of many people, including her own. Her course was laid out; she could not change it. First, there was the matter of fatal revenge; then, she would flee eastward since they would probably search westward for her where the nearest fort was located. It was too late to replace this particular woman whose return from the grave had destroyed her dream life and obsessive love!

Leah deceptively queried, baffling Shalee with the strange tone in her voice, "I didn't ask to love him, but I cannot halt these feelings. I didn't entice Running Wolf to rape me. I was so confused and afraid. I feared I would lose my mind. Do you know what it's like to lose all you have, to become a despised slave?" she scoffed, furtively eyeing Shalee for any clue to the puzzle of her prior existence.

Shalee gaped at the bewildering Leah. What was she up to now? Shalee refused to hear any more lies. Leah was anything but a defenseless, abused slave! If she thought for one moment she could delude her again, she was vastly mistaken. Shalee glared skeptically at Leah, then returned to her task.

"You don't believe me, do you?" Leah asked, stalling for time to retrieve the blade. Somehow she had to prevent Shalee's departure!

Shalee continued to ignore Leah's taunts and presence. She leaned over to pick up her blanket to dry her dripping hair.

With fierce hatred glazing her emerald eyes, Leah withdrew the knife and raised it, preparing to plunge it into the back of Shalee.

"Shalee! *Toka! Wayaketo!*" the warning thundered across the silence, warning of an enemy's presence.

Shalee whirled and straightened, her wide gaze taking in the swiftly descending knife. "Leah! No!" she screamed in a panic.

Shalee fell backwards to avoid the death which threatened her. Leah lunged at her prone figure, shrieking, "I'm going to kill you! You did this to me! I hate you!"

Running Wolf was granted a surge of energy and pounced upon the white girl, throwing both of them to the ground. Crazed, Leah squirmed in his grasp and sent the knife deeply and forcefully into his chest. A shout of pain was torn from the old chief's lips. Leah yanked the knife free and delivered another blow to his shoulder before he could roll free and avoid it.

Blood oozed from the wounds on Running Wolf's

chest. Weakened, he could hardly move. But Leah's hatred flooded her body with unnatural strength. With the chief too injured to battle her, she recognized her impending success over both enemies. She could finish him later. She held the ominous weapon tightly as she cast her menacing gaze upon the stunned Indian princess. As a wolf stalking his weaker prey, Leah edged toward Shalee.

"Leah! Stop it! You've gone mad!" Shalee warned the girl of her crazed actions, frantically playing for time.

A shrill and eerie burst of laughter came forth. "You will both die!" she boldly and smugly threatened.

"You can't do this terrible thing!" Shalee argued in alarm, completely cognizant of the girl's madness and brute strength.

"Who will stop me? Surely not that dying old man. When I finish with you, I'll cut out his savage heart! Gray Eagle was mine until you came back. If he learned to accept a woman who was once his despised slave, he can learn again with me! He'll be mine again!" she suddenly declared.

"He'll never be yours, Leah. Halt this madness and I'll help you!"

"With you and that simpering wolf dead, he'll turn to me for comfort, just like before. This time, he'll be too weak to resist me."

"You tricked Running Wolf and Gray Eagle, Leah. He'll never love you or trust you. He'll despise you for harming us, Leah. Think!" she urged the jittery girl.

"He'll think some enemy killed you two. I'll stab myself to prove how I struggled to save your lives. He'll be so grateful he'll keep me. Of course," she excitedly plotted aloud. "When he wonders why I'm bleeding, I'll tell him I'm miscarrying because of the fierce battle to help you!"

"Bleeding? You mean you're not pregnant?" she demanded, anger replacing most of her panic.

"Don't be silly! I've never been pregnant. My first child will be fathered by the Eagle himself, not that old fool!"

"It won't work, Leah," Shalee argued, hoping someone would sound the alarm. How did one reason with insanity?

"After viewing your bloody and lifeless body, he'll be so crazy with grief he'll demand I comfort him! How long can a virile man like that refuse my skills? Within a week he'll be begging to take me!" she crudely exclaimed. She came toward Shalee with the knife uplifted.

Terrified, but clear-headed by now, Shalee kicked her in the abdomen the moment she was close enough, having been told she wasn't pregnant, knowing there was no unborn child to harm. The forceful blow sent Leah tumbling backwards. Shalee's screams for help covered those of Leah's as the knife buried itself in the white girl's chest. Shalee was scrambling to her feet to ready herself for Leah's next lunge when several braves raced forward.

At the sound of their rapid approach, Shalee's eyes darted in that direction. She hastily shrieked, "She's got a knife! She stabbed Running Wolf! She was trying to kill me!"

On instant alert, the braves cautiously walked toward the prone figure. Leah did not move. With his foot, one brave rolled her over. Shalee smothered a scream as she observed the monstrous fate of Leah Winston: death at her own careless and vengeful hand. Her mind spinning, Shalee hurriedly went to the motionless body of Running

Wolf. Placing her ear to his heart, she shouted with relief and joy.

"Take him to his tepee! Fetch the shaman! Quickly, he's losing much blood," she shouted assuming command of this shocking situation.

Ramira watched over Bright Arrow as Shalee lingered by the side of Running Wolf, the once powerful man who was now struggling for his very existence. The medicine chief had done the best he could with the jagged wounds that refused to halt their ominous flow. The old chief was growing weaker by the moment, and they were helpless. Even the potent herbs refused to relieve his pain, serving only to inspire tormented jabber. Torturous hours passed.

Shortly before dusk, the medicine chief left Running Wolf's tepee to head for the Pezuta Tipi to chant and pray for the recovery of their beloved chief, leaving Shalee alone with the fallen warrior.

Shalee sat beside his sleeping mat, the dire events of this tragic day refusing to leave her mind. Her knees drawn up to her chest, her arms encircled them and her forehead rested upon them. Would the Great Spirit demand his life as payment for his loss of honor in the arms of the treacherous Leah? Leah . . . how sad for any life to end in madness and fierce hatred. She was actually going to kill her! All lies and deceits! If Running Wolf hadn't suspected she was in danger . . .

She came to full alert. Her head lifted as she stared at the ailing chief in utter bewilderment. What was he saying? Why would he speak his name? She held her breath as she listened to the incredible revelation of the monstrous secret that had haunted him for years.

"Powchutu," he called softly, his voice strained.

458

"Come, my son, I must tell you things before I die in such dishonor."

Shalee gaped at him. My son? Powchutu? He was surely delirious! Powchutu was a half-white scout, past enemy to her love!

She mopped the beads of perspiration from his wrinkled brow. "Rest, Running Wolf, my father. You are weak from blood loss. Shalee is here; she will care for you," she tenderly entreated.

"I must see him. Send him to me," he hoarsely commanded of the ghosts who plagued him, a ghost known only to him.

"Who, Running Wolf?" Shalee pressed.

"Powchutu. I must see my other son," he unknowingly replied.

"You have only one son: Gray Eagle," she softly debated.

"I have two sons. He was taken from me before his birth. I must speak with him. He must forgive me for denying him. He must understand. I knew of his life too late to spare him such grief."

"Who is this Powchutu you ask for, Running Wolf?" she helplessly inquired, dreading his imminent answer. Surely it was the drug talking!

"The scout at the fort. His mother carried him when she was sold to a white-eyes. I was not told of him until six winters past. I did not go to him and claim my son. I am filled with shame and anguish. He is known as half-breed and suffers greatly."

Shalee nearly swooned. It couldn't be true! Surely there was another Powchutu! Compelled to halt her traitorous thoughts, she questioned, "Does Shalee know this Powchutu?"

"Yes. Shalee is friend to my son Powchutu. He loves her and battles Gray Eagle for her possession. Shalee can find him and bring him to me. His blood is half Crow, not white."

Shalee fluctuated between nausea and faintness. Had Leah driven her insane? Surely she wasn't hearing this confession clearly! "Why did you deny him, Running Wolf? Why does Gray Eagle battle his own brother?" she hesitantly asked, praying he would not reply.

"He does not know about his brother. I have denied him since the truth touched my ears. When she wed a white man, I was not told she carried our son. She sent word before death called her. My pride cost me my son. I must see him and plead for forgiveness."

Gray Eagle and Powchutu were brothers? The half-breed scout, son of an Indian woman and a French trapper, was actually the son of Running Wolf; he was a full-blooded Indian? When she envisioned the scout from Fort Pierre years ago who had befriended her, loved her, and later betrayed her—her heart was ravaged with anguish. Now she understood why he favored Gray Eagle! His half-brother! How could Running Wolf be so cruel and selfish? How many times had Powchutu and Gray Eagle confronted each other in staggering battle? Powchutu had been her friend; he had died protecting her life and honor! He had loved her, no matter how traitorously and obsessively. If fate had devised otherwise, Gray Eagle would have dealt Powchutu his dying blow. What would her beloved say and feel when he learned the man who had tried to murder him and steal her was actually his own brother? How would he react to discovering his worst rival had been his father's son, his half-brother? How Powchutu's life would have been

460

changed by his rightful heritage! How he had suffered as a lowly and despised half-breed! A full-blooded Indian and son of a famed chief! Life was cruel and unjust!

"Powchutu is dead, Running Wolf," she sadly informed the hazy mind of the feverish chief.

"Did my son slay his own brother?" he cried out.

"No. He was slain by a white man. Why did you deny him his rightful name and place in your tepee? Why did you allow brother to battle brother?" she angrily demanded.

"It was too late to change feelings. Powchutu was white in heart and life. He despised us and aided our enemies," he feverishly babbled.

"No, he was not! He was always Indian in heart and body! You forced him to endure a life of hatred and denial. Why?"

"She married a white trapper; she lay with him while she carried my son. He was touched by the white; he was no longer my son. She took his love from me. She did not send word when her father sold her. She must suffer as I did. She made our son lower than the whites!"

"She did not suffer, Running Wolf; Powchutu did. It was wrong to condemn him to such a life. If not for the guidance of the Great Spirit, brother could have slain brother."

"Gray Eagle did not die from Powchutu's attack."

"He could have! When Gray Eagle came after me, he might have slain Powchutu if the white lieutenant hadn't! How could he live with such shame? Why didn't you send for him when you learned the truth?"

Long ago when the cavalry from Fort Pierre took her from Gray Eagle's tepee during a raid, she had met Powchutu as their half-breed scout. In her anguish of believing Gray Eagle had betrayed her love, she had turned to Powchutu: his image in many ways. Now, she knew why. Her heart rebelled against this heartrending confession.

"Where is my new son? I have another chance to prove myself," he raggedly murmured.

"Leah lied, Running Wolf; there is no child. Calm yourself; you are weak and injured," she entreated, fretting over his agitation.

"No child?" he echoed weakly.

"No, my father. Leah deceived us; she is dead."

"Evil slave . . . manhood burned with need . . . such magic and pleasure . . . couldn't resist such power . . . weak . . . shamed," he mumbled, barely coherent, rending her heart with his confessions.

"Speak no more of such things, Running Wolf. Others might hear. The past is dead. Do not break Gray Eagle's heart with such news."

On top of Running Wolf's betrayal with Leah, how would Gray Eagle respond to hearing his avowed foe and rival for her had been his brother? Thank God his was not the lethal blow to end Powchutu's life!

She suddenly realized if Running Wolf died, her husband would become chief of the Oglala. What should she do with such knowledge? God help her, for she did not know. . . .

The chief sank into merciful unconsciousness, his confession to be forgotten. Shalee observed Running Wolf until the shaman returned. Unable to bear the weight of her ravaged heart, she fled to her own tepee. If he survived, how could she ever look him in the face again, knowing the damage of his selfish lie? Yet, he was right in many ways. He hadn't known of his other son until shortly before her arrival, a time when she unfortunately stepped between the two men to increase their hatred and rivalry. How could any mother do such immense injury to her own son? Powchutu should have ridden at the side of his family. But it was too late to change matters, for Powchutu had been dead for years. The truth could give birth to so many new sufferings!

It was very late; so much had taken place on this fateful day. Bright Arrow was sleeping peacefully in Ramira's tepee, so she did not disturb him. She stretched out upon her sleeping mat, pleading for mindless slumber to enfold her in its protective and comforting arms. At last, she could partially understand the shortcomings of the old man. Two hours before midnight, sleep finally claimed her.

"Gray Eagle," Talking Rock called softly through the flurry of thoughts in the warrior's mind. "The scouts have seen and heard nothing."

Scout? his mind echoed, a curious feeling of resentment and coldness washing over him. He shook his head to clear it of such unbidden memories. Why should he recall such events tonight?

He forced himself to deliberate the white man's thoughts. He suddenly sat up, inhaling sharply. "We must ride, Talking Rock! Signal the others! We wait for the Bluecoats in the wrong place; they will attack from the other side of camp!"

While the Oglala warriors hurriedly mounted up, another curious episode was taking place in their camp. Shalee was suddenly aroused by a large hand clamped over her mouth to prevent her terrified scream. Her hands had been seized and pinned to the ground above her head. She was at the mercy of her unknown assailant in rich blue and bright yellow. She helplessly and frantically awaited her fate.

Would her love return to camp to find all dead, all he knew and loved destroyed while he pursued his avowed enemies? Remember me, my lost love, she prayed fervently. Bright Arrow . . . forgive me for not protecting you, my son. Great Spirit, help us!

The masculine voice whispered in English, "I pray to God I'm not in the wrong tepee. You've nothing to fear ma'am. I only need to talk with Shalee, Gray Eagle's wife. They say she's half-white and speaks English. Are you Shalee?"

Her trembling halted abruptly as she stared at him more in confusion than in terror. She neither struggled nor responded. "Damnit, woman! Are you Shalee? Can you understand me? There isn't much time before the soldiers attack here. You've got to alert your people or they'll be massacred," he softly alleged, fearing he had the wrong tepee and woman. Yet she appeared at least half-white.

Her look of horror told him she had indeed grasped his words. "I see you understand. You must be her. Hodges, the man who captured your son and husband, is planning to raid here tonight while your husband's out chasing shadows. It was a trick to lure him away. They plan to slaughter everyone and burn the camp. Warn your people to flee into the forest," he hurriedly advised.

When she attempted to speak, he prayed she would not betray him, not after the chance he was taking by coming here. God help him if it was a dreadful mistake, but he couldn't allow wanton slaughter. "If you call out for help, they'll kill me and nothing can save your people then. I'm expecting a promotion soon, which will grant me more power than Hodges. Then maybe I can end this senseless warfare."

As his hands released her, she sat up and stared at him. "Who are you? Why do you come here under the cover of night?"

"I'm Major Sturgis from Fort Meade. I tried to halt the attack tonight, but Hodges has as much power as I do, at least for the time being. He's determined to end the Eagle's reign no matter how. I can't permit the murders of innocent women and children. I hope you take this next statement the way I mean it, ma'am, but I can't afford for anyone to know I've been here. If they view me an Indian lover, they'll never obey me later. Truce can be very tricky. But I swear I'll push for one. Hopefully your husband will see me as a friend for sparing his camp and people. When this matter's settled, we'll meet and talk alone."

"The soldiers will attack tonight and slay all?" she asked in alarm, pondering whether she could trust this brazen soldier.

"Yes, at midnight. I'm sorry, but I can't stop them. You'll have to warn your people. For now, that's all I can do. I've got to leave before I'm discovered here and my word won't be worth a tinker's damn. Do you understand what I'm telling you?"

"Yes, Major Sturgis. I was raised white until six years ago. I understand. How can such immense hatred exist? I will tell my husband of your generous deed tonight. He also desires peace and happiness returned to his lands. He misses the singing, hunting, and joyful living which the advancement of the white man has denied for years. Life

465

is too short and precious to waste with endless warfare. I will take you to the edge of camp. You must go quickly. If peace is to be more than a dream, we will need a just man such as you. I shall never forget your kindness," she softly murmured, then smiled cordially.

"I can see Gray Eagle chose a worthy woman as his mate. She is as wise and gentle as she is beautiful." A genial smile relaxed his features and brightened his sky-blue eyes.

"I must give you something to protect your life if you face danger," she offered, retrieving a *wanapin* from a pouch. She walked to him and handed the necklace to the man whose generosity would save her people.

Sturgis took the proffered amulet and gazed at it. It was a small stone arrowhead suspended from a leather thong; a tiny yellow feather was tightly secured to the end where it was attached to the thong. "It will declare you *koda* to Gray Eagle. If any warrior confronts you, show him the *wanapin* and tell him, '*Shalee, koda, wookiye.*' It says we are friends and share truce. Even if they doubt your claim, you will be brought to Gray Eagle himself. My husband will never slay a man who shows such courage and honor as you do tonight."

"I am honored to be called *koda* to Gray Eagle and Shalee. The soldiers will attack from the east at midnight. Prepare to defeat or to flee them. Goodbye, Shalee. Perhaps we will meet again with peace between us."

"I pray it will be so, Sturgis. Go in peace and safety." They shook hands, then Shalee escorted him to the edge of the camp. She watched him slip into the concealment of darkness. She glanced up at the full moon; it was around ten-thirty. Could she trust Sturgis? Was he drawing them into a trap? Something told her he was not.

466

She must warn the others.

She hurried to the medicine chief's tepee and called his name. He came to her almost immediately. "A messenger came to warn us; the soldiers will attack here soon. You must summon the braves. We must flee for safety and hide until our warriors return." Shalee did not tell the baffled Indian leader that the messenger was white. He wondered why the warning was sent to her, but did not question her words or this unusual action.

Kaolotka instantly complied with her urgings. Within minutes, the braves were making plans to evacuate the camp. It was decided to head for the nearby hills, which offered more protection from weapons and enemy eyes. There, they could offer their people a better chance for survival.

The camp was awakened and cautioned to silence. The elders, women, and children were hurriedly sent toward the hills, which loomed dark and distant before them. Time short and valuable, most possessions were left behind. Horses bore the weights of the aged and weakened. Running Wolf was placed upon a travois, the danger of moving him known to all.

As the armed braves brought up the rear, the fleeing group halted suddenly. Furtively and rapidly approaching them was a huge band of dark riders! Shalee paled and shuddered. Were they betrayed?

Both groups were stunned by their unexpected meeting between camp and the hills. Almost simultaneously, the two groups recognized each other. Gray Eagle urged his horse forward to question this confusing desertion of camp. If there was an attack in progress, why was their flight so gradual and tranquil? They were not running swiftly! There was no sound of battle from the camp or treacherous fires lighting the darkness. Why did they seek the cover of the nearby hills?

Shalee left Running Wolf's side to rush to meet her returning husband. "The soldiers will attack at midnight, my love! You have returned in time to protect us!" She hastily threw the panicky words at him.

"How do you know such things?" he questioned in puzzlement.

"A messenger came to warn me. I told Kaolotka and the braves. We were heading for the hills to hide until your return. He said the soldiers lured you away. They wish to destroy our village and people."

"Who came to you? I sent no one," he reasoned aloud.

"The leader from Fort Meade, Sturgis. He tried to halt them, but they would not listen. He desires peace; he does not wish to see women and children slain. He sneaked into our tepee and told me this."

"He warned of their attack knowing we would ambush them?"

"My heart said he spoke the truth. I warned the others."

"I do not understand his ways, but he speaks the truth. When we saw their trick, we returned quickly. We have been camped in the hills since Wi showed his face."

"But he said they were attacking from the other side," she promptly informed him.

"This thought came to my mind. We were heading to defeat them. Go to the hills and remain there until this battle has ended. We will speak of this matter later."

"Please be careful, Gray Eagle. I love you," she whispered softly.

"Where is Running Wolf? Why does he not lead his people?" he demanded, suddenly realizing the chief's absence.

"He is ill, my love. I have watched over him," she reluctantly answered, wishing she didn't have to distract his mind with such evil.

"How so?" he instantly demanded, sensing her hesitation.

"Leah tried to slay me and escape. Running Wolf's body accepted the knife wounds meant for mine. He is very weak, but I think he will recover."

Astounded by this news, he snarled, "I will slay her!"

"She is dead. She fell upon her knife as she tried to kill me."

"Why did such evil and daring fill her this sun?" he pressed.

"This was the moon that proved all her words were lies, my love. She feared their exposure," she stated meaningfully. "She wished me dead before fleeing. The Great Spirit punished her. It is over now. Running Wolf will live."

"We must talk, for there is much to hear. Guard your life and our son's. You are my heart. I love you," he vowed, then rejoined his band to inform them of the impending attack. New plans were made.

One group headed for the hills and one for the darkened camp, one preparing for safety and the other for attack. All waited tensely.

Chapter Twenty-One

"Damn, what I wouldn't give for a cup of black coffee!" a nervous soldier snapped irritably.

"Me, too! This waiting chews on your gut, don't it?" responded his edgy companion.

"You think we're fools, like Sturgis said?" he asked uneasily.

"Any man who challenges Gray Eagle has to be! If we had any brains at all, we'd get the hell outta here pronto. I'd be shaking in my boots if I didn't know he was miles away."

"Whatta you say we ride back to the Ohio Valley when this is over? I didn't join the cavalry to kill women and children."

"Me neither! You ever done it before?" his friend asked.

"Yep! Once during a raid on the Cheyenne camp. Hodges said we weren't to leave no one alive. She was a pretty thing, young and scared. Turned my stomach. I ain't so sure I can do it again," he admitted.

"Don't you think it's a wee bit late for disobeying orders?"

"Hell, Josh! You don't know what it's like! You ain't never slit a woman's throat while she's casting them doe eyes on you! You ain't never seen a baby's head smashed into a rock! It takes weeks to stop seeing red ever time you shut your eyes, to stop hearing those screams. I

470

watched old people too weak to move run through with sabers. The stinch of blood and guts stays with you a long time afterwards. If Hodges is so set on butchering the redskins, why don't he try it one time!"

"You're crazy, Pete. We're at war here. If we don't kill hem, they'll kill us," Josh argued weakly.

"Am I? War is with other fighters, not their families. I got to get away from here when this is over."

"Don't ride off without me," Josh hinted genially.

"Why we doing this? I bet there ain't ten men who want to be here tonight. Sturgis is right; we're all bloody fools!"

Collins strolled over to speak with the two guards near the horses. "Won't be long now," he murmured, sadistic anticipation lacing his voice. "I'd give a month's pay to see the look on Gray Eagle's face when he rides into that camp after we finish there. We'll be famous, men. Collins and his daring band who wiped out the notorious and invincible Gray Eagle," he wistfully alleged.

When Pete's gaze flickered to the groups of men sitting around silently with their weapons forming conical stacks before them, Collins sneered scornfully, "You running scared, Pete?"

"Killing women and children while they sleep don't sit well with me, sir. But I ain't no coward," he panted in unleashed anger.

"What about you, Josh? You squeamish, too?" Collins disdainfully challenged, eyeing both men who were obviously not relishing this thrilling victory over their worst enemy.

"We'll obey orders, sir, but we don't have to like them."

"Then take a little reward for yourselves."

"What reward, sir?" Josh asked in confusion.

"There's some mighty pretty females in that camp. No need to kill all of them right off," he coldly insinuated

"You can actually diddle a female, then slit her throat?" Pete shrieked in amazement, shocked by the heartlessness of his leader.

"Why not?" Collins indifferently stated. "Ain't many females around here who don't have husbands or fathers. I got to find some relief somewhere. They're there for the taking, men."

"You make me as sick as this raid does!" Pete thundered before he could control his outrage. What would his mother think if he committed such savage atrocities?

"Cowards have dulled wits, Pete. You best get control of yourself, or you'll be a dead man afore morning," Collins warned. "Settle your nerves and have some fun. Least we can do is get a nice piece of tail for all our trouble."

Pete glared into the retreating back of Collins. "Let's get out of here, Josh. You know what'll happen after we enter that camp."

"You mean desert?" Josh inquired, the precarious thought having already entered his mind.

"That's exactly what I mean," came the easy reply.

The two men studied each other for a time. Josh cast a speculative glance toward the troop, which was beginning to prepare for the impending raid. He grinned boyishly at Pete. "Let's go," he agreed.

The warriors were befuddled when Gray Eagle signaled them to permit two young soldiers to sneak through their circle around the Bluecoats' camp. Having great confidence in their war chief, they allowed his curious act to

472

ass unchallenged. He knew the white man's tongue, and evidently the two men had said something to earn their lives. To leave their people at such a time surely indicated they did not wish to war against innocent women and children, as cowardly fear did not expose itself in the two vanishing figures.

Deciding to head for Fort Meade to explain their motives to the commander there, Pete and Josh would eventually learn of their close call with death at the same time Sturgis would discover that his daring action had not resulted in the destruction of Hodges' troops. He would be relieved to learn that Gray Eagle had reasoned out their ploy and foiled it himself. In spite of the attack, his courageous and generous act of mercy would inspire future talks for peace. In light of Collins' defeat, Pete and Josh would be viewed as lucky survivors of a tragic act of violence, their secret known only to Sturgis and the Indians. The two youths would be delighted and confused when Sturgis didn't press desertion charges against them.

"Listen up, men," Collins called out softly. "It's time we take that red bastard down a notch or two. Keep any souvenir or horse you want, but don't leave a single savage alive. Enjoy yourselves before you burn that camp to the ground. Might be a long time before you find a handy female around."

"You mean we can save some of the females for last?" one lecherous soldier asked for clarity.

"Only the pretty ones, Tankersly," Collins merrily joked. "Any questions?"

When no man queried or commented, Collins grinned. "Well, men, let's ride. We'll take 'em by surprise if we're careful. Take whatever action necessary, but don't

473

leave a sign of life when you're done. We ain't taking no female captives with us, so have your fill here."

The instant the last word left his sneering lips, a war whoop that could have startled the dead rent the air. The surprise attack stolen from them, the soldiers were denied the chance to successfully defend themselves. Fierce hand-to-hand combat ensued. Their flintlock rifles of little use at this close proximity and desperate speed, soldiers grabbed for their deadly sabers and pistols—weapons that could only fire once without reloading with ball and powder. The few shots they managed to get off missed their agile targets in the flurry of action.

Knives, lances, and arrows made deadly weapons that could be used quickly and easily. The Indians had bodies well-trained and developed, and keen instincts well honed. The soldiers never stood a chance against these masterful fighters. One by one, the lethal blows were deftly and relentlessly delivered. The roar of voices shrieking in pain and defeat filled the air. As if sensing the ominous meaning of this event, Mother Nature appeared to hold her respectful silence.

The reason for the soldiers' presence here was all too clear in the Indians' minds. They slew and maimed with an urgent need to right the wrongs done to them and to prevent future ones. Yells of warning and cries of agony were scattered over this perilous spot. In the beginning, the odds had been fairly even; but as time passed, the odds rapidly swung in the warriors' favor as the soldiers helplessly fell beneath their superior skills.

Another fact was petrifyingly clear to Collins: Gray Eagle had personally demanded to battle him. Each warrior he had rushed toward had grinned at him and refused to fight him. Within moments, he was encircled by five warriors who held lances aiming into his body. He was trapped, and no one made any attempt to battle him. Having heard tales of agonizing tortures at the hands of these Indians, Collins feared he knew his imminent fate too clearly. Determined to die quickly, he lunged at several men, only to be driven back into the center of this precarious circle by harmless nicks from those sharp lances.

"Cowards! Are you afraid to fight me? Does it take five of you to defeat one white man?" he shouted his contemptuous challenges, to no avail. Heart-stopping terror caused him to shudder. He was unable to do anything but watch his entire troop massacred, slain while he helplessly awaited a fate worse than theirs.

Several soldiers managed to reach their horses and mount them. Two were instantly yanked off to continue a bloody and useless battle. Another soldier screamed with searing pain as his back was stormed by countless arrows. Some escaped with warriors hot in pursuit, resolved no man involved in this incident would survive to participate in another one. From the troop, only three men would live to reach Fort Henry to report their staggering defeat to a white-faced Hodges.

As Red Cloud forcefully sent his knife into the gut of one soldier, he sneered coldly, "For Turtle Woman, white dog!" Over and over he plunged the blade into the dead man's body, until Talking Rock jerked him aside and shook him to clear his wits.

Little Beaver received the most damaging wound as a pistol hurled a ball into his left shoulder. Immediately he was encircled by three warriors, who prevented his death in his weakened condition. "Lie still, Capa Cistinna! Save

475

your strength and blood while we slay the white dogs."

Others received minor cuts and scrapes, but nothing serious. Soon, all Bluecoats lay dead or dying, except Collins. No one offered aid to those writhing in agony or supplied a release from their torturous fates. When all was settled, the other warriors slipped into the circle around Collins, ever increasing the circumference of its menacing fence of awesome points.

Collins whirled this way and that, watching the self-assured warriors with rising alarm. The warriors would taunt him with laughter and sneers each time he plunged forward to entice one to stab him, only to find himself shoved backwards without a single injury.

With only groans of pain to sever the silence, an opening appeared in the wall of truculent foes. The towering, bronze figure that stepped forward needed no introduction; it was none other than the mighty Eagle himself. The circle closed instantly behind him. Collins stiffened in dread. What would they do to him? His knees trembled with weakness, threatening to give way.

"What are you waiting for, you savage?" Collins' shaky voice demanded with false courage.

Gray Eagle smiled, mocking the vulnerable man who had dared to think of attacking his camp and slaying all who lived there. As if he possessed all the time in the world, Gray Eagle leisurely removed his breastplate of linked eagle-bones. Next, he casually removed his moccasins and *wanapin*. As he stood barefoot and clad in long buckskin pants, Collins wondered at his curious actions. Each item was passed to the warrior behind Gray Eagle and set upon the ground outside the circle. Assuming a spread-legged stance, Gray Eagle merely stared at Collins!

Collins struggled as he abruptly found himself imprisoned by several warriors who did nothing more than remove his shirt, hat, and boots! The human circle was completed once more. Collins glanced down in bewilderment, clad only in his deep blue pants. "What the hell are you pulling, Gray Eagle?" he nervously shouted.

The hearty laughter that left the robust chest of the stalwart warrior sent chills over Collins' lean and flexible body. Without warning, a heavy knife was tossed at his feet. Collins stared at the shiny weapon, but made no move to grab it. As a cobra before the hypnotic flutist, he observed the legendary warrior with intrigue and fascination.

A knife gleamed brightly in the right hand of Gray Eagle, the whiteness of his teeth sparkling just as brightly as he smiled ominously at the confused white man. "So, the legend fears one measly Bluecoat," Collins taunted.

"Gray Eagle fears no man, Indian or white, surely not a groveling dog like Collins," the vital voice mocked him in distinct English! "You wished to challenge and destroy Gray Eagle. Here is your chance. Do you only murder innocent women and children? Where is your pride and courage now, Bluecoat?"

Collins went stark white and shuddered. "You speak English?" he hoarsely inquired, utterly shocked by this unknown ability.

"I speak the tongue of white dogs. You have challenged me, Collins. Fight for your life. No warrior will help me. If you conquer Gray Eagle, you go free. If you fail, you die by my hand alone."

Astonished by this news, Collins sneered, "I don't believe you! If I kill you, they'll torture me, and we both know it!"

"I give my word of honor you go free if you defeat me. I speak no lies as white dogs do. If you cower in fear and refuse, I will let my warriors punish you for days until you die. It is a leader's right to be slain only by another leader. It will be so; Gray Eagle has spoken."

"You're saying if I kill you, I'll be set free?" Collins pressed smugly.

"I give my word. Fight for your life and honor, white-eyes."

Collins leaned forward and picked up the knife, his gaze never leaving Gray Eagle's. "Then come and take me, you filthy savage."

"The fight is to the death, white dog," Gray Eagle needlessly taunted, stepping forward.

Such struggles were familiar to Gray Eagle. He observed the white man closely. "Let's just see if you're as good as they claim," Collins murmured, studying the man intently.

Each man knew that a split-second delay in his reactions could cost him his life. A fighter needed to be on constant alert. Their eyes met and fused, never leaving each other's face. Both men dropped forward to stooped positions, feet apart, arms and hands hanging loose, and knees bent and flexed. Collins' face shouted his hatred, while the warrior's remained impassive. Torchlight offered a dazzling view of animosity and glittering blades.

They slowly and thoughtfully circled each other, each assessing the weaknesses and strengths of his competitor. Collins shouted and slashed out at Gray Eagle, missing his nimble foe, who easily dodged the thrust. Gray Eagle laughed merrily, making no attempt to send his blade home too quickly, playing with the life of his enemy.

Fury filled Collins. He knew without a shadow of doubt that he was no match or competition for this powerful Indian. Half-crouching, Collins began a new attack. He half-turned to throw the warrior off guard, then rapidly whirled and kicked at his groin as he lashed out with his knife. Gray Eagle chuckled as he parried the blows and sliced into Collins' left arm. Collins gaped at the swift flow of blood down his arm, then glared at the grinning Indian.

"You bastard! I'll kill you for that!" he thundered, rage inspiring strength and daring.

"Words cannot slay Gray Eagle." The taunt stung his ears.

Collins badly and desperately flirted with death, practically begging the noble warrior to end this charade. Gray Eagle refused to comply, dancing in and out as he nipped at the soldier's body. Shiny beads of moisture shone upon Collins' chest and face, while Gray Eagle's revealed none. Collins knew he was going to die, but he vowed to strike some injury upon his enemy's body first. Collins' upper torso was bare, and his numerous wounds could be viewed. Suddenly, feeling himself clothed in a liquid red shirt, he realized the warrior's sport at his expense: harmless slashes upon his chest, back, and arms.

Easily evading and injuring his foe, Gray Eagle knew the folly of distraction and excessive pride. A wounded animal was exceedingly dangerous. Collins was showing signs of fatigue and strain. It was difficult not to flaunt his superiority and imminent triumph. Muscles taut and cramped, Collins searched for some devious ploy to assist him.

The ultimate insult came when Gray Eagle dauntlessly tossed his knife aside and dared Collins to defeat him. "You arrogant snake!"

Collins came forward as Gray Eagle motioned him to do so. In the flicker of an eye, the knife was knocked from his grasp and his body hit the hard ground. He jumped up, his weapon out of reach. He lunged at the Indian, his breathing labored. Grunts of exertion came forth as they struggled. Acutely aware of his waning strength and the persistence of his rival, Collins fought wildly.

"Shall I halt while you pick up your knife, white dog? You are weak as a child without it," the puissant warrior scoffed.

"If you're fool enough to give me the advantage, why not?" Collins sneered, going for his weapon.

Collins raced forward, the knife held high. Gray Eagle seized his wrist and twisted forcefully, drawing a cry of pain from the white man's pale lips. The blow into Gray Eagle's stomach never fazed him, but Collins' fist ached. When the warrior followed his lead and delivered a staggering blow into his gut, Collins doubled over in agony. But as he went forward, he thrust his head into Gray Eagle's stomach. For the first time, the puissant warrior went down. Collins was upon him in a flash, the knife hurling down toward his exposed heart.

Before Collins knew what had happened, he was lying upon his back beneath the warrior, his hands pinned to his sides with the warrior straddling him. Collins resisted as Gray Eagle imprisoned one arm beneath his powerful knee. Catching his wrist in a grip of iron, Gray Eagle raised the hand holding the knife. His ebony eyes glued to Collins' horror-filled blue ones as he began to lower the knife. When Collins attempted to loosen his grasp upon

480

the weapon, Gray Eagle's hands squeezed over his to prevent his release.

"For a man who slays helpless women and children, you fear death greatly. Die in honor, white dog, for you never lived in it."

Collins thrashed to no avail as the gleaming steel was plunged into his heart by his own hand. He gaped at the warrior above him as the racking agony ended his life. His body went limp. Gray Eagle released his grip upon the dead man's hands, sending the shout of victory into the oppressive silence.

He stood up. "We ride for home, Oglala," was all he said after this stunning victory.

Shalee sat upon the stony ground with her forehead resting upon her raised knees, arms tightly encircling her legs. Her eyes were closed as she fervently prayed for the survival of her love. Time seemed to cease its passage as she awaited his fate. Sensing the importance of this span of time, everyone was still and silent.

"The warriors come!" went up the excited and elated shout.

Shalee's head jerked upwards; her eyes welled with tears. She could not pull her gaze from that of her husband as he strolled forward, his attention and gaze on her alone. Relief surged through her body, compelling her to her feet. With a cry of joy, she raced into his open arms.

He gathered her tightly against him and refused to release her for a long time. "It is over, Little One, for now."

Other cheerful warriors came forward to greet their loved ones and to take them back to camp. Shalee couldn't bring herself to inquire about the fates of the soldiers. Gray Eagle did not tell her he had placed their bodies upon their horses and ordered several braves to take them to within sight of Fort Henry as a warning against future treachery.

When Running Wolf was safely placed in his tepee under the watchful eye of the medicine chief, Gray Eagle took the hands of his wife and son and entered his own tepee. After their son had finally tired of hearing the tales of the day's cunning and battles, he fell asleep in his father's arms. Gray Eagle lay him upon his sleeping mat, gazing down in love and relief. No matter what future his first son chose, he would always love and respect him.

He turned to find Shalee's yearning look upon him. He came to join her upon their mat. As a smoldering green gaze fused with an igneous ebony one, they knew words could come later, much later. He reached for her and drew her close. Her eyes searched his lithe frame for any sign of injury. Finding nothing to mar its beauty, she smiled contentedly.

He pressed her down to the furry mat and kissed her thoroughly. As if to prove they had forever to live and to love, they came together in leisurely ecstasy, gradually feeding their smoldering embers until they flamed with blazing desire. His mouth savored the sweet taste of her lips and breasts, teasing each in turn. His warm hands stroked her slender, shapely body. She felt tense, yet utterly relaxed. She felt fiery, yet blissfully cool. Her body raged with delightful torment, yet it relished intense pleasure. She enjoyed this heady feeding, yet she ached with hunger. He was rapture, yet torture. How she loved this man who had stolen her heart so long ago.

As he explored her body, she reveled in the feel of his

482

vital flesh. His movements were deliciously slow and deliberately enticing. She yielded her all to his masterful onslaught. As their inferno built to an explosive level, he whispered his love to her many times. When he could halt the stormy tide no longer, it ravaged his control and shook them with sublime rapture. They clung together in fierce love and sailed along upon the now peaceful sea of brazen ecstasy.

When she lay curled into his arms, she started to tell him about Running Wolf and Leah. He silenced her with a kiss first, then with, "Sleep now, my love. We will talk of such matters with the new sun."

Exhausted, they slept until dawn announced her new face. The day began with recountings of their recent triumphs. The council met very early that morning. It was decided to attempt another buffalo hunt while the Bluecoats licked their wounds and regained their strength.

"First, we hunt buffalo. Then, the Blackfoot will join us for the Sun Dance. We must strike while the Bluecoats sleep from our wounds."

Shalee glanced up to discover White Arrow's lingering gaze upon Wandering Doe, who timidly returned his smile. Happiness filled her heart as she nudged her husband. Their gazes met and fused knowingly. "Soon, our brother will know the love and joy we share," he remarked.

Hand in hand, they strolled along. When they stopped to talk, Gray Eagle asked, "What happened while I chased our enemies?"

Shalee pondered how much she should tell him. She began cautiously, praying he would not suspect the critical point she would be compelled to overlook:

Powchutu. She described the fight with Leah and Running Wolf's courageous rescue. She exposed Leah's treacherous scheme. He smiled as those words struck a happy nerve. She ended her narration with the episode of Sturgis. Finding this event curious, Gray Eagle's full attention centered upon its meaning.

"You believed his words of peace?" he probed in a strange tone.

"Yes. He could have slain me and allowed us to die."

"I was there to protect you and the others," he corrected her.

"I did not know you were near, nor did he," she added softly.

"That is so. Still, a white man cannot be trusted."

"What about men like Joe Kenny and those two you allowed to escape?" she hinted gravely, pointing out his inconsistency.

"As always, Grass Eyes, you speak wisely and gently. Some whites are not bad," he conceded lightly.

She laughed merrily. "If they did not fear the shadow of the mighty Eagle and his hatred, other whites would lean toward peace. If you but hinted at truce, others would jump with joy."

"Your eyes cloud with wishful dreams, Little One. Gray Eagle is the Indian to them, not just a man."

"You can never be just a man, my love. You stand above others and all know this. If not for your prowess, the tribes would war separately against their mutual foe. You alone fuse them into one awesome force, which the whites fear. To make truce with you is to entice truce from others. They know you as leader; they must win your favor first. Many winters ago you told me one man could not control the destiny of many peoples. But you

e such a man. Where you lead, others follow. What you
ggest, others listen to. The word of Gray Eagle is
werful. Only you possess the means to inspire peace."

"You wish me to parlay with this Sturgis?" he asked
ietly.

"I wish our sons to know life as you once knew it. Only
ace with the white man can offer this. They will never
driven out and kept out forever. Peace is the only path
walk now. The destiny of the Indian is within your
nds, my love. Ask the Great Spirit to guide you in this
ave matter. Listen to His words, not the resentment in
ur own heart. Those who have died cannot return to
, but the lives of others can be spared. Is peace so
possible?"

"When we have hunted and returned, I will seek a
sion from Wakantanka during the Sun Dance. If He so
lls, I will parlay with Sturgis."

She hugged him until he laughed. "I cannot promise
ace, Shalee, only to seek the will of the Great Spirit,"
added, chuckling.

"That is all I ask, my love," she whispered tenderly.

The following weeks passed swiftly in laborious
tivity. This time, only a few hunting parties left camp
the same time. Braves were sent along to guard them,
hile one band of warriors guarded the camp. Three
eks later, the first buffalo hunt was completed with
eat success and without any hostile incidents.

The camp was busy with preparations for the Sun
ance and victory celebration when two events took
ace: Word came from Sturgis about a meeting between
mself and Gray Eagle, and Leaning Bush was placed
on the death scaffold. White Arrow politely waited for
week's mourning to pass before he approached

Wandering Doe for her hand in joining, but not befo
she had politely rejected Talking Rock's proposal. St
agonizing over the loss of his wife, Talking Rock read
accepted her refusal, also having learned of the affecti
between White Arrow and this girl.

She quickly accepted, with one stipulation: T
joining would take place as soon as a new tepee could
constructed, one without the ghost of her first mate, o
in which to begin a new life with her first love. Whi
Arrow calmly agreed. The joining was set to take pla
two weeks following the Sun Dance.

Shalee watched her husband as he rode away to me
with Sturgis under the sign of truce. The day crept b
giving itself up to dark as slowly and reluctantly as wint
had to spring. Night came, and he did not return. SI
dozed off and on, each waking moment fretting at h
lengthy absence. Why did he tarry? Had Sturgis' off
been a devious trick to lure him into danger? Had the
felt compelled to withdraw their offer and retaliate fo
the devastation of Hodges' men? Had Sturgis been sla
himself? Had they resisted his wisdom and used him
entrap her love?

Endless waiting and suffering! Why was she forced
sit by while her love confronted death and danger ever
day? She felt so useless and vulnerable.

Morning came, and still no sign of her husband. Sure
a simple discussion couldn't take this long! Tense, sl
went to bathe in the river. She stripped and dove into th
tepid water, delighting in its soothing arms. She swa
back and forth, tiring her body and energizing her spirit
She finally moved toward the bank. She rose from th
water and halted, the liquid surface lapping at her sma
waist.

A hand tapped her upon the shoulder. She inhaled i

486

alarm and instinctively turned to defend herself. She found herself staring into the smiling face of her husband. Roguish lights danced in his obsidian eyes. A beguiling grin curled up the corners of his sensual lips. Water glistened upon his bronze frame.

"You!" she shrieked, then playfully pounded upon his brawny chest. "Where have you been? I've been out of my mind with worry!" she frantically scolded him.

"You call playing like an otter in the river worried?" he teased mischievously. "You demanded I speak with Sturgis about peace. I did so."

He leaned forward and nibbled upon her ear, then sank into the water to gently ravish her breast. She stared at him in disbelief and mounting annoyance. "What happened?" she exclaimed in exasperation when he seemed content to make love to her right at that moment.

"First, peace with my wife." He devilishly continued his game.

"If you do not tell me what happened with Sturgis, we shall have war," she panted, slightly vexed with him and also enflamed by his actions.

"How can you think and speak of the white man's problems when I have a mounting problem of my own?" he jovially teased, closing her hand over his engorged manhood.

"Men! You leave for days while I worry over your safety, then you sneak up and try to seduce me?" she rebuked him.

"Peace is a thing of another sun, Shalee; our love is this sun. I have needed you and missed you. Sturgis spoke of truce and Gray Eagle spoke of truce. But others must talk and vote. When the tribes meet, I will give the words of Sturgis to them. I do not possess the power to speak for other tribes, not even my own without their

487

vote. Sturgis has much power now; he is leader of all whites here. He must convince them peace is needed. He will speak to his people and I will speak to mine. We cannot force truce. All must agree."

She smiled in relief and exhilaration. "At least that's a beginning," she optimistically stated. "Between you and Sturgis, I know we can find peace," she vowed confidently.

"It is good if peace comes. I also wish our sons to know such days as long ago," he admitted. "Does Wandering Doe make ready to join our brother?" he asked, behaving as if his prior line of thought was now forgotten.

"I've been helping her with the new tepee. All will be ready soon."

She leaned forward against him and placed little bites upon his shoulder. As if distracted, he remarked, "Chela, Brave Bear, and Black Cloud will come soon. They will join our celebration and observe the Sun Dance with their brothers the Oglala. There is still much to do."

Since he was acting as if he was ending their heated moment and was about to leave the water, she asked seductively, to refresh his mind, "Do you recall the first time we made love here after I returned from the dead?"

"Such thoughts could never leave my mind," he huskily declared.

She laughed cheerfully. "I was so afraid that day. I had forgotten what it was to love you without shame or restraint."

"Perhaps we should walk in the forest again today," he hinted suggestively, clearly.

She grinned. "Perhaps," she nonchalantly agreed.

"Come, Little One. It is time I show you how to greet your husband when he returns from a long and dangerous journey." He took her hand and helped her

488

from the water. He picked up a blanket and wrapped it loosely around her. He took her hand in his and strolled away.

Finding a lovely spot where they would not be disturbed, he halted. She did not prevent his hand from removing the blanket. He laid it upon the soft grass. He sat down, then smiled up into her leaf-green eyes. He reached up to take her hands to pull her down to him, slowly falling backwards with her atop him.

She laughed with carefree abandonment. "Did you have some new lesson in mind, my love?"

"How so when I have not grown weary of the others?" he mirthfully jested, ebony eyes sparkling devilishly.

Her breath caught in her throat and passion leaped into her lucid green eyes. Why did he always have this intoxicating effect upon her? How had she ever resisted him or briefly turned her heart against him? He was all she needed. "There are a variety of herbs to use in our food to enhance different favors as our moods and tastes change. Should we not search for loving herbs to stimulate us and to prevent future boredom?" she playfully hinted, unsuccessfully suppressing her giggles.

He was amused and delighted by her stirring game. His eyes danced with laughter and love. "Do you grow weary of me and my touch when we have shared only five winters? What must I do to halt such dishonor?"

"Teach me all you know?" she seductively entreated.

"All?" he echoed, then chuckled.

"Perhaps only what you desire me to know," she ventured sweetly.

Carefully and gently he rolled her to her back to lie half-on and half-off her naked body. His mouth closed over hers in a tender and inviting kiss. Soon, they were oblivious to all except their love and needs for each other. Over these past years, their love and passion had become enriched, had deepened and increased.

A light breeze played over their bodies, and slender fingers of warm sunlight teased their flesh. His kisses burned like the desert sun over her face and throat. His husky voice was enchanting and compelling, pulling her deeper into his spell. Her blood pounded instinctively for what he freely offered: fulfillment and pleasure.

Her hands wandered over his hard back and shoulders with light and tender touches, then hard and passionate caresses. She pulled him even closer and tighter against her eager body, enticing him to boldness. His teeth playfully teased at her lips and body, drawing little moans from her. For a time, he seemed content to masterfully explore every inch of her body, as she did his. He tantalized her over and over, stimulating her to yield to him completely.

As if never having enough of him, she mutely pleaded for more contact. Fires now leaped and burned within them. Total surrender was taking place, no reservations, no holding back. Her head rolled from side to side as he nibbled and fondled her taut breasts. He thrilled to the feel of her warm hands upon his body as she titillated him in similar ways. Brazenly and heatedly she gave and took, as he did.

When he finally eased within her fiery body, she accepted him with a fierce desire and feverish delight unmatched by any other woman. With each blissfully tormenting stroke, his body craved more and more of her. He wavered between deliberately leisurely probings and savagely desperate plunges. His body shuddered as he fought to control himself and his throbbing manhood. Each time his lips ravished hers or her breasts, the shaft quivered with the demand to frantically pierce her womanhood in search of exquisite rapture. Yet he held a tight rein upon his wild stallion.

Ensnared in this heady world of smoldering passion, he coached her with responses she knew by heart. Still, she thrilled to the words coming forth in that mellow and rich voice. Eventually, their bodies worked in perfect unison, the same goal in mind.

Her eyes blazing with desire and love, she hoarsely commanded, "Now, my love. Take me now."

His cue received, he deftly plundered her body until both found treasures beyond belief. Lips, bodies, and spirits intermingled—they exploded into total bliss when they could no longer suppress or restrain themselves. In love's golden afterglow, they lay locked together for a long time, savoring the sweetness and peace of this joyous union.

Shalee propped herself up and gazed down into the arresting features of her husband, calling to mind the past six years since she had come to this vast wilderness and met this powerful and irresistible legend. In the beginning, their love had been forbidden and savage. Later, they could not deny their passions and had defied all forces to obtain this brazen ecstasy they now shared. Brazen ecstasy . . . what could more appropriately describe the climax to their fierce search for love?

"What playful fox walks within your mind, Little One?" he asked, watching the glow that ever softened in her green eyes.

She provocatively trailed her fingers over his bronze chest, then laughed happily as she seductively murmured, "It is no fox, my love, only a mighty eagle soars here."

491

Epilogue

Late September of 1782 was tranquil in many ways. The days were mild and the nights were crisp. As if undecided about changing her face, Mother Nature was a lovely blending of summer and autumn. The fall buffalo hunt had been successfully completed and plans were under way for the coming winter. For a time, man and weather seemed at peace with nature.

It had been months since the awesome defeat of the soldiers from Fort Henry. Talks concerning a lasting peace dominated many tribal meetings, as well as lengthy discussions at Fort Meade, where Colonel Derek Sturgis now commanded the white forces of this area, including Hodges' replacement, Major Hollister Trent, at the ailing Fort Henry. No one knew for certain what had happened to Major Hodges; one day he simply vanished from sight. Some said he fled in fear of the Eagle; others claimed he met with foul play. Oddly, no one really cared.

One appealing fact caught the watchful attention of both white and Indian: During the peace deliberations no hostile episodes occurred. For a time, a fragile peace actually ruled the open Plains and lush forests, as obstinate and skeptical men verbally toyed with the seeming impossibility of it.

Running Wolf recovered from his knife wounds from the white girl who had tragically entered his life. Yet something was vastly different about the aging chief. He was quieter these days, often somber and withdrawn into himself. He never spoke the white girl's name again; nor did he ever mention the name of his other son to anyone. He would remain ignorant of Shalee's knowledge of his shame and heartache, for she would never tell him of his feverish confession. But it was clear something plagued the old man's spirit, gradually draining his energy. However, he was dearly loved, and times were presently peaceful; there was no urgent need to declare his son chief just yet. But soon, such times would come.

To Princess Shalee, the past was as dead as the unclaimed son who had lived and died as a despicable half-breed scout, a magnetic man whose rightful heritage had never been exposed or enjoyed. Shalee could close her eyes and envision the magnificent sight of those two brothers riding side by side, conquering all within their path and line of vision, brothers who had been similar in looks and character, brothers whose lives had both been touched and changed by the same white woman. If Powchutu still lived, she would have revealed his identity to her husband and have pressed for peace between them. It was too late. The weight of his rank upon his powerful shoulders, her husband did not deserve this added burden, which could not be removed or changed. Such tormenting skeletons would remain buried. With all her heart, she prayed they would. . . .

The day was destined to come when the fierce, but tender, Sioux warrior would rule this domain as chief. When that day arrived, Princess Shalee would be at his side. There was no turning back now; the English captive Alisha Williams existed no more. From this day forward, only Shalee—alleged daughter to Chief Black Cloud—lived and loved upon the Great Plains, her secret identity safe forever. . . .

Thoughts of Mary O'Hara and Joe Kenny often entered Shalee's mind. She prayed they had finally discovered the same love and joy that she and Gray Eagle shared, that White Arrow and Wandering Doe were gradually exploring. Surely Mary's love for Powchutu had ended with his untimely death. . . .

With Joe Kenny as Mary's husband, all living persons could finally allow the ghost of the scout to rest. How Shalee wished Powchutu's tragic existence had been different. He had truly loved Mary, as she had loved him. Sadness inspired Shalee to ponder his tragic waste, his lost destiny. Mary could have given him the peace of mind and powerful love that she could not, could not because she had met and loved his brother first. If only they had known a similar brazen ecstasy of love and passion. . . .

Peace, treachery, hostility, love, and passion . . . such powerful and often destructive forces . . .

Today was exceptionally mild. Poised near the serene river that had once raged from snow-swollen waters and stolen her from her love's side, Shalee was deep in thought as she recalled all that had happened since that fateful day last spring. A mellow voice called her from her reverie. She warmed instantly, then turned slowly.

Princess Shalee walked toward the invincible Sioux warrior who was her husband. She was happy and vivacious these days. She yearned for the son who had filled the vision of her beloved. Sun Cloud . . . Yes, they would surely have another child some glorious day. As for the other baffling visions, she wisely put them aside. They exchanged smiles before his mouth closed over hers, their lips forging a passion and love too powerful and unique for any force to destroy.

THE BEST IN HISTORICAL ROMANCE

PASSION'S RAPTURE   (912, $3.50)
by Penelope Neri
Through a series of misfortunes, an English beauty becomes the
captive of the very man who ruined her life. By day she rages against
her imprisonment—but by night, she's in passion's thrall!

JASMINE PARADISE   (1170, $3.75)
by Penelope Neri
When Heath sets his eyes on the lovely Sarah, the beauty of the
tropics pales in comparison. And he's soon intoxicated with the
honeyed nectar of her full lips. Together, they explore the paradise . . . of love.

SILKEN RAPTURE   (1172, $3.50)
by Cassie Edwards
Young, sultry Glenda was innocent of love when she met handsome
Read deBaulieu. For two days they revelled in fiery desire only to
part—and then learn they were hopelessly bound in a web of SILKEN
RAPTURE.

FORBIDDEN EMBRACE   (1105, $3.50)
by Cassie Edwards
Serena was a Yankee nurse and Wesley was a Confederate soldier.
And Serena knew it was wrong—but Wesley was a master of
temptation. Tomorrow he would be gone and she would be left with
only memories of their FORBIDDEN EMBRACE.

PORTRAIT OF DESIRE   (1003, $3.50)
by Cassie Edwards
As Nicholas's brush stroked the lines of Jennifer's full, sensuous
mouth and the curves of her soft, feminine shape, he came to feel that
he was touching every part of her that he painted. Soon, lips sought
lips, heart sought heart, and they came together in a wild storm of
passion. . . .

Available wherever paperbacks are sold, or order direct from the
Publisher. Send cover price plus 50¢ per copy for mailing and handling to
Zebra Books, 475 Park Avenue South, New York, N.Y. 10016. DO NOT
SEND CASH.

SWEET MEDICINE'S PROPHECY
by Karen A. Bale

#1: SUNDANCER'S PASSION   (1164, $3.50)
Stalking Horse was the strongest and most desirable of the tribe, and Sun Dancer surrounded him with her spell-binding radiance. But the innocence of their love gave way to passion—and passion, to betrayal. Would their relationship ever survive the ultimate sin?

#2: LITTLE FLOWER'S DESIRE   (1165, $3.50)
Taken captive by savage Crows, Little Flower fell in love with the enemy, handsome brave Young Eagle. Though their hearts spoke what they could not say, they could only dream of what could never be. . . .

#3: WINTER'S LOVE SONG   (1154, $3.50)
The dark, willowy Anaeva had always desired just one man: the half-breed Trenton Hawkins. But Trenton belonged to two worlds—and was torn between two women. She had never failed on the fields of war; now she was determined to win on the battleground of love!